LET'S DISAPPEAR

a novel

GARY L.
STUART

For information about this title or to order other books and/or electronic media, contact the publisher:
Gleason & Wall Publishers
7000 N. 16th Street, Suite 120, PBM 470, Phoenix, AZ 85020
www.garylstuart.com
gary.stuart@garylstuart.com

ISBN: 978-0-9863441-6-9 (print)
       978-0-9863441-7-6 (eBook)

Printed in the United States of America

Cover and Interior design: 1106 Design, Phoenix, AZ

Other Books by Gary L. Stuart

The Ethical Trial Lawyer

The Gallup 14

*Miranda—The Story Of America's
Right To Remain Silent*

*Innocent Until Interrogated—The True Story of the
Buddhist Temple Massacre and The Tucson Four*

AIM For The Mayor—Echoes From Wounded Knee

Anatomy of a Confession—The Debra Milke Case

Ten Shoes Up

The Valles Caldera

The Last Stage to Bosque Redondo

*Call Him Mac—Ernest W. McFarland—
The Arizona Years*

CHAPTER 1

She closed her umbrella and stamped the rain off her tennis shoes, just inside the main door to the Cranston Library. Hoping she could pass for eighteen, she squared her shoulders and stepped up onto her toes, trying to look taller. The thin-nosed man at the counter gave her that look—the one that says you don't have a library card, do you? Ignoring his sideways glare, she went straight to the card catalogue box next to the front desk. As he watched her, she opened one of the long four-by-four inch drawers, then another, and then another. Letting her breath out in a long gasp, she turned to the man, whose suspicions about her were printed on his forehead. Of course only she could see them.

"I wanna disappear," she said, with as much attitude in her voice as possible. His eyes narrowed in puzzlement.

"How old are you," thin-nose said, making it sound like a judgment, not a question.

"I'm eighteen, yesterday. Old enough to write a book about disappearing. That's what I meant. My character, her name is Vivian, she wants to disappear. I looked in the drawers thing, over there," she said, pointing to the Dewey Decimal card file.

"You got a library card?"

"No, but I'll take one out if you have a book about disappearing. I already looked and didn't find one. That's why I am asking you. Do you have a disappearing book—one that tells how Vivian could do it if she has to?"

"Young lady," thin-nose said, over the tops of his reading glasses, "that card catalogue is there only because I like it. But it's not up to date—we have a computer—you can search on it, not that beautiful old card catalogue. All of our books are indexed, in a modern database."

"Ok, I knew you did, but I like old things too, just like you. I searched on it last week but didn't find anything my character, Vivian, could use."

"Who's Vivian," he said, tapping the rubber end of his pencil against his front teeth.

"My character, I already told you that."

The Cranston Library was the only one in town, since the church library burned down four years earlier. The thin-nosed man, Perry Ricketts, used to work in both libraries. Now he had only one job, one he was proud of because it came with a title, Head Librarian, and a $3,265 monthly salary—not bad for Arizona in 2015. It was just after five and they closed at six p.m. on weekdays. No one was in the library, because of the rain, he thought. His voice was thin, entirely suitable for a librarian. Hers was husky and steadier than most high-school age girls. She looked freshly scrubbed. Although she could not see it from where she was standing, his brown tie had a soup spill about half-way down.

"Your character? Your character in what? If you're eighteen already, you must have graduated high school. From Cranston High, right? Now, my job is to help people, even if they might prefer disappearance over reading youth fiction. Is this a play or what?"

She looked down at the wet tennis shoes and crossed her arms across her flat chest.

"No, it is not a play. It's a book about Vivian and why she wants to disappear from things. But she doesn't know how and she wants me to figure it out. Actually, my character, Vivian, is writing a book inside my book. So it's a book about writing a book. Do you get what I mean?"

"Yes, I do. I surely do," the man said, now with a sort of smile on his face. "I'm the head librarian here; you may call me Mr. Ricketts. I didn't get your name."

"Didn't say one, yet. But it's Shortfield. See, Mr. Ricketts, this is important because Vivian needs to know about disappearing. We took a course online, about writing novels, and learned the most important thing is to have our reader disappear right into the story. You don't want your reader to even think you are writing, just write so the character is way deep into the story. Right? When I learned that online, that's when I knew what my character was up to, in her book, which she's writing inside my book, you know? See, the reader can disappear into your story if you write with verve. That's very hard to do, verve writing, I mean. But how can I get my reader to disappear into my story if both me and Vivian don't understand how to disappear ourselves. You know?"

"Well, I might be just the right librarian to help you. I read a book a week but only disappear into one maybe one time a month. But I must say I've never read a book where the author is telling a story about a character who is writing a book inside the author's book and wants both her reader and herself to disappear. Have I got that part right?"

"Pretty much, but here's one more thing to worry about. If I don't figure out how to disappear, then Vivian might just disappear without a plan, you know? What good would that do her? I think she should stay, but she wants to go. Once she makes her mind up, there's no talking to her. You know what I mean?"

"First things first, let's get you a card."

He handed her a three-by-five index card with little blank lines for personal details. She took it and studiously selected one of the short pencils he pointed to in the box on the counter. That was his name, Perry Ricketts. It was stenciled onto a folded tent thing, next to the pencil box—Perry Ricketts—Head Librarian. While she was writing her answers on the little card, he walked to a Dell computer sitting on the stand-up desk behind him. She could see he was wearing shoes with sponge-rubber soles and that his pants hung down over the back of the shoes. It looked like he was gliding over the linoleum floor tiles. She couldn't see the screen very well, but he was very fast on the keyboard. In a few minutes, he made notes on a little yellow Post-it note. Then he ran his pencil, eraser end down, through the note, and smiled one of those I-told-you-so smiles that people in charge were always giving her.

"This might be what you're looking for, Miss. Let me see your card, please."

She handed it over with her right hand and held her left out to him palm up so he could put the yellow Post-it note in it. It was no accident that yellow, green, and red Post-it notes were stuck on books, screens, and table tops inside Mr. Perry Ricketts's little work space. He took the registration card she'd filled out.

"Your name is Vivian Shortfield? Isn't that the name of your character?"

"No law against a novelist using her own given name for a character in a book. I asked Mr. Nettles, the English teacher at Cranston High, about that. No law against it, he told me. But my character's name isn't Shortfield. It's just Vivian."

"All right, Miss Vivian," Mr. Ricketts said, looking over her card. "I happen to be a friend of Mr. Nettles. We often read the same books, we do. But now that I study your card, I see you signed it but didn't date it. Would you mind?"

She took the card back and started to fill in the line, then hesitated and looked back at him.

"It's May 15, 2014."

She added the date and handed it back. He countersigned her card, scanned it into his computer, then printed a copy on card stock, showing both signatures. He laminated the card and gave it to her. "Now then, you are on record with us. You may take out two books at a time. Have them back in twenty-one days, please. If you need more time, we're happy to give you two extensions."

She took the Post-it note and walked to the stacks. Following the numbers on the note, she found the book she wanted and took it back to the desk. But Mr. Ricketts was gone. An elderly woman smiled and said, "I can check that out for you, Miss Shortfield."

"How did you know my name?" Vivian asked.

"Mr. Rickets told me you were in the stacks when he took his break. Did you find a disappearing book, my dear?" she asked.

"I did. I did. It's kinda old, but my character Vivian is older than me, and she's the one who wants to disappear. The title is *How to Create a New Identity*, and the author is 'Mr. Anonymous.' It's perfect."

CHAPTER 2

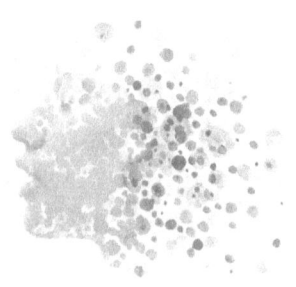

"But Daddy, you said we'd be safe here in Cranston for at least a year and I could finish high school here and . . ."

"I know I did, Viv, but now our situation is very different. We have to leave this town, get away from Arizona and we can't tell the marshal's office. We need to slip out of here at night, this weekend. Your last day of classes is this Friday, right? Today, while you're in school, I'm going to Phoenix, and get some of our money. You remember the safe deposit box I showed you in Phoenix, right . . . ?"

"Yeah. The one at Iron-Mountain-something on that twisty road by the fancy resort."

"Sure, you remember. And you remember where the key is, too, don't you? If they find us, they will force me into some other town way across the country from Baltimore. If that happens, you have to go to Phoenix yourself, get the money, then make a run for it."

"Why Daddy? Are they going to arrest us too, like they did your boss?"

"Viv, the FBI can hold a witness to a crime in what they call protective custody. That's me—I'm a witness to a crime, but not guilty of one. So they put me in protective custody—that's what the witness protection program is. And that's why we're stuck here in Cranston, Arizona, instead of our nice house in suburban Baltimore."

"I loved that house, Daddy. So did Mom. I loved my school there, but not the stupid one here. I wish we could go home."

"Well, you remember why we were relocated here, don't you? It was because my old friend and boss was charged with a criminal case in Baltimore and I was subpoenaed as a witness. It was supposed to be just a few months, but now something else has happened, and I don't know what to do. I do know one thing for sure. We have to get away from here. We have to disappear and no one can know where we've gone."

"Disappear? That's exactly right Daddy. I told you about my book. I'm going to disappear into the air like the air itself. Do you know why you can't see air? No, well, let me tell you why. It's because air is invisible. It's all around us, in us, and we're even made of it. Mr. Nettles said Shakespeare disappeared from the theatre by melting into thin air. That's what I want us to do, Daddy, melt into thin air. Vince, too. But can't it wait until after I graduate high school? This school is not very good. You and Mom home-schooled me for seven years, and I already know more than anyone in the senior class, and more even than some of the teachers."

"Viv, I wish I could explain it to you, but I can't. Something has happened and once I figure it all out I'll tell you all about it. But for now we have to get away."

We need to go next week when the semester is over and no one will miss you at school."

"OK. Remember Dad, I found that book about disappearing at the library. It doesn't cover everything, but you said it was very interesting, right?"

"It is, we can get new names and whole identities. The only problem with that book was it assumed that with a new name you could make a living. That's not true. All I know how to do is what I'm doing now, setting up corporations in Delaware. But you're right, the disappear book has some great ideas. Maybe if we could find someone we trust, we could figure everything out. And we have Vince to worry about too. Right? So don't tell anyone. We'll leave next week, as soon as you finish your last day at school."

"Daddy, you are looking so sad, is it Mom, is that what's making you look sad and wanting to get away from here?"

"No, sweetums, it's not that at all. I can't explain it yet, but something happened to my old boss, Mr. Goshkervic. I'll tell you later. I'm going to drive up to Phoenix today. By Friday, I'll have a plan. We can talk about everything once we're away from here and no one knows."

"But won't the marshals find out—they come down here and check, don't they?"

"Yes, they will. They'll find out we left and they will start looking for us. But your little book about disappearing will help us, right?"

CHAPTER 3

Three months later, two large men, in matching dark-blue suits, marched in the front door of the library as though they'd bought the building.

"We're looking for Perry Ricketts. Does he still work here?" they asked.

"He does," Ricketts answered in a lowered voice, signaling the taller of the two blue suits to honor every library's please-lower-your-voice rule.

"We need to talk to him right away," the smaller blue-suited man said, as he retrieved a black leather wallet with a badge and a picture on it from his inside jacket pocket. Mr. Ricketts was looking at the badge when he snapped the wallet shut. However, Ricketts was sure of the FBI stamp below the picture.

"I am he," Ricketts said.

The other blue-suit stepped forward, signaling that the shorter man was a junior partner who had done his job.

"Can you verify your signature on this card?" he asked, pushing a stiff laminated Cranston Public Library card toward him.

"What's this about?" Ricketts asked.

"Can you verify the signature or not?" the second blue suited man demanded.

"Yes, that appears to be my signature, but I've . . ."

"Thank you, Mr. Ricketts. You are not the subject of any investigation, but you are advised to cooperate with the investigation . . ."

"Investigation? What investigation? I mean, I can check to see if this card holder has any overdue books, but . . ."

The first blue suit jumped in, "It's about Vivian, Mr. Ricketts. When did you last see her?"

"Vivian? You mean the person named on this card? I don't recognize her name, but this is the card we issue to borrowers, and I'm sure that's my authorization signature on it. But, what is . . ."

"Mr. Ricketts," the larger blue suit growled, "this is an important federal crimes issue. We do not have time to entertain questions from librarians. When did you last see the girl you thought was Vivian Shortfield—the one you gave this card to? We do not want to take you in for formal questioning, but your lack of cooperation is being noted."

Growing alarmed and feeling a little faint, Ricketts stammered, "I really can't remember. The date on the card is stamped, that's how we issue cards, but that was, let's see, my goodness, it's been over three months. That's way overdue. I'm sure we've notified her. I don't understand why she hasn't come back in to return the book."

"You send overdue notices by post card?" the man asked.

"Yes, of course. But . . ."

"Well," the man interrupted, "if someone moves, but gets a postcard, and there is no forwarding address, the post office does not return it to the sender. Did you ever think about that?"

"No, I suppose not. This is a small town and everyone here almost always returns their books on time. I can check in the back if you like and see when we post-carded with an overdue notice. Those are in my office in the back. My goodness, we've never had a public safety issue in the library before . . ."

"Don't bother. Her name isn't Shortfield. How did she verify her name—driver's license, student identification, green stamps card, what? You did verify her name, didn't you?"

"I'm sure I asked her to fill out our standard card member form, then I typed the name on the Cranston card and gave it to her to sign. She was a high school student, wasn't she? We don't verify names here; we are just a lending library. We do charge fines for overdue books, but . . ."

"Hold up there, Mr. Ricketts, you don't understand. Our interest is in prosecuting federal criminal cases, not library rules, or overdue books. This card is evidence in the case we're investigating. It was left behind when our subject and his daughter left Cranston sometime in late May, or early June, of this year.

"Left behind? Are you saying this library card that we just issued last month to Miss Shortfield was discarded, or lost, or what?"

"Mr. Ricketts, I just told you her name isn't Shortfield. We found the card at a trailer park here in Cranston. But I'm telling you that in confidence. You are not to disclose that fact, or anything else you know about her, or her library card. And I must tell you again that, under federal statute, you should cooperate with us. Are you willing to talk to us? We want to know what you remember about her, and what kind of books she was interested in."

"My goodness, whatever is it you're investigating? I mean, this is a public library and you are making startling allegations about me, about how I keep our cards current. I mean, is it legal for you to ask me what kind of books our members read? Isn't that covered by the Constitution?"

"Mr. Ricketts, you don't understand. We're investigating a person who we believe may be involved in something completely unconnected to you, or your library. We cannot share that information with you, but most law-abiding citizens help us voluntarily. You want us to get a warrant? Is that it?"

The blue-suited men left five minutes later. They took Xerox copies of Vivian Shortfield's signed library card, and a copy of the database card identifying Vivian Shortfield's borrowed book, *How to Create a New Identity*. Mr. Rickett was quite proud of the system he had installed at the Cranston Library for back-tracking overdue books. They kept these copies ⌐¹ ˙ ˌetized by book title. Mr. Ricketts determined ˌortfield was the only customer in five years to ⸏ out. Now, just looking at the title, and the ⸏r pen-named, "Anonymous," triggered his ˈiss Vivian Shortfield and her book project.

The title seemed to interest the federal officers but didn't mean much to Mr. Ricketts. The subtitle and the author's name, on the other hand, got his literary juices flowing. The subtitle was three sentences long, stamped onto what looked like a library card on the front cover of the book:

"People create new identities for various reasons. Burdensome debts can be avoided, as can alimony and legal judgements. This book not only tells how to create a new identity, but also how to erase your past completely."

Equally intriguing, at least to Mr. Ricketts, was the name of the author. *"By Anonymous."*

What the FBI could not have known was Mr. Ricketts's lifelong habit of reading mysteries and trying to solve the crimes committed in them long before the last chapter. And now, the men in the blue suits had given him his first chance. Maybe he could solve the mystery of the missing library card and whatever other crimes or misdemeanors were afoot in the supercilious Federal Bureau of Investigation. Just because he wore red suspenders and didn't even own a suit didn't mean he could not investigate. He'd read every mystery every written by Dashiell Hammett, P. D. James, and Agatha Christie. He even fancied himself to be clever, like Hercule Poirot, without the mustaches.

My goodness, he thought, whatever was little Miss Vivian up to? His first glance at the book gave him the book's ISBN identifier, copyright date, and publisher's name—a small press in Secaucus, New Jersey. He looked it up

Amazon and learned the book had been out of print since 1991. But a used copy was available for $1.00. Shipping was extra. A week later, when the book arrived, Ricketts took the afternoon off, leaving his two older assistants in charge. He read the large-font, 110-page paperback in just under three hours. It would come to change his life.

Mr. Ricketts decided the overdue book might be the key to whatever crime was afoot at the FBI. Getting it back was secondary. But even so, there was library property to consider. He neatly divided the joint missions. First, he would collect the overdue fines and insist that little Miss Vivian return the book. Then he would solve the crime, or whatever it was the FBI was investigating. He called the high school, but it was on summer break. The nice lady who answered the phone said they didn't give information out about students. He had Vivian Shortfield's home address, so during his lunch break, he drove to her house. It was a trailer park. The very untidy woman who owned the park said they ran off, the girl and her father, a month ago.

His second task now became paramount. He would find out why she ran off. Maybe to Phoenix, he thought. Half the people who ever lived in Cranston had given up and moved to Phoenix. He started enlisting staff; the two older sisters who were his assistants at the library. Then he read his copy of his library's missing book. It was an epiphany of sorts to him. *You Are Who You Say You Are.* Was that true? he asked himself, over and over again. Is it that simple? It made no sense until he remembered what Vivian had said to him a month ago. "I wanna disappear." That's how she introduced herself.

The next day, sitting on the bench outside the auto parts store, arguably the most successful store in town, Mr. Ricketts strained, over and over, trying to recreate that single meeting with her. He was waiting for his closest town friend, Norman Nettles, the English teacher at Cranston High. Norman was inside buying a gasket, or something. Ricketts could not remember the girl's face, but he clearly remembered her outburst when he mistakenly said her character's name was her own name. No, she'd insisted. Her name was Vivian Shortfield, but her character's name was just Vivian. No last name. She said her English teacher confirmed that a character in a book could be named after the author. It was legal, she'd maintained. If Vivian wanted to disappear, the book in his hands could be the answer to both how and why she did it. She could be anyone she said she was—that was the book's central theme. Page five made the point quite well, he thought: "You must not only develop sound documentation, but also the proper mental attitude to most effectively utilize an alternative identity."

When Mr. Nettles came out of the store with a plastic bag of gaskets and a new flashlight, Mr. Ricketts told him about his conversation with Vivian Shortfield back in March and his visit from the FBI.

"I did have a student named Vivian in my English class, but you're got her last name wrong. It was Nau. Vivian Nau. A good student, but an odd one, for sure."

Mr. Nettles joined Mr. Ricketts on the hardware store bench, and they spent the next twenty minutes trying to sort out the inconsistencies in their collective memories of

Vivian. Mr. Nettles had not known that she was no longer in Cranston. And recalled little about her interest in writing a book.

"Yes, I think she talked a little about writing a book, but lots of high school students think about that for a few weeks, then it wears off, and they think about swimming with the dolphins, or something."

They agreed, in retrospect, that the girl probably did fit the notion of someone who wanted to disappear, and had apparently done just that. They agreed that she fit the missing library book's theme, especially "you are who you say you are." They agreed the next step had to be a call to the number on the card the FBI had left with Mr. Ricketts. As soon as they got back to the library, a block away, Mr. Ricketts called the agent in Phoenix, with Mr. Nettles listening in on the other phone in the work room. But the agent was out. Next day, he got a return phone call.

"Mr. Ricketts, I'm Cambridge, the FBI agent who talked to you last week about Vivian."

"Yes, Agent Cambridge, are you the tall man or the shorter one?"

"I'm taller. Why did you call us? Do you have information about Vivian?"

"I do. I think she did what she told me she wanted to do. She disappeared."

"Mr. Ricketts, have you talked to anyone else about this?"

"Anyone else? I talked to my two assistants here at the library, and I called Vivian's English teacher at Cranston

High, but that's all. You didn't say I could not talk to people. Am I in trouble over this?"

Cambridge told him to stop talking to people and asked him to drive to Phoenix the next day to "discuss the matter further." Phoenix was fifty-five miles northwest and not a place he liked. Too busy, he thought. Nevertheless, as he maintained a steady 55 miles per hour on the I-10 to Phoenix, he felt the presence of his imaginary colleague, Hercule. Pity there was no train, he thought. He remembered the movie version and the Orient Express as he drove past Chandler into the scorched desolate flat land of central Phoenix. Just after midmorning, he arrived at the FBI office in the north central part of town. There was a young girl missing, and maybe in harm's way, he murmured to himself as he pulled into the parking lot.

CHAPTER 4

The FBI office in Phoenix was in a high-rise building. The mall across the street could have housed half the businesses in Cranston. It was swathed in brown faux marble on the outside, had frosted glass windows, and was furnished with several grades of metal furniture on the inside. Mr. Cambridge was his usual intimidating self. The long and short of their conversation was that Vivian was somehow involved in what Cambridge continued to call a financial crimes case but would not divulge the smallest detail as to what that meant. Do not talk to any more English teachers about Vivian. Do not order any more books. That was that, he said.

"You have no reason to look into this matter—it's government business, not library business."

"But," Ricketts told Cambridge, "Vivian Shortfield has not returned that book. She owes a small fine now, and what's more, her name is not Vivian Shortfield. In

Cranston, we take fraud seriously. We are state funded, so this is government business . . ."

Cambridge was bowled over, nearing exasperation.

"Ricketts, you are dangerously close to an obstruction of justice charge. Don't investigate anything. Write that overdue fine off. And mail that book to us, the one about creating new identities. We'll take it from there."

"Do you have a library card, Mr. Cambridge? If not, I can mail a card for you to fill out. Then you can check the book out. Its Cranston Library property now, I cannot simply mail it to you. I could get in trouble with the Library Board for that."

Cambridge ushered Ricketts out, told him the FBI would get its own copy of the book, and reminded him he was not to talk to anyone about this matter. Ricketts felt secretly empowered by the brush off. The local gendarmes could not put Hercule off the scent, nor me, he thought. He knew one thing about the "matter." The FBI had no jurisdiction over an overdue book from a state-funded library. Vivian had purposefully hidden her true identity and likely still had that book with her, by whatever name she was using now. It was apparent the FBI did not know where she was—that's their business, knowing everything about everyone. But the library's business was the integrity of its public-lending policy. He had a responsibility to find her and get that book back. More importantly, he was no longer just a head librarian, he was Marceau, in the 2006 radio version of that famous murder on the Orient Express. Of course, he thought, there is no Rachett, and no murder to solve. Or was there?

Mr. Ricketts and his co-conspirator, Mr. Nettles, knew that the girl's father had done to the public school exactly what the daughter had done to the public library. They both gave false names to obtain state-funded services. But was that the crime the FBI was investigating? Mr. Nettles, wanting to be helpful like all teachers are, was able to bypass the assistant school principal, who had refused to give him any student information. He learned from the girl's gym teacher, Prudence Pastori, who knew every girl in the school by sight and athletic ability, that there were three girls last year named Vivian. One was a freshman named Vivian Abscott, who had bad acne all over her face and rarely talked in class. Mr. Ricketts immediately dismissed her. One was a senior named Vivian Escobedo, with dark olive skin and black curly hair. That ruled her out. The third, a junior, was named Vivian Nau, but she had withdrawn from school after the date on the Cranston Library take-out card signed by Vivian Shortfield. Cranston High did not have any students with the name Shortfield. No one named Nau seemed to be known by anyone in the downtown stores frequented by either Mr. Ricketts or Mr. Nettles. Maybe Mr. Ricketts did not know how to disappear, but he knew how to ask questions. The answers he seemed to get suggested that the Nau family knew very well how to disappear—their secret was never to tell anyone in town their name.

Vivian's address on the library card was the address for "Shady Acres." Mr. Ricketts had already been there. Mr. Nettles found out this was the same address on her school registration. And he also found out that for $310 a month, you could park your trailer there under any name you chose—no papers required.

Ricketts and Nettles went there together. They tried to engage the large woman in the office. She was dressed in a 1970s pink-green-red-and-blue streaky moo-moo and sat on an oversize aluminum stool next to the front counter. She could swivel back behind to the cash register and around to either side of the waist-high counter to reach keys for the electric boxes standing at each trailer space. She told Ricketts and Nettles she had no record of any guest at "Shady Acres" named Shortfield. But she had rented a space for almost a year to a man named Stephan Nau. He had a son, not a daughter. Didn't know the boy's name, and had never heard of a Vivian. The school records identified a Stephan Nau as Vivian's father. No mother listed. And the Shady Acres owner insisted no one who'd *ever* rented there was named Shortfield. Her first husband, who ran out on her two months after their marriage, was named Shortt. With two t's, she said.

"No way I'd ever rent to anyone named Shortfield, sounds too much like Shortt," she said.

However, they coaxed a little information out of her. Stephan Nau had rented a space in the back of the park. He'd insisted on a space in the back row, even though it did not have a single shade tree. And the man probably gave her a phony name. "Lots of 'em do," she said. Ricketts asked how long the man and his son had been there.

"'Bout ten months. They left off in the middle of the night when the school was over in May. But here's the crazy part," she said, "they pulled out in the middle of the night, and left some old clothes and newspapers in the recycle boxes we have for our renters. Funny thing was, they still had two weeks left on their front-end deposit. So I made a little extra money on 'em."

"Was the man, Stephan Nau, ever behind on his rent?"

"Not once, always paid with cash, never made friends with the other trailer people, and never caused no trouble, or his boy neither."

"What did he look like? And how about the boy?"

"Mr. Nau was what I'd call middling to normal. The kind you don't notice because there's nothing to *be* noticed about him. He was a little bony, I guess you could say, and must have had weak eyes because he always wore sunglasses. Could not tell you eye color because I never saw his eyes. Now his boy, he was like a mute, you know, just never had a word to say to me. He walked looking down. Saw him with his book bag going to school . . ."

Mr. Nettles asked, "School? What school? Do you mean Cranston High?"

"Can't say. Mr. Nau never said and the boy just never opened his mouth. He even looked away when I was anywhere close by. But my guess is he was in eighth or ninth, lots of books in his bag. And he always carried a little tablet and a ball-point pen you could click in and out. I saw him a few times, sitting at one of those picnic tables over there, writing in that tablet. Or else reading a book. In fact, now that you ask, I'd call that boy bookish."

Mr. Ricketts asked, "OK, you never saw his eye color, but what about his hair color?"

"Can't say. He always wore, and I mean always, a big flat-brimmed hat snugged down to his ears. I think he was crew-cut, but couldn't say for sure."

Mr. Nettles had a question.

"Did Mr. Nau have a daughter, of high-school age?"

"Already told you he had a son. Never saw a girl, just that skinny boy."

"And you said they left clothes and newspapers. Anything else.?"

"Yeah, they left those clothes and other stuff. Can't say what because the FBI took it all away when they were here two weeks ago."

Mr. Ricketts jumped back in.

"The FBI? Are you saying the FBI came here and interviewed you?"

"Damn straight they did. Two of 'em. None too friendly, neither."

"Were they wearing dark blue suits? One large man and another smaller one?"

"Paid no mind to the color, but yeah they were wearing Phoenix clothes and ties around their necks, if that's what you're getting at? Now if you two don't mind, I got business to attend to. This is a trailer park, not an information booth."

The school principal said it wouldn't do to discuss school matters, or students, with anyone except his teachers. So Mr. Ricketts never talked to the principal. That did not prevent the principal, a woman named Ida Lewinsky, from talking to her employee, Mr. Nettles. He learned and reported this investigative fact to Mr. Ricketts. Vivian Nau's records from a high school in Kansas never showed up. The principal's office wasn't worried because Vivian had only been a student at Cranston High for one and a half semesters before she dropped out.

Mr. Ricketts told Mr. Nettles not to tell Principal Lewinsky about the overdue book at the Cranston Library, or the visit from the FBI agents who were interested in a former student's father. Ricketts suggested that Mr. Nettles should only show a casual interest in Vivian because she had been a good student in his English class, and he was curious about why she left school. Ida, as all the teachers called her, said Vivian would not have been passed on to the senior class anyhow.

"You know," she confided in Mr. Nettles, "we could never verify her grades, or class credits. And since we could not verify her father's job, she might not have been an Arizona resident. So, that's a problem, you know," she said. While it was protected student information, the principal told Mr. Nettles about the address given by the father—the trailer park known as "Shady Acres."

Mr. Ricketts asked at the Post Office if they could give him a forwarding address for the father, but they said that's government information. Just like the FBI, he thought. Cranston only had one hangout for high school kids, a hamburger drive-in called *Hunger Bun*. No one there could remember a girl named Vivian. There was no listing anywhere for anyone named Nau. After looking for a week, Ricketts decided the book was wrong—you may not be who you say you are. Vivian Shortfield only *said* that was her name. But a person who claimed that name, Vivian Shortfield, was actually Vivian Nau.

Mr. Ricketts was sure of that. Over a gin and tonic, he told Mr. Nettles he had "talked to a live person."

"We have that much to go on," Nettles affirmed. "And don't forget, the FBI asked you about a girl named Vivian and was almost frantic to find out when you had last seen her, right?"

So she exists, they decided. *And* she's a character in a book. That's something both Mr. Ricketts and Mr. Nettles knew a lot about—books. Over several gin and tonics, the mystery deepened. We can find her in ways the FBI could not, they declared. What did *they* know about books?

Cranston had 4,100 residents and only one stationary supply store, "STITCH'S STATIONARY & COMPUTER SUPPLIES." It sold new and used laptop computers, paper, envelopes, pens, carbon paper, note books, and other office supplies. The owner, a disabled man named Stan Stitch, gave them their first clue to Vivian's identity.

"Mr. Stitch, we're looking for a girl, she was a junior last year at Cranston High. My friend, Mr. Nettles, had her in his junior English class. I met her when she took out a book at the library and told me she was going to write her own book. You sell writing materials and computers. Do you remember a student named Vivian Shortfield, or Vivian Nau coming in to your store and maybe talking about books?"

"No, Mr. Ricketts; don't know that name. But back maybe three-four months ago, a young boy came in looking for a cheap, used computer. Sold him a used Dell Inspiron laptop for $149 and an old portable printer for $20. He paid cash, bought two reams of printer paper, but never said his name."

"Wouldn't say his name? That's odd."

"Nah, not giving me a name ain't odd. Lots of people pay cash and I never know who they are. But this boy, he'd been in before, always buying notebooks and pens and stuff like that. What's odd was *why* he said he needed a laptop and a printer. Not that I asked him, he just volunteered he was a character in a book. That's' why he needed a printer to go with the computer."

"He was a character, or he was the author? I don't understand."

"Me neither. He just said the computer and printer was for a book and there ain't no law against being a character in your own book."

"Those were his exact words?" "Yeah, pretty much."

"How old was he? What did he look like?"

"Say fifteen, maybe fourteen. Short, runty, you know, like a 105-pound weakling. Spect he got picked on by every tough kid in town. Always wore a black cowboy hat, but didn't look like a ranch kid at all. Jeans, but no boots. Not a talker, and wore that hat so far down on his head, I could not tell you his hair color. He was white, that's all I can say about him."

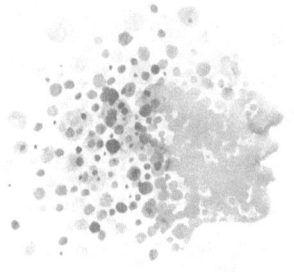

CHAPTER 5

Ricketts and Nettles left Stitch's intrigued by what they'd learned. A boy wanted to be an author and maybe a character in his own book? Just like Vivian Shortfield? Was the boy Stephan Nau's son at Shady Acres? Did they know one another? Mr. Stitch's answers stoked the fires of literary investigation. Where should they look? Mr. Ricketts suggested a meeting with his library assistants, Cecilia and Cynthia, twin unmarried sisters in their fifties. They were Cranston born, bred, educated, and hugely interested in the goings-on of everyone in town. They were not just nosy by nature, they were picky about everything and serious readers of genre fiction—not just mysteries—they also like John le Carré books and anything Tom Clancy wrote.

Cecilia and Cynthia, lifelong mystery readers, were willing to help, but had conditions. "First," they said, "we must be protected both in our jobs and in our reputations.

It would not do for townspeople to think that we are nosy or gossipy people, even though Cranston people are just that—nosy and gossipy. So we will help only if none of us is ever identified as part of a group interested in the lives of two former townspeople, Mr. Nau and his daughter, whom you presume to bear the first name, Vivian, and the given name, Nau."

"Well," Mr. Nettles said, "I agree with that. It would not do for my principal or her nosy vice-principal to think I was investigating a former student, either. Why don't we just all agree to keep this to ourselves, as much as we can?"

"Well," Mr. Ricketts repeated, "how about we form a private group? Let's call it Group X. We can all pledge to never reveal the members of Group X or its mission. Agreed?"

Cynthia and Cecelia nodded affirmatively and simultaneously. Mr. Nettles offered to write something down that would memorialize Group X's existence and function. Mr. Ricketts agreed with Cynthia and Cecelia, but vetoed Mr. Nettles' idea.

"No," he insisted, "to maintain our group and individual security, not to mention our reputations, there cannot be a written record of our intentions or our findings."

Three heads nodded simultaneously. Group X had just taken its first vote.

"Why," Mr. Nettles, asked the assistant librarians, "did you just suggest the possibility that neither the father nor his daughter might actually be named Nau, and that the daughter might not be named Vivian? You said Mr. Ricketts and I were presuming that."

"Because," Cecelia answered, "no one has seen a birth certificate or other identifying document for either the father or the daughter."

"And," Cynthia added, "we don't even know if the presumed father was in fact the male parent of the daughter. All we know is she was a high-school-age girl, with no known prior educational record or family history. They weren't from here; that's for sure. Or else everyone in town would have known them."

Mr. Nettles disagreed. "No, lots of people in town knew them, even if only for two semesters. He came to school and registered her as his daughter. I presume he was on campus on other occasions like most parents. You know, for activities, like most parents. Almost every student has extracurricular activities, and she probably did too. So, there must be many people who interacted with one or the other. I mean, Mr. Ricketts met her in the library. She was a real person. And like Cecelia and Cynthia said, people here are nosy. Since the man and his daughter were new to town, people would have been interested. Asked questions, nosed about. Right? And then there's the boy. Maybe he's not connected to the girl, but he had a similar story, you know, being a character in his own book, and all that. Maybe we can find out whether there was a connection. How could two kids—a fifteen-year-old boy and an eighteen-year-old girl—with a common interest in books, typewriters, and being characters in their own books—*not* be known by somebody?"

Always practical, Cecelia said, "Maybe they didn't want to be known around town."

"Maybe *they* are not *they*. Thought about that?" added Cynthia, the dreamer. "Maybe there's only one character in the book—a boy who acts like a girl. No law against that, is there?"

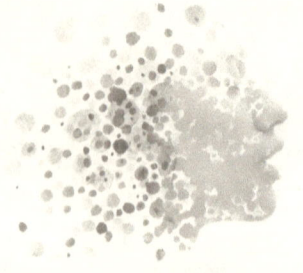

CHAPTER 6

The FBI Field Office in Phoenix was across the street from the federal courthouse, on Monroe Street. The special-agent-in-charge, or SAIC, a veteran named Marcellus Stanza, was not happy. He'd called a meeting of the two agents he'd assigned to investigate the case involving the US Marshal's missing protected witness, Stephan Nau, and his daughter. On the call he had his agents plus the deputy US marshal who had been making the weekly drive-by in Cranston, and a young lawyer from Department of Justice (DOJ). The deputy marshal and the lawyer were conferenced in over a secure telephone net.

"Cambridge," Stanza said, then paused to make sure the telephone people could hear him. When everyone chimed in, he addressed the group.

"I hope you have some good news about the Nau case. While everyone in the room, and on the telephone, has read your most recent update, I'm getting the feeling that we're further behind today than we were weeks ago, when the walk-away by Nau and his daughter was first discovered. Please tell us you're on top of this."

Suppressing the urge to loosen his tie, and squaring himself in the government-issue chair at the long table, Cambridge looked down at his notepad and checked off their current reality.

"The daughter, Vivian, finished her junior year, but has disappeared. The father, Stephan, pulled his trailer out of the trailer park in Cranston, but we're not sure of the exact date. It was before he made his last call into our office. They have a big lead, at least three weeks before the Marshal's office woke up, and figured they'd bolted. We put out a find-and-report APB on them to all field offices in the Southwest. But after fourteen weeks, not one office has responded. Both subjects and their crappy old trailer have simply disappeared. No one paid any attention to them in the nine months they were parked in the US Marshal's witness protection program. Cranston is a desolate little town—that's for sure. The Marshal's office here had visual coverage down there, twice a month, and a monthly telephone call with the park manager. She was a rough old broad, who didn't care what the tenants did as long as they paid their monthly plot fees, on time and in cash. There was nothing amiss. The father played his invalid role well—recovering from heart surgery—no contacts in town. The daughter was not liked in school but didn't care. She had her books. That's all she was interested in. The visual coverage confirmed that. We don't know why they skipped, or where they went. All we have is the book she borrowed at the local library. I reported on that two months ago."

"Right," Stanza said, "you digested the book. But nothing in the book hints at why the girl wanted it."

"Well, maybe, boss. There's more. She told that old librarian, Mr. Ricketts, she was going to go away, to disappear, and he found the book for her in their card catalogue. It's for people who need a fake identity. Hell fire, boss, it's not like the guy was the assassin in *The Day of the Jackal*, who was gonna kill Charles de Gaulle. But this girl may have fixated on the book. Let me just read the first sentence aloud in the book's Introduction. Quote: One need not be planning to kill Charles de Gaulle, as was the assassin in *The Day of the Jackal*, to take advantage of a false identity. The applications are countless, limited only by one's imagination. End quote. This girl, and probably our protected witness the father, may be living completely below the radar, and using techniques outlined in the book. Strange, I know, but what the hell, these people have been in hiding for a little over a year now. Maybe they learned the basics from witness protection and the US Marshal's Office. Could be now they're following the instructions in this book. Strange, but possible, right?"

SAIC Stanza took notes as usual. He ran tight meetings and frowned on free-flow discussions. His decided preference was to call on people who indicated they had something to say.

"Cambridge, I agree the book seems connected, at least on the surface. I also looked through the book. The author, who thinks he's a wit, is actually a nitwit. I don't know why anyone would take serious what a man who uses the pen name 'By Anonymous' says in a paperback book. But even if the girl and her father are following the damn book, what I want to know is, what we are doing to find them? Forget about the introduction and the reference to *The Day of the Jackal.* The part that gets my attention is the back cover. Pass the book over, Cambridge. I want to read it aloud so everyone here and our two guests on the phone can hear me."

He sipped the cold coffee on the table, coughed a little, and read aloud in his most authoritative voice.

> Did you ever wish you had just one more chance at life—the proverbial clean slate? Do you want to shake free from those alimony payments and your lousy credit record? With this book, you can trade in your old mistakes for a brand new start. You can create a totally new person—with bona fide birth certificate, passport, driver's license, credit cards, Social Security number—all you need to break with your past. Learn to project the image you want and prove you are who you say you are. You can have the reputation of being a successful, influential businessman with a prestigious address and corporate backing, or have an untraceable sheltered business savings account. Create either, without fear of being caught.

Agent Cambridge, looked uncomfortable in his standard-issue dark blue suit, the one with a visible sweat stain under one arm. He raised his hand.

"Well, that's the part I don't get. The US Marshal's Office already gave them false identities and a safe house to live in, even if it was on wheels. Nau is not the man's real name, or his daughter's. They are not legally bound to stay in the program, that's clear in the file. So, why run? And why now? And why by creating another set of false identification documents? And for the life of me, I can't figure out why the girl wants to write a book and be in it."

SAIC Stanza's frustration got the best of him. "Hey, listen up everybody. It makes no difference what the girl wants. Here's what is important. The FBI is the best investigative office in the world. This man and his daughter got the name 'Nau' from the US Marshal's Witness Protection Bureau. They are good at hiding people. We are good at finding people." Looking at the conference phone in the middle of the table, he asked, "Can you give us the current timetable regarding the retrial in Washington? And how important is the protected witness to the outcome of that trial?"

"Yes, I can give you the timetable, although the docket is always a little fluid in federal court here in Baltimore. The retrial won't come up until next year. No firm setting. I'm not sure why we're worried at this point. But I'm new to the trial team, and so I can't say for sure how important the protected witness, Mr. Nau, really is. But my sense of it is that if he does not show, and cannot be subpoenaed, lead counsel in the case will likely seek a continuance, which the judge is unlikely to grant. You will have to talk to Felica Navarro; she's lead counsel on this one. But she's tied up in another case right now, down in the Eastern District of Virginia."

"Boss," the larger blue-suited man said, "problem is we're looking for a man named Stephan Nau and his daughter, Vivian. But we know that's not their real names. And the DOJ and the US Marshal's office won't let us put out memos or APBs with their real names. Now, everyone in this room knows their real names, but we can't ask informants or anyone else for information about the real names. I don't get why we can't look for the actual people who took a flyer out of Cranston. Without that information, we're screwed and tattooed, as they say in the Navy."

"Cambridge, you're no longer in the Navy. You say you don't 'get' any of that? You're the lead investigator on this case. Your job is to answer each of those *why* questions. Read the book; that's what the daughter is doing. Who knows what her father is doing? You reported on the head librarian in Cranston, but is he helping or hurting us? Our file here is the standard need-to-know two-page summary. Tells nothing about the past life of Stephan Nau and his daughter Vivian. So, let's hear from the Deputy US Marshal on the phone. George, what can you add to this discussion?"

Everyone waited for a few moments. Then there was an audible click on the conference call speaker. "Marshal Ramsey, you still with us?" SAIC Stanza said.

But there was no answer.

"Well, maybe he disappeared too," Stanza said.

CHAPTER 7

Mr. Ricketts knew from Chapter 2 of *How to Create a New Identity* that the cornerstone of all identity in America is the birth certificate. Theoretically, all citizens have a piece of paper identifying them by name and vital statistics, and setting forth their state of birth, mother and father's names and, often, the name of the hospital where the birth occurred. If Vivian and her father wanted to change their identity, that's where they would have to start. The book described two ways to get a birth certificate other than the one acquired lawfully at birth. You could get a counterfeit one, or you could use what the book called the infant death method. He had assigned this Group X task to Cecelia and Cynthia.

Cecelia was first to report at their regular Saturday morning meeting, an hour before the library opened at ten o'clock a.m. "They won't use the infant death method to get new passports. That would necessitate two infant deaths,

one for Vivian Nau, and one for her father, Stephan. Both
would have to be the right birth years and have the same last
name. After all, it involves taking on the name of someone
who actually lived and died. It's a straightforward method.
Find someone who died but was born about the same time
you were. That means no other records to contradict you
when you claim to be that person. You apply for a certified
copy of the original certificate and make up a new identity
based on that name. The problem here would be finding
two dead people who fit the age requirement and who bear
the same last name. No, Mr. Ricketts, that would not be
simple enough for our elusive Nau family, would it?"

Cynthia, the more thoughtful sister, said, "Quite right.
Quite. Besides, the counterfeit-forgery method would appeal
to the father."

Ricketts asked, "Why do you say that? We know almost
nothing about him."

Both sisters answered at once. "But we do, we do."

Cecelia explained. "The father was not known about
town, rarely left his trailer, and didn't go to the school for his
daughter's things. That makes him a man either on the run
or obsessively private. The fact that they left in the middle
of the night, with two weeks to go on the rent, makes him
a man on the run. A year in a small town is a long time for
a man on the run, don't you think, Mr. Ricketts?"

"And counterfeiting is hard, and risky, but people do it
all the time," Cynthia chimed in.

"It's not hard, if you have the right supplies," Mr. Nettles
offered. "It says on page eleven of the book that it's easy to
order birth certificate forms, just like hospitals do. There

are restrictions, but there are ways to get around those. The book makes it look ridiculously simple. Once you have a form, you fill it in, create a fake signature, and use it to get a passport or a driver's license."

Mr. Ricketts, pouring himself a third cup of coffee and stirring in a packet of Splenda, asked, "Firstly, is it possible they are still using the name Nau, the one they gave at school? They don't know anyone here is looking for them, do they? And secondly, why would they want a passport? Maybe they don't want to leave the country. Maybe they just want to get out of Cranston."

Cecelia spoke while Cynthia nodded affirmatively, "Well, we know the FBI is looking for them. That alone puts them on the run. And it also tells us they would not still be using the name Nau. Which, in turn, tells us Nau is a false name. What we need to know is the name they had before. Who has that name?"

"Any law enforcement agency that gets the APBs—All Points Bulletins—from the FBI, that's how the FBI asks for help from state officers, like the city police here in Cranston, where patrol officer Leo Bustamante works. He is the only officer who reads books. A regular borrower, he is. Never overdue. Never fined. Likes Westerns and mysteries. He told me they had FBI APBs, but I didn't ask him questions that would have raised his suspicions about Group X's mission. However, I can report that the Cranston Police were never sent an APB asking about a student at Cranston High."

"If you didn't ask, how do you know they never got one?"

"Because of what I told him. Sometimes it's better to tell than to ask. I told him Cranston High was saying how proud it was that none of their students ever ran away from home. He said that 'was true for Cranston High, but not true for our chief rival over at Double Creek High in Superior. Lots of APBs on those kids.'"

Ricketts ended the meeting. He went back to his desk managing the library. They went back to cataloguing, shelving, and tidying things up. Little did they know the FBI was about to shift into high gear.

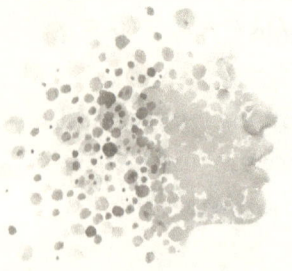

CHAPTER 8

The US Marshal's office in every state is inside a federal courthouse. That makes it especially convenient for facilitating witnesses in and out of government cases. It is also the nerve center for the US Marshal's "Witness Security Program." In the movies, they call it "witness protection." They hide people. Congress included the program in the Organized Crime Control Act of 1970.

"What n' hell are you saying, Marshal Ramsey?" SAIC Stanza hollered. "You saying you had eyes on both Nau and his daughter one week, in Cranston, and then two weeks later they just vanished? Nobody knew they were gone? Nobody knows where they went? And nobody can assure me that the man and his daughter will be found in time to take the witness stand again if the case has to be tried all over again in Washington, DC? Mr. Nau and his daughter got away from you in May. It's July now. You know I'm under a boatload of pressure from Washington because that trial has been postponed three times. Now it's back on the active trial docket. And the DOJ expects the FBI to find their chief witness. None of us ever saw the man, or his daughter. You knew them both. You ought to be helping us find them."

Marshal Ramsey didn't like SAIC Stanza because he always found someone to blame in every case. Fact was, the "eyes" on Nau comprised a drive-by through the RV park in Cranston once a week. Or at least a written note in the case log that someone drove by. Yes, there were also one or two random phone calls made during the two weeks before they bolted. The deputy marshal assigned to drive down to Cranston that particular week didn't go because he pulled a groin muscle in a softball game. Worse yet, the telephone checks went unanswered. Nobody worried about it other than to check a "no-contact" box on the Nau folder. What Marshal Ramsey didn't tell Stanza was that Nau had at least a four-week head start.

"We'll find them; it's only a matter of time. They left town in that big white elephant of an RV. We've checked every park and every sales lot in a five-hundred-mile circle around Cranston. It hasn't been sold, rented, gassed up, or seen anywhere. So, our operating assumption is that it's under wraps somewhere, and they have another vehicle. They've been in that damn thing since they signed the witness-pro doc two years ago. As I understand it, the man and his daughter lived in a real house back in Virginia for more than three years before the first trial. When was that, summer of 2013? They must be country folk or wandering gypsies, I don't know. However, odds are, they have abandoned it somewhere out of sight. We've got every federal and state law enforcement agency in the Southwest looking for it. But we can't post their pictures anywhere because they are protected by law. You know that. Our APB just describes them as a forty-year old white male and his seventeen-year old daughter. Their names are also protected, which makes the search that much harder."

"Marshal Ramsey, you are authorized to reveal names to other federal agencies, you know that."

"Yes, I do, and we have. But that creates two problems. First, state law enforcement doesn't know their real names. Doesn't matter because the likelihood is they are using fictitious names anyhow."

SAIC Stanza exploded. "Likely? Is that what you think—it's merely likely they have fictitious names? Crap, we know damn good and well they *are* using fictitious names. They checked a book out of the library to tell them how to escape from you!"

"A book? What are you talking about?"

Stanza opened his desk drawer, picked up the thin five-by eight paperback, and slid it across the desk. Ramsey picked it up, looked at the front cover, turned to the back cover, and read the first sentence aloud, "Do you ever wish you had one more chance at life—the proverbial 'clean slate'? You can create a totally new person—with *bona fide* birth certificate, passport, driver's license, credit cards, Social Security number—all you need to break with your past. Learn to project the image you want and prove you are who you say you are."

Ramsay tried to quell the growl in his stomach, "And you know they are following the plans in that little book *how*?"

"We know it because a bookish little librarian down there in Cranston talked to us about it. He's looking for them too. He wants his damn overdue library book back! I think your marshals better get off their butts and find my witness before that damn librarian does."

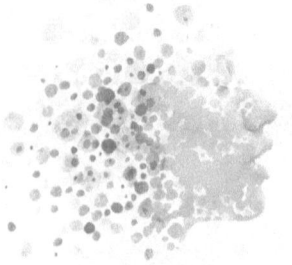

CHAPTER 9

A week later, Stanza had not heard from Marshal Ramsey, which he understood given their testy relationship. He left a voice message for Ramsey to call him back and then walked down the hall to the men's room. From there he made the loop around the floor to the back hallway and stopped by the lunch room and poured himself a cup of luke warm coffee. Just like the Nau investigation, he thought. When he got back to his office his secretary was standing in his doorway looking like she was about to faint.

"Where've you been," she blurted at him. Director Ashurst called and insisted I find you ASAP.

"Did he say what he's calling about?"

"Yes, it's about that WITSEC bolt from Cranston. He sounded very anxious."

It was only the second time in his twenty-seven years with the FBI that *the* Director of the FBI called him, except for conference calls with multiple agents. He knew before taking the call that his job might be on the line.

"This is Agent Stanza, sir. I presume you're calling about the Goshkervic case and our missing witness, Stephan Nau. I have the file on my desk. Would you like a short briefing, or is there something specific I can help the Director's office with?"

"Stan, this is not my office calling, this is me. We don't know one another well, but our interactions have been good over the last three years since I approved your SAIC appointment in Arizona. So, let's cut the formality. My friends call me Brad. Now, you're alone in your office, right Stan?"

Bradley Anderson Ashurst had led the FBI as director for just over two years and had another eight to go on his ten-year term. He was one of the few directors who had actually been an FBI agent for his entire career. His thirty-three years in service gave him an agency perspective no prior director had ever had. With that experience came an institutional reluctance to share information with other agencies unless it might adversely impact national security. And even then, the impact had to have a global connection before Ashurst would seek outside help.

"Yes, Mr. Director, that's right and . . ."

"Have you read the three new 302s on Mr. Nau? I know you read the originals the Baltimore SAIC filed in April, but these are new; these three witnesses were added in anticipation of the upcoming trial in Baltimore. I was just told your office was not provided with these until yesterday afternoon. I'm sorry things got screwed up in Baltimore, but there may be more to this case than your office understood when the missing witness evaded the Marshal's Office. He's been gone for a long time now.

Sucking in a deep breath, Stanza made the right decision—don't try to bluff the boss.

"No, sir, I haven't read them myself. I learned late yesterday afternoon that they'd come via secure-net-five. Copies were made and read by my number two last night. He's tied up in court this morning, so I could not talk to him and . . ."

"All right. That's understood. Read them today, and call me back this evening. You're three hours behind us, so try to reach me before 1800 hours your time. I'll still be here. Don't want to overstate this, but you'll see when you read the 302s that what all of us thought was a large domestic financial crimes case is looking more and more like a South American money laundering case. It has CIA operatives and FinCIN agents mounted up. Your missing witness, protected-named Nau, true name Manchester, may or may not have known what was happening with his company's parent. But there's a possibility he learned something that would have scared the crap out of him. And there's a possibility that he may know that his company actually did more business with a bank in Panama than any other currency trader in the US. The Panamanian bank was called *Banco de Transfercias de Divisas*, which loosely translated means the bank of currency transfers. To complicate matters, the target in the Baltimore case, Fritz Goshkervic, is no longer with us. My understanding is your office has no recent tracking of the missing witness, right?"

"Yes, sir. But I met with US Marshal George Ramsey last week and tried to light a fire under him. But, sir, if I may, what did you mean when you said the target, Mr. Goshkervic, is no longer with us?

I'll give you a more thorough update tonight. In the interim, you should know as you read the 302s that Mr. Nau's boss, Fritz Goshkervic, who had copped a plea to avoid a conviction, made a really bad deal."

"Bad deal? He avoided prison time, didn't he?"

"Yes, but yesterday Goshkervic boarded a private Learjet in San Antonio, Texas. The flight plan indicates a nonstop to Panama City. The plane blew up over the Gulf last night. Two pilots, two passengers on board. No survivors reported. The National Transportation Safety Board's (NTSB) team is on station, and Homeland Security's bomb squad will be sorting things out. But the explosion was spotted on FAA radar, and the debris covers a five-mile area already. There's limited press on it, because no one's connected the dots yet. If, as we suspect, this is a Sinaloa Cartel hit, then our missing witness, Stephan Manchester, might be next in line. These boys kill everyone in sight when enough money is involved."

"Boss, why was the plane headed for Panama if the hit came from Mexico?"

"Why Panama? Because that's where the Sinaloa Cartel launders its money. Tons of money; we don't have a ball-park number yet, but Financial Crimes Enforcement Network (FinCEN) is thinking that the Panamanian bank "dry cleans" more than a billion dollars a year. So, whatever plan Mr. Manchester used to hide from you *and* the US Marshals better be a good one. He could be lined-out for a long-barrel sniper shot wherever he is. The guy's pretty smart—he's eluded us and the US Marshal's office for months. But now, he may have the Sinaloa Cartel on his ass. We need to find him before they do."

CHAPTER 10

"Daddy, I think you picked a peach of a place for us this time," Vivian said, sitting outside the new "Jumbo" they'd bought in Yuma, two months ago. "And I like the color of the new Jumbo, too—he looks pretty in blue."

Jumbo was what Vivian and her dad called the old wreck of a house trailer that had been their home in Cranston. They'd lived in Jumbo ever since the US Marshal's office bought it for them, just before the first trial in Washington two years ago. Two days after they left Cranston, they parked Jumbo in a big abandoned rock quarry twenty miles off the I-8 Freeway between Cranston and Yuma. Somebody would find it there, someday, her Dad thought. By then, he hoped he and Viv would be the new people she'd invented in her book. The one she'd never publish because it was part of their disappearance.

Her dad had traded in the 2007 Dodge Ram pickup for the 2010, twenty-four foot Winnebago RV in Yuma. They only gave him $500 in trade for the Dodge pickup because he said he didn't have the title with him. I'll mail it to you when we get back home to Texas, he told 'em. Actually he had it in one of the boxes of stuff in the bed of the pickup, but didn't want to sign anything the US Marshal's office could use to track them. Cash only, he said. Everything we do, we do in cash. He said that a lot. Viv knew that because it was in the Cranston library book. Cash is fungible, not traceable. Credit cards and anything you sign can help people find you when you don't want to be found, Mr. Anonymous preached.

They'd read Chapter 10 together. She read and he took notes. Viv thought this chapter, entitled "Losing a Past Identity," was lots of fun. Fun to read, fun to think about, and exciting to put into their new lives, on the run.

"Daddy," Viv said, "This chapter asks two questions. I don't know the answer to either one. Can we talk about them?"

"Sure," her dad answered, "but maybe later."

"Daddy, you said that before. I would really like to know why we had to leave Cranston in the middle of the night. You seem like you're hiding something from me."

"OK, Viv, what are the questions?"

"Well, these come from Mr. Anonymous. First one is how badly do you want, or need to disappear? The second is how much would someone spend to try to locate you?"

For a minute, her dad just sat there, staring out the window at the hazy blue sky.

"OK, Viv, I'm sorry for keeping this from you, but it's because we had to get away and I didn't want to stir things up, you know what I mean, don't you?"

"You were worried about Vince? Is that Daddy?"

"Yes and because, well because we know what stress does to you. But the truth is we had to get away because something really bad happened to my former boss, Mr. Goshkervic, and I was afraid to tell you. You know, because it would scare you."

"Scare me? Something bad about Mr. Goshkervic?"

"Yes, Viv. He died in an airplane accident while the plane was flying over the Gulf of Mexico, about a week before we left Cranston. I only found out about the plane crash when I read an article that came out a newspaper in Houston, Texas. It was a private jet with two passengers and two pilots. All four were killed. So, well that scared me to death. He was my friend and . . ."

Vivian hugged her Dad as he started to tear up. "Daddy, that's so terrible. But what does that have to do with us, or staying in the witness program in Cranston."

"Viv, I hate to tell you. Please don't get too scared. It was a bomb. Somebody bombed the plane and killed everybody on board. I'm really scared, for me and you. If they bombed the plane to keep Mr. Goshkervic from testifying, what about me? Are they looking for me now? That's why I had to get you out of Cranston. Disappear, you know. Just like in that library book. My old boss, Fritz Goshkervic, stole some money from the company we both worked for. He was denying it. But I was going to have to tell the judge and the jury what I knew. So, if Mr. Goshkervic was murdered to keep him from testifying, and he's dead now, will they be coming after me?"

Vivian sensed what had happened to her dad. Not all the details, but at least enough to see how and why they had to move to Cranston. Vivian knew a lot more now than he had told her when they first went into witness protection. He'd told her then that he'd been the assistant treasurer in a company in Baltimore that traded in commodities around the world. Now, she was eighteen, they'd escaped from Cranston and had been living in national parks, trailer parks, RV parks, and big rig parking lots for almost three months. They were on the road, almost all the time. Together.

"Daddy," Viv said after he got two bottles of water from the little fridge in the RV, "I was only sixteen when we had to leave Baltimore. Now I'm eighteen and I think you should tell me more about what happened."

"My company, Hurlitt International, bought and sold future contracts on products in the energy space—natural gas, crude oil, and refined products dealing in futures and options. We were also active brokers in gold and rare metals. The company I worked for didn't actually own anything. They just connect buyers with sellers in an electronic exchange center. Say, for example, an investor here in Arizona wanted to buy some gold as an investment because he thought the price of gold was going to go up. He could buy gold ingots from a gold mining company, store them in his garage, wait for it to go up in price, and then sell it at a profit. If you are a commodities trader, you buy gold when you think it's going to go up and sell it when you think it's going to go down. Our company was a boutique operation, specializing in fossil fuels and rare metals. We had customers from all over, although mostly in South America. I was an accountant and really good with numbers, and how to deal with large amounts of currency from foreign countries. I didn't buy or sell or trade commodities for the company. I just got paid a good salary every month for keeping the books. My boss, Mr. Goshkervic, was the chief financial officer at the company. I didn't know it while I was working there, but he figured out a way to skim money away from our company by trading for his own account, without telling the company. When he made money, he kept it. When he lost money, he assigned the trade to one of the customers and they took the loss."

"But," Viv interrupted, "you never did anything like that, or anything wrong. You already told me that two years ago."

"Right Viv. I'm just the poor shmuck who learned about the scheme and told the president of the company. He called the FBI and they arrested my boss. I testified at the first trial, and the jury convicted him. But one of the prosecutors lied to the judge and failed to disclose exculpatory evidence to the defense lawyers. So, the appeals court reversed the conviction. You know they were going to have another trial. But bombing that plane, well I just don't know. I know the federal prosecutors don't want me anymore. But who killed Mr. Goshkervic? Are they going to come after me now? Do they know about me?"

"Daddy, I don't think we can answer that. But we can still be careful and disappeared. Right? I remember when you sold our old Dodge pickup in Yuma and bought the Winnebago RV? They know our names do they?"

"No, he only gave me $500 for trading in the pickup. And remember, I told him I didn't have the title."

"So, Daddy, how could the man get his money back. I mean without a title?"

"Sweetums, that's how the used car business works in border towns. Our Dodge truck was worth maybe twenty-five hundred dollars. He probably took it to the MVD office and told them he bought it for scrap, and needed a duplicate title. But since he didn't know my name, they would not give him one. So he would then sell it for scrap, for maybe $600. He's made a hundred dollars on the deal. The scrap dealer probably had a way to send the truck to Mexico where they are not that particular about titles and things. That scrap dealer guy might have gotten a thousand cash for it. It's really just all about doing business in cash. I told the salesman we were going to spend a year or two in Mexico. Lots of people headed into Mexico dealt only in cash. Didn't bother him none."

After taking the road south to San Luis, they'd stopped and spent the night at a rundown RV park, making sure the owner knew they were headed south to spend the summer in Mexico. Next morning, they took US 2 back to Yuma and followed the Arizona side of the Colorado River north up to Kingman, where they turned back north and east to St. George, Utah. They just stayed there for a few days, then drove east toward Nevada and from there over to central California. They spent the next six months driving back and forth from Nevada and California. Finally, now that the winter snow was gone, they were back in St. George.

The Grand Canyon RV Park in St. George was less than a mile from the north rim and busy with hikers and trekkers in the summer. Viv looked the part, with new hiking boots, trekking poles, and a new REI 70-liter backpack ready for a five-day trek down into the canyon. In a way she couldn't express in words, here, on the Utah side of the Grand Canyon, Viv felt safe.

She'd worn her blond, frizzy hair short the year they spent in Cranston. Her dad called her mop top. When she wanted to, she could rake her hair back and upwards. Whether she wore a baseball cap or her beat-up black cowboy hat, she could instantly become a gawky fourteen-year-old boy. She was thin-lipped, with good teeth, but was moderately duck-footed. That attribute allowed her to take on a boy's persona. She had the gait of a boy, but when called for, the grace of a girl. The one very girl-like thing she did was giggle rather than laugh. So, when she wanted to be taken for a prepubescent boy, she avoided laughing at all costs. When the tomboy in her gave way to Vivian, the evolving young woman, her laugh made her unquestionably feminine.

The next morning, after learning about Mr. Goshkervic's murder, Vivian spent more time than usual in the Winnebago's three-foot-square bathroom. When she emerged, her hair was cropped shorter than ever. Her Dad noticed.

"I cut it as short as I could, Dad. You knew I would."

He did.

"Did you and Mom ever come here, you know, before . . . ?"

Vivian's voice trailed off. A few moments passed in that awkward silence between them whenever the subject of *before* came up. Her dad never knew how far to take the conversation. He was torn between full disclosure to his sometimes-fragile, sometimes-strong daughter. So often, he gently glazed over their new life on the road in "witness-pro" since Angela's death two years ago. He could talk to Vivian easily enough, but had difficulty talking to Vince.

"No, Viv, we never traveled this far west. We thought about a Southwest trip, before you were born, but it never panned out. But Viv, I am excited about us hiking down the North Kaibab trail to the Colorado River at the bottom of the Canyon. Lot fewer people—less risk for us."

"Dad, when do you think we'll be safe? I'm glad we escaped from Cranston, but do you know yet where we're going?"

"Sweetums, we're on the run so nobody can find us. Not the US marshals and not whoever killed Mr. Goshkervic. We're safer when we keep moving—no roots in the ground, you know. And there's always the thing about you sometimes acting like a boy. Like cutting your hair really short. I hope you're remembering the doctors we saw when you were ten years old. You do, don't you?"

"Sort of, Dad. But who cares about that?"

"You're right. No one cares. Just remember what remember what Dr. Garcia told us in San Francisco. He said you need to be comfortable in your own skin—even if others aren't comfortable in letting you do that"

"Right, Dad, but I can't do anything about Vince. I wish I could just pick one life. But I remember everything

Dr. Garcia told us. My life is real. Vince's life is fiction. You know my book is real for both of us, and for you. It's a true story, even if I'm calling it a novel. I could be Vince as long as it keeps us safe. The real me, the one you and Mom brought into the world, is Vivian. That's what it says on the government-issued birth certificate, right Dad?"

He resisted the urge to hug his daughter, never being quite sure how Vince felt about hugs. He just continued filling up the canteens and checking his day pack.

Then, breaking the silence, he said, "I know our life is a fiction and your book is true, at least it's true to you. Let's just play it safe for another month. I hope Vince doesn't show up. But if he does, well, let's just see if that happens."

"Sure, Dad. My book isn't even half finished. How could it be?"

CHAPTER 11

"Mr. Ricketts," Cecelia asked softly, "my sister and I think Group X should meet after school this afternoon. We have an idea about the missing library book."

The library closed at six o'clock every night because state libraries were not thought of as vital in Arizona's conservative budgetary climate. Once the doors were locked, the four members met in Rickett's office.

"Cynthia, what have you to tell us?"

"Well, I was reading Chapter 4 in Mr. Anonymous's little book. It is a simplistic little thing; you know; just over one hundred pages—large font—not literary quality writing. That chapter covers 'ancillary documentation' and explains how to get the so-called 'cards of life.'"

"Cards of life? What's that mean?" Mr. Ricketts asked.

Cynthia, looking slightly askance at him over her half-rimmed reading glasses, smiled. "Mr. Ricketts, Mr. Anonymous is writing about all kinds of cards in his little book, including library cards. He calls all of them cards to establish a false identity. Mr. Nettles, did you know people use fake student IDs for improper purposes? We didn't either. Library cards are covered in the same section that covers Social Security cards. Isn't that interesting? What occurs to me—well, to both Cecelia and me—is that probably the library card that this girl, Vivian, filled out was not just to read, not just so she could check out books. The Cranston Library card was step one for her, you know, like a coming-of-age thing. Because they didn't mingle, had questionable histories, and no educational records, we think the girl and her father were hiding here in Cranston from who-knows-what. This book, which is poorly written and shallow, probably gave them false hope. Let me read a sentence aloud from page thirty-two. 'Having a library card almost ensures that you are a stable, well-educated, trustworthy citizen.' Yes, she wanted that particular book. But she also wanted us to think she was all those admirable things. After all, she didn't simply steal the book. She got a proper card and checked it out. But the card itself, irrespective of which book she used it to get, was just as valuable as the book was. It meant she could pass for a stable, well-educated, and trustworthy person. What we're wondering about is whether her father also wanted to project those same qualities. If so, why didn't he also get a card?"

Cecelia nodded her head in agreement. Ricketts squinted and, ever so slowly, turned his head from side to side.

"Not sure about that, Cynthia, not sure at all. It could be argued that a stable, trustworthy person would have returned the book by now. It's way overdue. There's a three-dollar fine for that, you know. And she is only eighteen, so maybe the decisions about false identities, and false cards are her father's doing, don't you know?"

Cecelia jumped to her sister's defense.

"Well, Mr. Ricketts, maybe we're wrong and you're right, but have you thought about this. Maybe they are not stable, but want to appear stable. Maybe they aren't trustworthy, but want to make people think they are. Maybe the family's old identity was unstable and untrustworthy. Maybe the new identity, starting with the library card and the book, gives them protection from whatever they are hiding from here in Cranston. Oh, my dear, that was a little speech, wasn't it? Sorry."

"That's all right, Cecelia." Ricketts said. "We know the FBI is onto them and wants to find them for FBI reasons, whatever they may be. The FBI was insistent that I not interfere with justice, but I told them we have a just reason to follow the trail because we are custodians of books and little else in America is as important as that. You say library cards and Social Security cards are covered in the same chapter. I think one's Social Security card is government-issued and carries more legal stature than does a library card."

"Perhaps not, Mr. Ricketts," Cynthia responded, even though the comment was directed at her sister. "But have you checked to see whether the man known as Stephan Nau at the high school also has a library card?"

Suddenly feeling queasy, Mr. Ricketts got up from his chair and walked to the front desk, which was only about twenty feet away. Checking quickly, he seemed relieved when he came back into the office and faced Group X.

"I'm happy to say Stephan Nau does not appear to have applied for a library card."

Cynthia frowned, showing her disappointment. "No, Mr. Ricketts, the test I was suggesting is whether the man known at school as Mr. Nau took his daughter's fake name, Shortfield, here in your library?"

"Oh my, I never thought of that," he said, as he went back to the large cabinet behind the counter. He found it immediately, and brought it back into his office. "Miss Cynthia, you must be promoted to detective first-class at once. Here is the card issued to a Stephan Shortfield over a year ago."

Mr. Nettles asked, "Did he sign it?"

"Yes, of course," Ricketts answered. "We ask for signatures from all library members. Why, is that important?"

"Well, I'm not a detective, or a librarian, I'm just an English teacher. But wouldn't you think that if you compared Mr. Nau's signature on the school documents with the one in your hand under the name Shortfield, the handwriting might be the same? And if that's the case, hasn't the man defrauded both the school and the library? And what if he signed other documents in other places, like the offices of public health in Phoenix? Could we tell if it's the same man because the handwriting is the same? Isn't that what the FBI would do if they knew what we've discovered here in Cranston?"

Group X was silenced, if just for a minute. Mr. Ricketts poked at the idea. "Well, even if the signatures are the same under different names, what value comes from discovering that fraud on public institutions?"

Cecelia, perhaps hoping for a promotion of her own, said, "The value is not in knowing he signed using different names here in Cranston, the value is having his signature in two different places in Cranston. What if those names and signature styles were to show up in places where you get identification documentation from government agencies? Like, for instance, what if Mr. Nau said he was Mr. Shortfield to get a library card, and then used that card to get, say, a driver's license in the same name? Might one compare the signature at the library with the one at the motor vehicles department and determine they were the same person?"

"Perhaps," Mr. Nettles said, "but would the people at motor vehicles tell you anything?"

"Perhaps," Mr. Ricketts, answered, "they would if you gave them Mr. Shortfield's library card and asked for a duplicate driver's license. Unfortunately, we don't have his actual card. We just have our copy in our card file. And besides, it would be a crime to apply for a license under a false name."

"But it's no crime to ask if you could get a duplicate. The crime would be to actually get it, you know, by paying a fee and all that. It's no crime to ask questions. Like, 'Could I get a duplicate license by showing you my library card? It's the only identification I have.' No crime there, I should think."

And that's how Group X found out that Stephan Shortfield got an Arizona driver's license at the Cranston MVD on February 12, 2014. And by looking for the name

Stephan Shortfield in the Pinal County Courthouse, they found out he had petitioned the court for a name change in March 2014. Judge Lincoln H. Cash granted the petition and issued an order for his name to be changed from Stephan Shortfield to Stephan MacLawn. The court petition confirmed that the reason given by the petitioner was to return to his family's historic Irish name.

Cynthia discovered this and called it pure blarney. Cecelia found out that Steven MacLawn had used his new driver's license, issued four days later, to open a savings account at the Cranston Public Employees Credit Union. Actually it was a debit card that he could use like it was a credit account. When asked how she accomplished this, she said her first cousin, Agnes, was the manager. She was also a gossip gold medalist. She said Mr. MacLawn had been a very good customer with a sizeable balance until recently when he said he'd been transferred to a new job in Texas. They were sorry to see him go, she said—six-figure balances are rare in Cranston, don't you know.

Even so, Group X could not acquire a Social Security number for anyone by any name. Belatedly, Mr. Nettles learned by reading Chapter 5 of the book that American citizens are not legally required to carry Social Security cards. While it's not exactly legal, you can buy a blank Social Security card through several form catalogues. If you do that, you can order an attractive-looking card with any name and number on it. Any name and number you give them. No one checks. No one can. It is what Mr. Anonymous calls a "good identity validator and one that is easily manipulated!".

Mr. Ricketts, normally a calm person, was outraged. "What nonsense is that? Social Security numbers represent a private account, held by every citizen so the government can track paid-in benefits for our old age. It's a wonderful government savings program. My favorite president, Mr. Franklin Delano Roosevelt, an enlightened man, made the Congress set it up as a matter of national social conscience. Surely it cannot be that easily manipulated by people hiding from the government."

"But Mr. Ricketts," Cynthia chimed in, "citizens are not required to divulge their Social Security numbers and private companies cannot ask the government for a list of people's Social Security numbers. That's why it's a perfect tool for people on the run, or people who just want to fool other people for whatever reason."

"Yes, Cynthia, but that's the point, isn't it? People must have a number to open a bank account, or get credit at a store, or establish themselves for any number of reasons."

"True enough, but people, you know, are a little foolish. You see, there is no reliable way for a bank, a store, or a credit agency to check on whether the number you give them is accurate. Mr. Anonymous says millions of people have more than one SSN. He encourages people who want to create a new identity to just make up a number and give it to stores over the phone. They can't check. They always just assume it is a proper government-issued number. Many times it is not."

"Well," Ricketts said, dejectedly, "that is all the more reason for us to continue our investigation. If Vivian and her father are fooling us about the library card, and fooling everyone else about his SSN, then we might never get that book back. We must learn more. Let's all think of ways to ferret out the truth and meet here again in my office, same time next week."

CHAPTER 12

Three months later, Group X had lost interest because when none of them came up with any new ideas. The FBI had not called. The only new information they had was about the boy who bought the typewriter from Mr. Stitch. Eventually, they agreed, this boy probably wasn't from Cranston. He probably went to school someplace else, maybe at Maricopa. Cynthia and Cecelia thought he was probably home-schooled; lots of religious people in rural Arizona are, they said.

So, on July 3rd, the day before the Cranston Fourth of July parade passed by, Mr. Ricketts picked up the morning mail at the Library's big box at the Post Office. He was very surprised to see a tan envelope addressed to The Cranston Library, Cranston, Arizona. The sender's name was neatly printed on the upper left corner—Vivian Shortfield. It was postmarked, Phantom Ranch, The Grand Canyon, Arizona.

Inside the envelope was a typewritten letter and twelve dollars. Two fives and two ones. The letter read:

Dear Head Librarian,

We are sorry we couldn't return the library copy of the book, *How to Create a New Identity*. We found it very useful and we continue to find good ideas in it. I think your overdue book fine is $3 per month. Please find twelve dollars to go towards my fine. I hope by the end of the year we won't need the book anymore. I will mail it back to you then. You found this book for me and I can tell you it was a lifesaver.

Sincerely yours,

Vivian & Vince Shortfield

Mr. Ricketts called Group X to order and showed them the letter. Everyone was delighted with the new development.

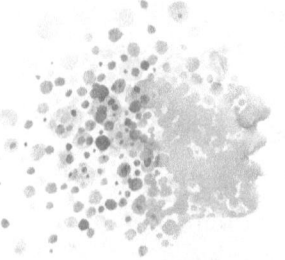

CHAPTER 13

Eight months to the day after Vivian and her dad escaped from Cranston, he signed a month-to-month rental agreement on a condo in a new vacation community five miles from Jackson, Wyoming. They'd spent the last eight months driving to and from RV parks, campgrounds, short-stay hotels, and RV and eighteen-wheeler lots located next to Indian casinos all over California, Nevada, Utah, and Wyoming. They'd taken baby steps toward establishing a new business, one that seemed opportune for them, and one that no one else in America had ever tried. The idea was Viv's, but her dad put flesh on the skeleton drawn by Viv in her book. The book was now about a hundred pages long and showed real promise.

The family business, creating legitimate LLCs in Delaware, was doing OK. They'd made $3,600. It was run from an online account under a fake ID and a passcode that Vivian said Vince would change monthly. Stephan had cashed out his retirement plan at Hurlitt International, sold their house, and cashed in his insurance policies. That generated $362,000, which he'd deposited in his checking account at Wells Fargo in Baltimore, under his given name, Stephan Manchester. When he first became a protected witness, and the US Marshal's office had relocated them in Cranston, he went to a Wells Fargo branch in Phoenix and closed out his Baltimore account. It was under his real name, Stephan Manchester. He took a cashier's check for $72,000 and the rest in cash, which caused a stir at the bank. They made him wait three days, which meant another driving trip from Cranston to Phoenix.

The cash, in hundred dollar bills amounted to $290,000. Stephan wanted a private, secure place to hide the cash. He took off the bank wrappers, counted the money into stacks of hundred dollar bills. He used new rubber bands to hold each stack of $10,000. He had twenty-nine stacks. Then he went to a REI store in Salt Lake and bought a fireproof bag. The bag cost $105. It was made of metalized aluminum/Mylar and measured twenty inches long by eleven inches wide, and was seven inches high. The fire-proof guarantee was clear, but he knew he'd never make a claim on it. Once he secured the thirty-six stacks of newly rubber banded hundred dollar bills, he did both an online and a personal search for a place to store the PacSafe roller bag.

What he found surprised him because it was not a bank; it looked like the ultimate safety deposit box. They called it *Vault Mountain*. When he and Vivian saw it in person they agreed it had the look and feel of a medieval dungeon. Deeply embedded in a mountain in north central

Phoenix, surrounded by tons of steel, concrete, and rock, the front door was a 7,000-pound steel vault door in front of ten-inch steel-reinforced walls and floors. It claimed a state-of-the art security system, consistent humidity and temperature control, and armed guards on duty 24/7. And most importantly, it was privately owned; no Social Security number, or driver's license required. *Vault Mountain* did not ask about the contents of the Mylar bag. They simply allowed him to stuff it into the tin box they provided. Then they tagged the box with a computer-generated thirteen-digit number and sealed it with four-inch-wide, red-and-yellow security tape. Any effort to open the tin box would cause the tape to self-destruct, leaving the words "opened" and "void" on both the affixed surface and on the security tape. Lastly, they gave him the thirteen-digit number embossed on a one-quarter-inch-thick piece of heavy card stock. All that Stephan, Vivian, or anyone else needed to retrieve the bag, or change its contents, was that number. Stephan had another $25,000 in fifty-dollar bills hidden inside their RV.

When he and Vivian escaped from Cranston, he had that $72,000 cashier's check with him. He cashed it in Blythe, California. He worried that the government might discover the transaction in Blythe, but Vivian reminded him that even so, they could not track, or find the cash. After their stay on the north rim of the Grand Canyon, they drove to Jackson Hole, Wyoming because it seemed perfect for their life in hiding. Wyoming is America's smallest state. It draws more tourists than residents. They'd camped around Jackson Hole several times over the three months that it took to make a final decision about where to plant a few temporary roots. The fact that the FBI and the US Marshal's Office had never gotten close to them was because they moved from one place to another every other week, and sometimes every other day. And they always paid for everything in cash—no credit card accounts for the FBI or the Marshal's Office to track. They used prepaid phones, made-up names, and fictional Social Security numbers.

They used only first names, Viv, or Vivian, Stephan or Ship. They made no friends and never attracted attention from anyone. On the surface, they were just another small family on vacation, minding their own business, and being stand-offish when asked questions of any kind. Rural people were more friendly than city people, and readily took no for an answer.

"Morning, folks. New to our little town?" they'd be asked.

"No, just on vacation passing through," her dad would answer.

"Mighty fine," the man, or lady would say, "I can give you some ideas if you want."

"No thanks," Dad would say, "we got a book."

And that's how Vivian continued to write her disappearing story.

Jackson, Wyoming seemed perfect. Founded in 1894 and serving as the county seat of Teton County, it was as transient as any place they'd visited in the last year. There was no real count of how many people actually lived in Wyoming year around, but more people lived outside of a town than in one. The county swelled and dissipated between summer and spring due to the proximity to Grand Teton and Yellowstone National Parks, the National Elk Refuge, and highly popular ski resorts.

"Jackson Hole" was a nickname for the valley surrounded by Yellowstone National Park on the north, the Tetons on the west, the Gros Ventre Mountain Range on the east, and the Wyoming Range on the south. Her dad particularly liked the culture of the valley—deep Western heritage overlaid with tourists, visitors, lots of money, deep secrets to keep, and an obsession with privacy.

Viv, now eighteen but mature beyond those years, spent much of her time in small community libraries reading books at little tables or in secluded reading nooks. When asked if she wanted to take a book out, she'd decline with a smile. "We're just staying at the campground, or the hotel," she'd explain. The part-time local library volunteers always respected that, and discouraged conversation of any kind— just like librarians, worldwide. She read both fiction and books on criminal law, procedure, corporate governance, and especially anything remotely suggesting a hidden life. A month before her dad picked the valley known as Jackson Hole for them to settle in, she told him how they might live the next five years.

"Five years," he said. "Why five years? Why not ten, or two?"

"Dad, I'm eighteen and you're headed for fifty. No self-respecting plan lasts longer than five years. Corporate America lives on five-year plans, and most of them are changed after the first two years. Congress rotates every two years, the presidency lasts four, and only God knows how long anyone lives. And of course, there's Vince. Who knows how old he is, or how long he will stick with the plan? My plan needs one year to implement, one to grow big, and three to give us a stake that, if invested wisely, can carry us forever."

Her dad got up, went into the house to get another Diet Coke, and returned to his wicker chair on the front porch. The little stream across the dirt road gurgled in the afternoon lull, and everything seemed content in their little world. The closest neighbor was two football fields away. All the lots were four acres, and so far only twenty out of the hundred lots had been sold. Jackson was five miles away. They were safe.

Easing down into his chair, he mused. "Viv, you've latched onto more information, read more books, made more lists, and spent more time with your handheld calculator than anyone in Wyoming. But there's no financial stake that could carry us forever. Markets go bust, crooks steal, the government takes more, and who knows what inflation will do in my lifetime, much less yours."

"Daddy, Daddy, for a smart accountant, you reject mathematical projection. Besides, when I said forever, I meant the foreseeable forever, not the hypothetical one. If we can find the right associates, build the right corporate structure, and invest in treasury notes, municipal bonds, and debt instruments, we can live on the yield and never touch the principal. That's sound financial planning for the foreseeable future, don't you agree?"

"Viv, I think your plan, at least the sketch you've given so far, is brilliant. But before we get too deep into it, what did you mean about Vince—his age, and whether he'll stick with the plan? Can we talk about that?"

She hated Diet Coke. For her, hydration was a strict regimen—she ran 3.1 miles every morning—half a 10K. She carried a quart water bottle with her everywhere. She drank tea with meals, every meal. But she never nagged her dad about his addiction. She went into the kitchen, filled her aluminum bottle with ice and water, and came back to the porch.

"Did you know, Dad, that Vince used to like pop, but he only drank the real stuff, the full-sugar version? Remember him fishing around in rental fishing boats for the real stuff, which you never put in the cooler?"

He laughed. "Sure I remember, Viv. Sometimes he was more like me than you. Probably still is, although he hasn't been around since we escaped from Cranston."

"Dad, he was always more like you than me, not just sometimes. Vince is here, not on the porch, but back in the house, on my writing stand. You know that, right? He's not gone, he's in hiding, just like us. Without Vince, I could never have made this plan. I wrote it on his typewriter, the one he bought with his saved-up allowance money back in Cranston. Here's something I bet you didn't know. When Vince needed money for popcorn or movie tickets on Saturday morning, he always got it from me. You bought his clothes and food and stuff, but I bought him happy stuff. That typewriter was way beyond my budget, so he bought it with his own money. That's the only time he did that."

"And your point is?"

"My point is that Vince was a financial planner. He knew the difference between invested capital and operational expenses. He sees the soundness in my financial plan, but you have doubts. We need capital, which can only come from two sources—money from customers and money from investments. Our long-term capital will build up over the five years. Our operating capital will increase over the five years, but will be spent on us, the owners of the company. Our investment capital will not be spent—it will spin off money forever, the reasonably foreseeable forever. And Vince cannot be an owner, because he's not an adult, like me and you. But he will be a beneficiary of invested capital because he will always be here, just invisible while I'm here, you know?"

"OK, Viv, I'm all ears," he said. "Let's go past the outline. Tell me exactly how we'll implement your plan."

"OK, Daddy, here it is. I think there are large numbers of people in America who would love to change their reality. The reasons are almost endless. Bad marriage, bad job, bad educational choices, bad parents, siblings, friends, bosses, or just bad luck. Most of them are not criminals, or even suspected of criminal acts—like you. You were an innocent witness to a large financial fraud, so you needed protection, security, and time. The government gave you, me, and Vince a temporary secret life because they needed your testimony. But my plan is not about government witness protection, or witness security. My plan is to create a private company giving private citizens a new, different, wholly secret life. They run away and hide from their old life. They do it to get away from the land of bad things they used to live in. And our new company creates that new life and charges a fee. It's that simple."

"The idea," he said, "is simple. But I asked you how we're going to implement the plan. That can't be simple."

"Actually, Daddy, it is simple. It's simplistically simple, I guess. We become a limited liability company in Delaware because that state doesn't make the owners of the company reveal their names in the articles of organization. All they insist on is the name of the company and the name and address of the company's registered agent in Delaware. Almost all of them are law firms located in Dover. It starts with that simple act. We hire an agent. We file articles of organization under our name—that is, our company name—and we're in business."

"But names aren't simple, Viv. We've worked hard to change our names—our real names before my boss got arrested—to the ones we got in Arizona when we changed them legally before that judge in Pinal County. Are those the names we're going to use for the new company?

"No, we don't use what I'll call human, or person names. We only use a corporate name, which we make up, after we make sure no one else is using it. The name for our first limited liability company will be Disappearance, LLC, a Delaware Limited Liability Company. Do you like it?"

"I suppose so. Just one word, disappearance? Or is the full name The Disappearance Company, a Delaware blah blah blah?"

"Right, just one word."

"Well, this is your plan so I'll leave that part to you, but what is our business?"

"Dad, don't you see the simplicity at play here? The name of our company *is* our business. That's what I told the head librarian, Mr. Ricketts, I wanted to do—disappear. He found the book that gave me the start of this plan. But that book, while I loved it a year ago when I knew nothing about business, is too simple. It's mostly about how a person can make up a new human—or person—name, and how to prove it to anyone who asks. My plan is way better than that. We don't change people's names; the courts do that legally. Then those people come to us for ways to make money while staying anonymous. What I've discovered is how to do that as a company, not as an individual. Everyone treats companies different than they do people. Companies can sue, be sued, hire, fire, do business, make deals, get paid, have bank accounts in other states, or countries, and do anything that people can do."

"No, Viv, not anything. They cannot get married, have children, love the mountains, or write books, like you can."

"I beg to differ, dear Daddy. Corporations get married by merger. The have children by forming subsidiaries. They love by being loyal to their corporate mission, and they issue stock certificates and annual reports, which are how corporations write books. Sometimes they cook the books, too. We'll get to that later."

The problem with Jackson Hole turned out to be a nosey manager and loud neighbors. Their condo had joint walls with neighbors on either side and another one directly overhead. The upstairs neighbors had two teenagers, who had a very loud stereo system. The couple on the east side fought a lot. The single woman on the west side was quiet but seemed to have gentleman callers at all hours of the day and night. None of them stayed long, but it meant lots of men walking up and down the hallway. The upstairs neighbors' teenagers were seventeen and eighteen and they tried to get to know Vivian. She didn't like their music, or their politics. Mostly she didn't like the fact that they were hunters and talked mostly about the thrill of dropping an elk with something called a thirty-ought-six.

The other thing was the rental manager's insistence that Dad increase the security deposit from $500 to $2,500. Dad objected and said he thought everyone in the building was on a $500 security deposit.

"Yeah," the always-cranky manager said, "but you're the only one that doesn't have a credit rating. I called Experian and Trans-Union both. One of 'em, can't remember which, said you had no rating. The other said they never heard of you. So, I gotta have extra security on you. Maybe you're an escaped bank robber for all I know. You always pay in cash, you're the only one, so . . ."

Dad cut him off.

'We're paid up to the end of the month. We'll be out by then.'

Dad decided they should go to Boise. "They have a good college there, and we can go back to living in the baby blue Winnie."

CHAPTER 14

Group X lost its focus on Vivian and her missing library book. But still, every other Saturday morning, they met over coffee and donuts at the library for an hour before the front doors were opened. They occasionally talked about little Miss Vivian, but with little interest. Surprisingly, they found another reason to meet—the discovery of a common interest in the stock market. All four were frugal and put away a good part of every paycheck. They were all faced with the challenge of how to get ahead on a government salary. They all liked their jobs and didn't want to do anything else. So they decided to do what many other small groups in America were doing now that the stock market crash in 2008 was no longer plaguing Americans—they formed an investment club.

They signed a general partnership agreement that limited the partnership's business to investing, for mutual benefit, in equities, mutual funds, and bonds. All four were equal partners. All buy-and-sell decisions had to be unanimous. The decision to hold a position came by default. They opened a partnership bank account at the First State Bank of Cranston, on Apache Boulevard, a block down from the library. All four were joint owners with right of survivorship. They did that because of a little ditty Cecelia made up; "Last One to Die Gets the Pie." Ricketts and Nettles readily agreed since they were at least ten years younger than the twin sisters. They planned to distribute all dividends and interest income annually, and agreed to make a year-end decision on whether to declare a cash distribution by selling one or more invested positions. They started out with a $5,000 per partner capital contribution. Nettles and Ricketts were surprised when Cecelia and Cynthia expressed concern that was too low. While no one disclosed personal net worth, it became clear in the first couple of months that the sisters had much more money already invested in the market and could likely buy and sell their higher-paid partners.

The day before they were to meet and make year-end investment club decisions, Mr. Ricketts got a brightly colored box in the US Mail, from a UPS store in Boise, Idaho, with a cheery Merry Christmas stamp in lieu of a return mail address. Inside the UPS box was a letter and a smaller box that said, "Read Letter First—Then Open Me." The letter said.

Dear Mr. Head Librarian Perry Rickets,

I know what a bother I have been to you and that you probably worried a lot about my overdue book. You were kind to find it for me and I repaid you by not returning it on time. It is, I am ashamed to say, almost twenty months overdue. Yikes! Enclosed is $48.00 which, with the $12.00 I sent earlier, should reinstate me as a library card holder. I wanted to tell you why I so loved the book you found for me. My father, my brother, and I were in Cranston under false pretenses due to a legal entanglement my dad had in our home state. He did nothing wrong but was an important witness in a legal case. His life had been threatened, so the US Government offered to protect him under a federal statute called the Witness Security Act. You can look it up, I'm sure. My dad didn't want any more government security last year, so we left the program voluntarily. I'm sure the FBI and the Marshal's Office contacted you. I'm sorry for that. We're going to stay disappeared, but we have a new business, and hope to attract qualified investors soon.

Merry Christmas,

Vivian & Vince

Inside the other box was the overdue book, *How to Create a New Identity*. Paper clipped to the front cover, Mr. Rickets found a crisp cream-colored business card with embossed printing on the front side. Disappearance, LLC, a Delaware Limited Liability Company. Below the corporate name was the name, address, and telephone of a Dover law firm called Boulders & Scrantin, PLLC, registered corporate agent. On the back side of the card was a handwritten note. *"We help you to live life twice."*

CHAPTER 15

The home office of Houston International Savings and Loan, Inc., is just one of three drab-looking rental suites in a Baytown strip mall on Garth Road. Baytown is a working-class suburb of Houston. The local S&L is conveniently located next door to a busy Pac 'n Mail store. The third suite is a law firm called Withers & Associates, which claims expertise in construction loans and bankruptcy. While it's not obvious to the public, what really connects the three different businesses is the hallway at the back of each tenant space. It allows the single owner of all three entities remote access to each separate facility. Julia Santerra-Evans owns the building, and runs all three businesses. Collectively, the three companies employ four people. They get generous bi-monthly paychecks drawn on the house account at Houston International Savings, but no healthcare coverage, or 401K accounts. They have very little to do and almost no supervision. They call the S&L by its acronym, "HIS," double entendre for its female owner.

Julia, a fully-licensed Texas lawyer, was a solo practitioner. There never was a lawyer named Withers, and her law practice was a front. She was a good lawyer, a good shot, and had a concealed-carry permit for her Glock G19s pistol, a weapon initially designed to provide the US Army with the very best personal protection sidearm in the world. By early 2016, the G19s had been available to law-abiding citizens like her. She was a registered broker/dealer at Houston International Savings, which had a front office teller and cashier named Abe, an elderly black man. And she was the owner/manager of the franchise Pac 'n Mail store, which had two staffers—always temporary—and rotated every other month by Julia. All incoming and outgoing mail came to the Pac 'n Mail, where it was sorted and then delivered twice daily via the back hallway connecting the three businesses. While HIS had a typical front-office look, complete with a teller's caged-window, it had no local customers. Its posted fee schedules were three times as high as other S&Ls in Baytown and the greater Houston area. In a word, all three companies were shells.

The strip mall had one vacant space, posted for lease through a Houston real estate agency. All calls to that agency ended quickly since the square-foot rental price was much higher than competing space anywhere in south Texas. The deed to the strip mall itself was vested in a Delaware LLC, with a statutory agent in Dover, the capital city of Delaware. The Delaware agent paid all taxes, utilities, and maintenance costs by invoicing Withers & Associates.

The oblong, four-stall strip mall had one feature that differentiated it from almost every other building in that part of Texas. Built in 1953 by South Texas Cement Industries, the building's exterior, slab, and roof were constructed entirely out of poured concrete. Electrical wiring was housed inside three-inch steel piping and the entire 4,000-square-foot building was heated and cooled via floor ducts with a 1950s-model heat pump cabinet. Functionally, it served service businesses well. But from a security perspective, the entire building was a concrete bunker with zero Internet access. That's because the ten-inch poured concrete walls inhibited all but nearby cell tower signals. Each tenant had a single landline phone jack, which provided AT&T service. One unlisted number was common to all three tenant spaces, but the landlord, Ms. Santerra-Evans, prohibited the tenants—who were all employed by her personally—from using the landline under any circumstances.

Julia had a steel desk in her office with a reinforced drawer fitted with an old-style combination lock. Inside that drawer she kept a variety of security and secure devices, including a Glock G19S, and an ASE-MC501 ComCenter Iridium satellite phone. She used the phone daily, but only fired her gun on the Clear Creek Gun Range, every Saturday morning.

Julia had been at her desk, with the satellite drawer wide open, for six hours. It was now almost 10:00 a.m. She had a thermos of black coffee and a bag of carrots. She'd watched the breaking news on CNN's *New Start* program with Chris Cuomo and Alisyn Camerota on her cell phone screen for ninety minutes. The news flash was about a crash of a private jet somewhere over the middle of the Gulf of Mexico sometime after midnight central time. Little was known about the crash. Switching back to the network channels in Houston, she saw they all confirmed the crash and reported some debris visible at sunrise, but nobody seemed to have a fix on either the plane's location or the fate of its occupants yet. So why was her satellite phone not ringing? She had asked for immediate confirmation that her orders had been followed completely and that Mr. Goshkervic was fish food. She wanted visual confirmation that the bomb her team had planted exploded on signal from the fishing boat she'd arranged at the proper GPS coordinates at precisely 0900 hours Greenwich Mean Time, or 2:00 a.m. Houston time. And she wanted confirmation that her fee had been wire transferred from Panama City to her offshore account in Paraguay.

CHAPTER 16

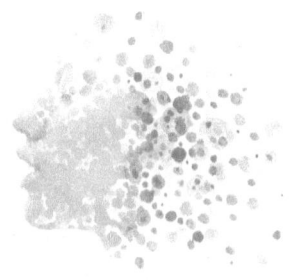

Group X, now fully engaged in twice-monthly sessions about investments, remained mildly interested in Vivian and her book. After receiving the long overdue book a month ago, Mr. Ricketts was excited to say he'd just heard from her.

"Well, my friends," he announced when everyone was settled around the conference table at the library, "I have most interesting news for you. I've made contact with Vivian Shortfield."

Everyone expressed surprise and turned to their leader to hear more. "After we got the book and her nice letter, I wrote to her, in care of that UPS store in Idaho. The address was on the box. I used her official library name, knowing full well it was an alias, and didn't expect it to ever get to our little Miss Vivian. But it did. Yesterday, when I picked up our mail, I found a small envelope mixed in with the stack of junk mail. I didn't sort that stack until this morning and was very surprised to see a note from that same company she mentioned in her last letter, Disappearance, LLC, with its return address in Dover, Delaware. But the postage marks show it came from Boise, Idaho. Let me read it to you, it's short but sweet.

Dear Mr. Ricketts,

I got your nice reply and am happy all is well in Cranston. My dad does not know I'm writing to you, so please don't write back using our mail drop (that's what he calls the UPS store in Boise). We could correspond via general delivery at the main United States Post Office in Boise. It's at 770 S 13th St, Boise, ID 83708. I'll get in trouble with Dad if he finds out, because we're still disappeared, even though the stupid trial is over with in Baltimore. I'm worried about him for the first time since we escaped from Cranston and from those awful marshal deputies. I don't mean personally awful; one of them was nice when he checked on us. But being checked on like you were in jail, or something? It's for the birds. Like crows. I don't like crows, or deputies very much. Anyhow, I'm very much enjoying disappearance and our new business is starting to make money. A man that owns a rafting company up here has made a two-thousand-dollar investment in our company. Dad said that was for 0.05 percent of our stock. I guess he liked our business plan, which I mostly wrote. Dad says we'll either go bust or make a million dollars. He's a very smart man, so I bet we make a million. Please, if you ever see him, say hello to Mr. Nettles, my English teacher at Cranston High. He encouraged me to write my book. It's almost a hundred and fifty pages long already. I ought to finish it in two eons. If I live that long.

Sincerely yours,

Vivian

Cecelia was first to speak. "What a sweet girl. She sounds like such a fine, honest person. Mr. Nettles, you're the only one that knew her, aren't you proud of your student? What with writing a book after learning English from you?"

"Yes, Cecelia, she was sweet, but she was also very quiet and reserved in the classroom. I always had the feeling she didn't want to be noticed. She just did her homework, spoke up only when called on, and left class as soon as the bell rang. I never saw her with other students in the hallways, or the lunchroom. But I did talk to her a few times because she was so sure she'd write a book. She said every time that she was a character, and I told her that was just fine, but it would be hard to write about yourself. She had a strange answer. Something about she could be someone else and still be herself. I didn't follow up with her. She was interested in composition, but not so much in English literature."

Cynthia, ever so practical, said, "Well this is a meeting of the Group X Investment Club, not the Cranston High English club. But we could do both. Why don't we write to her and ask to see her business plan? We could consider an

Angel investment. Cecelia and I would be willing to invest $500 each for one half of a percent interest in a million-dollar company. We'll still be here in two eons, right Sis?"

The club had come into existence on the upswing of the business cycle and in the fifth year of a bull market. They were up almost 20 percent and had a little over $4,000 in cash they could invest, or distribute. No one favored disbursement. Mr. Ricketts was given the go-ahead to write back and get the business plan.

CHAPTER 17

It had been almost eight months since they'd made their escape from Cranston, and no one seemed to be looking for them. Two months moving from place to place in Jumbo II, one-and-a-half months in Jackson Hole, Wyoming, and now another three months in Boise, Idaho. They felt disappeared. Not that they actually knew whether anyone was still looking. It just seemed like the FBI and the US Marshals had forgotten about them. That sense was fortified by the fact that there was no longer a trial in Baltimore to worry about. But Viv, as always, had questions.

"Dad, why did your boss, Mr. Gosh something, I can never remember those funny names . . ."

"Goshkervic," her dad said. "It's Polish, I think."

"OK, gosh-cur-vick," Viv said, drawing the syllables apart phonetically. "Why, hasn't there been any news about what happened to him?

"Viv, Sweetums, I don't know. I've read the *Baltimore Sun* online every day, and other papers too, looking for more about the case, or about the airplane bombing over the Gulf of Mexico. No news from back there. All I can think of is that maybe since Mr. Goshkervic is dead, God rest his soul, maybe the case against him is dead too. And if that's so, then maybe they don't care about us anymore. I was only a witness in the case, not a target like my boss."

"Maybe so, Dad. No news is good news, right?"

Let's hope so. But speaking of news, I have some for you."

"Good or bad?" Viv answered.

"Maybe it will turn out to be great news. I got a text yesterday from a commodities trader up in Seattle. I saw a notice on a job-search website. I could hardly believe it—it sounded like my old job. But it's as far away from Baltimore as you can get, unless you count Alaska. Anyhow, I called their HR office three days ago and they texted me back yesterday."

"Hold on. Just hold on, Dad," Viv said, holding her hands to her ears. "You called a company and gave them your phone number? You didn't tell them your real name, did you? What are you doing? They're gonna find us now—they can do that with just a phone number."

"No, Viv, I think we're safe now. The case is over. They don't need me to testify because it's over—over! We don't have to hide anymore. Heck, I doubt they are even looking anymore. And besides . . ."

Vivian stood and started pacing around the coffee shop. She didn't know whether to cry, or stomp out and go home.

"Dad, how could you? You didn't even tell me? What about our plan and Disappearance, LLC?"

"We can still do everything you've outlined and planned and worked so hard on. It's just that we don't have to hide out ourselves. We can still sell the plan to people who need to hide out—disappear, as you put it. I mean what we still need is money. I know you checked out Boise State University here and didn't think it was right for you. So, let's think about Seattle. You could go to the University of Washington, with your GED. We talked about that. You built this great plan to help us put together a new financial stake. We still need that even if I could find a new job out here, 3,000 miles away from Baltimore."

"Seattle? Well, I guess I'd like that—Boise is backward, Dad. And it's kinda creepy with militias and all that anti-government talk. What's the name of the company in Seattle?"

"It's called North-by-Northeast Commodities, Inc. They're small, only three traders. The HR office is probably only one person, the guy I talked to on the phone. They have a bookkeeper, and a student, who's part-time from the University of Washington, a finance major. They don't have a CFO, and their accountant is quitting because she's going to have twins, and wants to stay home for a year. The guy really sounded nice."

"Still," Viv said, sitting down across from him in the booth at Blinkie's, their new favorite coffee and books hut in Boise, "you should have told me before you called them. Anyhow, we think our LLC business should be strictly online—no analog stuff."

"We?"

"Yeah, me and Vince. It's really important, Dad. We can do things over the Internet that are impossible in the old analog world you grew up in. Course, some stuff we have to do by snail mail. For instance, we can send stuff using the post office in Boise and use it as a mail drop too. Are you going to move us to Seattle?"

"Can't say."

"So, Dad, as long as we're talking about doing things without telling people, I told Mr. Ricketts he could send me books or other stuff by general delivery at the main US Post office here. Before Mr. Gosh-whatever got killed."

"We both did things to give us a better future, Viv. Whether we go to Seattle, or stay here, we can do this Disappearance, LLC, thing anywhere."

"They have UPS stores everywhere. But, Dad, I've been thinking about when we talk to customers about setting up LLCs, or investing in our business. We gotta do that online, in the cloud, so no one can track us, or find us. Stay disappeared, right?"

"Well, I'm thinking we could come out into the sunshine, although maybe moving to Seattle means lots of rain and fog. But our business has to be legal, and we don't want to ever have to hide out again. Doing business online is legal unless it's a fraudulent business."

"OK, but there's no sunshine up in the cloud, Dad. The part of the Internet I'm thinking about is dark. 'Dark' as in not visible to the analog world. But Vince and I, well mostly him, have been thinking about the 'Darknet.' It has more promise than doing a paper-only job in Delaware."

"Vince," Dad moaned, "is spending way too much time in Internet cafes and fixating on computer stuff."

"Dad, he's eighteen going on thirty as far as the digital world is concerned. He knows more stuff, hacks more systems, and can code with the best of 'em down there in Silicon Valley. He's our future."

"You aren't doing what it sounds like are, are you, Vivian? Vince is only a character in your book—we agreed on that compromise years ago, actually four years ago, when you were fourteen going on fourteen-and-a-half. He's not my future; you are. When he first showed up when you were eight—or maybe it was nine—your mom and I barely understood what was happening. Remember, three doctors talked to you. I loved you then, and I love you now, more so with your mom gone. But where are you taking Vince now?"

"Dad, it was three doctors. One thought I was nuts. One thought I was making stuff up. And one said I was traumatized. But you and Mom accepted me for what I am. Vince is a character, isn't he? But he's so real to me. It's like I once was him, instead of him being me in the book, and up in the cloud, the Internet cloud. He's always surfing up there, you know. He logs on then glides like an albatross for hours. I don't know why it matters at all. He's helping me understand how to stay disappeared, just like he helped you fool the marshals, and the creepy lady at Shady Acres. Remember, he thinks he's writing a book too. But he's a character in my book, even though I suspect he thinks he's writing the book, and I'm just a character in it. Can we quit talking about that and get back to the Darknet, and how it fits into my business plan for Disappearance, LLC?"

"Sure, Viv, whatever you say."

For the next hour, Vivian walked him through the legal and digital maze she had been expanding way beyond her first rough sketch of Disappearance, LLC.

"Call it, Disappearance LLC, version 2.0," she said.

At ground level the Darknet is a computer network with restricted access used for illegal peer-to-peer file sharing. In the analog world, files, legal files particularly, are shared in print or PDF form over the Internet, which is not dark. The Internet is for everyone. Buyers, sellers, cops, witnesses, spooks, preachers, sinners, everybody who can type and knows how control-alt-delete works when your screen freezes. All those people do the Internet visibly. But others, like Vince, have pierced the Darknet and can surf and manipulate invisibly.

The plan Vivian had etched out would keep her, her dad, and their new digital company invisible. It might make them a lot of money, too. She knew their first LLC had to be formed in Delaware because Delaware law let them hide their ownership—lawyers call it membership—from everyone except the registered agent in Delaware. She'd figured out a way to keep their identities private even from the agent himself. But now she walked her dad through the rest of the plan.

They would access the Darknet from computers. If they went to Seattle, they would use MacLawn, as the family name. That was the one the Judge in Cranston had approved. They'd use it there for what she called "analog" stuff.

She educated him on computers, just like long ago he taught her cost accounting. Every computer has a name—only it's called an IP address, and is just numbers. But it's the same thing. A human is vulnerable if bad people know his real name. A computer is vulnerable if its IP address is known, or can be discovered by some other computer.

That's where the Darknet comes in. That slippery crow in the cloud can be accessed only with specific software, configurations, or authorization, often using nonstandard communications protocols and ports and . . .

Dad had been patient for maybe fifteen minutes. But she could see him grinding his teeth. He only did that when he was anxious about something, or wasn't getting what she was saying.

"You with me, Dad?"

"No. But even if I was, I don't see what this has to do with your business plan. I mean, why can't we do everything over the good old United States Postal System? I mean, really, who knows anything when I send a letter?"

"Well, Dad, whoever gets your letter knows you sent the letter, right? And even though it's a private corporation, the US Postal Service's budget gets governmental approval. It cooperates when the government wants something from it. Personal letters, fine. Registered letters, no. It's a business risk we don't need to take."

Viv spent another ten minutes advancing the Darknet thesis. There are three different kinds of Darknets, friend-to-friend that share files, peer-to-peer that share connections, and privacy networks like Tor. Tor is where she thought they had to go. Dad started grinding his teeth again. Viv moved over, sat next to him, and put her hand on his arm.

"Daddy, remember when I told you I didn't understand why the government could make us hide out until you could testify in the case in Baltimore, and you said it was complicated, and I should just trust you? Well, that was two years ago. Now everything is different. And now you need to just trust Vince on this. But to help you see why we need to do business on the digital Darknet rather than in the visible analog world, let me just tell you a little more."

It took an hour. But in that hour, Vivian's digital plan emerged. Because so much of the world was now digital, almost everyone had a computer. And almost every computer user could access an amazing wealth of information. What most people over thirty didn't get was there was an entire world that's invisible to your standard web browsers. The tools needed to access that invisible world were easy to find if you knew where to look. Vince did. At fifteen, or however old he was, he was already an expert. He only had a few friends, but they were all deep into the Darknet. They wanted to browse the Web invisibly, mostly to keep their parents in the dark. Parents were clueless, his digital friends thought. They didn't know a huge percentage of the Internet was not accessible through standard search engines. So, if you were interested in things like heavy porn, Bitcoin laundry, narcotics, hackers for hire, stuff like that, you tooled up, and engaged Tor. Viv shocked her Dad, without meaning to, just by letting him know she knew things he'd never imagined. The Darknet allowed her, and Vince, to operate in total anonymity. Without being tracked. If they wanted to visit a website that sold drugs or weapons, they could. They could even hire an assassin. She told him about one black-market site, on the Darknet, called Silk Road, an online black market best known as a platform for selling illegal drugs. It was hit after a crackdown by the FBI.

"The FBI? Are you saying the FBI uses this Darknet too?"

"Yes, Dad. But we aren't on it yet, and when we go there, the FBI won't know we're there. And if you're right in thinking we're safe now, they won't care. You know, they broke the Silk Road only after thousands of hours of work. But our plan will be invisible because we're not subject to Foreign Intelligence Surveillance Act (FISA) or any other government program. We'll just be one of millions who want to do what we do privately."

"I still don't get how you avoid the basic rule that all computers have—IP addresses."

"Me, neither," Vivian said, "But Vince thinks differently than the rest of us do. He built his own computer. When he's here, he drags it around in his backpack to wherever he can find a free Wi-Fi connection. Or he just hacks into someone else's connection. His system operates with a static IP, not Dynamic Host Configuration Protocol (DHCP). He says it just takes a few minutes to manually input the IP details into a system and then change it minutes later. He has administrative rights, you know."

"No, I didn't know. Who gave them to him? Not me."

"Dad, be serious. By manually configuring his computer and disabling DHCP on his router, each time he accesses Darknet, he reinvents himself every time he surfs. It's like shopping at a big mall. No one can track you because you're a different person in each store. That's Vince when he surfs. He'll be building our Darknet presence while you and I are setting up domestic LLCs that are hidden, even on Darknet. That's genius."

"But Viv, I can maybe see how something's hidden on that Darknet thing from people who don't know about it, but once you're on it, can't you see whatever's up there? And if you and Vince can get there, what's to stop the government—the FBI—from logging on?"

"Dad, here's how Vince sees Tor. It's a network of nodes that route Internet connections through a bunch of computers before they connect you to the website you're accessing. So, the signal trail you're leaving behind could come from anywhere on the planet. Know what Tor stands for? Don't try. It stands for 'the onion router.' It's like an onion with many layers because it layers encryption while routing you up into the light cloud and then up into the dark one even higher up. When the connection you want is finally reached, one of the computers opens it and there is, like, you know, another box inside waiting for you to open it. Could be many boxes—each one securely locked—only opened by you, the addressee. The computers in the middle—doing the routing—never see, or know either the sender and the recipient or the contents in the final box, the one on the website you're headed for. Does that make sense to you?"

"Viv, you're saying our website, Disappearance, LLC, is in a box on the Darknet. Do I have that right?"

"You can think of it that way. But what's really happening is that your entry into and exit from the box is hidden from the planet. Only the computers know parts of the route and they can't talk to one another to track you. Neither can the government."

CHAPTER 18

As soon as his boss got off the phone, Stanza called his assistant in.

"Karen, I need three things right away. One, hold all my calls. Two, get me the 302s that came in late yesterday from DC, and three, text Agents Cambridge and Lin. Tell 'em to come to my office the second they get back from court."

Karen, recognizing the urgency, didn't waste time answering. She just whirled on her three-inch platform shoes and headed for central filing. Ninety seconds later, just as he'd poured a fresh cup from the Bunn coffeemaker on the sidebar in his office, she returned with three rubber-banded files with Goshkervic file stamps. He moved them to the center of his desk, laid a fresh legal pad just to his right, pulled a new rollerball red pen from his desk drawer, and opened the first 302.

The FBI was likely the only investigative police agency in the world that steadfastly resisted modern technology's vastly superior solution to the decades-old 302. At a time when recording a conversation was as easy as whipping out a cellphone or an iPad, the FBI policy on electronic recording of witness interviews was unwavering. No agent was allowed to electronically record confessions or interviews, openly or surreptitiously, unless authorized by the SAIC or his or her designee. This practice originated from the unacceptable risks posed if defense lawyers could obtain accurate electronically recorded information. FBI policy demanded that FBI agents take written notes and later type up a summary report—the infamous Form 302. Almost all important interviews involved two FBI agents and a single interviewee. Federal judges described the prosecution-favored practice as eschewing the objective for the subjective. It would always be two FBI agents' word against one suspect's unrecorded and unnoted recollection of his confession or other incriminating remarks. They honored the Fifth Amendment but did not record the suspect's waiver of his constitutional right to remain silent.

The first 302 summarized an interview dated May 14, 2015. The subject, a woman named Alice Bluegown, worked for Hurlitt International Services in the human resources office. She had not been previously interviewed because no one knew that she had anything to report about the Goshkervic case. She was not a witness at the first trial. She never worked for Steven Manchester, the accountant in the CFO's office, whose birth name was changed to Stephan Nau when he went into WITSEC. She never worked for defendant Fritz Goshkervic, or any of the broker-traders in the company. But she knew a good deal about how the company reimbursed its employees for business travel expenses. They interviewed her as a follow up to Goshkervic's expected testimony at the upcoming retrial.

At the first trial, Goshkervic had insisted that his job was purely financial management, and that he neither knew nor dealt directly with any of Hurlitt's clients. One of the company's largest trading clients was a Texas company headquartered in Houston: Plankton Resources, Inc. Ms. Bluegown confirmed for the FBI that she'd processed five different reimbursement packages for airfare, car rental, hotel, food, and entertainment expenses for trips Goshkervic took over a three-year period from Baltimore to Houston. The agents matched up the expense vouchers including the names and employers of clients and guests, all of whom were connected to Plankton Resources, Inc.

When asked if she had any other information about Mr. Goshkervic, or Plankton Resources, Ms. Bluegown said no. The agents terminated the interview. However, later that afternoon, Ms. Bluegown called the number on the card she'd been given and volunteered that, while driving home, she'd remembered one other thing.

"About Mr. Goshkervic?" the agent asked.

"No," she said, "it's about the other employee you asked me about, Mr. Manchester. You didn't ask me about his travel expenses, but I processed his reimbursement, too. He went to Houston twice, with Mr. Goshkervic. They stayed at different hotels, and he flew separately. I only thought about it when I remembered Mr. Manchester made several calls from his hotel room to a bank in Panama City. As far as I knew, our company didn't have any commodity clients in Panama. Just thought it was odd," she said.

The other two 302s covered two separate interviews with a confidential informant. His name was not in the reports—just the reference "CI." One report, dated a week after the first trial, was five pages long. The second, dated ten days ago, was a single page. He started with the oldest, as was standard operating procedure in the FBI.

It referenced an interview conducted at the Baltimore Metropolitan Detention Center between the same two agents who had interviewed Ms. Bluegown and a CI, obviously a jail snitch. He had become friends with a man named Otero Valenzuela, who claimed to know Goshkervic before he went to work for Hurlitt International. The man was doing a forty-five-day sentence for DUI and said he was a professional gambler.

He told the agents that he played table-stakes poker in a private game on Friday nights at the historic Lord Baltimore Hotel. The game had been staged in various suites at the hotel for decades. It would start around ten on Friday night and would often last till the wee hours on Sunday. Players would drift in and out. You had to know the concierge personally before he would tell you the suite number and how many players were at the table.

Most pots were between three and four thousand bucks, so, as the CI put it, "the Johnnies drifted in and out for thirty-six hours." Beer and bourbon shots were served by skinny chippies for $20 a pop. No guns or loud talking were allowed while you sat on couches waiting your turn for one of the seven guys at the table to drop out. A professional dealer was slapping the cards and changed the deck whenever a Johnnie wanted a fresh one. That's where the CI said he met Goshkervic, who, he said, "had a good face for the game and usually did OK. He never came in until maybe 11:00 p.m. or midnight on Saturday. He either did good right away or lost a bundle if he stayed until the sun came up. Anyway, the regulars all seemed to know this Goshkervic guy and his business trading futures and options at a trading house in the financial district. Sometimes he would talk about the trade at the table, just to break a guy's concentration on the cards."

The snitch's main point was that if you traded enough at Goshkervic's brokerage, they could set you up with a wired account in Latin America. Maybe you could keep the dough away from your better half. Maybe even the IRS, he said.

The third 302 was a one-pager about the same CI jail snitch. It was dated a week ago. The last four sentences made him reach for the telephone. The agents' summary referenced a couch conversation at the Lord Baltimore between two players waiting to sit in the game. Both knew Goshkervic. Both were clients at Hurlitt International's commodities trading shop. One of them told the other, "You hear about Goshkervic getting his ass blown up in that plane crash south of Galveston Bay? Dumb shit shoulda known. He's been playing with Panama money for a year. Dumb shit shoulda never threatened them greasers."

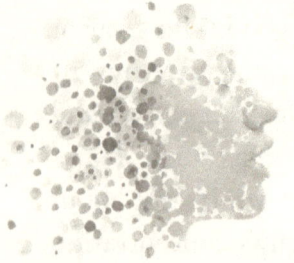

CHAPTER 19

Galveston Bay is the seventh-largest estuary in the United States, and Baytown pays daily tribute to it—most often in the form of trade but sometimes in bodies. The fishing's pretty good there, but once in a while someone hooks a corpse. Galveston Bay is connected to the Gulf of Mexico, surrounded by sub-tropic marshes, and holds more secrets than the old Iron Curtain.

Julia's life blood mixed easily with the salty mix in Galveston Bay. She was as salty as the bay water fifty feet from her back deck. Since she was just a few miles away from the Greater Houston metropolitan area—the fifth-largest in the United States, with a population of over six million—it was easy to hide but she still had access to massive resources and opportunities. It had a huge international port, spread across the northwestern section of the bay. Locals touted it as the biggest in America, but it was really only the second-busiest port in the country by overall tonnage.

It produced more seafood than any bay in the nation except the Chesapeake. Julia had never visited the Chesapeake, or anywhere else. She hated the rest of the world, never read newspapers or books, but loved seafood and killing. While known to cartels, gangs, mobs, and South American generals, Julia was barely recognizable in south Texas, except for her few neighbors along Missouri Street backing up to Black Duck Bay. She was occasionally seen going in or out but had made it clear to everyone who knocked on her door that she hated the world and everyone in it, especially those who knocked on her door.

Her law office in Baytown, snugged in concrete between her other two businesses—Houston International Savings and Loan, and Pac 'n Mail—was the ultimate sham. Her name was not on the door that contained the brass plaque—Withers & Associates, PLLC, Attorneys at Law. Hardly anyone ever knocked on the door. But for the few who did, the receptionist was always welcoming. Julia had gone to law school at St. Mary's University in San Antonio, known mostly for its wide-open admission standards. If you could pay the tuition, you'd be accepted. She passed the bar on the second try. She did not practice for two years while she lived in Mexico with her boyfriend, a gunman for the Sinaloa Cartel. There was a rumor she killed him and was well-paid for it by the cartel. It might have been her first hit. Shortly after that, she returned to Texas, visited her mother in Brownsville for two months, then opened the Withers & Associates office in Baytown.

While they had varied over the years, each woman hired by Julia as the firm receptionist had three things in common. She lived in the neighborhood, needed a good salaried job, and never questioned Julia's orders.

She always used the same greeting, "Hello, welcome to Withers Law. How can we help you today?"

Ninety percent were walk-in clients who needed but could not afford a lawyer. Those prospective clients would explain their problem in a few sentences or in a long out-pouring of the legal difficulty they, or someone they "knew," were experiencing. Once that was clear to the receptionist, she would consistently say, "I'm so sorry, but this firm does not take those cases. We only do investments in international financing, and we do not take cases except on referral from existing clients. Sorry, we can't help you."

Truth was, even though Withers & Associates reported six-figure fee revenue on its annual tax return, it had no legal clients. Probate was as close to law practice as Julia ever got. Most of the time the revolving receptionists never saw her. She communicated, if absolutely necessary, only when the receptionist dared to knock on the office door. Usually not even that worked. Several of them had met her only when they were hired, quit, or were fired for knocking on her door. None of them could have ever given a consistent description of what their employer even looked like. When hiring a new receptionist, she wore a variety of wigs, face-altering make up, and dark sunglasses; she offered limited conversation. But she paid very well while offering no benefits of any kind. Every Friday was pay day. A cashier's check made payable to the receptionist of the week, drawn on the law firm's account at Houston International Savings and Loan, would be on the reception desk. Most of them walked next door and cashed the check immediately. None of them asked questions about Julia. Somehow, it seemed likely that the teller next door lived the same life as did the receptionists in the middle office and the shipping clerks in on the other side. None of them chatted with one another. The few who tried got termination notices attached to the following Friday's paycheck.

The receptionist on duty Friday, January 12, 2016, was named Maria Basta. She was very surprised to hear someone knock on the front door less than a minute after she walked in. She spoke through the door on the intercom. Whoever was there sounded Spanish and said he was a client. She opened the door to find a huge, sloppily dressed man.

"Oh, good morning, Senor," she said as she opened the door wide. She had just hung her coat on the rack but still held the umbrella in her hand. "How can we help you today?"

"Tell her it's Chaco Hernández," he said, pointing at the door behind the receptionist's desk.

"May I tell her what this is about? What is your legal matter?"

"Jus tell her."

"Well, I'm afraid we cannot take walk-in clients, Mr. Hernández, you see . . ."

The man appeared to weigh well over three hundred pounds and was not young. Walking right past Maria Basta's desk, he opened the door to Julia's office, walked in, and closed it behind him. Maria was so startled she could not immediately decide what to do. She waited for a minute, then rang Julia on the intercom. She had started to explain what had happened when Julia interrupted her.

"No, Ms. Basta. I know this gentleman. It's all right. I won't be needing you any more today. Take the day off. Leave now."

Julia turned to the big man, festooned with mustaches, who stared at her through blurred and narrowed eyes.

"Chaco. It's been what, two years? Why are you here?"

"Because they sent me. I was here in Houston last night on something else. They called me at the warehouse. Said go to your office first thing this morning. Said to tell you to call them, with me sitting with you. I dunno what. But you know me, from Nicaragua, so jus call 'em. Don't make him mad. Or me. Jus make the call."

Julia punched in the combination to her steel desk drawer, opened it, and took out the sat phone. Reaching further in the drawer, she slid the Glock to the front, and pulled out the small leather telephone directory. Selecting a number, she made the call, said good morning, and listened for a minute.

The man on the other line, Leopoldo de Santos, was famous for two things: he was always close to his sat phone and he was a man who always anticipated what you had to say.

"OK, Julia, is Chaco there with you?"

"Yes, he is."

"Put the phone on conference so he can hear."

She did.

"Chaco, you sitting there with Julia? You know my voice now for what, your whole life, right? How's the weather over the Gulf? Not so many clouds out there today, is that right?"

Chaco said something in his rapid guttural Spanish, only understandable by senior members of the cartel, like Leopoldo de Santos.

"Now, Julia and Chaco, you listen please. I have to tell you even if there's no clouds up there to bother you, there is some shit clouds coming down here. Julia, you got paid in full for that fucking gringo named Goshkervic, but now his friend needs to feed the same fish. *Comprende?*"

"No, I don't understand. What friend are you talking about, and why did you bring jeopardy to me by sending Chaco to my office?"

"Julia, I'm sorry to be a bother by sending Chaco, but there was no time to set up a conference call. Lucky for us, Chaco is up there on other business. We want him to do a guy. This is his hit, not yours. But we want you to plan it all out for him. And we want you to go with him. We don't have time to plan something like we did with Goshkervic. We know where the *hijo de un poco* is. You must make all the travel arrangements and go with him. He can't do this part alone because of language, and he's not a planner; he's a doer. We want it done today, if possible, and we want to send a message to the American FBI. Chaco will do this thing in public so everybody knows not to fuck with us. I'm very upset that we have to do this thing two times. You did the guy in the Learjet for us last summer. Now Chaco's gonna do the other one. That's the way I want it."

"So two things. One, what's this man's name, and where is he? And also, how come you want Chaco to do this thing. If the man's here, I could do him without Chaco's help."

"We didn't know about the man. His name is Stephan Manchester. But now he's going by Stephan MacLawn. He also worked for that commodities trader in Baltimore. He was not known to us except as a witness against the other guy, Goshkervic. But now we just learned Manchester knows too much. So you and Chaco have to do him today. You get paid the same fee as before, no split with Chaco. He kills for us all the time. You get him up there, plan it, and get him back to Houston. We'll get him home from Houston by boat."

"Where's the target?'"

"Boise, Idaho. We don't have an address yet, but we think the target is staying in an older Airstream RV. And we got a driver's license photo, which we'll PDF to you in few minutes. If we get anything else, we'll call you on the SAT phone. You take charge of Chaco."

"How did you find this man with two names. Manchester and MacLawn?"

"Because he's a dumb shit. We think he ran from Baltimore to keep from testifying at Goshkervic's trial. We don't care about that. But maybe he knows something we don't want him to know. What he did was proof he's a dumb shit. He called another commodities broker in Seattle just two days ago. They help us out in the dry cleaning business. Not such a big volume as Hurlitt in Baltimore but, you know, it's a West Coast connection, so when we have packages up there, we use North-by-Northeast in Seattle. Only one broker there. He's our front man up there in Seattle. He called us and so now we're calling you."

"OK, two more things. Who supplies the gun? And why use Chaco? I can contract the job out of Vancouver. They could get a team of Chinese down there in two hours. They would have to arrange for guns in Seattle though, probably."

"We use Chaco because he don't need a gun. He uses *la garrote*; that's part of the message. And also because if he gets caught, he don't talk, right Chaco?"

"Leopoldo," Julia asked, "What about me? What if I get caught?"

"Don't get caught; you won't get paid. Also, Chaco will have to kill you. You won't like his wire around your throat."

CHAPTER 20

It took two meetings over four days for the members of Group X to review the business plan Vivian had sent back to Mr. Ricketts. All four members had read the plan, which didn't take long since it was only three pages. Mr. Nettles described the plan as two parts hope and one part fantasy. Mr. Ricketts thought the plan was a codification of the book Vivian was either writing or an abstract from the book she borrowed about creating new identities. Neither indicated a willingness to invest in Disappearance, LLC. But the sisters, Cecelia and Cynthia, thought there was enough in the business plan to at least justify a discussion by the four members.

As was their pattern, Cecelia went first, posing the issue. "We have given a lot of thought to Ms. Vivian's business premise. As we see it, Disappearance, LLC, is a highly differentiated financial planning device for anyone who wants to make money without telling the government, or other nosy entities or individuals. While Ms. Vivian sees the business as catering to individuals for whom privacy and secrecy are paramount, we think the market is much broader than that. It's a way for people to lawfully avoid federal and state individual income tax by doing business only as a corporate entity. That's the core of Vivian's shiny apple. Pay corporate tax rates, not personal income tax rates. And do it without anyone knowing who owns the corporate entity conducting the business. The genius we see in the idea is that every small business in America could benefit from this format. Barber shops, candy stores, landscaping work, you name it. The kind of business conducted is irrelevant to the way you conduct it. That's salable anywhere in the country. And her pricing plan is so low, the market could easily generate thousands of buyers in a year or less. If we assume Disappearance, LLC, is entirely automated, all business is done online, and all payments are made via online banking, then it is entirely possible for one person, highly adept at e-commerce, and with a solid package of documentation acceptable to the corporation commission in Delaware, to set up scores of new entities in a single hour. Add the same time to create online bank accounts, and it seems possible to deliver a fully operational LLC to the client hundreds of times every week. Even if you assume modest numbers, say 200 LLCs per week at $100 each, you have a gross revenue stream of about $20,000 per week, or $1,040,000 per year. Assume an 80 percent margin and the net profit is over $800,000 per year. Even if our estimates are off by a factor of ten to one, this notion of Ms. Vivian's is a cash cow worth $80,000 in the first year. Two-thousand dollars would buy us a 0.05 percent stake, or approximately $4,000 the first year. That's a 100 percent return on investment. Questions, anyone?"

Mr. Ricketts and Mr. Nettles could not wait to contest the sisters.

Mr. Nettles, took the shot. "Even if you're right on the revenue side, where's the market for this service? I mean how many people have any of us ever known who wanted to disappear or conduct their business secretly over the Internet?"

"Dear me," Cynthia said, "I'm sure you're right about people wanting to disappear or conducting business secretly. Only criminals or people of low moral character would want those things. Ms. Vivian fixates on that kind of people. But Cecelia and I think she is missing the real market: honest citizens who just want to be corporate taxpayers at 15 percent rather than personal filers at 25 percent or higher. If Ms. Vivian can do that for a $100 flat fee, the market is so big as to be incalculable. Frankly, we think she will face a staffing challenge, but we know about automation and form filing over the Internet. It's machines doing all the work, once the coding is done."

Mr. Ricketts had a different objection. "My worry is legality. I don't see how Ms. Vivian can be right about simply creating LLCs under Delaware law as the full solution. These hundreds, maybe thousands of people who buy the product have to do business in their home states. She says nothing about that in her business plan. Isn't that the Achilles heel here? I mean, the people who want the private LLC set up in Delaware aren't doing business in Delaware.

Take Arizona, how would an Arizona business make this work with a Delaware LLC?"

Cecelia took this one on. "We're talking about 21st century business here, not Greek mythology, Mr. Ricketts. We called our own trust lawyer, who practices in Tucson. He said the easy solution is the creation of a revocable living trust here in Arizona. Then use that trust as the member listed in the Articles of Organization. Of course, you would not want to use a family name, like Cynthia and I do under our existing family trust. You would, he said, want to use a generic name that does not disclose the identities of the trustor, trustee, or beneficiary. Then you set up a trust account in an online bank, open up a UPS mailbox account, and use your lawyer's office address to forward the mail. It's perfectly legal. He says it's quite easy and would take less than 2.5 hours of his time."

Ricketts and Nettles disclaimed any interest in actually becoming a Disappearance, LLC, customer but did agree to a $2,000 commitment for a Group X investment of 0.05-percent share in the business. Mr. Rickets was authorized to handle the investment by a unanimous vote. He said he'd get a letter off to Ms. Vivian at her general delivery address in Boise, Idaho.

CHAPTER 21

The Phoenix FBI office was bustling with activity when SAIC Stanza called the Director of the FBI at exactly 6:00 p.m. Phoenix time, as directed earlier that Thursday morning. Stan had his three most senior officers in the room; all of them would be taking notes.

"Stan," the director said, "thanks for getting back to me on time. I have my deputy director, Abe Kahn, here. Also present for this conference, I have Mercedes Langa, the lead agent from FinCEN on this matter. Now that I've got you on, we'll conference-in the CIA at Langley—his name is A. M. Gallo. But first, who's in the room with you in Arizona?"

"I have agents Cambridge, Lin, and Sterndusky with me, Mr. Director. We've all read the new 302s and I've upgraded the status on the Manchester/Nau search to paramount. But we have no recent calls or reports on his whereabouts, and . . ."

"Hold on, Stan, let my assistant conference-in Mr. Gallo, then she'll call roll for the log here."

It took a couple minutes to conference-in Langley. Everyone on the FBI side knew the lag was so the CIA recording system could be uploaded to whomever else the spooks wanted to hear the brief but not be part of the record. And everyone on the CIA side was equally aware of the FBI's historic opposition to recording its agents. This meeting would be digitally stored at Langley and filed in a cabinet on paper in Washington. Once the roll call was complete, Mr. Ashurst resumed his direction of the meeting.

"First," the director said, "let's hear from SAIC Stanza. Stan, bring us up to date on the sit-rep out there in Arizona."

"For the record, I have to report total silence here. We have no recent calls or sightings of Mr. Manchester, no idea as to his current location, and no information about his daughter. But once the new 302s came in yesterday, we reinstated the APBs. I've added two agents to the search here, and we've made sure every field office in the Southwest is fully briefed and engaged in finding the missing protected witness."

The CIA agent, speaking in a polished East-Coast higher-education voice, interrupted.

"Might I ask, Agent Stanza, would you give us a geographical sketch of what you mean by 'the Southwest?' Does that include the West Coast?"

"No, sir, technically it does not. Our service area is Arizona, New Mexico, Texas, Colorado, and Nevada."

"So, might I inquire of the director, what's the level of investigation on the West Coast, specifically, California, Oregon, and Washington?"

Director Ashurst was quick to explain.

"While Stan's accurate in defining our districts, you can rest assured the entire western half of the country is on alert for Mr. Manchester. But since he was under the protection of the US Marshal's Office in Arizona, when he bolted from the program, that office has original assignment in locating him."

"Yes, well, by my inquiry I didn't mean to suggest limited investigation. It's a sense of urgency I'm inquiring about. For example, do all field offices in the 'entire western half of the country' have access to the most recent 302s? They suggest the missing Manchester might be the next target. Or do they think we want him back because we might need his testimony, as was his original focus?"

"All offices, nationwide, have summaries of the case, and a clear statement of why we want this man found. The recent 302s have not been distributed nationally because they are limited to the larger issue of why this witness might be at risk from a drug cartel. Now, let me pose a question. I presume the CIA's interest in this case is not based on the financial crimes in the original indictment against Goshkervic. Can you fill us in on the extent of your interest in the case?"

"Sure," the man from Langley said. "We track known money laundering worldwide. The Goshkervic case was originally of no interest to us—domestic crime, you know. But when it became known that Hurlitt International Services, Inc., was a subsidiary of a certain Panamanian consortium, with international banking as its core offering, we matched it up with two other cases, one in Los Angeles and another in Seattle, that have carryover issues."

"Hmm," said Mr. Ashurst, "what got your attention?"

"Hurlitt changed law firms between the trial and the appeal. That's unusual, isn't it? The Hurlitt appeal was briefed by a Seattle law firm, which, except for this one case, only handles appeals in the Ninth Circuit Court of Appeals. But the Hurlitt case was appealed from the district court in Maryland to the Fourth Circuit Court of Appeals. We weren't tracking the parties. We got a sniff because the Seattle lawyer's firm is well known in money laundering cases and global wire fraud but has no history in cases involving commodities trading. It's a private firm, but it seems to act as general counsel for problems arising out of the global stack of cash deposited in Panama City banks. That lawyer has been tracked on several trips he made from Seattle nonstop to Baltimore on a Learjet normally hangered in Houston. The agency has been tracking that tail number for two years. It was the same jet that Goshkervic was on. It's just a few pieces of flotsam in the Gulf of Mexico now."

"Well, that interest must have been fevered when the connection was made between people in Baltimore and people in Panama City."

"Yes," Mr. Director, "I can tell you it was a bingo moment here at Langley."

"OK, then. Let's go back to SAIC Stanza, and let him finish his current brief."

"Yes, Director Ashurst. It's good to hear that both CIA and FinCEN are in the mix now. I will be in personal contact with every SAIC in my district this evening and tomorrow morning. And, now that I've been cleared to do so, we're engaging all law enforcement agencies and giving them both the missing man's real name, Stephan Manchester, as well as his protected witness status name, Stephan Nau. We're asking local authorities to report on all transients, tourists, and new residents based on the demographics of the man and his daughter. But, the CIA interest is unclear to me. What was the 'bingo moment' you just mentioned?"

"Yes, but this is strictly on a need-to-know basis. Your senior agents are cleared as well, but the files from this point forward should be under your personal lock and key. The commodities broker, Hurlitt International Services, turns out to be a wholly owned subsidiary of another American company, domiciled in Delaware, called Autocrancis Currency, Inc. It was formed in the sixties as a holding company. It may own as many as 200 other businesses that span the entire national financial and insurance industry. In the seventies, it went global and started buying up currency exchanges and finance companies in Pacific Rim countries. Its principal office was in the twin towers in New York. After 9/11, it moved its operation across the river to Newark and began accumulating banking and funding connections in the Caribbean and Latin America. What may have looked like a small financial crime in Baltimore now looks like a large secret money case on a global scale."

After the phone conference ended, the junior-most field agent in the Phoenix field office asked the question the other two had wanted to ask but didn't want to appear ignorant of other agencies in front of SAIC Stanza.

"Stan," Agent Lin asked, "I know I should know more about FinCEN than I do, but I'm having trouble following the discussion we just had as it relates to the Treasury Department."

"Well, don't think you're alone. We have about 220 active files in this office. Phoenix is the sixth largest city in the country. But FinCEN is not involved in any of our cases, up to now. So, this is a first for me, too. The mission of the 'Financial Crimes Enforcement Network' is to safeguard the American financial system and the US Treasury from illicit use and to combat money laundering. It has a large research and data storage business. It promotes national security by analysis and dissemination of financial intelligence. Have you worked on any cases yet involving the Bank Secrecy Act?"

"No, sir, not yet."

"Well, we do get involved in some cases under that act, given our proximity to the Mexican border. I looked it up this afternoon because I knew the FinCEN agent would be on this evening's call. The short name, 'Bank Secrecy Act,' is formally identified in the US Criminal Code as the 'Currency and Foreign Transactions Reporting Act of 1970.' It requires all US financial institutions to assist US government agencies to detect and prevent money laundering. Hurlitt is a commodities trading company and its license and regulatory scheme demands full compliance with the Bank Secrecy Act. But my limited understanding is that it focuses mostly on cash transactions."

Agent Lin said, "Well, even though I haven't worked any investigations involving financial crimes, I am just fresh out of law school—only have eighteen months on my law license. I can add something from my white collar crimes course on this point."

"Fire away," Stan said.

"Yes, sir. Specifically, the act requires financial institutions to keep records of cash purchases of negotiable instruments and file reports of cash purchases of those negotiable instruments of more than $10,000. They have to report suspicious activity that might signify money laundering, tax evasion, or other criminal activities. They do that by filing CTRs—currency transaction reports—on anything over more than $10,000 in cash. My guess is that the commodities trader in Baltimore wasn't doing business on the commodities exchange in cash. But it was also supposed to file a different report, called a CMIR. I think that stands for 'Report of International Transportation of Currency or Monetary Instruments.' Maybe here the Hurlitt company was using a domestic bank that was shipping or mailing currency or other monetary instruments over ten grand into or out of the United States. If so, they had to file reports. Sometimes those reports are sent by FinCEN to law enforcement agencies to investigate violations of the Bank Secrecy Act."

"Or maybe," SAIC Stanza said, "it was running the other direction. Maybe some bank in Panama was shipping foreign currency banked down there in Latin America up here in the states to launder in the commodities exchange. In any event, it's not our focus. We have to find Mr. Manchester. So get to your sources now. Don't wait for tomorrow."

CHAPTER 22

After a rain-soaked landing in Boise, Julia and Chaco deplaned and headed for the rental car lot next door to the terminal. While Julia's first language was Spanish, she refused to talk to Chaco except in English. He didn't like English, which was fine with her.

"Wait outside, over there, on that bench," she said.

"*Acaba de obtener un gran coche*," he responded. Then he picked a different bench, under a sheet metal awning. Pulling a stub of a cigar from his outside flap pocket on his filthy cameo jacket, he chewed on it and waited for Julia.

She had intended to rent a full-size sedan, something with tinted windows, but his growled instruction changed her mind.

"I need a mid-size car, maybe with an uncomfortable back seat," she told the rental agent, who seemed perplexed by the request.

"Ma'am," the barely-out-of-high-school boy behind the counter responded, "we have Fords and Mercurys in mid-size, but they have regular back seats, with three belts. We rent a lot of Jeeps here, too. They're all four-wheel drives. The roads in Idaho can sometimes be difficult, especially in heavy rain, like today. And the backseats might be harder than regular passenger vehicles. Some people don't like them because getting in back is harder than in regular cars, which are lower to the ground."

"Get me a Jeep, with a manual shift, if you have one."

"I do, but it's a cloth top, with a flat bench backseat. It only has two belts on the bench. And there's a luggage box behind that, but it's not too big."

Fifteen minutes later, Julia walked outside with her backpack hanging from one strap, motioned to Chaco, and walked to the black Jeep with the gray top, two rows over. She tossed her backpack on the front seat, got in, and started it up. Chaco had not moved. She drove the Jeep through the checkout drive, showed the gateman her license and the paperwork on the rental, and made the circular drive around Airport Way to pick up Chaco. Pulling up right in front of his bench, she braked, clutched the gear shift into neutral, and pointed to the back seat.

"You sit there; in case the FBI chases us. You can cuss them out from there, since you don't use guns, and cannot shoot their sorry asses."

Like the five-hour flight, with the plane change in Salt Lake, they did not talk to one another in the Jeep. She gave directions. Chaco followed them, silently. But they had come to an uneasy peace between them by using silence to smother their dislike for one another. Julia drove first to the center of town. They took Broadway Avenue into downtown, crossing the Boise River near Bronco Stadium. Chaco pointed, and asked, "Soccer?"

"Football," she said. "It's a collision sport. You'd like it."

She took his question as a positive. He'd used English. So, she backed off a little.

"Chaco, we're going downtown first. The GPS on my phone says it's 5.2 miles. We're going downtown to a big hotel so I can ask them some questions. Maybe it's better if you don't go inside with me, *que no?*"

"*Si*, Julia. Don't worry about me on this job. You make a plan, I'll follow it."

She drove down what looked like the main street in town and found what she was looking for. The Grove Hotel was large, probably a four-star, looked to be maybe ten, twelve stories, and had a big underground parking lot. As she drove to the down ramp, she could see it was bustling with people, even though summer officially ended on Labor Day two weeks ago. They parked the jeep, took their backpacks, and started walking toward the elevators. She'd told him in the Jeep to take the stairway up, not walk with her, and find a bar no more than two blocks away on the north side of the hotel entrance.

"I seen one already. Bar Gernika, on the other side of the street, one block up. I'll be there," he told her.

She'd seen it too. It wouldn't be his kind of bar, but he would make no trouble. She took the elevator up, crossed the lobby, and got in the short line at the registration desk. When it was her turn, she asked where the concierge desk was. The black-suited man pointed to the far side of the desk at a woman talking on a corded phone while waving her other arm in the air, as though she were directing traffic. Julia walked over, stood a few feet away from the animated blonde, and waited for her to finish her call.

Three minutes passed, and the blonde hung up, moistened her lips with something on the end of a little blue vial, and gave Julia her patented can-I-do-anything-for-you smile.

"My husband's napping in our suite," Julia said, flashing her own bright-white smile at the blonde. "So I thought I'd come down and ask your advice about this charming little mountain town. Our first trip here, you know. Can you direct me to where I might find two things?"

"Certainly, Madam, certainly. What things are you interested in?"

"My husband is a CPA. We're here on vacation from back east. We're going to do some rafting, but my husband works even on vacation. So I need an office supply store where they sell accounting ledgers and the like. Also, I would be interested in a place where we could go, in our rented jeep, that would be very private. You know, like an RV park or campground that catered to people our age. And there should be a nice bar nearby. We often find interesting and compatible couples in those places. You know, couples that like the out-of-doors and are open to different styles, if you know what I mean."

"Well, I can tell you where the closest business supply store is. Two blocks from here on the same street. Just drive west two blocks to Staples. As for RV parks with bars close by, try Quinn's Pond. Just take Thirtieth Street north up to the Boise River. You'll find lots of RV parks and even some campgrounds, but I'm not sure they have overnight spots there. I can give you a complete list, but you could get the same one on the Internet, from your suite. Are you on the twelfth floor, the club floor?"

"Yes we are, of course. The suite's a bit tight, but the view is glorious."

"So, glad you're happy. Now, as for nightlife, Boise has all kinds. Perhaps The Balcony Club would fit. It's got lots of action, if you know what I mean. And there's a country-western club called 'Humpin' Hannah's.' Just the name alone draws some people inside."

Julia thanked the foolish lady and went to look for Chaco. She had no interest in nightlife. Her questions were just throwaways to distract the concierge. What she was interested in were places where their target might have stayed in the RV he'd purchased in Yuma. That detail would never have reached the ears of the Sinaloa Cartel in Mexico if Mr. Manchester hadn't tried to convince the salesman he and his daughter were going to Mexico when they traded in their 2007 Dodge pickup for the 2010 Winnebago. The used car dealer assumed the car was hot when the seller said he'd lost the title. But it only cost him $500. He moved it to a chop-shop in San Luis, Mexico, that did business with the Sinaloa Cartel. They traced the Dodge VIN number to a Stephan Nau, in Phoenix, Arizona. That led them to a trailer park in Cranston, called Shady Acres. The fat lady there was only too happy to give a description of the Dodge owner, and his son, who she thought was called Vince. The Sinaloa Cartel had friends in the US and they put the word out to look for a baby blue, twenty-four-foot Winnebago. Several had been spotted, but only one looked promising. It was driven by a man who looked like the photo of Stephan Nau they had from the MVD in Phoenix. And the man had a female passenger as he parked at a Staples store in Boise, Idaho. That was all Julia needed—an easy-to-spot RV and a photo of the man they came to kill. On the down side, they were in a town full of outdoor enthusiasts and gun-toting militias.

CHAPTER 23

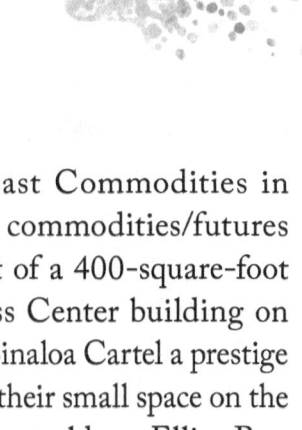

North-by-Northeast Commodities in Seattle had a narrow slice of the commodities/futures business in Seattle. Operating out of a 400-square-foot office suite in the Seattle Business Center building on Seventh Street, the center gave the Sinaloa Cartel a prestige address with a stunning view. From their small space on the fourteenth floor, the four employees could see Elliot Bay, the Space Needle, a sliver of Mount Baker and, of course, Downtown Seattle. It was right in the middle of a business hub, filled with companies in the shipping, biotechnology, and financial services sectors.

Its location and presumed-legitimate place in the commodities world gave the company access to wealthy people with both ready cash and a need to outsource their portfolios. They did it by offering only "managed futures accounts." By narrowing the offering this way, they attracted a few dozen legitimate clients who wanted to diversify their portfolio without the day-to-day management of traditional trading accounts. They dealt exclusively with funds managed by a third-party 'Commodity Trading Advisor.' What made these CTAs attractive was their similarity to mutual funds. They could be diversified across a variety of different commodity types. Alternatively, they could concentrate on a single group of futures contracts such as the oil markets or the grain markets. Their come-on was personalized treatment of investors who needed diversification and were willing to take a little risk to get it. One of the two traders in the office promised legitimate clients that he was a CTA who would stick closely to their individual needs and risk tolerance. The other trader laundered Sinaloa Cartel money to and from Panama.

Stephan MacLawn bought a United Airlines round-trip ticket from Boise to Seattle for $211. The Uber ride into town cost $12. He ate the egg-salad sandwich Vivian had made for him on the ride up and spent $9 for a Starbucks panini and a bag of chips on the ride back to Boise. In between, he spent less than an hour on the job interview with North-by-Northeast. They offered him a job as a bookkeeper and cashier. It came with flexible hours, $76,000 in annual salary, a relocation stipend of $7,500 to spend however he liked, and a benefits package that was far superior to the one he had at Hurlitt International Services in Baltimore. The only reason he didn't accept it on the spot was he'd promised Vivian he'd talk it over with her first. He'd do that tomorrow morning in Boise. And he'd call them back and accept the job by 2:00 p.m. Pacific Daylight Savings Time.

Vivian heard her Dad unlock the door to the extended-stay apartment they'd been in for the last two months at ten minutes after midnight. She knew he'd be tired, so she just stayed in bed. Now, it was almost 7:00 a.m. and she couldn't wait. Dressing quickly, she went downstairs from the loft to the kitchen; she didn't drink coffee, but he did. She knew from living in the trailer that coffee would wake him up without her banging on his door.

The Extended Stay America franchise on Vista Avenue in Boise was a half-mile away from the airport where, without knowing they were that close, Julia and Chaco had driven past their apartment the day before, while Vivian's dad was in Seattle. The apartment cost $63 per night, had one bedroom, a nice bathroom, and a small living area attached to a larger kitchen area. The loft had a pull-out sofa bed, a two-foot wide closet, and a skylight. It came with free Wi-Fi, which Vince loved, free breakfast, which Dad loved, and a bathtub, which Vivian loved.

"So, Sweetums," her dad said, "I smelled the coffee and had to get up. You already knew that, right? What's new with you?"

"Don't play dumb, Dad. I'm all twisty inside my head. Are we moving to Seattle or not?"

"Depends, Sweetums. Do you want your dear old dad to try to live on $76,000 a year, plus a $7,500 moving allowance, plus a benefits package almost as good as the US Senate gets? If I took it, you'd have to get used to living in the most beautiful city I've ever seen. It makes Baltimore look like Detroit. And the view of the snow-capped mountains all around will take your breath away. If all that sounds OK to you, then I'll call them this afternoon and accept the job."

Vivian jumped up from the vinyl-topped table and gave him a big hug and a kiss on the cheek.

"Way to go, Dad. Can't wait to tell Vince."

"You know Seattle is a really important Internet place, don't you? Vince will love that part. Microsoft's just a few miles away, and Amazon's just up the block from where I'll be working. I saw a list on the wall at the airport and wrote the names down while I was waiting for the flight back here last night. Twitter, Snapchat, DropBox, Redfin, Zulily, Big Fish Games, Nintendo, Tableau Software. The list was from something called the Geekwire Top 200. I knew you'd, I mean Vince, would want to know the names."

"That's great Dad, I'll tell Vince right away, soon as he gets back. He's surfing, been gone all night."

"So, look. There's some stuff in the engine well of the Winnebago I need to take a look at. Want to drive up to Quinn's Pond with me?"

"Sure, but I need to stick around here till Vince comes home. I got some talkin' to do with that boy, I do, I do. Can you wait a few?"

"OK, let's see. I need to shower, shave, and make a list of things I want to cover with my new boss at North-by-Northeast when I call them this afternoon, then I'll go to the Winnie, and . . ."

"Why wait until this afternoon, Dad? Call 'em right now."

"Suppose I could. But I said it'd be two this afternoon. Best stick to the plan. Don't want them to think I'm easy to get. Jeeze, would you believe it? Seventy-six-thousand-dollars per annum! That's $292 a day, and I get the same pay for my fourteen days off a year, not counting all the holidays the stock market takes off."

"Dad, we're going to be rolling in the dough for sho. I'm figuring we'll make twice that, once we get Disappearance, LLC, fully marketed. It's doing pretty good now, but we need more umph on Tor. I bet even the port-a-potties have Wi-Fi in Seattle. Vince can work from anywhere. We are taking the Winnie to Seattle, right?"

"Sure we are. In fact, I think I'll call that tech guy at the RV Park, you know the one you say looks like me. He's been trying to fix the satellite dish on the roof of the Winne for three weeks. He should have the parts in by now. I gave him the extra key ring so he can fix it without me being there. Maybe he's already got it done. But for sure, we can't drive into Seattle without Internet coverage, right? What would they think we were, pumpkin heads from Kansas?"

"You know why the guy looks like you, don't you, Dad?"

"I think he's my size, with Scandinavian roots, and has the same hair color as me. But when I look in the mirror I see me, not him. So why do you think we look alike?"

"Because, from the neck up, you have the same facial structure. Your eyes and forehead are set almost identically. Neither of you has a noticeable Adam's apple, and you both have dimples and crinkles around the eyes. I read in one of my change-your-identity books that those facial markers are how you can make fake driver's licenses. I betcha you look like his twin on an MVD photo."

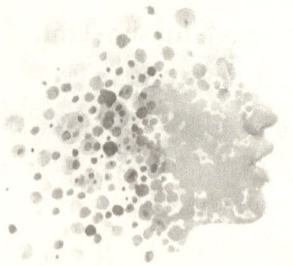

CHAPTER 24

It had taken Julia and Chaco almost five hours driving from one RV park to another all over Ada County. The Wikipedia page for the county said it contained over 200,000 of Idaho's population. After the first four hours, Julia was starting to believe most of them had trailers or RVs parked in the scores of parks they found. One by one, they got out and started at different ends of the paved parking spots, although about half were not paved. They found several dozen fairly new Winnebagos, nine of which were blue. But only three were baby blue, and only one of those had Arizona plates. One of the three, at a park nine miles from Boise, had three skinny teenagers close by, all high on pot, and all from Montana. Another baby blue Winnie, with Washington plates, was owned by a state policeman. They parked fifty feet away and finally saw the owner emerge; he was dark skinned and bald.

So, that left the one at Quinn's Pond, the one with Arizona plates. There was no park manager and no office to ask for details. One of the tenants, a hefty woman in sweat pants, owned a thirty-foot Fox River unit. She told Julia the owner of the blue Winnebago with Arizona plates wasn't living in it any more. He rented it out by the week but came by once or twice a week to check on it. She said the manager ran two parks and lived in the other one, across the pond—a ten-mile round trip. Julia found a playground with a hot-dog stand about two hundred yards away. With binoculars, which she always had in her backpack, they could watch the Winnie from the playground parking lot. She'd told Chaco to stay at one of the tables and she'd watch from fifty feet further back.

About 11:30, a pick-up truck, with a ladder rack on top, stopped alongside the Winnie. A tall man got out, fished around in the bed of his truck for something, and then walked to the RV door, opened it with a key, and went inside.

Chaco ran to the Jeep. "Is it him?"

"Can't say," Julia answered. "I only saw him from the front at first, then by the time I got the binocs on him, his back was to me. So, here's the plan, Chaco. We will drive over there very slowly. The road is straight, so if he comes out, we'll see him. You sit up front now. Don't do anything till I tell you."

Julia started the Jeep, put it in first, and moved forward as slowly as she could go. A truck pulled up behind them and honked. So she pulled over almost into the bar ditch. Now they were only about fifty yards away. There were trees on both sides of the road, but from where they were stopped nothing blocked their view of the Winnie and the surrounding RV park.

"You get out, Chaco. Leave your backpack here. Walk over there, but stay in the trees along this side of the road. I think you can see from in there everything I can see from here. If he comes out, I'll see him through the binocs. If it's him, I'll turn on the headlights as a signal. If you don't see my headlights, it means it's *not* him. You got that! No headlights, it's *not* him. But if you see them, then you go. Do him! I'll watch from here. Then, you make sure he's dead; I mean sure because you take his fucking pulse, right? Then you just come out and walk toward me. I'll pick you up between here and there. Got it, Chaco? Do you have any questions?"

He didn't even look at her. He shucked the backpack, felt in his right front cargo pants pocket for his wire, and got out without a word. He walked into the edge of the tree line. She could see him making his way toward the Winnie. He stopped about thirty yards away. Chaco was in his silent zone. She trained the 8x lens, slightly adjusted the focus, and panned back from Chaco in the dark trees to the baby-blue Winnie in bright sunlight. She couldn't see his neck from this far away, but she knew those huge veins were pumping, and that he was wrenching his hands into fists and grips. She knew too that he was controlling his breath, easy in, and with pursed lips, easy out. Very slow. Getting ready.

Exactly seven minutes later, the RV door opened. She had the binocs up and the MVD photo of Steven Shortfield between her teeth. She focused immediately on the man as he stood in the Winnie's doorway, eighteen inches off the ground. Lowering the binocs without taking her eyes off the man, she picked the photo out of her mouth and held it at elbow's length in front of her. It was him! Slowly, not wanting to lose her line of sight to him, she used her left hand to reach for the headlight switch on the dash. Looking down for a fraction of a second, she turned the headlights on and pumped the floor switch, turning the brights up and down.

The man stepped down from the Winnie and walked to the back of his truck. Lowering the tailgate, he climbed up into the back and started to unstrap the twelve-foot orange aluminum ladder. He'd just got one strap loose when Chaco, running at a surprisingly fast pace, reached the truck. She hadn't seen Chaco move. But all of a sudden, there he was, jogging toward the back of the man's truck. Putting his hands on the lowered truck gate, he vaulted up into the back of the truck. Just as he did, Julia saw and heard another loud truck pull up alongside the man and Chaco.

Chaco, seemingly oblivious to the other truck, stretched his twenty-four-inch-long strand of wire, holding firm onto the half-inch bolts that slotted the killing tool on either end. He looped the wire from behind, over the top of the man's head, and jerked back. The hapless man tried to scream, trying desperately to get his fingers under the wire and away from his neck. But Chaco extended his elbows out to both sides, compressing the man backward into his own chest. As they stumbled backward together, Chaco leaned back and the smaller man in his grasp was lifted off his feet.

As if in a death dance, they jostled and bobbed backward toward the open tailgate.

Two men jumped out of the other truck, hollering incoherently. Julia sat, transfixed by the horror thirty yards away. Chaco ignored the men screaming up at him from the side of the truck and kept sawing into his captive's neck. The wire had flushed down into the shattering skin, bone and blood now gushing from the other man's neck. The smaller of the two men on the side of the truck appeared to be reaching for something behind him in his camo waist pack. The other man tried to grab Chaco's leg from the side of the truck. Chaco kept his backward pressure as he and the man in his steel grasp stumbled backward toward the tailgate. Chaco sawed the wire back and forth from right to left, as the man's throat ruptured and black blood flew up and back onto both of them, some of it spewing over the side of the truck onto the two passers-by. Chaco and the man inside the wire noose lurched backward, flying backward off the tailgate. Chaco landed on his back, with the other man splayed on top of him like a bloody sleeping bag. Chaco roared like a wounded bear as he kept sawing through the other man's skin, muscle, ligaments, and eventually bone.

The passenger in the truck reached the now blood-soaked pile on the dirt just behind the tailgate. Instead of trying to stop the attacker, he pulled a .357 magnum from his waist pack and fired three shots into Chaco's head. Other people, hearing the shots, began running to the bloody scene. Three men were in the dirt. One man was nearly decapitated. Another one, lying under the first, had his head blown nearly off. The third, the driver of the second pickup truck was on his knees, vainly trying to separate the bodies. The man with the .357 flipped open the chamber, ejected the remaining rounds into the bed, and laid his gun on the tailgate. Reaching into the rear pocket of his Levis, he flipped his phone open, and dialed 911.

No one noticed the brown jeep with the gray top start up, make an orderly U-turn, and head west, toward the airport.

CHAPTER 25

Fbi headquarters in Washington first learned of the Boise, Idaho, killings nine hours after the bodies were tagged and bagged. They became the medical examiner's problem; the crime scene was cordoned off by yellow tape. It took the big rain two days later to wipe the blood from the dirt fifteen feet away from the now-deserted baby-blue Winnebago.

Boise had about 225,000 residents, which made it by far the biggest city in the state. Eighty-nine percent of the residents were white, the remaining 11 percent were defined in the 2010 federal census as "Hispanic origin, of any race." The man garroted to death was white. His killer was obviously Hispanic. That's about all the Boise police department knew about either victim when they turned the case over to the FBI.

Violent crime in Idaho was rare. Boise only had three murders in the previous nineteen months. There had never been two violent killings at the same time, anywhere in the state. Without any evidence whatsoever, the FBI presumed Chaco was from out-of-state simply because no one could identify him. He had almost nothing in his pockets and was heavily tattooed, especially around his neck; prison tats, mostly *en Español*.

The call to the Boise FBI field office resulted in a scramble for jurisdiction. The FBI had jurisdiction over crimes that crossed state lines and over criminals who commit violent crimes, such as gang members. Three things suggested Chaco met the FBI protocol. He had a rubber-banded roll of 100-dollar bills taped to the inside of his left thigh. His fingerprints didn't find a match on federal or Interpol databases. And his weapon was a garrote. No one had ever been killed in Idaho with a garrote. The Boise police did a quick Internet search on the unknown killer's choice of weapon.

A garrote can be made out of rope, fishing line, nylon, guitar strings, or piano wire. A stick can be used to tighten the garrote, which is a Spanish word referring to the stick, not the wire. Since World War II, garrotes have been used as a silent means of killing. Special forces in all nations train operators in their use. The typical military garrote had two wooden handles attached to a length of flexible wire. But Chaco's was different. His was a double-loop garrote, called *la loupe*. It was double coil of wire that, when dropped around a victim's neck and pulled taut, meant sure death to the victim because, even if a victim pulls on one side of the coils, he only succeeds in tightening the other. The post-mortem would eventually confirm those mechanics, since his head was nearly sawed completely from his torso.

The FBI office in Boise quickly established that the garroted victim was not the owner of the RV he was working on that day. The day of the shooting had been consumed by forensic examination of the crime, outside the RV. Those forensics matched what the "non-involved" eyewitness reported to an anxious television journalist on Boise's local channel KTVB, an NBC affiliate. He and an unidentified friend "happened on the killing ground by accident," the flushed reporter said, on live TV. As the camera panned the crime scene—two trucks and a twenty-four-foot recreational vehicle, 150 yards from an easily recognizable local water park—the breathless reporter described only the aftermath. No one at the actual scene was willing to go on camera. So the reporter denied knowing anything except that "we have two bodies, one shot to death and one almost beheaded. We'll have more details at ten."

The station used the grisly deaths as the lead on its five o'clock news. Their on-scene report made it local because the first victim was a local handyman, "name not yet revealed pending notification of next of kin." He was described as a "handyman who fixed motor homes and trailers in several parks and rental facilities in the Quinn's Pond area of north Boise."

Once it accepted jurisdiction, the Boise FBI SAIC emailed via Secure Net 6 a report to FBI HQ in Washington, DC, and all other SAICs in the country. Only the Phoenix SAIC's office responded within minutes. The next morning, less than twenty-four hours after the Idaho killings, SAIC Stanza briefed his team in Phoenix.

"Here's what little we know. The local man garroted and nearly decapitated, identified as Vic-1, is Jason Bloomington, age forty-four, Idaho born and bred, white, no criminal record, and a community college graduate in mechanics. The second man, identified as Vic-2, is an overweight Hispanic. No name yet. Fingerprint and photo identification under way. He was killed by a passerby, identified in the Boise FBI APD as EyeWit-1, with a .357 magnum revolver. His name is Stunt Jaueger, white male, aged twenty-seven. Fired three rounds point blank into Vic-2's head, blowing much of the skull and part of his face off. Both vics died within minutes of one another. So, gentlemen and Agent Lin, we have two victims, two killings and, as yet, no hard information about motive on Vic-1. It's the first death-by-garrote case in Idaho, and maybe anywhere else except for Florida. It's clearly a premeditated murder. The second case, death by multiple bullet wounds to the head, has a probable motive—to try and save Vic 1. Seems to be an attempt at preventing a crime, but we logging it as a possible homicide for now."

Agent Lin interrupted her boss. "Possible homicide, boss? Why?"

"Because, Agent Lin," Stan said, "we don't know enough to disregard him. The APB says Witness-1 was a passerby, just happened accidently to be driving by. They took a short statement and interviewed him downtown. We have the 302. They are calling it a possible homicide because, after giving the statement, Witness 1 left town. The 302 says his name is Stunt Jaueger. But follow up calls to his cell are going to voice mail. He said he was just a tourist and that he was headed north up to Coeur d' Alene to do some fly fishing. We know nothing about him. He was told not to leave the area, but he apparently ignored that. There will be a coroner's inquest in Idaho, and he will be an important witness. But until he returns a cell call, it's a "possible homicide."

"So," Agent Cambridge added, "Mr. Bloomington is garroted by an unknown Hispanic male, who is shot to death by Mr. Jaueger, address unknown, who flees the scene shortly after shooting the Hispanic male. Both victims die within seconds of one another. There are two witnesses to both killings. One is the .357 magnum shooter. What's the name of the second witness and what'd he say about Witness-1?"

"Witness-2 is a twenty-two-year-old Boise State University student. Hopes to graduate next year with a sociology degree. His name is Ivan Zagal. Born in Boise. Never lived anywhere else. He owned the truck he and Mr. Jaueger were in. He says he met Stunt Jaueger in a bar the night before the killings, but didn't know his last name until their interviews at the Boise FBI office shootings. Says the guy was a big spender and bought several rounds of drinks for him and his college pals at a sports bar called Humpin' Hannah's. They closed down the place night before the killings. Jaueger had no car and apparently no place to sleep when they left the bar at 2:00 a.m. So Zagal offers the couch in his apartment, and . . ."

Agent Sterndusky, usually reluctant to interrupt anyone, jumped in.

"Boss, I don't mean to interrupt, but I don't see the connection to Arizona, yet. What am I missing?"

The SAIC opened his iPad, clicked on the projector cable, and displayed a photo on the screen.

"This is a photo of the Vic-1, Jason Bloomington. It's his MVD photo from Idaho. Anyone recognize him? No? OK, I'll put another MVD photo side-by-side on the screen."

SAIC Stanza fumbled a bit but in a minute found what he was looking for on his iPad and projected it onto the screen.

"Now, does anyone recognize the second MVD photo? Cambridge, how 'bout you? Either one look familiar?"

"No, except that they look a little alike. Who's the second guy? I can see his name there on the MVD photo, Stephan MacLawn. Who is he?"

"Good catch. They do look alike. The second guy is Stephan Manchester, also known as Stephan Nau, or Stephan Shortfield."

"Jesus H. Christ!" Agent Sterndusky, shouted. "And we know this how?"

"Because last May, the man we lost track of in Cranston that the US Marshall's office knew as Stephan Nau, did a legal name change in Pinal County Superior Court. He changed his birth name, Stephan Manchester, to Stephan MacLawn. Told the judge he wanted to restore his family's Irish heritage. What question does this raise for us?"

Nancy Lin asked, "Why didn't he change it to his Cranston name, Stephan Nau?"

"Because his Cranston name was a phony name, created by our friends at WITSEC. He would have made a false representation to the court had he used Nau as his real name. He told the truth—his real name was Manchester. The question I was hoping to get was why did he use MacLawn? Remember, he was also known as Stephan while he was in Cranston."

"Well, damn. I should have caught that," Agent Cambridge said. "Shortfield was the name the girl, Vivian, used to get the library card. That's where we started in this case. And now we've sort of come full circle."

"How did we get the Arizona MVD photo?" Lin asked.

"It was a follow-up attachment to the APB that came in yesterday, from FBI-Boise. They got it out of the glove compartment of that blue 2010 Winnebago that Mr. Bloomington was doing the work on. I'm thinking he died because of something that you should now be able to see in the photos on the screen. Can't you see it? These two photos could be, with different clothes and different lighting, the same man. Maybe Bloomington got garroted because Vic-2 thought he was offing Manchester. And if that's right, what the fuck is going on here?"

"It's a professional hit. We're probably going to find that Vic-2 is a paid assassin," Sterndusky, answered.

SAIC Stanza wrapped up the session. "OK everyone, get at it. I can tell you that FBI HQ is now actively investigating, as is both FinCEN and the CIA. Cambridge, go back to Cranston and shake the weeds there. Lin, you need to go to Yuma. You'll see in the workup from Boise that the VIN number on the Winnebago confirms it was sold in Yuma to Stephan Shortfield just a few days after his alter ego, Stephan Nau, bolted from Cranston. Lin, I'd like you to call someone you trust at our HQ in DC. You spent five years there before escaping to Phoenix. See if they are making progress there. I want you to focus on Vic-2, the unidentified Hispanic male with the terror weapon, a double-loupe garrote. Find his house and blow down the door."

CHAPTER 26

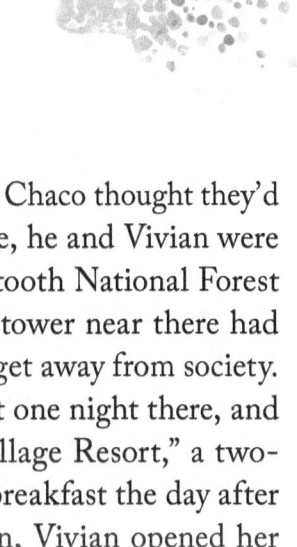

On the day Julia and Chaco thought they'd found Stephan Manchester in Boise, he and Vivian were 150 miles away, hiking in the Sawtooth National Forest near Obsidian, Idaho. An old fire tower near there had been restored for hikers looking to get away from society. Perfect, Vivian thought. They spent one night there, and a second one at the "Mountain Village Resort," a two-star motel, despite its name. Over breakfast the day after Chaco garroted Jason Bloomington, Vivian opened her laptop to check something and found the explosive story about the killings. The sensational articles were all over the Internet. Flash and splash photos of the bodies and her loveable baby-blue Winnie had gone viral. She read bits and pieces of the story to her dad, who seemed not to comprehend the reality.

"No, Dad. It's no coincidence. They were trying to kill you! Jason looks like you. Look at this screen, Dad. His face is up on the Internet, right next to yours, anyone can see how someone could mistake him for you."

Her dad's arguments seemed endless to Vivian.

"We have to go back," he moaned.

"No we don't," she said, in coldly measured language.

"We have to help them find out who killed Jason," he pleaded.

"No, Dad. He's dead because bad people thought he was you."

"But, don't you see, Viv, we have to get our things from the Winnie. They aren't looking for me anymore. We are free now because Mr. Goshkervic is not on trial. He's dead."

"Right Dad, he's dead. And you're alive, but only because they killed someone yesterday in Boise, they thought was you. Can't you see that?"

Her dad looked at her like he was sitting with a stranger. His face was suddenly drawn and white. He tapped his fingers incessantly on the vinyl table top in the motel's coffee shop. He reached for the coffee mug, but it tipped over and spilled over the table. He started to wipe the spill with the small paper napkin, but Vivian stopped him.

"Stop that. The waitress will clean the mess. I can't give you all the answers right now. You go check us out. Pay cash. I'll get our little rental truck filled up at that station across the street. But you have to drive while I use my iPhone to find out whether your old boss Fritz Goshkervic was behind this. Then, when we get to a town big enough to have an Internet café with high speed broadband, Vince will surf the Darknet for the real story behind the killing. Dad, don't you understand what's happened? Whoever was behind it—I can't hardly say it—they used a garrote to kill Mr. Bloomington! We need to get as far away from Idaho as possible. And right now."

They drove in shifts for the next two days, on back roads, and without ever breaking the speed limit. They never went into a grocery store together. While Dad drove, Vivian curled up in the back seat below the windows, using cell towers to surf and making notes. In two small towns, they stole rear license plates from cars parked in long-term spaces at airports. Finally, they reached Minot, North Dakota, where they parked the rental jeep in the extended-stay lot.

Viv drove and told the lady in the parking booth that she needed a space for five weeks because, "I'm gonna disappear to Brazil to study my Spanish, and get really good on the guitar."

The lady in the booth apparently didn't know that Portuguese is the official language in Brazil. Neither did Vivian. She just made it up on the spot.

Fifteen minutes after Vivian walked to the airport terminal, Dad followed her instructions. He unwound himself from the floor in the back, got out, and carried his bag to the other side of the airport. He stayed there until Vivian called him from The Hampton Inns and Suites, a half mile down Broadway from the airport. Vince had rented a room there, she told him. Dad, just knock on Room 109, she had instructed. Vince will let you in. It would turn out to be a long time before he would see his daughter again. She had disappeared completely.

CHAPTER 27

Julia took the next flight out of Boise; it happened to be to Billings, Montana. She didn't care. As long as it was away from Idaho. When she landed in Billings, she was surprised to find it was Montana's largest city, with 110,000 residents. A brochure at the airport information desk proudly proclaimed that Billings had more hotel accommodations than any area within a five-state region. It hosted "a variety of conventions, concerts, sporting events, and other rallies."

Julia asked the septuagenarian behind the desk, "Where's the taxi station?"

She asked the taxi driver, "Where's the bus station?"

She asked the ticket agent at the Greyhound bus station, "When's the next thru bus south to Omaha, Nebraska?"

After only asking a handful of questions, she was on a half-empty bus two hours later. Google Maps on her cell phone said she was in for an 840-mile-ride to Houston. It would eventually take the better part of three days from Boise to Houston, counting food, restroom breaks, delays due to poor terminal management, and a little bad weather. But she got what she wanted most: invisibility, and a back-door trip to Baytown. She knew the most important thing about riding in a transcontinental bus—guaranteed anonymity. She was never asked her name, or for proof of identity. She paid for every lousy meal in cash and she never engaged a passenger, or a waitress in conversation. She could have been a mute for twenty-two hours.

In Omaha, she checked into a battered woman shelter, which offered a locked door to the sleeping room, a communal with five beds, and one bathroom. None of the women stayed for more than a day. She stayed the night and left the next morning before breakfast. Using made up names on the spot, everywhere, she hitched a ride at a big truck stop on the south side of Omaha. The driver with really bad teeth owned an eighteen-wheeler bound for San Antonio, Texas. But she got off in Las Cruces, New Mexico, disappointing the ugly driver who'd hoped she'd get into the filthy bed in the back of his giant cab-over diesel rig. There, she called Uber on her cell phone and negotiated a $356 fee for a one-way trip to Houston. Once in the back seat of a nearly new Prius, she offered the driver a fifty-dollar tip if he'd just shut up and drive. She was exhausted, she said, after a rafting trip down a crappy river. Finally, three days later, she got out at the front gates of Rice University in central Houston. Once the Uber driver was out of sight, she walked to the Texas Medical Center where she found a taxi line at the front door. She went inside through the

ER entrance and then back outside through the front door. The hospital greeter thought she was a recently discharged patient and hailed a cab. Forty minutes later, the heavily bearded driver with the white Turban dropped her off at her home in Baytown.

Once safely inside, at almost midnight, she took a shower, changed her Boise clothes, fixed a catfish salad, and set the alarm on her cell phone. When it buzzed her at five a.m., she drove to her office and called Leopoldo de Santos on her satellite phone. He answered in two rings, but in a hushed tone.

"Hold on Julia, I'm still in bed. Not alone. I will ring you back in just a few minutes. Don't go anywhere."

Three minutes later, she punched the talk button of the cumbersome sat phone. "It's me," she said.

"So, Julia, I am relieved to hear your voice. Of course we learned about Chaco killing the wrong man, and then some gringo gave him three *balas* to the head. I've made one, just one, call to your sat number every morning at seven for the last three days. Where you been?"

"Where have I been? What did you think? They caught me and I spent three days in the fucking CIA black and blue camp? No, I had to escape from the big fucking dragnet they had out for me."

"But how could they know about you, Julia? You didn't get caught there when Chaco got his head blown off."

"But they had Chaco's body. Not too hard to track him back to the airport in Boise. He flew there on his real name—we had to do that—you didn't give us any time to do it differently. And once they did that, they could also track me on the same plane. Again, because you were in such a big fucking hurry—not time to do a better plan. Now, I'm exposed, because you made me fly up there with Chaco."

For a full minute, the sat phone was silent. Then, with a deep inhaled breath, Senor Leopoldo de Santos responded. "So, Julia my old friend, I'm very happy to hear your voice, but also I'm disappointed you fucked up in Boise. Chaco has been with us his whole life. He served my father and uncle before coming to my service. So, what happened?"

Julia talked without Leopoldo interrupting for five minutes. She took full responsibility for giving Chaco the go-ahead by flicking the light switch on her rented jeep. She had no explanation for a man who could have been Steven Manchester's twin brother coming out of his RV when he did. And she could not even begin to explain the bizarre oddity about the tourist with the .357 magnum blowing Chaco's head off to save a man who was probably already dead inside Chaco's la loupe garrote. She offered to go find the man who killed Chaco, and kill him herself, for no fee.

"So, you listen close now, Julia," Leopoldo whispered from 1,544 air miles away. "I did not know you had a soft heart for Chaco. But this is very important. Do not do one single thing about the man who killed Chaco. Don't ask about him of anyone in *Norteamérica*. If he walks in your door someday, don't talk to him. He is being taken care of down here. Jus you forget him, *que no?*"

Leopoldo assured her that her fee would be paid, the usual way, by wire transfer to her account in Panama. He assured her a second chance at killing this Mister Manchester, or MacLawn as the newspapers were calling him. But he made clear if he called her again, please to remember, she'd already been paid for the killing.

"We do not pay twice. Only once. If we give you two chances and you fuck it up again, we will kill you, not pay you. *Que no?*"

"Yes, Senor de Santos, I understand," she said.

CHAPTER 28

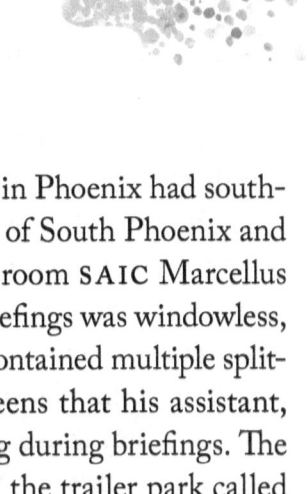

The FBI field office in Phoenix had south-facing windows, with a mixed view of South Phoenix and the dry Salt River. But the interior room SAIC Marcellus "Stan" Stanza used for high-level briefings was windowless, had one steel-reinforced door, and contained multiple split-screen computer monitors and screens that his assistant, J.A., was very adept at manipulating during briefings. The images of the crime scene in Boise, the trailer park called Shady Acres in Cranston, a used car dealership in Yuma, the Extended Stay America franchise on Vista Avenue in Boise, two pickup trucks, one MVD photo of Stephan Manchester and another Idaho MVD photo of Jason Bloomington were displayed in split-screens on five monitors.

Once his team was seated with five mugs of half-day old coffee in front of each, Stan asked in reverse order of seniority what "location-connectors" they could see in these images. They all knew FBI jargon—location connectors were links that, if read correctly, could lead the FBI to a current location of a missing person.

"Agent Lin," Stan said, waving a yardstick at the bank of monitors, "you've got the youngest set of eyes in the room. What do you see in these seven photographs?"

She'd been staring at the monitors for ten minutes while the rest of the team came in and guessed her boss would call on her first, given her tenure as an FBI agent. She tried as best she could to sound knowing and confident.

"Sir, I see the Boise crime scene, two vehicles, two trailer parks, an Arizona MVD photo of Stephan Manchester, and an Idaho MVD photo of Jason Bloomington. Seven pics. But they're not arrayed in the right chronological order."

"OK, tell J.A. how to rearrange them chronologically."

Sally Lin turned to J.A. "You've got the Arizona MVD photo last. Move it to the left so that it's in first place. Now, put the Shady Acres trailer park in second place. Move the Yuma used car dealership to third, make the Extended Stay America hotel number four, place Vic-1's, Jason Bloomington's, truck on number five, then display the other truck—the one Stunt Jaueger was in, our .357 magnum shooter—in sixth place, and end the array from left to right with number seven, the Boise Crime scene."

"Nice job, Lin. Now tell us why you think this pic story is in the right chronological order."

"Well," she said tentatively, as though she knew her boss disagreed with her chronology order, "this all started with the man we knew as Stephan Nau, whose real name was Stephan Manchester. We know now that he legally changed his name to Stephan MacLawn in Cranston before he bolted from WITSEC. So, I put him first. Obviously, he was staying at that trailer park, called Shady Acres, so I made that pic second. He traded in his Dodge pickup in Yuma for the 2010 Winnebago that we can see in the last photo. I wish we had a pic of his truck, the one he let go for $500. But we don't. And . . ."

Stan interrupted, "Hold on a sec. Why is MacLawn first? We're part of the task force on the murder case in Boise, Idaho, right? So, why start in Cranston instead of Boise?"

She knew this was a test, a rookie test, and that the SAIC was making sure this office was not straying too far from their part in the task force.

"Boss, I started with the intended victim in Idaho, Mr. MacLawn. I presume other field offices are digging into the murder of Mr. Bloomington—primarily the Boise field office. You didn't put up a picture of the garrote killer, Chaco Hernandez, or Mr. Jaueger, the passer-by who blasted Chaco into eternity. I thought our piece was to identify the whereabouts of Mr. MacLawn because he bolted and nobody knows why. Presumably, his disappearance from Cranston will help explain his reappearance in Boise."

Stan, turning to the other agents at the table said, "Everybody agree with Lin's chronological order, and her assessment of what our role is?"

Cambridge, always ready to correct a rookie, rose to the occasion. "She's right boss. Well, she's at least half right. We need to find out *why* Maclawn bolted, not just where he bolted to. And we need to know why MacLawn bolted again after his handyman got garroted in Boise. My gut's telling me both bolts are for the same reason, but for one problem."

"Which is?" Stan asked.

"*If* MacLawn, the father of the girl who wanted to disappear in Cranston, was in the program because he was an important witness in that commodities fraud case in Baltimore, and *if* he bolted to avoid testimony in that case, why would he stay in hiding once the Baltimore case was over? I mean really over—Fritz Goshkervic got his bad ass blown apart in that Learjet over the Gulf of Mexico. I can't see our missing witness bolting from Boise for the same reason he bolted from Cranston."

Agent Lin said, "I'm not at all sure the two bolts are the same. Maybe he bolted from Cranston because he was afraid to testify again. And maybe he bolted from Boise out of a different fear. I think the six weeks he spent out in the open at that Stay America joint in Boise tell us he thought he was safe. He wasn't really hiding then. But the second his repairman got garroted in Boise, he went on the lam again. I think he was scared—first his old boss gets murdered in a Learjet—then his repairman gets murdered in Boise. And neither murder was your garden-variety killing. Both may have been messages to parties unknown."

Agent Sterndusky chimed in. "Maybe the Learjet explosion message was intended to put the fear of God into Manchester—the guy we now know as MacLawn. And maybe he didn't get the message. So, whoever killed Goshkervic had to kill him too. What we don't know is who killed Goshkervic. It sure wasn't the 300-pound gorilla with the double-loupe garrote wire."

Agent Lin held up her hand and got the nod from Stan.

"Jeeze, I hadn't made that connection. If both killings are connected, either by the victim and the intended victim, or by what they both knew, who would want to silence both of them—not Chaco Hernández, right?"

Stan answered, "Sure, Sally, but Chaco is well known as one of the Sinaloa Cartel's favorite killers. We are not tasked to follow those connections. Yes, the cartel is the prime suspect in the explosion and the garroting case, but our assignment is narrower. FBI HQ is deep into the cartel connections, with help from FinCEN and the CIA. I just talked to Abe Kahn, the deputy director in Washington yesterday. He will keep us posted, but cautioned me against asking questions or making it known that we think Manchester's double disappearance and the Goshkervic murder are directly connected. They may be, but if so the connection has to be made out of DC, not Arizona. It's not just expertise, it's turf."

Cambridge had been silent long enough.

"Boss, I've reread all the APBs, the 302s, and I went over our first interactions with the US Marshal's office last night. Maybe we're looking for the wrong person. Maybe it's not Stephan Manchester we need to find, maybe its Vivian Shortfield, his daughter. If we can find her, we'll know her dad is close by, right?"

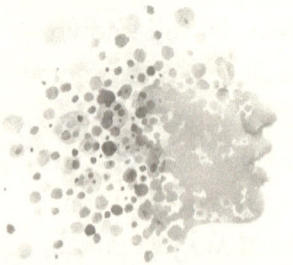

CHAPTER 29

Vivian had instructed her dad to make his way from the Minot, North Dakota, airport to The Hampton Inn and Suites, just a few miles away. Just knock on the door to Room 109, she'd said. When he got there, that disconnected-from-reality feeling that Stephan Manchester had first experienced nine years ago came back. He had to knock twice. He could hear loud music inside. Vince, who'd always been a somewhat morose boy, quickly looked away as soon as he let him in. Stephan was startled by the change since he'd last seen his son, at the bottom of the Grand Canyon months ago. At Phantom Ranch, Vince wore his sixteen-year-old persona, the one he'd developed in Cranston so his sister could be the only one in high school. Today he looked every bit the eighteen-year-old boy version of Vivian. He was slack-jawed, stoop-shouldered, and dismissive. He seemed to be wholly unaware they had just driven 1,006 miles, from Boise to Minot, taking turns hiding under a blanket in the rear seat. And he seemed oblivious to the fact his sister was not there. Vivian had intimated that Vince might show up.

Stephan's life, structured around Vivian after his wife died, was about to disassemble. Stephan had only seen Vince twice since they escaped from Cranston. But he was still the same, talking trash sports, acting out, and spiting noisily into sinks, toilets, and wastebaskets. He belched, farted at will, and asked no questions of any kind. Stephan tried not to jar Vince by openly asking about Vivian. Vince acted as though he didn't have a sister, or at least one he could remember. The opposite was true of Vivian. She loved to talk about her little brother, a year or two younger than her, but always there when she needed him. She never seemed to know when he'd show up, or where he'd been, of even why he was in their lives. But at least she knew about him. Stephan always wondered what she really knew, and what she imagined, about her elusive little brother. As he stood there looking at the eighteen-year-old-version of Vince, he was pretty sure Vivian would have been as dismayed as he was. But like his daughter, Stephan knew better than to challenge Vince in any way. He told Vince he was very tired and wanted to take a nap.

Room 109 was one of those three-room suites that had popped up on most Interstate highways in the last ten years. One bedroom. One bathroom. And a communal room of varying size, depending on which chain you picked. It had a kitchenette, eating bar, a pullout couch, one swivel chair with an overhead reading light, and a thirty-six-inch TV with a limited number of cable channels plus the local news network station. It was larger than the one in Boise, and newer. Stephan went into the bedroom, leaving Vince the pullout couch. He knew the day might come when Vince would take the bedroom. Where Vivian was warm and caring, Vince was calculating and cold. Vivian was very smart, but Vince's genius, especially with technology, was frightening.

Stephan went into the bedroom, closed the door, and found his rucksack on the bed. The fact that it had obviously been thrown there, upside down, and with one of the straps hanging off the side of the bed told him Vince had unpacked the jeep, not Vivian. He unzipped the nylon pouch at the bottom of the pack and pulled out the small laundry bag. Inside, he found two ballpoint pens, a notepad, and the well-worn leather binder stamped *My Diary* on the front cover. It once had a small working lock that inhibited the curious from opening the front and back covers, but it had broken about ten years ago. Just touching it brought back the stationary store in Baltimore where he and Angela had bought them together. One for her and one for him, she'd said.

"We have to make notes about what the doctors tell us about Vivian's condition," she'd said. "Your notes will be about the big things like diagnosis and prognosis. Mine will be about helping, not hurting, so Vivian can lead as normal life as possible despite her affliction."

That's how Angela had always thought or it—an affliction—not mental—just afflicting. We can help her live with it, she'd said, over and over, until she died when Vivian was ten. As he thumbed through his notes, he wished, as he had many times in the last eight years, that he'd kept Angela's own diary notes. But he left them in the metal box at the cemetery where he and Vivian had laid Angela's ashes to rest.

The first of three psychiatrists to examine Vivian was absurdly young, just thirty-four, and only one year out of his residency and fellowship in pediatric psychiatry. Stephan's notes consisted of words and phrases Dr. Sterling had used to explain what was afflicting their daughter. As he read the cursive note—*afflicting*—he remembered how quickly Angela had seized on the word. At the time, it was very comforting. They had been thinking that Vivian might be transgender. Instead, the young doctor, sitting with them in his cramped little office, told them about DID. *Dissociative Identity Disorder.*

His notes, taken in pencil on the cream-colored paper, had faded some. But his shorthand was clear. *Multiple Personality Disorder. Not sure Viv has. New name is dissociative identity disorder. Hypothesis—maybe childhood trauma—hypnosis would work—bring her out—both of them—maybe more identities. Time will tell.*

Angela told the doctor about the fifteen hours Vivian had spent in a cave after getting lost on their disastrous Thanksgiving trip into the Prettyboy Reservoir area not far from Baltimore. She was just nine then, Angela said. They'd been hiking with another couple, who had a seven-year-old boy, named Chester. Vivian and the boy hit it off right away. While the parents spread their backpacked lunch on the park bench, Vivian and Chester walked down the fifty-foot slope to the short spillway from the reservoir. Somehow, Chester fell in and Vivian ran away. Both families panicked. Within a half-hour park rangers and an EMT team arrived. Later that night, Chester was found, three miles away, drowned. The following morning a different search team found Vivian, crouched down inside a small rocky cave almost completely covered over with thick forest undergrowth. She later said she heard people all around calling her name, *Vivian, Vivian, where are you?*

It took six months for Vivian to talk about anything. She never admitted sleeping in the cave that night. She gritted her teeth and glared at anyone who asked her about it. Finally, a neighbor who'd often taken care of Vivian coaxed the truth out of her. She'd told Chester not to get too close to the spillway. When he fell in and disappeared, she tried to find him. Then, she said, "I disappeared too. Crawled into the cave. Afraid his mom and dad would think I killed Chester. *Poor Chester.*"

Dr. Sterling explained how severe childhood trauma can create a mental split, or "dissociation" as a defense against that trauma. He thought, guessed, speculated that maybe, possibly, Vivian had *two, or more selves* and each *identity* has its own mood, memories, behaviors, and experiences. Angela asked about treatment. *Psychotherapy,* he said. *No,* Angela said.

The second psychiatrist they took Vivian to, Dr. Gladys Gillinson, offered more insight into Dissociative Identity Disorder. DID. It's different than Multiple Personality Disorder, which is more like a disease, where a person has it, or does not have it, she said. Angela didn't think much of Dr. Gillinson. She said the term dissociation was used to describe the split in consciousness that results when patients are exposed to traumatic events. And Dr. Gillinson insisted on differentiating between the patient's body, and the patient's mind. In dissociative identity patients, several distinct states of mind, or personalities reside in one body. Each personality has its own sense of self and its own habits of thought, emotions, and memory.

Angela thought that was a little crazy. She asked Dr. Gillinson if the identities were aware of each other. Yes, and no, she said. Some do. Most don't. While one personality is in control, the other is in the background, in the back of the mind, vaguely aware of what the current personality is doing.

"Can the not-in-control personality see what the current personality sees?" Angela had asked.

"Perhaps," Dr. Gillinson had muttered. Dr. Gillinson didn't like being questioned about her diagnosis—took it as a challenge. "Maybe the inside personality, deep inside the brain, can sense what's being seen, but it would be foggy, not really images, but fragments of images."

Stephan and Angela decided Vivian was always in control, and Vince only showed up when Vivian needed him. So they did not return to Dr. Gillinson' s office. In fact, they gave up on looking for answers, mostly because Vivian was so cheerful and seemed to be over the trauma of watching Chester thrash against the brown water as he disappeared down the causeway at the Prettyboy Reservoir.

What no one ever told them about was that Dissociative Identity Disorder rarely resolves spontaneously. Or that it happens more to females than males. Later, Angela would read a good deal about DID, but not Stephan, much less Vivian. Angela knew that sometimes one personality would work against the other, in say, both mental conflict, and physical self-harm. She read case studies where one personality tried to undo what another did, bringing new meaning to the acronym DID. In almost all cases, one personality lacked memory of the other, creating memory gaps and making one personality feel as though the more dominant one was trying to kill them. Or, worse yet, one psychiatric nurse practitioner said, both personalities might come to feel as though they did not exist for the period of time when they were not in control. She called that amnesia of the amnesias. In time, Stephan and Angela forgot about that.

The third and last doctor to see Vivian was the one who discovered Vince. He was a transgender specialist in San Francisco, Dr. Garcia. Vivian never doubted she was born female. She identified with her sex. Dr. Garcia told Angela and Stephan that he understood Vivian did not want to be a boy. But she loved the things boys did that were denied to girls. Horseplay, guns, spitting, and ignoring parents' admonitions. Boys were bolder and got away with more things. His records confirm Vivian's history—from age four or five, she often playacted she was a boy. She didn't name herself or dress differently, she just did boy things. And, Dr. Garcia thought, it was important that Vivian's playacting started when she was that young. It made it easier, five years later when she was traumatized by Chester's death, to go back to playacting about having a brother, Vince. But it wasn't playacting then, it was the brain reacting to trauma. After five interview sessions with Vivian alone, and two sessions with her parents, Dr. Garcia assured her parents their daughter was not transgender. He recommended they seek psychotherapy. That would help her manage her emotional reaction to stress, especially threats to either one of her parents. When Angela died five years ago, Vivian seemed to handle it well, but her imaginary little brother, Vince, disappeared for a full year. In time, after Angela died, Stephan realized Vince was not imaginary. He was one of Vivian's alters—a different and very dissociative identity.

Stephan finally went to asleep and woke up in the dark. His watch said 9:30 p.m. and his stomach screamed at him. He brushed his teeth, changed his shirt, and went into the front room. Vince was nowhere to be seen. He walked next door to Denny's, ate a chicken fried steak at the counter, and walked back to Room 109. No sign of Vince. He went back to bed and heard someone come in at 3:20 a.m. Hoping it was Vivian, he opened the bedroom door just as Vince dropped his backpack on the middle of the small kitchen table.

"Where have you been?" he asked.

Vince walked to the little fridge and took out one of the sixteen-ounce bottles of Pepsi. Holding it with two fingers at the neck of the bottle, he looked sideways at Stephan, as though he was trying to decide whether or not to bother answering. He took an exaggerated swig from the bottle.

"Been surfing for ya, Dad. Ganight."

Then he turned his back, went to the couch, flopped down with his shoes on, and switched off the lamp on the little desk beside the couch.

Stephan woke up early the next morning, opened the bedroom door, and saw that Vince was sound asleep on the pullout. He was wearing what he had on last night, but had taken off his filthy tennis shoes, which he wore half laced, never tied. His backpack was on the bed with him but locked with a stainless-steel bicycle rope lock to the metal frame under the six-inch mattress. Stephan remembered that Vivian had told him how paranoid Vince was about losing his computer and the external hard drives he carried around with him. Stephan closed his door, took a shower, got dressed, and went out into the kitchen area. It was messy, but not dirty. He was hungry and remembered a coffee shop back up the street toward the airport. Opening the door as quietly as he could didn't work.

"Where you going, Dad?"

"Oh, good morning, Vince. Tried not to wake you. I'm going to get some breakfast. Wanna come, or can I bring you something?"

"Not a good idea. We should stay inside. Least you should. Cops or private dicks poking around, I figure."

Stephan stepped back in and closed the door.

"Vince, where's Vivian?"

"We can stay here for maybe a week, I dunno. How much cash you got on you? This is costing $119 a day."

"We have quite a bit of money. When will Vivian be back?"

"Dad. I will be gone most of the time doing the Disappearance, LLC, thing. You can't go out until I smell around for cops, or private dicks, you know?"

"What do you mean the Disappearance thing? Vivian told me you were working on a private network. I forget the details, but she said it was on tar, or something like that."

"Tor. Dad. Tor. How much do you know—you got the basics, right?"

"Yes, the basics. But I'd like you to tell me more."

"Cool, Dad. Me teaching you. The shoe on the other foot thing, ya know. Tell you what. Nobody's looking for me. I'll go get breakfast at the dining room, bring it back here, and give you the ABCs of T–O–R."

Forty-five minutes later, after Stephan had finished his Cheerios with nonfat milk and Vince had stuffed the third sprinkled donut down his throat, the first of many lessons began.

"OK, Pops, let's say I'm surfing from an Internet café, on a rental computer, and I log on to a website somewhere. Who knows what I'm doing if nobody is in the café except me?"

"Pops? That's what a son calls his father these days? Sounds like the fifties, to me."

"No, Dad, 'Pops' is what hackers like me call old guys like you. The word we use is *numb-nuts*. Ya know, like you can't explain shit to a numb nut. Don't mean no disrespect, Dad. It's just that when we're explaining the unexplainable, it's frustrating. Don't take it personal. 'Pops' are people who show up at awkward times, ya know. They pop out at the end of a browsing session when you're using Tor."

"OK, Vince, I kinda like 'Pops' anyhow. Makes me feel my age, ya know? I'm going to need a lot of English-to-English translation while you're teaching me about Tor, and other wizardry, Internet things. For starters, what are 'nones'?"

"Nones," Vince said, without looking up from his iPhone, "are that humongous bunch of adults who answer, 'none' when hackers like me ask how much they know about the Internet. But, hey, three years ago I was a 'none' myself."

"You've been a hacker since you were fifteen?" Stephan asked.

"I been using tech since I was ten; Viv taught me. While she was sleeping, I guess. I started taking electronic things apart when I was eleven. Sometimes I think I wasn't born till I was ten. Before that, it was just Vivian. Remember, Dad? Anyhow, nuff about family history. Let's talk the future—that's today."

Vince launched into a monologue that fascinated Stephan as much as it surprised him. He didn't think Vince was given to more than a couple sentences at a time. But he discovered that Vince liked talking out loud; he just didn't like conversations, with anyone.

"Tor is quintessentially *something*, ya know. It's the big diff up there in the cloud when a dude wants *more* than privacy. He wants anonymity. Know the diff? Most C-drive dorks only use computers for local stuff, like writing letters, which is stupid, or gaming, which is OK for little kids. They do not, I repeat, do not know the diff between privacy and anonymity. Once you shift gears out of neutral into like D12, in the fastest Porsche on the planet, you gotta be in the cloud jamming on those keys like they was turbo-charged. Oops, Pops, gotta go, gotta go."

Vince pushed away from the eating bar, farted, and went into the bathroom. Stephan took the occasion to clear the counter and put the two cheap ceramic bowls, one coffee cup, and the flatware into the kitchen sink. He turned on the TV and was moving up and down the channel selector when Vince came back. He could hear the toilet flushing, so Stephan quickly turned the TV off and took his seat at the counter.

"So, here's the diff. Up in the cloud, if you are the kinda guy who settles for just privacy, you click on the tab marked 'private.' It's usually up in the corner of your browser. You know about browsers, right Pops? No matter. If you're in the cloud, you used a browser to get there. And you needed an ISP to use the browser in the first place. But hey, dorks don't give a shit about ISPs or browsers. They just want privacy while surfing the Net. They think they get it by clicking on that 'private' tab. But while they get a little bit of privacy from that tab, it ain't really private. Ya know why? No, I didn't think so. Even if the website he's surfing privately—meaning they don't track you, or tell the CIA you're up there—he is known. Lemme repeat that. He *is* known. By who, you ask? Who knows he's there? His ISP does. That's because his computer has an IP address. I think you get IP addresses; different than URLs, right? No matter."

Vince's monologue was interrupted by a knock on the front door.

"Dad, go in the bedroom," Vince said.

Vince went to the door, opened it, and told the house-keeper they'd be out in a half hour, to come back then.

"All clear," he said. Stephan came out and took his stool at the counter. Vince continued.

"OK, we were differentiating, right? So who gives a shit that your IP address is known by your browser? And by your ISP? Well, kids do, ya know. And adults who want anonymity do, ya know. That's because if you're open, it's like having your fly unzipped. Your junk is visible. Well maybe not visible-visible, if you're wearing underwear, but everybody knows you got junk there, behind the zipper, and barely covered by nylon *Under Armor,* ya know? Here's the thing. Privacy is overrated. Sure, your folks can't see where you went in the cloud because you hit the private tab mode. But the IP address gives you away, and the web browser talks to other web browsers. Next thing you know, you are targeted, like in the old days, when a door-to-door salesman shows up on your doorstep."

Vince spent ten minutes talking about Google Maps, per-click ads, Yahoo trolling, and how easy it is for someone to find out if you have herpes. His analogy was that it was like a gun locked away in your garage, where nobody can see it. Not a bad thing, he argued. But if it's loaded and hanging off your belt like a fanny pack, somebody can take it off you. It's the method of execution that matters, he insisted, mostly to himself. Finally, he got back on point. Stephan would discover, over the next week's daily teaching sessions, how easy it was for Vince to get off point.

"You know about VPNs? Don't answer that. VPNs are virtual private networks. Emphasis, Dad, on private. It's a technology that creates a safe and encrypted connection over a less-secure network, like the Internet. VPN technology lets remote users securely stuff data inside a business. We're already using VPN technology to advance Disappearance, LLC, business, right? You know that already. If you use the right software and know your shit, like I do, then here's what you get. Our data in our business travels through secure tunnels. Our customers have to strictly follow our authentication methods—including passwords, tokens, and other unique identification methods. So we control access. But, hey, that don't mean we are anonymous. We're just private, not anonymous. Know why? Nah, you don't."

Opening his third bottle of Pepsi, he took a swig, plunked it back down on the counter, and went into the bathroom. When he came out, they could hear the toilet flushing loudly again. Stephan thought he'd ask the Hampton's Inn plumber to take a look at that. Vince vetoed the idea.

"You're disappeared, Dad, remember? OK, where was I? Anonymity. To get that, you need tools. One of them, my personal favorite, is Tor. But how we get there, gets us back to that IP address thing. You following me? Right, I can see it in your eyes. Not yet glazed over like most guys your age, no disrespect intended. You need to think of an IP address like it was a phone number that talks. Ya know, like a phone number that allows other computers to call you and recognize you when you're calling them. Get it? What happens when you forget a telephone number? Can't call the dude, right? But you could call another dude, whose number you still remember, and tell him to call for you. So, switch gears with me now. You're on the Internet, but you do not, I repeat, do not want to use your IP Address, so none of the dudes up there can call you back. You don't want them knowing your IP address. Ta da!"

Another monologue. The essence? Use Tor. Why? Because Tor masks your IP address. If you're up in Apple's cloud, they do not mask your IP address—hell, they capture it, sell it, use their Appleness to screw you with it. Tor is a conduit. It lets you connect to somewhere else through several layers of IP addresses. Remember Dad, Viv called them "onions layers."

Vince decided he needed a nap because, he said, he worked mostly at night. Stephan would discover that meant Vince was only available for teaching from about nine until about noon every day. He slept in the afternoons, didn't eat dinner in the room, and spent his nights at various Internet cafés where he could log on to Tor from someone else's computer. The IP address that got masked was never his, it was the Internet café's. Screw them, he explained. That afternoon, Stephan used his own computer to reach the regular old adult Internet, using Bing. He still did not know how to use, or reach, Tor. Screw Tor, he thought, channeling Vince. But he was intrigued by onion routing. And he learned on his Internet searches that onion routing was done by an "originator."

To create and transmit an onion, Wikipedia said, "the originator selects a set of nodes from a list provided by a 'directory node.'" Stephan logged onto a different website to find an old guy definition of "node." "A node is a basic unit used in computer science. Nodes are devices or data points on a larger network. Devices such as a personal computer, cell phone, or printer are nodes. When defining nodes on the internet, a node is anything that has an IP address. The chosen nodes are arranged into a path, called a chain, or circuit, through which the message will be transmitted. To preserve the anonymity of the sender, no node in the circuit is able to tell whether the node before it is the originator or another intermediary like itself. Likewise, no node in the circuit is able to tell how many other nodes are in the circuit and only the final node, the 'exit node,' is able to determine its own location in the chain." That seemed straightforward. Things Vince could do easily. But Madame Wiki said there was more.

"Using asymmetric key cryptography, the originator obtains a public key from the directory node to send an encrypted message to the first entry node, establishing a connection and a shared secret, called a 'session key.' Using the established encrypted link to the entry node, the originator can then relay a message through the first node to a second node in the chain using encryption that only the second node, and not the first, can decrypt. When the second node receives the message, it establishes a connection with the first node. While this extends the encrypted link from the originator, the second node cannot determine whether the first node is the originator or just another node in the circuit. The originator can then send a message through the first and second nodes to a third node, encrypted such that only the third node is able to decrypt it. The third, as with the second, becomes linked to the originator but connects only with the second. This process can be repeated to build larger and larger chains, but is typically limited to preserve performance."

Stephan inhaled as deeply as he could. This stuff, he thought to himself, takes the oxygen out of the room. Vince would later dumb it down as much as he could. But there was still more to absorb.

"When the chain is complete, the originator can send data over the Internet *anonymously*. When the final recipient of the data sends data back, the intermediary nodes maintain the same link back to the originator, with data again layered, but in reverse such that the final node this time removes the first layer of encryption and the first node removes the last layer of encryption before sending the data, for example a web page, to the originator."

He had no idea what this last part meant, but the whole process seemed to bubble up through his accounting brain. It was tantamount to double entry accounting. He'd done that for years while he was with Hurlitt International in Baltimore. He made some notes on his yellow pad, and then, using Notepad on his computer, typed the notes into sentences.

> Double-entry bookkeeping requires every entry to an account mirror a corresponding and opposite entry to a different account. When Hurlitt took in earnings of $50,000, recording it on their books required two entries. A debit entry of $50,000 to an account called 'Cash' and a credit entry to an account called 'Revenue.' Both accounts were visible to the accountant. Neither account was hidden—that is, encrypted.

This got him to thinking. About anonymous accounting. What if the first entry into Cash was in plain open text, and the second entry into Revenue was encrypted? And what if the encryption was done in reverse? That is, the cash account was encrypted, but the revenue account was in plain text? Well, he guessed, if the accountant was the originator of both the cash account and the revenue account, then he would have the *session key*. To his orderly way of thinking, the session key put the accountant in control. Without him, no one could see the double entry accounting. They might find the $50,000 in revenue, but not the corresponding entry into cash. So the credit entry would not be offset by a debit entry. So, as he moved it around in his brain, maybe Tor could do something the IRS could not: match cash against revenue to discover tax evasion. Brilliant, he thought. Maybe, he rambled.

He logged off Bing around four o'clock in the afternoon, while Vince was asleep. He used the house phone to order an extra-large pepperoni pizza and two thirty-two-ounce Pepsi "thirst busters," one unleaded, and the other fully-leaded. Then, he put a twenty and a five-dollar bill on the little table beside the front door. When he heard the knock on the door thirty minutes later, he went into the bathroom, left the door open a few inches, and hollered.

"You the pizza guy? Doors open. I'm in the shower. Your money's on the table, with a little tip."

When he heard the door open then close thirty seconds later, he came out. The pizza was OK, the Pepsi was cold, and he watched TV till nine. Then he went to bed. Somewhere between three and four the next morning, he heard Vince come in, stomp around for a few minutes, get the other two-thirds of the pizza out of the fridge, and turn on the TV. When he woke up at seven, as always, the TV was still on but the sound was muted. The empty pizza box was on the floor, upside down. The thirst-buster was gone, as was one of the sixteen-ounce bottles from the little fridge. He closed the door to the bedroom and read a novel on his Kindle until ten. Then, hearing Vince come out of the bathroom, they had another teaching session.

Stephan spent the next four mornings listening to Vince's lectures on the Internet. But he spent his mornings in the public library in Minot, reading old-fashioned books about skip tracing, disguises, and the art of going incognito. Some of it was fiction, some was how-to-do books. After four days and adding thirty-five pages of notes to *My Diary* Stephan took back his role as dad.

"Pack up, Vince. We're going to Washington, DC. We'll sell the Jeep cheap, so no questions are asked. We'll take the bus to Chicago and catch the train from there to DC."

"Hey, Dad, what the fuck. You gone crazy on me?"

"Crazy? No, but I am going skip tracing. Tell Vivian to come back."

CHAPTER 30

On the long bus and train ride from Minot, North Dakota to Washington DC with Vivian, Stephan continued to fill in blank pages in his *My Diary*.

One, find out what happened to Goshkervic's case.

Two, find out if the Feds know who killed him.

Three, if they don't know we need to find out who he was.

Four, find out who sent the maniac with the throat wire to kill me.

Five, find out why they want me dead.

Six, call the FBI and tell them.

Under "suitable living accommodations," he penned in "old-folks home for me" and "youth hostels for Vivian."

In her case it would be a series of three-day stays in youth hostels, weeklong Airbnb rentals, overnight stays at the YWCA in DC, and a community kids-safe-center in North Bethesda. For himself, it would be a one-month stay in an upscale, well-established assisted living facility in a good neighborhood in DC.

Vivian mastered the subway and local bus systems and would meet her dad in a different place at least every other day. He bought Cricket phones and matching iPads for them in Chicago. She set them up by creating simple code words that could be texted to either device via open Wi-Fi and roaming cell towers. Stephan's cover was simple and designed to protect him from the people who had tracked him to Boise, Cranston, and Jackson Hole. He became a senior citizen in need of an assisted living home and even worked out a new voice with a low, almost guttural, New York accent.

He searched until he found a nice clean room for himself, with oxygen support, part-time use of a wheel chair, good meals, and residents who'd respect his need for peace and quiet. Vivian posed as a student researcher working on an independent study of government regulatory and law enforcement structures at the federal level. Vince would never show up.

When he and Vivian got off the train, exiting from separate cars, at Union Station in DC, no one would have connected one to the other. She looked her age and wore athletic clothes, skier's sun glasses, a wool cap pulled down over her ears, and a hoodie two sizes too big. She shouldered the obligatory backpack festooned with national park badges and peace patches. And she walked with long, purposeful strides, without looking at maps, or signposts. Anyone paying any attention would have assumed she lived there.

In stark contrast, Stephan drew attention from everyone who saw him take tentative, carefully placed steps down the two metal steps from the train to the concrete platform. He was clearly a senior citizen. Round shouldered, consumptive looking, with the deadpan look of a man lost in a strange and new urban environment. He cupped his hands over his ears while everyone else ignored the train noises all around them. He wore large hearing aids, attached on one side to the back of his head by a small black wire that ran into what looked like a round brown telephone plug. His wispy white hair on the sides of his bald dome stuck out on his left side, but was plastered down on the other. As soon as he stepped onto the platform, he licked the fingers on his right hand, and slicked-down gray-white hair sticking out behind his right ear. He could feel people looking at him.

A minute or two later, the porter stepped down with two bags, one a duffel and the other a beat-up twenty-eight-inch roller bag that had once been green but now looked camouflaged with oil, mud, and other more disagreeable stains. He had a red-cross medical alert bracelet on his right wrist and an oversize Timex on the other. The watch had what looked like clear strapping tape over one side of the face, but the watchband, made of bright red nylon, looked shiny new. The porter told him there were baggage handlers around.

"Don't you worry yourself none," the old black porter said, "one of 'em will find you soon enough."

It was almost five minutes before a man in his twenties, chewing gum, walked up with a baggage cart.

"The woman who got off your train told me you'd be needing help with those bags, old timer. Where you headed?"

Stephan had to repeat the address twice, with the baggage handler moving closer to his lips.

"Oh, yes sir, old timer, I hear you now, I hear you now," he said, forcefully chomping his gum. "Take you to the *Land of Oaks* house. Well, I'll take you out front to the taxi stand. You got taxi fare, right? Yes, sir, I'll take you outside to the taxi stand, and the kid there in the yellow vest, he'll call you up a taxi. That guy will know where the Land of Oaks is."

Stephan asked the chewing-gum man to slow down twice, but gave him a ten-dollar tip when they got to the taxi line fifteen minutes later. The shiny yellow cab looked almost new. The driver, a dark-skinned woman with a big smile, swung his suitcase and the duffel into the trunk and held the right rear door open while Stephan bent himself awkwardly into the back seat. He struggled to get the seat belt across his chest, seemingly could not find the red-topped clasp next to his left hip, and then pushed out a long breath of noisy air.

The cab driver waited patiently in the driver's seat. When Stephan settled himself in the back on the passenger side of the car, he looked up at the rearview mirror at the blank look on Stephan's face.

"Well, sir, where we going this fine April day in the nation's capital? Not the White House, I hope. The baggage man said Land of Oaks. Is that a hotel, or what?"

"Sand Oaks," Stephan said, "not Land of Oaks. My hearing went years ago, and now my voice only carries as far as I can spit. Sand Oaks. I have the address on the envelope I got confirming my room."

Stephan looked first in his jacket pocket, then in his front right pants pocket, and finally in his tote bag, which he'd set on seat beside him. With a grunt of success, he handed the envelope over the front seat to her.

"Oh yes, sir. Now I see it. Sand Oaks, an assisted living place, 4601 Eisenhower Boulevard, NW. I know exactly where that is. A fine, big building for sure. It's out there almost to Stanton Road in Northwest Washington. I've been there before. It's next to an urgent care clinic. You say they confirmed you a room there? You moving there?"

Stephan explained he needed help in his living situation. She said she could see that. In less than a half-hour, she pulled into the entrance to The Sand Oaks. The wrought-iron entrance befitted the elegance of the four-story, red-brick building pictured on their website, which claimed, "Our gracious Italian-style residence was designed to combine comfortable surroundings, personalized assistance, twenty-four-hour support, and a full range of services and activities."

Stephan had made the arrangements from a pay phone in Chicago, three days ago. He'd explained he needed assisted living in a safe DC neighborhood. Implying he was a university professor, he said he had a niece in DC, who would, from time to time, visit and that he'd be in need of pulmonary care for his COPD. But, he said, he was mostly ambulatory, and other than his breathing was in pretty good health. He expected to stay in the DC area for six months, until winter, when he'd go to Florida. His Washington hiatus, he explained, was to work on his memoirs about life in government service. He'd be doing more research too, he added. And yes, of course he knew their pricing might be high, just from the services listed on their website. He would bring a check with him for the first month's stay—$6,400 plus applicable taxes. That's fine, the woman on the line said, asking whether his first name was spelled Stephan, or Steven. P H A N, he said, and then corrected her spelling of his last name—Holmrstein, not Holmstein. Gotta pronounce the r, he said. There was no mention of identity verification, just bring us a cashier's check, they said.

Stephan was met at the locked front door by a pudgy man in an inexpensive suit with a pencil mustache.

"I'm Alfred," he said.

"Stephan Holmrstein. I talked to your Admissions Director, Ms. Strougin. She assigned me to a studio room on the third floor, but I don't remember the number. I have the check she asked me to bring. Should I give it to you? And can you get someone to bring in my things? The taxi driver left them out there, on the curb. And I'm a little out of breath. Can you get me a wheelchair and someone to push it to my room?"

Somewhere between Chicago and Washington, up in the dining car, Stephan had given his daughter a glimpse of what he'd learned in his four-day adventure in the Minot City Library. He'd read up on skip-tracing, a much-misunderstood world, before the Internet came along, he said. Skip-tracing is finding someone's whereabouts. Mostly, they hunt down debtors who run out on a bill, or the rent, or fugitives from justice. It's an acquired art form now because ordinary people, thanks to the availability of Google searches and social networks, don't need private detectives, they just need skip tracers. And, he told her, in the new online world of chats, tweets, and texts, communication is quick and rarely verified. You can bank online and get customer service from government without knocking on government's door. Phone companies and public utilities do not want you coming to the office; they want you doing your business online. If they believe you are who you say you are, they'll do everything without ever laying eyes on you. The front-door man at the Sand Oaks facility just proved that. He took the check, put it in his coat pocket, got Stephan a wheel chair, took him to room 3129, and said his things would be brought up shortly. Within the next half hour, Stephan was unpacked and on his way to the dining room at exactly five o'clock. He was who he said he was.

CHAPTER 31

At dinner on his first day at The Sand Oaks, the dining room host seated Stephan at a table for two with a gentleman named Bryce Belington, who actually *was* in his eighties. A retired lawyer, he was afflicted with advanced macular degeneration, type-2 diabetes, and rheumatoid arthritis. But his mind was sharp, his memory excellent, and he loved to talk. After exchanging names, medical diagnoses, and what they used to do for a living, Stephan turned the conversation to legal research and got some helpful advice.

"So, Bryce, how long ago did you retire from the law business?"

"Eleven years ago, the day I turned seventy. I was down to about 20/500 visual acuity, starting to have trouble tracking my A1 counts, and the knuckles on my fingers inhibited keyboard use, so I left the partnership at Logan Circle, and Martina and I started traveling. When I couldn't do that, she checked me into this place—great food, you'll like it here. And she moved to our daughter's house in Florida. She always hated the winters up here anyway."

"You practice here your whole life? Private practice, was it?"

"No, not all of it. I went to GW Law, joined the Justice Department in the seventies, spent ten years there, went to the IRS for ten years, then I joined the Skeller firm here doing white collar crime cases. But by the time I joined the firm, I didn't feel comfortable in the courtroom anymore, so mostly I did pre-indictment work. We had young DOJ lawyers moving from government to private because the money was better. They handled the courtroom cases. Not that we had that many. You interested in the law, Mister Holmerstein? Thought you said you retired from the accounting business."

Just then, the chef stopped at their table to introduce himself.

"Manfred, mind if I interrupt so I can say hello to our newest resident?"

Turning to Stephan, the portly, goateed cook continued, "Mr. Holmerstein, my name is Gottfried. I've been the executive chief here for three years. Was the lamb to your liking this evening?"

"It was. It was. Didn't expect to find lamb on the menu," Stephan said.

"I roast lamb on Friday nights. Turn it into stew on Saturday. Do the same with pork loins on Sundays, and with beef on Mondays. You'll notice other parallel choices during the week. Some of the old timers here joke with me about roasting or stewing. 'Is that all you do, Gottfried?' they ask. Know how I answer them, Mr. Holmerstein?"

"No, sir, how do you answer the old timers?"

"I say, I got fried for that. Get it?"

Stephan grinned, but he didn't really get the joke. His table mate helped him out.

"Mr. Holmerstein, our chef plays with words like we do with scrabble on game night here, every Thursday. His name is Gottfried. His joke is got fried. You'll get used to corny jokes like this soon enough. Lots of jokesters in this room. Some of 'em research jokes on the Internet just so they can try new ones at dinner."

The joking chef wandered over to another table, where he drew a laugh about something. Stephan answered his new friend's question.

"No, I'm not interested in the law, just one particular case. I was an accountant before I retired. Worked up in Baltimore for a few years, before I went west to Idaho. Had a friend there who had some kind of legal problem, but I haven't heard from him for a few years. Can't find an address or phone number, so I thought I'd go to the library or the court building and see what I can find on him."

"You know anything about legal research, Mr. Holmerstein?"

"No, but I thought they'd have a librarian at the Washington City Library, and if necessary, thought I might go to the courthouse here. It was a federal case, after all. I can look up cases there, can't I?"

"Well, sir, you are computer savvy, aren't you? If you are, then you don't need to traipse all over town to libraries or court houses. Just Google law.com, or findlaw.com. I expect you could even try typing the name of the case on Google and see what pops up. Probably everything except the lawyer's fees. And even that is available on some cases. Say, here's a better idea. Have you ever heard of LexisNexis.com?"

"No, can't say I have," Stephan answered.

"Well, you're in luck. Did you know that young lawyers almost never go to court anymore and that law firms no longer even have law libraries? In my day we all went to court and we all spent half our time in the law library. But today, there's LexisNexis.com. Hellfire, man, there's even Lexis Nexis Advance. No offense intended, but even an accountant from Idaho could find anything ever written about a case, and everyone involved in it by just logging onto Lexis Nexis Advance. But you'd need a logon user identification and a logon password. And that's a pretty pricy thing, these days. My firm pays several thousand dollars a month just to keep current. The old farts like me get it for free; we use it to keep track of stuff on every case that hits the newspapers. Retired lawyers everywhere get their legal news on Lexis Nexis Advance."

"Well, I can't afford a paid subscription, so maybe I'll try the Internet sites you mentioned. If I don't get anything there, I'll taxi my way downtown."

"No sir, you don't need to go down there. There's politicians everywhere you step in downtown DC. And they'll step on you if you don't get out of their way. I mean everybody's in a hurry these days. Tell you what, if you strike out looking for your friend on the Internet, meet me in the bar tomorrow night, just before dinner, say four-thirty. I'm always there. A wee cocktail before dinner is good for the liver, don't you know. If God didn't want us to drink, why did he give us two livers? You can borrow my identification name and password. I'll give you a quick primer on Lexis Nexis Advance, and you'll be in business."

CHAPTER 32

Vivian met her dad, as they'd agreed when they got off the train the day before, at the entrance to the Smithsonian at ten o'clock. Part of their "security plan" for Washington was to not mention names, places, or addresses over the Cricket phones he'd bought for them in Chicago. Vince had warned her that any good hacker could listen in on a Cricket phone call, but it would take a few hours. They'd also agreed there would be no hugs in public places. So, when he saw her waiting for him at the Smithsonian Castle on Jefferson Drive, he just walked up and started talking.

"You OK, Sweetums?"

"Sure, you?"

"Yeah, The Sand Oaks is quite beautiful, the dining room is excellent, I have a view of a garden with cherry trees starting to bloom, and I made a new friend at dinner last night. Let's walk inside and find a place to sit down and talk."

Over the next hour, they shared what little information they had to trade. She told him the DC YWCA was a dump and she was moving to a youth hostel on the other side of the Smithsonian Natural Zoo. It's the International Student Center on 18th Street, she said. She needed a specific assignment. He told her to go to the Securities and Exchange Commission and run their list of names against their database of SEC cases.

"Dad, why are we looking for data points on money laundering? Was that what Mr. Goshkervic was charged with?"

"It's complicated. He was charged with insider trading, a violation of the SEC law. But somehow there was money laundering involved too. I'm just getting the basics of money laundering down myself. Here's what I've learned in the last week. Money laundering is the process of taking the proceeds of criminal activity and making it appear legal. They call it the "lifeblood" of crime because, without cleansing money made illegally, the business side of crime fails. Drug money laundering gets a lot of attention in the press, but it seems like money laundering sustains every criminal activity that involves profit."

"For profit? Isn't all crime for profit, I mean stealing and stuff like that?"

"No, there are crimes of passion or vengeance. So, in those cases there might not be any illegal money involved. But, as someone once said, 'Crime is a cash business.'"

"So, Dad, where does money laundering fit in the murder in Boise? Was that poor man killed for money? Is that what we're looking for here in Washington?"

"I don't know much yet. But you figured it out right away—he was killed because they thought he was me. The only reason could be that I was a witness in the Goshkervic case. And that case involved wire fraud, money laundering, tax evasion, and insider trading. I think I know enough about the tax and insider trading parts of the case because I was the one who discovered what Fritz was doing. But I never knew how it was connected to the money laundering part of the case. I could not see it when we were living in Baltimore. And there was no way to get to the bottom of it hiding in the West. So, coming here is dangerous, but necessary."

"Dad, I know how important this is to you, but if it's really dangerous, don't you think we need a get-out-of-here plan?"

"No, Sweetums," he said. "I just want to be here long enough to figure out what Fritz was involved in that got him killed. The maniac with the garrote wire was just a hired killer. Whoever hired him must be tracking me now. I think we're only safe if we stay on the move. So, if I can't find anything here, in one week, we'll move up to New Jersey, or maybe one of those little towns down on the Chesapeake."

"But Dad, if your research really can be done online, why are we staying in a place full of important people and millions of police? From just walking around for the last ten days, I can tell you that everyone looks at everyone here. All those acronyms, SEC, FBI, CIA, MP, DEA, HMS? They even pay attention to me and there's thousands of girls here that look just like me—students, secretaries, waitresses, and who knows what?"

"Well, Viv, you've been extra careful, like we talked, right?"

"Sure, Dad, always aware of my situation, always changing my route, never talking more than I have to, and never letting anyone engage me in a conversation. It's kind of fun, actually, but all the things you asked me to do got us nowhere."

"And no one has asked you what you're doing here? That's still true, right?"

"No one cares about me in the least. I'm dressing down, looking upper-low class, chewing gum in public, slouching when I walk, and avoiding eye contact. Fun, right? But Dad, if no one is looking at me, does that mean no one is looking at you? Are you situationally aware, too?"

"Right, little girl, I'm aware so much my eyeballs hurt. Let's give it one more week. You call me every day at noon. I'll call you evening after six p.m. That way we both know we're safe. One more week; if I still don't find anything, we'll change costumes and scoot out of here."

CHAPTER 33

Stephan spent the next three days doing online research from open Wi-Fi venues like branded coffee houses, Internet cafes, museums, and public libraries, which were all over Washington. Every day he added notes to his *My Diary*. He was proud of himself for creating notes that most people would not understand. He wrote short phrases and single words, never a complete sentence, and he didn't write down dates, except on the first page. He wrote only in pencil and didn't bother with punctuation. One night, when he called his daughter at 11:59 p.m., he read her that day's notes.

> "lousy breakfast place white cement five lanes across Iron bars Ugh Breath smells Five names none matched Don't think F here Two miles away South of oxygen tank Martin prince Spread pillows Hours and hours Beach M D is stitched in"

"Ok, Dad, let me guess what you found today. I wrote down the words as you talked. You went out for breakfast because you've told me breakfast at Sand Oaks is always great. You went somewhere on the National Mall because there's more 'white cement' there than anywhere in the world. You walked across Pennsylvania Ave—it's 'five lanes' wide. Not sure which building there had 'iron bars,' but it must be only one, or you'd have used other words. Poor people were there—with bad 'breath smells.' And trash— 'ugh.' You had 'five names' to look for, but none of them 'matched.' And you think Fritz Goshkervic, that's 'F,' was never there—so that's a big clue, and a conclusion, too. You've always said the Lincoln Memorial was breathless, so I'm guessing you were south of there—'Oxygen.' You were close to the 'Martin' Luther King memorial, or maybe a statute of him—'Martin prince.' I think 'spread pillows' is a disguise for spreadsheets. And after reading spreadsheets for hours and hours, you went back to The Sand Oaks. That is what 'beach' means, Sand. Am I right?"

"Viv, my oh my, what a little genius you are. You got all of them mostly right, except for my last entry. It was 'MD is stitched in.' Any guess as to that?"

"None, Dad. I wrote it down but there's no little light bulb shining in my pointy head. What's that mean?"

"It means that *My Diary* is hidden in the bottom of my canvas rucksack. The one we bought at that Peace Surplus store in Minot. I keep it in the room. Never carry it around town. The bottom of the rucksack is made of two canvas layers. So I cut into it and made an opening from the bottom. I take it out by undoing the stitches. After I finish the day's notes, I slide it back in. Then I stitch the layers back together. You remember that if anything happens to me. Now, we've talked over ten minutes on the phone and Vince insisted we don't talk more than five minutes ever. So, I'll call you back tomorrow at the crack of lunch time. I love you."

CHAPTER 34

Vivian waited for her noon phone call from her dad. When it didn't come by twelve-thirty, she dialed his number. No answer. She called again five minutes later. Stay calm, be aware of your surroundings, don't panic, she kept telling herself on the bus ride from the DC YWCA across town to the Sand Oaks retirement home in northeast Washington. As usual, she got off the bus two blocks before it passed the cross street to the retirement home. Seemed a normal day in residential Washington until she got a half block away and saw the yellow crime-scene tape cordoning off the curved entryway. She started running past the big oak trees and stopped dead in her tracks. Two fire trucks, an ambulance, and several police cars blocked her way.

Trails of smoke lazily drifted out of the giant hole in the left wing of the building. Bricks were widely scattered on the lawn, and one tree that had been only a few feet away from the wall lay splintered ten yards out onto the lawn. The blackened bricks around the burned-out hole in the wall told her everything.

"That's my dad's room!" she screamed as she pushed her way through the crowd of onlookers and ducked under the yellow tape trying to get to the front door. A blue-uniformed police officer grabbed her from behind and held her tight to his chest. Screaming, wailing, and kicking backward at her captor, she wailed at him.

"Lemme go! Let me go! That's my dad's room. It's . . ."

Another officer, a black female, barked at the man still holding her from behind. "Let her go. I've got her now."

Vivian felt his arms drop just as the lady dressed in black SWAT clothes reached for her. Too late. Vivian dropped to the pavement with a thud. It seemed like just a minute, but it actually took the paramedic almost ten minutes to revive her. When she came to, she was on a gurney in the back of an ambulance headed for the closest hospital. The lady SWAT officer was seated across from her in the back, with two hospital-garbed EMTs.

It was hard for Vivian to focus, and her head throbbed like she'd been run over. The EMT's words came in slow motion. She heard most of it.

"You fell and hit your head. Try not to move. You're in a neck brace. Just in case. Can you see me? Hear me? Try to squeeze my hand. We'll be at the hospital in three minutes. IV line in . . . soon . . ."

Her dad's voice seemed to ring in her head between spurts of sound from the EMT, the siren wailing above her, and the black SWAT lady holding her hand. Do not tell them anything. Can't trust anyone. Just be quiet. Be still. Vince will be close by. So, she closed her eyes, and her mouth.

Vivian stayed in the trauma room inside the huge ER at George Washington University Hospital for four hours before she got up the courage to speak.

"Where is my dad?"

One of the green-garbed nurses heard her from the other side of the curtain that surrounded her bed. She'd been fully awake the whole time but kept her eyes shut and moved as little as possible. Her head ached and she felt the small bandage over the cut on her forehead. But she could move all her limbs and her brain worked. Actually it was on fire with what became organized thinking once they took her off the ambulance's wheeled gurney and plopped her onto a bed. She knew her dad was dead, simply because he was not here. They must have her name from her Boise driver's license in her purse—they had been calling her name all afternoon. Vivian, can you hear me, can you open your mouth please, can we get you anything, your vitals are fine, you only have a cut on your head, no damage, X-ray is perfect, can you talk, there are some people here who want to talk to you, are you ready to talk, can you talk?

Within a minute, the curtains parted and the nurse came in with the black SWAT lady and a man with a gray beard and dark suit carrying his hat and a small brief case. "We need a private place to talk," one of them said. The nurse accommodated. They rolled her into a small treatment room smelling fetid. A large round plastic tub with a floppy top used to discard bandages and used medical equipment took up half the wall space.

Gray beard said, "Ms. Shortfield? That is your name, right? Shortfield? We have to talk to you about . . ."

Vivian, grimaced but spat her question at the man.

"Where is my dad? Is he dead? Why won't anyone tell me?"

"Is Stephan Manchester your father? If so, we can tell you. But we have to know who you are and why you collapsed at the Sand Oaks retirement home earlier today."

"He is my father. I was coming to visit when I saw the police cars and the hole in the wall in the same wing where he lived and . . ."

The SWAT lady shooed the stern-faced man away, put her hand on Vivian's hand, and moved closer to her.

"Vivian, just hold onto yourself, my dear. I'm gonna give it to you straight. Your father is dead. He was blown up in an explosion at his retirement home. The man with me, Agent Burlein, is from the FBI. They are taking over the investigation, but I'm the one who picked you up off the pavement. And they are letting me talk to you with them so I can report to my boss, the DC police chief, what happened to you. I know they gave you some pain medication. Are you thinking straight, or is the medicine still working on your brain?"

"I'm OK," Vivian mumbled. "Can I please have some Kleenex? And some water. I fainted because I saw the black bricks and knew there must have been an explosion. Who did this?"

Agent Burlein responded. "We don't know that yet. Can you think of any reason why someone would want to kill your father?"

Vivian glared at the man. Still holding onto the woman's hand, she answered his question while looking into her eyes.

"They killed him by blowing him up. Just like they did to his old boss at Hurlitt International. He showed me the newspaper about it. You know that, don't you? They blew up a plane just to kill Fritz Goshkervic. Then they tried to kill Dad in Boise. Are you going after them now?"

"Ms. Shortfield," the man said, moving closer to the end of the bed so she had to look at him, "this is not a conversation we can have in a hospital room. I'll talk to your nurse and make sure it's medically permissible for you to be checked out of here. I will escort you to the FBI office downtown and we can continue the interview there. We won't need DC Police assistance there," he added, looking at the SWAT lady.

Vivian shook her head slowly, took several deep breaths and said quietly, "Are you arresting me for the death of my father?"

"No, of course not. But we still . . ."

"Then, I'm not going to the FBI office or anywhere else with you. I would like you to leave my room. I want to talk to this lady. I'm sorry, ma'am, but I didn't get your name."

"That's all right my dear. My name is La Fonda Wilsea. I'm a police sergeant with the DC police. We would also like to talk with you, but only if you want to help us. We can wait until you're feeling better."

"No, I want to answer your questions now. But the FBI has never been helpful to me, or my father. So, as soon as he leaves, I'll answer your questions."

Sgt. Wilsea said, "All right, if you feel up to it. Let me talk to this gentleman out in the hallway. While I'm out there, I'll get you some fresh ice water, or would you like a soft drink?"

"Dr. Pepper would be nice," Vivian said.

When Sgt. Wilsea came back into Vivian's cubicle in the ER, Vivian was gone. The nurse said they never saw her leave, and she didn't go out past the triage nurse at the swinging-door entrance from the lobby. All they saw was the young man who'd been in visiting her.

"Who was he?" the SWAT lady asked.

"Dunno," the nurse said. "We didn't see him come in; we thought you sent him to talk to her."

"Describe him," she insisted.

"Just another DC kid, Levis, hoodie, sun glasses, Baltimore Orioles baseball cap—looked brand new. In a hurry."

She was gone, but her backpack was still in the room.

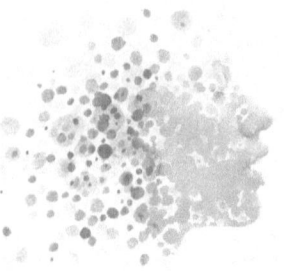

CHAPTER 35

Three weeks after Stephan's murder in DC, Marcellus Stanza, SAIC in the Phoenix FBI field office, received the FBI HQ file. He called a meeting attended by Agents Cambridge, Lin, and Sterndusky to discuss the interim findings.

"OK, listen up guys. You too, Lin. We finally were blessed by DC-FBI with their findings on the Stephan Manchester hit at that old folk's home in DC . . ."

Cambridge interrupted, "Can't say 'old folks,' boss. That's discrimination, you know. Gotta call it a retirement home, even if some of them ain't."

Shaking her head from side to side, Agent Lin corrected him. "Agent Cambridge, it's age discrimination you have in mind, and The Sand Oaks was an independent living facility. You can't say retirement home—none of them thought it was their home."

"Cut the squabble," Stan said. "This report is twenty-nine pages long, and I've only got thirty minutes to brief you. How about you all just shut up and let me give you the highlights? Main point. Crime-scene forensics, witness confirmation, and correlation with other ongoing investigations about Mr. Manchester in Boise, Houston, and DC all agree on two points. Lots of unknowns. Point one: This was a hit, carefully arranged, leaving little hard evidence behind except the things they wanted us to see. You all know from the weekly station briefing memos that Manchester died two weeks after checking into The Sand Oaks under the name Stephan Holmrstein. DC cops initially thought it was due to the explosion that blew out the double window and lots of bricks into the front yard of what Lin thinks was an independent living home. They were wrong. Point two: Manchester died the same way as Jason Bloomington, the trailer repairman in Boise; strangulation by garrote wire. Manchester was dead *before* the explosion happened. Post mortem puts his death about a half-hour before the fire alarms went off."

"Suspects?" Cambridge asked.

"Maybe. The killer left the double garrote wire. It had Manchester's DNA on it. It was duct-taped onto the portable oxygen tank that the killer used to set off the explosion. Langley thinks they were actually sending us two messages. One was that Manchester is connected to his former boss, Fritz Goshkervic. That message came from using a bomb, just like the hit on Goshkervic. The second message was leaving the garrote wire behind. It's identical to the one the killer used in Boise to kill the man who looked like Manchester but wasn't Manchester. Now, the second point of agreement is that both hits were directed by someone in Mexico, probably the Sinaloa Cartel down there. They have operations all over Mexico, and the US; they do their banking in Panama. They launder drug, gun, and protection money on a very sophisticated basis. Killing is not their main enterprise, but they always send messages when they kill someone. Leopoldo de Santos calls the shots, puts out the hits, and sends the messages. He sent Chaco Hernandez, whom we know was the Boise hitman. His garrote is still in an evidence locker in Boise, but one just like it was taped on an oxygen tank in Manchester's room in DC. Message delivered . . ."

"Boss," Cambridge interrupted, "what's the message?"

"Message number one was to quit looking into the Goshkervic case. I don't mean his death; I mean his federal criminal case that was up for retrial in Maryland. If the Sinaloa Cartel is sending its killers to *Norte Americano*, it's likely because Goshkervic and Manchester knew something dangerous to Senor de Santos."

"And message number two?" Lin posed.

"That one's more speculative, not evidence based, if you know what I mean. FBI Director Ashurst thinks it is intended for someone who has never surfaced in this case. It's not a message to us—that is, to FBI Phoenix, or FBI DC. It's a message to whoever Manchester was working with in Boise, and DC."

Lin came back. "Working with? What's that mean, boss? Nothing we discovered down here, or in Boise, suggested Manchester—or Nau, or Shortfield—was connected. He was just a witness in the federal case in Baltimore, right? Or did I miss something in the 302s?"

Stan started to answer, but Cambridge jumped in.

"Holy moly, boss. Maybe FBI HQ is right. Maybe the message is to bow out—quit messing with the Goshkervic case. If that's it, maybe it's to his kid, you know, the daughter down in Cranston. What was her name? We learned about her from the librarian Ricketts. Don't remember her name, but it started with a V or maybe a W."

Lin corrected him. "It was V. Her name was Vivian. Manchester's daughter. She checked out the library book on how to disappear, and the nice librarian—at least I thought he was nice—was a little protective of her. Her name was in the Boise APB. There were no 302s, but vitals and description were in Boise's file report. Once her dad disappeared from Cranston and then disappeared again right after the hit in Boise, there's no record, not even a hint about where she is. Maybe that's who the message is to."

Sterndusky, who preferred to keep his own counsel, surprisingly spoke up. "But how would she get the message? How would she know about the garrote wire? Isn't that the message?"

"OK, guys, slow down here. Maybe we're onto something. The newspapers in Boise splashed the garrote killing. Then, the newspapers in DC talked about the garrote wire as part of their crime coverage. Somebody in the DC metro police leaked that to the press. We know the daughter was with her Dad in DC and in Boise; she'll get the message clear enough."

"She was there? On the day her dad was killed? Is there a 302 on her?" Cambridge asked.

"No 302. In fact, she refused to be interviewed by the FBI at all. The agent and a DC cop went to the emergency room to talk to her. She apparently fell and hit her head on the driveway when she learned her dad was killed. It's confusing, but she reportedly said the FBI was 'not a friend to her dad.' She took a disliking to our agent. He tried to get her statement at the ER, but she balked. Said she'd talk to the DC police, but not him."

"Do we have that?"

Stan answered Lin's question.

"No, she disappeared from the ER before that happened. We know her dad was doing legal research in DC. She may have been helping him. We have a 302 on a retired lawyer, an old guy living at The Sand Oaks down the hall from Manchester. He let Manchester use his LexisNexis logon to search for information, legal information. I'll text DC and follow that up with a phone call tomorrow morning. Meanwhile, one of you needs to go back down to Cranston and see if anyone has heard from the daughter, Vivian. Do we know what last name she's using these days?"

Nobody knew.

"One other thing, boss," Lin said, "I'm unclear about the garrote wire and the oxygen tank explosion in DC? What's that story?"

"The twenty-nine pager from FBI-HQ says a service man from a medical supply office showed up with two portable oxygen tanks for Mr. Manchester. He delivered them to the room, while Manchester was in it, about 11:45 a.m. He signed out at 11:51. They have a locked front door and a sign-in requirement. Thirty minutes later, at 12:15 p.m., everyone heard the big bang, which blew out the window in Manchester's room. The DC crime scene includes pics of the garrote wire duct-taped to the other tank, the one that didn't blow. The explosion came from the tank that had a small FM receiver taped on. It set off set off a spark, sent by remote control. That spark ignited the oxygen in the tank, which caused a large fire and the blow out of the window. But, as I said, Manchester was not killed by the explosion, he was strangled before the boom. His daughter arrived after the DC fire and police teams got to the scene."

"OK," Lin said, "I have two questions. How long had Manchester and his daughter been in DC? And why did the killer rig the oxygen tank to blow up if he'd already garroted Manchester?"

"Because, the killer, wearing an oxygen supply uniform, had been told to make sure this killing made front page news. The explosion alone would ensure that. Also, he knew the fire would set off alarms and get the press to the scene right away. Once that happened, the press would cover the garrote story—much sexier than just an oxygen tank bomb. The file says he'd been at The Sand Oaks for about two weeks, maybe a little longer."

Lin continued. "That probably means the killer, and his bosses down in Mexico, did not know the daughter was there in DC, with her dad. And that means they didn't know how long Dad had been there, either. Is FBI-HQ tracking her now?"

"Don't know. But your speculations make me think you're the right agent to go to Cranston and see if she's surfaced there."

"Sorry boss, but I'm taking personal leave starting tomorrow to check on my mom. She's hospitalized in DC, remember."

"Right, sorry about that. But how about I send you to DC on FBI business instead of on personal leave? You can go to FBI HQ and read the whole file, look at their pics, go to the chapter, and talk to the DC trooper who almost got an interview from Ms. Vivian. I'll clear that with DC HQ. And Cambridge, you go down to Cranston and pick up whatever you can down there."

CHAPTER 36

When she got to Washington, Agent Lin didn't just read the paper file in the DC FBI office, she looked at everything inside Stephan Manchester's rucksack, which had been boxed up and stored in the evidence cage on the fourth floor of FBI HQ. She knew it was there from the paper file, but what surprised her was that Vivian Manchester's backpack was also there, just one box over on the same shelf. The evidence clerk said DC police sent it over when the FBI took over the investigation. Both revealed new information and changed the course of the investigation into two murders and multiple disappearances. She started putting the pieces of Vivian's puzzle together at the George Washington University hospital while visiting her ailing mother. She matched what she found in the backpack and rucksack with what the medical librarian found for her in the small medical library for patients at the hospital.

Stephan's rucksack had a hidden pouch carefully sown into the bottom of the sack. His *My Diary* was there, along with two medical articles written ten years ago. She read his notes about Vivian getting lost in the cave when she was nine after her childhood friend, Chester, drowned in the Prettyboy Reservoir. She read Manchester's notes about his daughter. And she read the medical articles, written eight years ago, about Dissociative Identity Disorder. She made her own notes about all of it and was struggling to connect the missing pieces. She'd been spending the part of each day with her mother at the hospital. One day, when she could not find an open table in the hospital's cafeteria was packed, she noticed a door in the back marked "Physicians & Staff Seating." Hoping they would not mind, she took her lunch tray and briefcase through the door. There were no empty tables there either, but there was one open seat at a table for two.

"Hi," she said to the woman in the other chair, wearing a white coat and a friendly smile, "would you mind if I joined you? I'm not a doc, but you know the main room is full, and . . ."

"Hi back," the woman said. "I'm Eliana Socorro, happy for the company."

"Thank you, I'm Sally Lin."

The other woman continued spooning her soup while thumbing her iPhone. Lin set her tray down and opened her briefcase with her notes and copies of the medical articles about dissociative disorders from *NAMI*, *Psychology Today*, and *Wikipedia*. While munching her grilled cheese sandwich, she added a few words to her notepad.

*DID—a mental disorder—2 or more distinct person-
ality states—usually with memory impairment—not
imaginative play in children—can be pathological—
rarely resolves spontaneously—mostly diagnosed in
female children—sometimes used in criminal cases
as insanity defense—some cases therapy—induced
iatrogenic presentations.*

As she pushed her soup bowl away, Agent Lin's lunch companion said, "So, you're not a doc, but you read articles about DID. Do you have a family member here with that disorder, a child maybe? Sorry to be nosy, but I'm a pediatric psychiatrist here. DID is a rare diagnosis, but I've seen a handful of cases over the years."

"Dr. Socorro, am I ever glad I happened on to your table. I'm here visiting my mom, but these articles are job related. Could I ask a question or two?"

"Sure, I have about twenty minutes before I have to be back upstairs, on the peds floor. How can I help you?"

Agent Lin took her badge out of her jacket pocket and laid it on the table.

"I'm an FBI agent from Phoenix, Arizona. Like I said, I'm here to visit my mom, but there is a case that our office in Arizona is working on. Actually, it ties in to a more recent case here. One aspect of the case is a young girl, aged eighteen, who apparently was diagnosed with dissociative identity disorder when she was nine. I just discovered that fact yesterday. I got these articles from your great little patient's library this morning. But all I know about the diagnosis is what I read this morning. I have questions, and I'd like to make notes if you don't mind."

"Happy to help the FBI anytime. Actually, I have helped two times. Children sometimes commit horrendous crimes and an FBI agent in Baltimore is married to a college roommate of mine. Fire away."

"Well, the Wikipedia article uses the term 'alters' and says that each alter may have a separate autobiographical memory, independent initiative, and a sense of ownership over identical behavior. What's that mean in lay terms?"

"Autobiographical memory is a memory system consisting of episodes recollected from an individual's life. It's often episodic personal experiences, or specific objects, people, and events. These experiences or things tied to a particular time and place are interspersed with the patient's semantic memory, meaning general knowledge and facts about the world."

"OK, that's helpful. I can figure out independent initiative, but I'm not sure what they mean by a 'sense of ownership over identical behavior.'"

"Right. That's a bit more complicated. Remember that each alter, and there can be many, owns what they do or say, once they are out. If the primary identity does something, the alters may, or may not remember it as their own act. Please understand, this is oversimplification. What one alter does might be unknown to either the primary identity, or another alter."

"But, Doctor Socorro, it's just one patient, right—one primary identity? Does the patient just forget when her alter does something?"

"Call me Eliana, please. And I'll call you Sally. OK? Now, in DID treatment, we know that each patient is different from all other DID patients. But in most cases, the identities, or alters as they are commonly called, are frequently, if not universally, unaware of each other. They establish this by compartmentalizing knowledge, and memories. That makes their lives chaotic. When they don't remember what someone tells them they did, they feel shame, or fear, or many other emotions. But there's always a primary identity who has the patient's given name. In almost all cases, the primary identity tends to be passive, dependent, and often depressed. The alter of that identity may be aggressive, overconfident, and hostile. But the primary identity, even if she knows she has an alter, can be quite accepting, almost comfortable with knowing she has an alter. It's a relief, almost."

"Wow, Eliana, does that mean that the primary identity, let's say it's an eighteen-year-old girl, might know about another girl, her alter, and be comfortable with that?"

"Could be. But it doesn't have to be another girl. Some primary identities, at least ones in therapy, can be aware of multiple alters of different gender, age, and very different personalities."

"Do you mean the alters talk to one another?"

"No, Sally, I doubt that. Being aware is one thing, and that is rare enough. But talking is different. Many primary identities hear voices, but they rarely answer. Mostly they can't identify the voice, and they rarely think it's their own voice. Remember, while not everyone agrees with the actual etiology, or cause of DID, it is always a reaction to trauma.

And, sadly, sometimes the trauma that induces a dissociative identity disorder is inappropriate psychotherapeutic technique."

"OK," Sally said, "is there an age component here? Can older people be afflicted, too?"

"There is some medical literature tying DID to memory processing connected to PTSD, in similar ways it happens in children with DID. To start with, we know a little about memory processing with PTSD patients. Some of it is pathological. And faulty memory processing is often present in DID cases. Some clinicians see it all as trauma-based and stress-based dissociation. But the clinical definition of DID today is generally reserved to cases of severe physical or sexual abuse during early to mid-childhood."

"How many confirmed cases of DID are there in America?"

"Not sure, but in my fellowship training five years ago, the number was quite small; memory says only about 250, or so. Most clinicians have never seen a case, but still, we know enough about it to want to rule it out when treating depressed, or suicidal children. We're always trying to find ways to help children cope with extreme stress. Maybe the largest problem is that people, parents especially, are often disinclined to seek treatment because doctors, or other first responders do not take their symptoms seriously. That's why dissociative disorders are called 'diseases of hiddenness.' They're hiding from the symptoms their children exhibit. And the children quickly accept that."

Lin sipped her cold coffee and made a note. Then she turned to Dr. Socorro.

"Wow, a disease of hiddenness. In the FBI world I live in, every crime is hidden at first. Little by little, evidence shows up. Eventually crimes come out into the open. Once discovered, the perpetrators hide. Once we find the perps, we have to present the evidence to the DOJ, which hides the evidence until a grand jury is called. Maybe we're in the same business, Eliana."

"Oh my goodness, no. I think your FBI investigates criminals, but I don't think they treat them. That's my job."

"You're right about that. Do you have time for two more questions?"

"OK, just two."

"I know from medical articles I read this morning that the symptoms of DID include significant memory loss, out-of-body experiences, mental health problems, a lack of a sense of self-identity, and a sense of detachment from emotions. Is there one predominant symptom that would be present in every case?"

"Sally, I think you're reading the NAMI list, which is written from a treatment perspective and intended to help parents. It's oversimplified for good reason. Parents need time and a deeper understanding of what chaos might be whirling around in a child's head. Let me just say that those symptoms, while well-intentioned, are not helpful to the clinician. DID reflects a failure by the primary identity to integrate essential components of identity, memory, and consciousness into a single multidimensional self. It's about control. When in control, each personality state, or alter as they are called, can be seen by a clinician as if he or she has a distinct history, self-image, and identity. In every case, when an alter shows up in therapy, often under hypnosis, they present in stark contrast to the primary identity. Certain circumstances or stressors can cause a particular alter to emerge. When that happens, they tend to deny knowledge of one another while at the same time being critical of one another. To complicate things—at least according to case studies, not my own experience—the emerged alter may appear to save the primary identity, or to avenge some harm the primary is suffering from."

"What kind of harm?"

"Serious harm, like death of a loved one, usually a family member, or a threat to the primary identity the alter believes is imminent, but is either ignored by, or unknown to, the primary identity. Sorry, but I've got to get upstairs."

"Could I walk with you to the elevator and slip in my last question?"

On the way to the elevator bank, Agent Lin got the answer to an ominous phrase in the literature—the amnesia of the amnesias. It's forgetting the fact that you forgot something. In DID patients, sometimes the primary identity has amnesia related to an event that an alter remembers all too well. The primary identity can be crippled because she cannot remember, while the alter is traumatized because she can.

CHAPTER 37

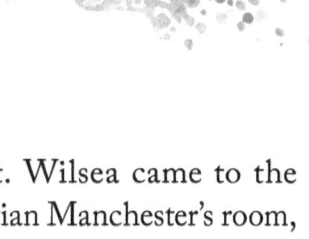

The day after Sgt. Wilsea came to the YWCA front desk asking to see Vivian Manchester's room, a young man approached the same clerk asking a different question.

"Where's my sister's backpack?" the boy in the green hoodie asked.

"Sorry, but who are you asking about?"

"I'm asking about her backpack, not her," Vince snarled, with spittle trailing a bit out of the left side of his mouth. "I know she's bolted. But her backpack ain't with her."

"All right," the clerk said, sensing this guy could be trouble. "Tell me her name and I'll check our baggage room for you."

"It's Vivian. Ain't telling you her last name because she has several. But her backpack is orange and red, and the bottom's all duct-taped. Just look for one like that, and I am in a hurry, if you know what I mean."

The clerk had no idea what he meant, but he turned his back and went into the six-by-six baggage room behind the desk. A few minutes later, he came back and told the boy they didn't have a bag with the first name Vivian on it, and none were orange and duct-taped. The boy said she had it two days ago, when he was in her room. It was the end room on the third floor—had a dirty window looking out on the dumpsters in the back. Go look there, he directed the clerk. The boy glared at him when the clerk said the room was empty. The police were here yesterday, asking about her, he said. The boy ran out into the street.

Next morning, just after seven a.m., Sgt. Wilsea got a text message on her cell phone. "Meet me at the front door to the Smithsonian at ten when they open. Vince."

She traced the number—it was a Cricket phone using a prepaid card—bought at Target, on 14th Street just a few blocks from the YMCA where Vivian had been staying. So, she went to meet Vince, with backup in a van parked in the Smithsonian driveway. She was wired. Two agents in the van had eyes on her as she walked to the front entrance to the Smithsonian, at five minutes to ten. The usual long line, maybe fifty people, were waiting to get in. At five minutes after ten, she got a text. "I'm inside, by the men's room. Vince."

When she found him slouched against the wall, she thought he must be starving. He looked emaciated, with ambiguous lips—could be a boy, or a girl. His forehead, from what little of it she could see under the green hoodie, seemed to merge abruptly into his temples, splashed with dark brown hair, thick, but stringy. Looked like he hadn't showered recently.

"I'm Vince. I want my sister's backpack. You gonna give it back to me?"

"Vince, nice to meet you. I spent some time with your sister, Vivian, while she was in the hospital after her fall, and . . ."

"She didn't do nothing wrong. You better give it back."

"All right, Vince. You're right, she didn't do anything wrong. But we didn't finish talking to her at the hospital. We need to finish that."

"She ain't talking to you anymore. She sent me to get her backpack."

"It's no longer at the police station. The FBI took it. They're investigating your father's death . . ."

"So am I. I want the backpack, and my dad's stuff too."

"Well, Vince, I'll work with you on that. Let me see your driver's license first, so I know for sure who you are."

"Ain't got one. Not old enough. But you're just shitting me. I'll get it back my way."

Before she could react, Vince whirled backward, ran through the South Pavilion, past the Asiatic Exhibits, and out the emergency exit. The alarm sounded, and scores of people began to rush out into the Pavilion. Sgt. Wilsea never saw Vince again.

A week later, someone checked both Vivian's backpack and her dad's rucksack out of the FBI's Active Case Evidence Room. Located on the fifth floor, that heavily fortified room was accessed daily by more than a dozen young people hired to push carts, pick up files or boxes, and then deliver materials to offices all over the gigantic FBI Headquarters. The boy who checked out the packs had an FBI Form 2323(a) initialed by an agent on the third floor. That agent was not working the Manchester killing, and would later deny ever sending any of the office runners upstairs to the Evidence Room. The boy who presented the form had put both packs into his cart. They found the cart later that day in a broom closet on the second floor. The boy had only been on the payroll for two days. All his hiring papers were false. The emptied backpack and the rucksack were left in his delivery cart. According to the evidence log detailing the contents of the rucksack, the following was now missing and presumed stolen: Stephan Manchester's *My Diary*; his handwritten notes; twenty-three emails; a list of employees at Hurlitt International Services, LLC; the indictment of Fritz Goshkervic; the corporate filings related to Hurlitt's corporate parent, Autocrancis Currency, Inc.; and thirty-one pages of notes made by Vivian Manchester. Of course, they had all been scanned and digitally stored, so nothing was lost.

As soon as Agent Lin heard about the theft from the Evidence Room and saw the list of what the boy took, she realized the connection. Vince now had all of the information that might explain why his dad and sister were in Washington. And she suspected that Vince was looking for the same thing the FBI was—the name of Stephan's Manchester's killer. What she could not fathom was why

Vince, an eighteen-year-old boy, would want that information. He must not have been in Washington while his father and sister were researching, she thought. She was still missing pieces from the Vivian puzzle she was trying to lock together.

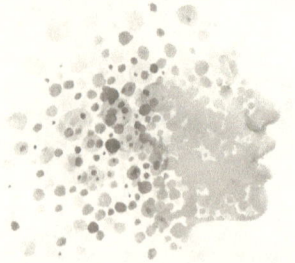

CHAPTER 38

Agent Cambridge made the forty-two-mile drive from Phoenix to Cranston in just over an hour. He thought that wasn't bad considering the slowdown from the five-car pile-up on I-10 that hit about noon. He maneuvered his way through the mangled vehicles at five miles per hour. Finally, at 1:00 p.m. sharp, he parked in the Cranston Public Library lot. Taking care to brush the crumbs from the blueberry scone he'd bought at the Starbucks, located inside the Safeway, two blocks away from the library, he walked up the steps to the front door. He'd used his cell phone to call the library from the accident scene on I-10, asking if the Head Librarian Perry Ricketts was available. They said he was out to lunch but would be back at 1:00 p.m. Never one to pass up a snack, Cambridge bided his time at a Starbucks inside a grocery store.

Nothing about the library, or Mr. Ricketts, had changed since Cambridge first visited the library fifteen months earlier.

"Good afternoon, Mr. Ricketts," Agent Cambridge said, flashing his FBI badge at the bald-headed man who still looked the cameo part of a small-town librarian.

"Oh, my," Ricketts said, mischievously, "what is it now? Surely you cannot still be investigating the loss of our library book that Miss Vivian checked out."

"We never looked for the book, but we are still interested in Vivian Manchester. You knew her as Vivian Shortfield back in May of 2014, when I was last here. We know now her real name was Manchester. I want to talk to you about her. Is there someplace we can talk in private?"

"Surely so, Agent Cambridge. Come to my office. I'd offer you coffee, but I know you've already had your mid-day coffee at our Starbucks. I was there at Safeway, buying oranges and a half-gallon of milk when you came in, about a half-hour ago. Just follow me, please."

Over the course of the next half-hour, Agent Cambridge learned a lot about Miss Vivian, as Ricketts insisted on calling her. He learned about Group X, which Ricketts had started with his colleagues, in a small-town effort to recover a library book. He was surprised to hear about the correspondence between Miss Vivian and Ricketts and was amazed when copies had already been made for him, as soon as Ricketts got back to the library from the grocery store. He was genuinely surprised to learn how Ricketts,

Nettles, and two library employees had been running a parallel investigation, looking for Vivian while the FBI was looking for her father. But he was astounded to learn of Vivian's enterprise, starting limited liability companies that could evade public scrutiny, and that these small-town citizens were in on the ground floor. Over the course of a half hour, Cambridge took careful notes about Group X, its members, its discovery of Stephan Nau's participation in WITSEC, the US Marshal's witness protection service, the APBs that had been sent out about the missing Mr. Nau and his daughter, and that they had actually talked about FBI Form 302s as though they were common knowledge. Turns out, everyone in the group had read numerous Wikipedia pages about the FBI, DOJ, and the US Marshal's office, while collecting all the local gossip about the disappearance of a high school student, and her elusive father in an old Airstream trailer.

"And you actually got that library book back, the one about disappearing?"

"Surely so, Agent Cambridge. Although she didn't say so in her letter, we are quite proud of our little Miss Vivian for evading her government watchers. We understand she and her father had every right to give up the program after Mr. Nau no longer had to testify in that court case back east. New Jersey, was it?"

"No, Mr. Ricketts, it was not New Jersey. The case that first brought him into WITSEC was in Maryland. What else do you know about it?"

"Nothing else. We lost contact with her a year ago. I hope they are well," Ricketts said.

Cambridge was tempted to leave it at that, but suspected there was more to be learned by giving them what was now public knowledge.

"Did you, or the members of your Group X, know that the man you called Stephan Nau was murdered in Washington, DC, just a few weeks ago?"

"Murdered? Murdered, you say? No, sir, no not at all. My goodness, what will Cecelia and Cynthia say? What about Miss Vivian, has anyone told her? Where is she, and also . . ."

"Mr. Ricketts, I told you about the murder because it was widely reported in the East Coast papers. Vivian, the daughter, was at the scene of the murder shortly after it occurred. She fell, or something, and was treated at a local hospital. But she disappeared from that hospital before her formal FBI statement was taken. You have not heard from her, have you?"

"Disappeared? Again? Oh, me! And you have lost track of her again, haven't you?"

Agent Cambridge went back to Phoenix and wrote a 302 on his conversation with Mr. Ricketts.

Little did he know that while he was typing that 302, Vivian's alter was back in Arizona.

CHAPTER 39

Vince got off the Greyhound bus at the downtown Phoenix terminal just as the eastern sky started to tinge with pink, streaking across the city. He'd been sleeping on Greyhound buses, and eating at their terminal lunch counters for three days, as he made his way across the country from DC. He'd changed bus lines, directions, costumes, and his plan many times, but now that he was here, he felt secure. He badly needed a shower. This is bastard HQ, he thought. That fuckin' FBI office is here, those assholes that chased us from Cranston to the North Rim, over to Boise, and finally to DC where Dad was offed. Now I'm gonna fuck 'em up. Right here where Dad hid our cash stash, right here where I'll build a new high-tech hacker station. This is gonna be the epo center where I do to them what they did to us—Dad, Viv, and me. Here's where we get even—the assey fuckers.

"Are you a member here?" the fat black man at the YMCA center on First Avenue asked.

"Maybe I am," Vince answered.

"OK, what's your name? I'll just get your number on the computer."

"Well, my name ain't gonna be on your computer, but my dad's name is. He used to bring me here, when I was just a kid, ya know. His name is Nau. Stephan Nau. Look him up."

The man couldn't find a membership under Nau, but offered to start a new one for Vince, who said his name was Vince L. Agin. He paid $36 cash, in advance, for a two-night stay in the men's community room—hot shower down the hall—cafeteria on the south side of the building—and basketball gym upstairs. Vince ate his usual breakfast of cheese on white, coffee with half-a-cup of cream from little plastic tubs, and by himself. He used the phone at the end of the hall to call Vault Mountain on Cavecrick Road. "Iron Vault Mountain, how may I help you today?" the automated digital voice answered. After the usual three-second pause, she continued.

"If you already have an account with us, please press one, if you'd like to open an account please press two, for information on our highly secure bullion and valuable document storage, press three for all other matters, press zero, and our office staff will . . ."

He stabbed the zero key twice, then took in a deep breath. When a man answered, Vince asked about their bullion storage facility. He knew it was fluff, but they said it was the finest, most secure, rock-embedded, vaulted-steel-encased, fire- and waterproof facility in the country.

"Yeah, but is it modern, I mean keyless, ya know? Accessed by encrypted passwords on a thumb drive, ya know?"

"Well," the man stuttered, "my young friend, our bullion boxes are state of the art when it comes to entry. Every box has a deadbolt specifically engineered to provide Fort-Knox-grade . . ."

Vince interrupted, "What makes you think I'm young, or your friend? Making assumptions about people over the phone ain't good, ya know?"

"Sorry, sir, no offense meant. But our vault holds an ANSI Grade 1. The bullion and high-grade securities boxes have a resistive touchscreen, an anti-pick shield, and a strong motorized bolt that automatically locks and unlocks when a user code is entered. The special Bullion Room has built-in alarm technology that senses movement of the door or any weight above two pounds on the floor . . ."

"Hey, man, sounds good, but is it wireless or hard wired?"

"Well, I'm glad you asked. We use Z-Wave, a wireless technology that makes us better than any bank in the country. While you cannot access your box, physically, our system allows you to connect from your home via computer, tablet, or smartphone with the service provider of your choice. I'd love to show you our facility and . . ."

"Hold up, Dude, I ain't dressed for going out right now, ya know what I mean? I got another question. What about space for my digital backups? I don't mean a box for an external hard drive, I mean like a VPN in a private cloud, but no syncing auto, only uploading, or down by me, no one has access, encrypted by me, holding the key, no scanning privileges, ya know?"

"Yes, sir. We do indeed, we do. We have a fraud-proof identification system to protect your backup data from any unauthorized individuals. With twenty-four-hour monitoring of heat, motion, smoke, sound, and vibration by means of state-of-the-art security systems, your data is completely safe in our facilities. We offer a current, updated HFC-125 fire suppression system. And broadband access, once you log on."

"OK, dude, can I swing by unannounced, after eight p.m., when I get off work? My schedule is erratic; you know . . ."

"Yes, you can. We're open for normal business from six in the morning until ten at night, and we allow access to the facility on a twenty-four-hour basis for existing customers with Level-One holdings."

"Cool, man. But hey, I almost forgot, my dad already has an account with you. He's back east right now, but wants me to come and check on his stuff. I have the key and his account number. So that's cool, right? I just stop by?"

"Well, we'd have to authenticate your father's account, but as I'm sure he's told you, all accounts have beneficiary, and secondary access. What's your father's name? I'll check to see who has access."

"Nau, Stephan, that's my dad."

The line went to music for a full minute. Vince stepped away as far as the corded phone would reach. Another man was on the bench, signaling him with a hand motion that he needed the phone. Vince just glared at him.

"Sorry to hold you up, sir, but I've checked your father's account. He listed his daughter, Vivian Nau, as a joint holder. So she could come in anytime and have full access to his bullion box. But he did not open an online account, I'm afraid. She'd be the only one we'd allow in the Bullion Room."

Vince hung up. The next day, Vivian, dressed in new running shoes, a Nike hoodie, and sweat pants, with a tight pink newsboy cap on her apparently bald head, making her look like a cancer survivor, arrived at the Vault Mountain during lunch hour. She presented her driver's license, waited to be authenticated, was shown into the vault room. Using her matching key to unlock the box, she took the fifteen-by-twenty-by-eight-inch steel box to a seat at the table. Then she removed $200,000 in paper banded one-hundred-dollar bills from the box, and stuffed them into her gym bag. Her Apache Cab was waiting at the curb. She told the driver to take her to the downtown Phoenix metro bus station. From there she walked two blocks to the YMCA, and down the hall to Vince's room. Twenty minutes later, Vince walked out the front door, wearing the same shoes and sweat pants, but without the pink newsboy cap over his dark brown hair.

He walked a few blocks north to the Burton Barr Central Library. There, he used the fifth floor computer space to look for obituaries. Thirty minutes was all it took on www.myheritage.com to find obituaries for three one-year old males who died the same year he was born—1999 in Arizona. While in DC, he had purchased fifty blank birth certificate forms from an online hospital supply store. It was simple, he just pretended to be a hospital administrator who had run short of blank certificates. He bought blank seals from a different provider. The three male deaths he found were for white babies with Anglo-Saxon names. He ran the names of the parents through a variety of social media sites and business sites with no mention of the families anywhere. So, he created authentic-looking, but completely fake birth certificates for the three deceased children: Charles Layton Montgomery, Andrew Nicholas Nolan, and Kyle Harrison O'Leary. The names of the doctors, nurses, and parents were made up, as were the dates of birth, and paternity details. All had 1999 birthdates and claimed to have been issued in small to midsize Arizona towns. The hospitals were real, but all of them had either closed, or were merged into larger institutions.

He headed south back to the Greyhound Bus station, with $198,000 inside a well-worn backpack, one that he'd just bought at the YMCA's Lost and Found room.

CHAPTER 40

Agent Sally Lin convinced her boss, Stan Marcellus, that she should be the case agent in Arizona Field Office on the Manchester case, but it was a hard sell.

"Come on Stan, you know I am ahead of anyone here. It's possible I'm out in front of anyone in DC."

"How so?"

"Because DC has assigned just one agent to deal with the case there. And he's come up against a wall. They see the Manchester killing as an inexplicable attack on a visitor, by persons unknown, for unknown reasons, and with no viable witnesses or suspects. They cannot see any connection to Manchester's history down in Cranston, or his short stay up in Boise. But all of it is connected. What ended in DC started down in Cranston. The documents we scanned from the daughter's backpack and her father's rucksack all point to here, and Boise. And, from my way of thinking, they suggest that the son and daughter are likely targets because they know their father. We don't. Not yet. But DC will never spend any time here, or Boise, and has no interest in the collateral victims—the son and daughter."

"What's in the scanned docs from the backpacks that makes us more likely to solve the murder than DC can? They have the docs, too. And remember, this actually started in DC, not here. They asked to get involved as soon as the Marshal's office realized the WITSEC witness bolted."

"Boss, I remember all of that and I have given it a fresh look in light of what happened in DC. It's still fuzz and noise, but I'm starting to see clear patterns. The path from Cranston to Boise to DC is like dots on a murder map. The last dot is absolutely connected to the first dot. I just need to spend half time on this case, which means you need to shift a few of my other cases to Cambridge, or Sterndusky."

"OK, but run your conclusions by me first before linking your counterpart in DC. And be careful. The son and daughter are also victims and have well-defined rights under federal law. You can't treat them just as possible investigative leads in this case."

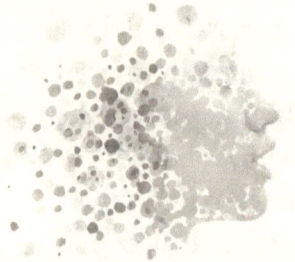

CHAPTER 41

Vince walked the twenty-one blocks from the Downtown Phoenix YMCA to the Phoenix Greyhound Bus Station on East Buckeye Road. He stopped at two Circle K stores, a Walmart, a Staples store, and a Mexican restaurant. At each stop he bought something inexpensive, and paid for it with a hundred-dollar bill. He ended up with a bag of snacks, two writing pads, a red ballpoint pen, a green chili burrito, and $472 in small bills, plus a pocketful of change. He threw the change in a trash container; he hated the jingle of change in his pants pockets, especially in sweat pants. When he got to the bus station, he bought a one-way ticket to Lordsburg, New Mexico.

"Watcha going there for, young feller?" the bored-looking ticket agent asked.

"My brother lives there, haven't seen him for two years. You ever been there?" Vince asked.

"I went to El Paso once, years ago. I think the bus passed through Lordsburg. Didn't like the name; seemed unreligious to me. But no, I ain't actually been there less you count riding a bus through it as being there."

"Right, that don't count. I've passed through a lot of towns on lots of Greyhound buses, but that's not the same. To have been somewhere, you have to get off the bus, don't you?"

The bus was an express, so it didn't stop at every small town on I-10 between Phoenix and Lordsburg. One stop only—Tucson—thirty minutes to gas up, eat another cheese on white, a bag of Fritos, and a root beer. Vince had switched from Pepsi to root beer after his dad was killed. Couldn't take all that caffeine any more. It was daylight so Vince naturally went to sleep on the bus. He woke up in Lordsburg two-and-a-half hours later. He didn't even see the town until he felt the bus coming to a stop, hissing the airbrakes, and sliding up against the curb. Vince got off, stretched, and headed for the one-horse bus stop. The other five passengers who got off in Lordsburg went to the parking lot. Vince went inside, used the men's, bought a pack of gum, and asked the ticket agent where he could catch a taxi.

"Right here, of course," the bespectacled agent said, pushing his glasses back up his nose. "My cousin has the best of the four cabs in Lordsburg. I'll call him for you. Can I tell him where you're headed?"

"No," Vince said, turning his back and walking back outside to the passenger's bench. The Tucson bus was just pulling out, headed for El Paso. For a second there, Vince thought that's what he should have done. His mind was sending him hints about Texas, like it did when he'd forgotten something—usually something about Vivian.

As he sat there, chewing gum, an older black Lincoln Continental pulled up, with a sign mounted on the passenger door.

Lordsburg Taxi—Nothing Fancy—But We Go Everywhere.
505-867-6651

"Howdy, young feller," the driver said. "My cousin said you'd be needing a taxi. Where you wanna go?"

Vince took in a measured breath. "You're only the second person to speak to me in this whole town, but both of you called me a 'young feller.' How'd you like it if I called you an old fart? Never mind, I'm being a dick, don't pay me any attention at all, none at all. I need to get a driver's license. Do you know where that is?"

"Course I do. Don't get your britches all twisted up. You're wanting the DMV. It's on Main Street, in the 800 block. That's eight blocks from here. Cost you five bucks. OK?"

Vince got out at the DMV and was surprised to see only three people there. One was getting his vision checked, an old lady was arguing with the clerk about her suspended registration, and the last one was getting his license renewed. He'd been rehearsing his story in his head all the way from Tucson.

"Driver's license? But you're not from here? Why you want a New Mexico license?"

Looking at the lady in the 3XL sweatshirt with "Aggies" on it, Vince tried to smile at her. "Well, see, my family is moving here from Topeka, Kansas, but not until next month. I've been going to school at ASU in Tempe, but I'll be switching to a college in Las Cruces in August. I don't have a license yet, because my dad said no license until I can afford a car."

"We require proof of age. Do you have that?"

"Yes, ma'am, I do."

He unslung his backpack, pulled the now-well-crumpled birth certificate out, and handed it to her.

"Kyle Harrison O'Leary," the clerk read. "Born November 13, 1999. Winslow, Arizona. In a Catholic Hospital, too. That's nice. How long did you live there?"

"Dunno," Vince said. "My dad never said. He died a while back. Didn't leave much, but I did find this old birth certificate in his mother's old bible."

"Well, you got it all crumpled in that backpack. Anyhow, it don't matter now. I'll start the paperwork. First you have to take the New Mexico driver's test. You been studying for that?"

"Yes, I got the little yellow book on it last week and have read it more than once. What else do I need to do?"

"You need to pass a vision test and a driver's test. Go over there, where that eye machine is. The man with the white shirt will test you. If you pass, he'll tell you where to wait for the driver's test. Is your car here?"

"Don't have a car. They said I needed a license before I could buy a car. Is that right?"

"Can't say. But we don't normally provide cars for test drives. But the guy that gives the driver's test might help you out. Go on and take the vision test. I'll ask Gabe if he'll test you in his car. He won't ask, but you ought to give him a cash tip, for the use of his car."

Forty-five minutes later, Vince had a valid New Mexico's driver's license with his picture on it, and the Irish name of a little boy who died nineteen years ago in Winslow, Arizona. He walked back to the bus station, bought a ticket to Las Cruces, a hot dog smothered in Hatch green chili, chopped onions, and a bag of Fritos. They didn't have root beer so he settled for Dr. Pepper. His iPhone maps app said Las Cruces was 121 miles due east on I-10 and would take one hour and fifty-two minutes, but they made it in record time, one hour, forty-six minutes. On the way he reread the three-page sheet he'd printed at the Burton Barr Central Library in Phoenix on the vehicle he'd come all this way to buy. And he could get it registered in his name because he had a valid driver's license with his picture and Kyle O'Leary's name on it.

The man trolling for buyers on the big open lot at Holiday World in Las Cruces watched Vince as he got out of the cab. Vince slung his backpack over his left shoulder and walked through the three dozen RVs on the front lot. When Vince paid no attention to any of them, the salesman, with his left arm in a cast, walked out to give him a hand.

"Didn't see anything to your liking?" he asked.

"No," Vince said. "I'm looking for the 1997 Airstream RV your website says is for sale."

"Oh, I think that one's out in the back lot. We keep our older RVs back there. I can see you already printed the specs on it. Let's go back and see it."

Vince was set on this one because the picture looked almost like the Jumbo that Dad had for them back in Cranston, almost two years ago. God, Vince thought, I loved Jumbo—and now here's one pretty much the same. As Vince stood there, the salesman, who said his name was Carlos, made his pitch.

"Senor, you got a good eye for value, a damn good eye. This was never used rough, even though it's nineteen years old. It's got your roof air conditioning units, two of 'em on the roof, a furnace and water heater in the two big doors on the driver's side, your auxiliary battery, brand new, double electric step and—get this—*two* TVs, and a roof antenna and . . ."

Vince interrupted, "You don't need to tell me what I already read on your website. What I don't see is no satellite dish up on top. I gotta have that."

"Well, sir, you have come to exactly the right place for that. Our shop can install that for you, but it will take a day or two to order the electronics from Albuquerque. Now, you can take it as-is, and drive her up there yourself. Your pleasure."

"What I want is a Winegard PA6002R Pathway X2 Automatic Portable Satellite TV Antenna with DISH ViP 211z Receiver. You got a Walmart in this town?"

"No, but they got one over at Deming."

"Well, you can order that for me, from the Walmart in Deming. They offer free shipping and it will be here in two days. But here's the deal. I'll pay the $566 for the dish, but you have to install it for free. I'll pay the $14,999 price you list on your website, in cash, today. You fill up the tank, and

I want to drive it out of here this afternoon. I'll be back in two days so you can mount the satellite TV antenna. Deal?"

"Well, by God, if you don't take all. Damn straight we have a deal! You want to drive it first, don't you?"

"Why? Is something wrong with it?"

"No, sir. It's just fine. We've had it for about a month. The boss himself took it in trade for a 2015 Ford F-150 outfitted with a brand-new Lance cab over unit on top, that was a real beauty. It had . . ."

"Not interested in that. How long will it take for you to do the paperwork? I'd like to be out of here by five-thirty. Ain't had my dinner yet."

It took until almost six p.m., but Vince, now known as Kyle Harrison O'Leary, drove to a campground just north of Las Cruces, off I-10. His new driver's license worked. He had the title mailed to general delivery at the main post office in Phoenix. He stopped by Denny's on the way to the campground and had a chicken fried steak covered in gravy, with biscuits, and the mandatory paper cup filled with chopped green chili. They also had root beer. It was nearly a perfect day for Vince.

The next morning, Vince drove Jumbo II forty-five miles to El Paso, Texas. First stop was the Texas Motor Vehicle Department where he used his second fake birth certificate to get a Texas driver's license, with a street address he made up by driving down a side street and arbitrarily assigning a house number to a vacant lot. He passed the vision, and written tests, but didn't have to take an actual driving test. He didn't have a car, yet, he told the uniformed lady in booth number 13. When he left, with his photo on his new

Texas license under the name Justin Bradley Luther, she said, "Yawl take care now."

"Fuckin' A," he said, under his breath.

After a late breakfast at a huge local restaurant called Texas Red's Restaurant, Vince walked across a six-lane roadway to the El Paso County Fairgrounds to a barn about the size of your average Walmart. But instead of consumer goods and supersize TVs, this was a gun show for private sellers, not firearms dealers. Guns of every size, shape, and killing power—no background checks—no paperwork except a paid invoice made out to the name on your driver's license and a local street address. Vince had both. He paid $540 for a Smith & Wesson .44 Magnum revolver. It was nickel plated, six and one-half inches long, six-shot double action. He bought a box of shells and a flat metal case with foam inserts that would mold to the shape of the gun. It had a digital lock; he set the code at 666. He'd never even held a gun before, much less fired one. But he had a plan for this one. They told him he could carry it in the case, unloaded, in Texas, New Mexico, or Arizona. Put the shells somewhere safe, but not visible, they said. The gun seller, who called himself a provenance for Smith & Wesson handguns, wondered why he needed a .44 mag. Big gun for a kid, he said. It's for my dad, Vince told him.

At a different booth, he bought ammo. This took more time than buying the gun because the guy behind the counter was a Texas talker.

"Now, you listen here, young man. I'm the only sumbitch in this whole barn that knows ammo like a bear knows how to shit in the woods. Did you know the .44 Magnum round was an instant success and has remained popular even after losing the title of most powerful production cartridge? The ammo right here in this case first became a massive hit when it was featured in Clint Eastwood's *Dirty Harry*, bringing the power and grace of the .44 special to the forefront of American gun-admirers' minds. Did you know that?"

"No, can I just buy a box? I got cash."

But the man would just not shut up.

"Check out our lineup of .44 FMJ ammunition as well as .44 jacketed hollow-point rounds for sale. See here in this bin you got your . . ."

Vince raised his voice, "Sell me that box right there, right now, or else I might hit you with the butt of the empty gun inside this tin case."

Vince was in El Paso for two reasons. He had the gun. Now he needed the technology to get to the point where the gun would make a difference in his life. For starters he needed a used computer. He parked Jumbo II at a Starbucks, loaded up on a grande vanilla latte, an apple fritter, and two bags of chips. Sitting at the little table inside his nineteen-year-old RV, he used his iPhone to surf for the kind of computer he needed. It had to be used, but refurbished, and free of the crap that came with a new computer. He found his answer in the El Paso online yellow pages. El Campo Used Computers—1230 El Campo Drive.

They had three refurbished Dell Optiplex 780s with Windows 7 Pro. Wow, Vince thought. These guys know their shit. Windows 10 was crap, not to mention unsafe for hackers like him. The ad claimed they tested the refurbished hard drive and the RAM. They also renewed the thermal paste on the CPU heat sink, and created a recovery disk set. Motherfucker! An Intel Core 2 Duo E8400 3.0GHZ processor, 500GB Western Digital Hard Drive, 4GB PC-12800 Memory, Wireless Network Adapter N, Windows 7 Pro, Microsoft Office 2010 Pro, CyberLink Power DVD, CyberLink Power2Go, Adobe Reader, Flash, Recovery Disk Set, 2 USB Front Ports, 6 USB Back Ports, Game Control Port, Lan (Internet) Port, VGA Port, ESata, HDMI, Audio Ports Front and back. And they'd upgrade the memory to 8GB for a modest price over the $287 out-the-door price. The ad described the warranty. Four-month warranty on parts and labor, battery excluded. Warranty does not cover damage from abuse, droppage, liquid spill, cracked screens, or hammer damage from the wife. Dude's got a sense of humor, he thought.

He knew from his hacker buds in Boise that the Dell Optiplex series were a higher quality computer than the consumer grade sold by retailers. And, the ad said, they had one all set up in their shop for data recovery/hard drive testing. Come see it. Play with it. You'll love it. They said. So he did.

"Hey Dude, how they hanging?" the acne-scarred kid asked when Vince knocked on the glass door of the tiny store with the hand lettered sign—*El Campo Computers for Shooters.*

He had to knock because the door was locked, even though the open sign was facing out onto the sidewalk.

"Low and slow," Vince said. "I saw your ad. About the Dell Optiplex running on win-seven. I'm down for that."

"Cool, we got three. One I upped myself, and two more still in Dell's shitty boxes from Austin."

"I'm only interested in one that I can, ya know, use for getting to Tor, and shit like that."

"That's cool. You from around here?"

"No, I live in Las Cruces. Got my algo-algo-rhythm there, but couldn't stand the humanities shit at that Aggie school, if you know what I mean."

"Got it, Dude. You can call me Woods. Lemme flip the safety off this shooter for you."

"Ok, Woods, if that's what they call you. The sign on your door says computers for shooters. What's that mean? Oh, and by the way, you can call me Customer. You down with that?"

"Down as a feather, man. I got a sense about you. The sign on the door is to tell some people, like you, that we understand tech shooters. You know, dudes who shoot first and ask questions later. Dudes who like Tor and can find secrets about clams, if you know what I mean."

Over the next half-hour, Vince made a new friend, the first one he'd made since Vivian put him to sleep in Boise. Woods admitted to frequent use of a tool called Metasploit. Actually, he said, it's a collection of exploit tools.

"I use it to build other tools, if you catch my drift. It's free. Tor has a portal. I use it to check for vulnerabilities at different platforms, if you know what I mean."

Neither Vince or Woods would stoop to using the civilian term "hackers." But they spoke the same language—that never-ending search to uncover the weaknesses in your system and penetrate some other dude's data stash. Woods claimed Metasploit was the top hacking tool package. With this child at your fingertips you can simulate real-world attacks to tell you about the weak points in some other dude's server farm. As a penetration tester, he claimed, it pinpoints the vulnerabilities with Nexpose closed-loop integration using Top Remediation reports.

In a rare sharing mood, Vince gave Woods a small look into his own use of tools like Metasploit, but better.

"I'll take your word on it, man, but for me, Acunetix is the answer. You know about it?"

"I heard something, but ya know we are all different. I don't mean Texas. Shit, man Texas is all the same. I'm from San Francisco, but my mom dumped my dad and drug my sorry ass down here two years ago. I'd be back there, by the Bay, they say, but my finances ain't that good right now. I ain't no friend of Texas."

"True. New Mexico ain't Texas. Acunetix is a web vulnerability scanner. It scans and finds out the flaws in a website that could prove fatal. Seriously, man, it's multi-threaded, crawls through websites as you watch on your big-ass monitor, and finds malicious cross-site scripting, SQL injection, and other vulnerabilities. It comes with a login sequence recorder that allows me or even dudes from Texas to access the password-protected areas of websites. And get this, man, the AcuSensor technology inside this software will reduce your false positive rate. Check it out," he said.

Vince left Texas with a new driver's license, a computer for shooters, and a gun that would blow a two-inch hole through a six-inch brick. The license cost $35, the gun cost $350, the bullets $60, and the computer $287—total $732. He thought of it as a down payment.

When he got back to Las Cruces, Vince drove Jumbo II to a different campground, on the west side of town called LOZ Spaces. They had twenty-seven cement slabs, ten feet apart, with water and electricity hook-ups for $29 per day. He paid for one day, took his first shower in the Jumbo II's wet shower, used the microwave to cook spam inside a plastic dish, and drank two bottles of root beer. He spent a restless night on the Jumbo II's bed, which turned out to be a six-inch foam pad on a plywood base. He told himself he'd get a soft mattress and two feather pillows first chance he had. That turned out to be the next morning. He drove back to Holiday World, where they had his Winegard TV and Internet satellite dish ready for installation.

"You got a subscription for this, young feller?" the installer said.

"Not yet. Can you help me with that?" Vince answered.

That took longer than mounting the receiver on Jumbo II's topside did. But at the end of the day, Vince had both Internet and TV coverage inside his new rolling home. While the dish antenna was being mounted on the RV, he tested the Internet signal with a cheap new computer tablet he bought at Walmart. He watched a game show on TV that night and spent a boring hour surfing the Net. He'd decided to wait until he was back in Phoenix to test his new Optiplex computer—then he'd have his own private gateway to Tor.

Next morning, he drove north on I-25 to Albuquerque, where he bought two boxes of canned food, six frozen pizzas, a case of bottled water, a case of Virgil's root beer in bottles, an ice chest, and a dozen bags of Fritos. He spent the night parked in a casino parking lot west of Albuquerque. He had breakfast at the casino, then drove west on I-40 through Gallup, and on to Flagstaff, Arizona. He parked at a truck stop and got directions from there to the DMV office. It took him forty minutes to make it there on foot, where he took a number, and waited his turn to be called.

"How can we serve you today, sir?" the dark-skinned woman with big hoop earrings asked.

"I just turned eighteen," Vince said. "And I finally learned how to drive. I'm ready to take my driver's test and get a license," he said, trying to give her the biggest smile he could.

"Name please?"

"Andy Nolan."

"I need proof of ID for a driver's license. Do you have your birth certificate?"

"Yes, ma'am."

He put his backpack up on the counter, fished the rumpled birth certificate out, and handed it to her. She entered the information into her computer, then asked for his current address. He told her he was a student at NAU and had been assigned to McKay Village, but he didn't have a room number yet. Get it tomorrow, I hope, he said. Not to worry, we'll just put down Unit 1 on the form. You can change it later. Then she gave him a small booklet with Arizona driving rules in it. He passed the vision test, but they didn't ask him to take a driver's test. They photographed him with his hat off and his hair standing up. He tugged his lower jaw to the side, just as the photo box blinked at him. In less than an hour he walked out of the DMV with his photo on a licensed issue to Andrew Nicholas Nolan. The NAU campus was just across the street. He wondered how hard it would be to get a student ID. Using his new ID and explaining at the booth in Ashcroft Hall that he was a new student, he got his picture on an NAU student ID card along with a number that gave him a discount in the book store. He stocked up on notebooks and got a textbook on computer coding. He bought some NAU-branded workout clothes, a new hoodie, and a new backpack. On the way back to the truck lot where he'd parked Jumbo II, he passed a used clothing store operated by Goodwill. He bought used canvas work pants, a grey down vest, a heavy work coat with washed out oil stains on one arm, and a pair of Army lace-up combat boots. And he bought two pair of gloves—one pair canvas and one pair leather.

He packed the new clothes in the small hallway closet and stashed two of his three driver's licenses, all with the same picture, and home addresses in three different states inside a waterproof bag. As he drove south down the long hill to Phoenix, he thought about Vivian. He bet himself she was really proud of him. He was whoever he said he was, three times over, just like it said in her book, *How to Create a New Identity.* He'd spent most of the last three days working out the strategy that would let him get even, for himself and Viv, with the dick who garroted his dad. All he needed now was the dick's name and his neck size. His garrote would be virtual, but still lethal.

CHAPTER 42

§ally Lin got back to Phoenix the day before Vince became Andy Nolan, a freshman at NAU. She was still focused on Vivian, but was inching her way toward a clearer picture of Vince.

"I'm sorry," SAIC Marcellus Stanza said when she finished her oral brief of the highlights of her two-week stay in Washington, DC. "You spent eleven days back there at FBI HQ on duty and three days with your mom in Arlington. I am having real trouble with the patchwork of names and guesses you put in this report. You really think the daughter, Vivian, had this dissociative disorder, and that this guy no one's seen, Vince, is a—what did you call it, her other?"

"No, Stan, this is all in the present tense. Vivian *has* DID, the acronym for dissociative identity disorder. Vince is an *alter*, not an *other*. She is the original identity and he is her, except in a very different alter personality. They both exist, because one of them does, in two different identities. I spent a lot of time, at night off the payroll, reading up on this syndrome. And I got a lot of help from that doctor at Johns Hopkins, Dr. Socorro. Their father was—I'm sure, based on the data we recovered from his rucksack—investigating the federal case in Baltimore against his former boss. I am persuaded that's what got him killed. And I think his daughter, and her alter are now doing exactly what we are doing, following up that investigation about the father, Stephan Manchester. We want to catch the killer. They want to kill the killer."

"Is that your professional opinion, Agent Lin? Is there one shred of evidence to support your claim?"

"There's no evidence, at least not yet. But their tracks are all over DC. They know some of what we know—that the garrote killer in Boise who mistook his victim for Stephan Manchester was a man named Chaco Hernandez. That name is in *her* own handwriting on Vivian's notepad in her backpack. They know whoever strangled their father in DC is connected to Chaco some way because of the garrote wire wrapped around the oxygen tank. I think, without a shred of real evidence, that the two killings are connected—one in Boise, the other in DC. But I don't know how. When we figure that out, we might solve two murders. That's what we want, two crimes solved. But I'm afraid that Vivian and her alter, who some people thought was her brother, are motivated by revenge, not by federal criminal charges."

"Sally, let's say you're right. Boise and DC are connected murders. But how did an eighteen-year-old girl, who imagines she has a younger brother, make the connection that even the FBI has not yet made? It's a working thesis, yes, but without evidence, we have no investigatory path to follow. Am I wrong about that?"

"No," Sally said. "But Vince is not an imaginary brother. He's real, at least to her. He might see her as his sister, or he may think he's the only child in the family. The diagnosis is very complex. What is very rare is a child with this diagnosis being acutely aware of her alter identity. I think Vivian may be aware of Vince. It's theoretically possible he is aware of her. And to push theory to its limits, it's possible that her father was aware of Vince and even interacted with him, especially in times of stress, when Vivian might have temporarily disappeared."

"That's a boatload of theory, Sally, but even if it's what we are facing in reality, how does that help us solve Steven Manchester's murder in DC?"

"Stan, you just said we have no investigatory path to follow. HQ DC is on point for this investigation. But at one time, the father, daughter, and alter-slash-brother were under our jurisdiction. And we lost them. Now, maybe we've found what's left of the family—the daughter, Vivian, and maybe the son, Vince. That's our path to follow. It may lead back to DC. Or somewhere else."

"OK, say you're on to something. Where do we go from here?"

"Maybe Manchester disappeared from WITSEC down there in Cranston because he did not want to testify against his former boss, Fritz Goshkervic. He hid out in Boise, Idaho. Maybe he thought he was safe there when the Goshkervic case was closed. Or, maybe somehow he learned about the bomb in the private plane that blew his boss into the Gulf of Mexico. Maybe he didn't. But he sure got a hell of a shock when the poor handyman, who happened to look like him, got garroted in Boise. That shock would have been traumatic enough to make Manchester disappear. Again. But what we didn't know until we got the contents of the backpack and the rucksack in DC was what the shock of that death may have triggered in Vivian. It may have been the trigger for Vince, the alter, to take over for Vivian. DID is all about a young child dealing with the trauma of death, or abuse. The primary identity is sometimes displaced by an alter when that happens. Maybe that's what happened here. Vince arrives when Vivian undergoes the first shock in Boise, and then again when the second shock hits her in DC."

"So, what now? Are you an FBI agent or a psychiatrist?"

"I'm an FBI agent who knows a psychiatrist. Dr. Eliana Socorro said I could call her back anytime. I think it's time."

CHAPTER 43

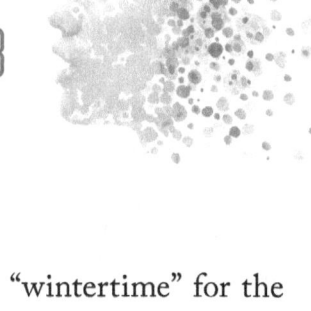

In Phoenix, July is "wintertime" for the locals. In the northern states, blizzards and ice storms often keep the locals inside. In Phoenix, they stay inside in the middle of July when the temp reaches 115 degrees outside. In parked cars, with the windows up, the temp can be 140 degrees. That's why almost everyone has a garage in front, and a swimming pool out back.

Vince found a trailer park in Apache Junction, thirty-six miles east of downtown Phoenix. The area was lightly populated, but popular with snowbirds from January to April. Life was slow there and even hotter than Phoenix in the summer. The Sunny Days RV Park bragged it was an "active 55+ park," with over five acres of full-hook-up pads, fifty-amp service, swimming pool, and concrete patios. But when Vince pulled up in Jumbo II, most of them were empty. It was July, ya know.

"I'm looking for a quiet crib to do some writing this summer," he told the teenager manning the front desk at eleven o'clock in the morning.

"Well, I dunno," the kid said, "my folks own this and my summer job is to work the desk in the mornings. This is what my dad calls a retirement home. It's supposed to be for really old people—they love it here in winter, then they go back home in summer."

"I'll be outta here in a month, Dude. It looks like you got lots of space. And I pay cash."

"Let me call my dad," the boy said.

An hour later, Vince parked on the last row, about a quarter mile from the swimming pool and recreation center that would have been busy in March. There were no other RVs or parked house trailers in the back twenty rows. The fifty-amp electricity service and the inverter that Vince had installed in New Mexico worked just fine for the AC unit on the roof. And once he calibrated the satellite dish, his Internet connectivity was up. A bit slow compared with a good Internet café, but still workable for surfing the cloud and logging on to Tor. He stocked up on groceries, more canned food, frozen pizza, and small cardboard boxes with cereal and nuts. He figured he could spend all night on the Internet and sleep all day. I'm after you bastards, he said to his refurbished Optiplex, as he logged on to Tor.

He spent the first full night at the fold-away table searching for names and places he associated with his dad. His search was based on the contents of random notes and printed pages he took out of his dad's and Vivian's backpacks from the FBI building in DC. After looking for about three hours, he could not find out why Dad didn't want to testify in the case. Stephen Manchester was not involved in the insider trading that his boss was doing. If that's the case, why not testify?

He found nothing in the US press about Chaco, so he switched to Mexican and Latin American papers, which also had lots of stories about men named Chaco Hernandez, apparently a common Spanish name. But one story got his attention. It was about Panamanian banks and their connection to the Sinaloa Cartel. He used a translation site on Tor to translate all the stories to English. One of them was about Latin American men who were accused of murders and connected to the Sinaloa Cartel. Senor Hernandez was on the list. In fact, he was on the top of the list. Motherfucker!

The American papers had only two articles about Goshkervic and the bombing over the Gulf of Mexico. They interested him since his dad, while digging into the Goshkervic case, had been bombed too. And the bomb had a garrote wire, just like the one that killed the handyman in Boise.

Vince remembered that guy. His name was Bloomington according to the *Idaho Statesman*, Boise's largest newspaper. Vince only remembered the first name, Jason. He didn't think he looked like his dad, but the Boise newspapers made the connection. The more he read, the more he came to believe that the connection between Goshkervic's death and his dad's death was what happened in Boise, not in Baltimore. So he switched search patterns. He discovered the press knew nothing about Chaco Hernandez, the garrote man. Why don't they? he wondered.

By his third night Vince had his answer. The assholes in Boise don't give a shit about my dad, he thought. And the handyman's murderer, this Chaco dickhead, was done by the dude with the .357 Mag. Motherfucker! The papers said the dude's name was Stunt Jaueger. Who names their kid Stunt? And what n' fuck is Jaueger? A Nazi name? Well, they ain't so interested anymore. Fuck everybody up there in Boise. Chaco wasn't from there, so somebody hired his ass to go and off my Dad, 'cept he was a dickhead, and garroted the wrong man. Who sent him? Now that's something the FBI spies gotta be looking for. And the police in Washington, too. I need to talk to that lady cop back there, the one that wouldn't give me Viv's backpack—the one with two big guns—one yellow and made of plastic or something, the other a black Glock, or block or whatever the fuck they call those big-ass guns that fire a million shots all at once. Her name was Sgt. Wilsea, and he had her card. Somewhere. He'd have to find it. Maybe she knows.

Next morning, Vince called Sgt. Wilsea on a throwaway phone he'd bought in Albuquerque, with a phone card that was good for 120 minutes.

"No, I don't want to talk to anyone else," he said. "It's only that lady cop, Sgt. Wilsea, that I'm willing to talk to, ya know. I got a right, says so in the Constitution, don't it? She asked me about a murder and now I got something to ask her. You gonna get her on the phone, or what?"

It took twenty minutes, but Sgt. Wilsea called back.

"This is Sgt. Wilsea. Is this the same handsome young boy I talked a few weeks ago about his dad, Mr. Stephan Manchester, and his sister, Vivian? Do I have that right?"

"Yeah, you wouldn't give me her backpack, but you did give me your card. So, I'm calling back. I got some questions for you."

"Fine, Vince. You don't mind if I record this call, do you?"

"I'm recording it too. Don't trust cops to tell the truth, ya know. You know my dad was doing research on some stuff there in Washington, right? Then he gets killed for that. Who did him? That's what I want to know."

"I don't know anything about that investigation. The case was taken over by the FBI, but you already know that, don't you? My guess is they haven't solved it yet, because there's been no press release about it. They are good at that, the FBI are. They like publicity."

"Bullshit, lady. You're just covering up for them, aren't you? How come you're on their side instead of being on me and Viv's side? We lost our dad, ya know."

"Vince," she said, "we are on your side. But we tried to talk to Vivian and she ran off. I tried to talk to you and you ran off. I would be happy to sit down with you right now and tell you what I know, but it isn't very much. Could we meet somewhere and just talk?"

"No. Don't want to meet. I ain't there, anyhow. If you got nothing to say, I'm gonna hang up."

"Wait, young man. Don't hang up yet. I could tell you a few things that'll ease your loss, if you will also answer one question for me."

"What?"

"Did Vivian have anything to do with getting her stuff out of her backpack while it was inside the FBI building last month?"

"That's none of your business. She's entitled to her privacy, ain't she?"

"Well, you could just say no, she didn't do that. That's all I want to know. And I'll tell you something that might help you right now. The case is being investigated here by the FBI, but there's another agent, who lives in Arizona and who is also working on the case. I am willing to give you her name and number. I know she'd like to talk to you. Her name is Agent Sally Lin, and you can call her at the FBI field office in Phoenix. In fact, I could call her for you and ask her to call you. I think she knows a lot more than I do. Just tell me Vivian didn't interfere with the investigation at the FBI headquarters here in Washington."

"Nah, she didn't. But she could of if she wanted. That's her stuff, ya know."

CHAPTER 44

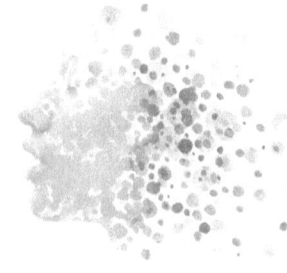

Agent Lin spent three days traveling back and forth between Cranston and Phoenix. She did follow-up interviews and wrote 302s on everyone that Agents Cambridge and Sterndusky had talked to two years earlier. It was worth the trip; she found some new facts and one new investigative lead.

The interviews with Mr. Ricketts, Mr. Nettles, and the Cranston High School principal, Ida Lewinsky, revealed nothing new. But the interviews with the elderly twin sisters, Cynthia and Cecilia, at the Cranston Public Library were helpful. They told her about Group X and the foolish "but fun" effort with Nettles and Ricketts to track down Vivian and the overdue library book. She learned that Dad got an Arizona driver's license at the Cranston MVD in February 2014. By looking for the name Stephan Shortfield at the Pinal County Courthouse, Group X discovered that dad had secured a legal name change in court sometime in March of 2014. He went from Stephan Shortfield to Stephan MacLawn.

At the courthouse, Agent Lin read the petition Shortfield had filed two years earlier, in which he claimed he wanted to return to his family's historic Irish name. So, under his new court-approved name, Steven MacLawn drove to the MVD and got a new Arizona driver's license. With that license, he opened a savings account at the Cranston Public Employees Credit Union. Surprisingly, the twins got this from their cousin, a woman named Agnes, the manager at the credit union. She told Cynthia and Cecelia that Mr. MacLawn eventually withdrew his "sizeable six-figure balance," in cash, because he'd been transferred to a new job in Texas. That turned out to be a month before he vacated the Shady Acres trailer park.

Lin also re-interviewed the manager at the Shady Acres Trailer Park. The obese woman looked even heavier than she had been in July of 2014, and she added new facts to the case. She suspected the boy, whose name she never bothered to learn, was gay. She insisted she'd never heard the name Vince, or Vivian. But she said she once she saw him one time wearing what looked like a plaid skirt, and a wig. He was "either a fag, or had a part in that stupid school's play." Either way, she thought he was gay and was happy the dad took off in the middle of the night. Didn't want people like that at Shady Acres, she said.

Mr. Stitch at the stationary shop had an entirely different sense of the boy who bought the used Dell Inspiron laptop for $149.

"You're sure, Mr. Stitch, that the boy didn't mention a name when he bought the computer?"

"No, ma'am, he did not. And I didn't ask, neither. He was paying cash. No warranty on used computers. No need for a name."

"And you never had a customer named Nau, Shortfield, or MacLawn, right?"

After a two-minute look at his store computer, Mr. Stitch confirmed those were names unknown to him.

"But the boy was a little odd and had a mouth on him."

"Mouth?"

"Yes, ma'am. He did. Course kids these days talk like that, but this boy didn't look people in the eye. And threw out F-bombs all the time."

"How many times did he come into your store?"

"Can't say it was often, but he always bought something. Like notebooks and pens and stuff like that."

"So what made you think he was odd?"

"Well, not odd, maybe, just unusual. He told me he was a character in a book. That's why he needed a printer to go with the computer."

"What kind of a book?"

"Didn't say what kind."

"Was it a library book, by any chance?"

"Didn't ask where he got it, either."

"Mr. Stitch, you've been helpful. I'll leave you with my card, so if you remember anything else, you can call me."

When she got back to her office, the Ops director told her she had two calls, one from Cranston, a Mr. Stitch, and one from a Washington police officer named La Fonda Wilsea. Stitch remembered something.

"I tried to call out to you when you pulled out of my parking lot, but guess you didn't see me waiving at you in your rearview mirror. Here's the thing, though. I remember seeing that boy that bought the computer, one other time, but not in my store."

"Where was that?" Agent Lin asked.

"Well, he was at the Cranston library. I guess waiting for it to open one morning. And it was, well you know, eerie, I guess."

"What was it?"

"The library opens at nine every morning. I got there that morning too early; I was just stopping by to deliver some supplies to Perry. You know, small legal pads and those little short pencils, without erasers, that he likes. I knew the library would not open for another fifteen minutes, but I parked anyhow and went to the front entrance. The library has five or six steps to climb up from the sidewalk to the front door. Below that is a half floor drop down into the basement. That's their storeroom, and that's where I always took the supplies. They stored everything down there. Usually someone is working down there in the mornings even before they open the main door up above. So I walked down there, and whoa. There was that boy, half-dressed."

"Half dressed? What do you mean?"

"Well, that big black hat he always wore was upside down on the cement, his big black boots were off, sitting next to a shopping bag, and he was changing his pants, I guess. His Levis were on the cement, next to a pair of tennis shoes with chartreuse green laces. He jumped up when I almost stumbled over him."

"What do you think he was doing?"

"Had no guess at the time. He just yelled a profanity at me, finished pulling his Levis up, grabbed the shoes, and the stuff in the shopping bag, and took off at a run. Never saw him again. I expect the reason I forgot about it was that he never came in the store again. That and the name he hollered at me."

"What was it?" Agent Lin asked.

"Hate to say it to a lady, but it was motherfucker."

She traded two rounds of missed calls with Sgt. Wilsea in DC before finally connecting late that afternoon.

"Agent Lin, I'm sorry about playing phone tag, but I have something you ought to know about. It involves that murder at The Sand Oaks, where the man from WITSEC was the victim."

"Yes, sergeant, I remember your name in the record. You took the man's daughter to the hospital but never got a statement, right?"

"Yes, I talked to her, but just about her condition. She refused to talk to me about her father or what, if anything, she knew about his death. What I'm calling about now is a phone call I had the day before yesterday with her brother, whose name is Vince. Have you talked to him?"

"No, have you?"

"Yes, he called me. Wants information about the case. I told him the FBI has the case, not the Washington, DC, police. I offered to put him in contact with you."

"What specifically did he ask you?"

"Well, to put it in his vernacular, he wanted to know 'who did our dad.' I wrote the conversation up and sent it over to the FBI. I could also email it to you."

"No, don't do that. I'll get it from HQ. How did he sound? You talked to him once before, right? Any change?"

"Both times were very short, both were sort of cryptic. He sounds like a young teenager, claims to know everything, cocky, but still frustrated that his dad's murder isn't solved."

"He asked about 'our dad.' In the plural, right, 'our dad'?"

"Yes, we talked for a minute about his sister Vivian. He sort of talked about her a little. He was pissed off because I couldn't give him his sister's backpack. I knew by then that the FBI had it, and I told him so."

"Did he sound threatening? Unstable?"

"No, I wouldn't put it that way. He was more pissed, like all kids get these days. I got the feeling this is all he's thinking about, and that he's investigating his dad's murder. I don't think he's even eighteen yet, is he?"

"Sergeant, there's a lot I can't tell you about the family, and the case. But I am extremely appreciative that you called me and that you tried to get him to cooperate with us. Keep it to yourself, but there's some agency concern about what the brother or sister might do. Stress following a parent's death is always terrible, but in this family, there might be more to it than just bereavement."

"Like what?"

"Sorry, Sergeant, but this is a need-to-know situation and FBI HQ is being strict about ongoing matters. I'm sure you know what I mean."

"Yeah, Sally, I do. I heard some kerfuffle about items missing from a rucksack, or a backpack. Can you comment on that?"

"What did you hear?"

"Just cop talk, you know. The DC police and the FBI work together on hundreds of cases every year. There's always a little pillow talk going on. All I heard was that your evidence room back here was not as secure as the top-floor people wanted it to be. No specifics."

Agent Lin thanked Sgt. Wilsea again and gave her the Phoenix office number to call if she remembered anything else. She opened her laptop and wrote 302s on both conversations. Then she found Dr. Eliana Socorro's card at Washington University Hospital and left a voicemail asking her to call her back at her earliest convenience. To her surprise, she got the return call just twenty minutes later.

"Agent Lin, this is Eliana Socorro in Washington, you left me a message?"

"Yes, I did, Doctor. Do you remember our conversation a while back in your cafeteria?"

"Of course I do. I mean, how many FBI agents ask me about dissociative identity disorders? I was only too glad to help. It's Sally, right?"

"Oh, thank you for remembering my name. Most people just freeze up when they get a call from the FBI. The young girl and her alter that I asked you about are, well I'm not sure exactly, but they act like they are trying to investigate their father's murder on their own. I'm using the plural, because while it's very confusing, we're getting signals that both the daughter and the son are somehow in communication with one another. Is that possible? I'm very confused."

"Possible? No one can answer that question as a general proposition. Every case is different. But I can say that in most dissociative identity patients, there is no communication between the person and one or more alters."

"So, one doesn't know about the other? Is that what you're saying?"

"No, that's not what I mean. This disorder depends for its accuracy on one person who exhibits and expresses several distinct states of mind or personalities. They reside in one body. Each personality has its own sense of self and its own habits, needs, insecurities, emotions, and memory. But there are rare cases, reported cases in the medical literature, where the primary is aware of the alter, and even more rarely, vice versa. Communication, as opposed to mere awareness, is exceptionally rare."

"But you can't rule it out, is that right?"

"Sally, nothing in a rare disorder can be ruled out. We know very little about DID, other than it is a legitimate mental disorder, and one that can be very destructive for the patient."

"Oh, that is helpful. In the case I'm working, I have concerns for other people."

"You mean the DID patient's parents? Other siblings? Is that what you're worried about?"

"No, in this case, the parents are deceased, and there are no known family members."

"What psychiatrists worry about, especially in children, is harm to themselves. Next, we worry about harm to parents. But if there is no family, then our focus is entirely on the patient."

"Dr. Socorro, are you willing to be a confidential informant in this case? If you are, then I can be more specific. But you have to assure us that what we ask and what you say will remain confidential. Can you do that?"

"Yes, of course. I could see the stress on your forehead in the cafeteria, and I hear it in your voice now. Just tell me how I can be helpful."

"Thank you. This is a murder case. The young girl who may have this dissociative disorder has a known alter. Our growing concern is that they are completely unwilling to talk to us or cooperate in any way in the investigation because, as bizarre as it might sound, they might be trying to solve the case themselves. There is no FBI case in history where these speculations have occurred. As a lawyer, I can tell you that the Latin term, *sui generis*, is applicable here."

"*Sui generis*? Sorry, Sally, my Latin is a bit rusty."

"Eliana, that means one of a kind."

"Oh, well in my world, I see patients all the time who are unlike any other patient I've seen. Do you know much about comorbidity, Sally?"

"I think it means a disease or affliction that exists alongside some other condition. Right?"

"Close enough. Patients with DID are diagnosed frequently with other comorbid disorders. It's quite common, actually. There are overlapping symptoms and many differential diagnostic possibilities. You can have a patient with DID and an alter who appears to have a borderline personality disorder while the primary identity shows no signs of it. Many DID patients present with either schizo-phrenia or rapid-cycling bipolar disorder. Sometimes both. It's extremely challenging for the treating physician to be sure whether the primary personality might be adversely affected by treatment for an alter's comorbid diagnosis."

"So, hypothetically, in the case I'm investigating, might it be possible for Vivian to suffer from DID, and her brother, assuming he's an alter, to suffer from some other comorbid disorder?"

"Hypothetically, the answer is such a comorbid com-bination is unheard of. I've never read of such a case. But your question is whether it's possible. Of course it's possible. DID is a twentieth-century diagnosis; we're learning more about DID every day. Who knows? Maybe the patient has DID, and the alter is psychotic. One could be nice, the other mean. The danger is both to the primary identity and the world she and the alter live in."

"Are you saying Vivian is in danger of being harmed by Vince?"

"Vince might not see it as harm to his sister. He may be aware of her in most situations. But he could kill her, without knowing it, or intending it."

"How could that be?"

"He could commit suicide. Remember, we're talk-ing about a person with multiple personalities. The Vince personality, perhaps driven to self-destruction by his own schizophrenic mood, addled by his psychotic state, perhaps crippled by desires driven by his borderline personality disorder, loses all sense of reality and jumps off a cliff. He dies. But so does Vivian."

"Oh Lord," Sally said, stifling an urge to cry, "that could happen, couldn't it?"

"Honestly, Sally, I don't think it could happen; I'm talking medical theory here, not real life probability. The issue here from a psychiatric perspective is that Vivian is not in treatment. She's not talking to anyone who might moderate her symptoms, or help her not drift in and out of her own self-consciousness. That's an oversimplification of a very complex psychiatric calculus, but untreated, Vivian is captured by her own history—one where death is unbearable—and avoidable by escaping to an alternate personality—Vince. You should do what you can to get her into treatment."

"Dr. Socorro, I am an FBI agent trying to solve a murder case. I cannot do anything about treatment."

"Right, I understand that. But you raise an interesting legal question. What if Vince harms someone else, rather than harming himself? What if he seeks revenge against his father's killer by finding and killing that person?"

"Well, the first question would be jurisdictional. It might not be an FBI case. It might be a local matter. We wouldn't be involved then."

"But, Sally, that's not what I'm curious about. Assume the crime is in the FBI's jurisdiction. Who do you arrest for a crime Vince committed? Him? Or do you arrest Vivian?"

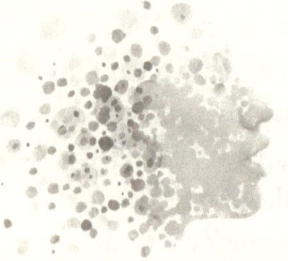

CHAPTER 45

Vince looked skeptically at the guy with the Stingray device in his lap at the skateboard park in Gilbert, Arizona, a suburb on the east side of Phoenix.

"You the man I talked to last night about grabbing cell phone talk?" he asked.

"I be him. I be him. You late, man. We said high noon, just like in the movies, man. High noon was an hour ago."

"No," Vince said, "high noon was only fifty-three minutes ago. I been here watching you from up there, on the grandstand."

The man looked older than his digital signature made him out to be on the "Getting Back at 'Em" website on Tor. Vince realized he was over forty, with graying wisps of hair sticking out from under the skull cap. He had two teeth missing, sat sloppily on the bench, and wasn't looking around for his customer, like he should have been.

"Watching? What you watching for, man? Shit, you don't want what you said last night, I got other buyers. You the Man, is that who you are? This Stingray is legal, so what you watching for?"

"Don't care about legal," Vince said. "I do care about getting ripped off from old timers like you who probably ought not to be on Tor at all. It's for young hacking, cracking dudes like me. And don't call me 'the Man.'"

"Hey, don't get upright. I brought the Stingray, like I said. You want to look at it or not?"

A Stingray is a phone tracker. Vince had never seen one and only learned they existed three days ago. The International Mobile Subscriber Identity-catcher, like the Stingray, had been used by cops for years, but were only now being used by skip tracers, private dicks, and guys with grudges about their women. There were brands other than the Harris Corporation, but the word in the cloud was Harris made the best machine. They were both passive digital analyzers and active site simulators.

"How's yours work?" Vince asked.

"How's it work? Shit man, you don't know how it works? You don't know, but you be a buyer? You're suspect to me, man, suspect."

"Chill, chill. Not trying to rile you," Vince said as he sat down on the bench next to his potential seller. "I'm just careful, ya know, careful. And if the truth be told here, I don't know shit about how it works. I never seen one. But I think it will help me with a current need, ya know. Need. Not want. Need. Humor me a little, will ya? OK? Explain how it works, then if it actually does work, we can talk price."

"Ok, better attitude, man. Here you go. You can mount this in your ride, or on your back, if you get a hand-carried version. This one's not hand carried. It pretends to be a cell tower and it kicks the shit out of all the other real towers close by, when you on it, jamming and cramming. You know what I'm saying? When you turn on active mode, this machine forces whatever cell phone is close by to disconnect from its real service provider cell site and hook up with the Stingray. You get to mine the numbers called, sometimes the names on both ends, like when they leave voicemail. But you got to know your digital shit to make it work."

"Not sure I know what you're saying. How do I listen in to what the people are saying?"

"I knew it! I knew it! You are some kind of amateur punk kid, ain't you? Listen in? You think a Stingray machine gonna let you hear words and shit? This machine, which will cost you fifteen hundred small ones, just gives you numbers. Gives you what grownups call data. It's for cops—they want to know which numbers you call and which numbers call you. If they want to hear you talking and shit, they got to have a warrant."

"All, right, maybe I'm just a kid, but you ain't got no call to say I'm a punk. I could smash your head in for that. But I won't. How *could* I listen in to a phone call, do you know?"

"I know how to tap a phone line, like a house or apartment, but I thought you were interested in cell phones. They don't have lines in the walls, like houses do. Shit, if the dude you're following, or some bitch you think's cheatin' on you, you got to get close enough to hear 'em, or else you sucking hind tit, if you know what I mean."

"Any other way to do it? Any way?"

"So you a skip tracer? You just huntin' people down on retainer basis? Sure. You want to know what people are saying? Only way is to just ask them who they talking to and what they're saying back. That's the old fashioned way."

"Hey, old timer. I don't need your Stingray machine. I ain't no damn skip tracer, but I am interested in finding a dude—a really bad motherfucker. Maybe you could do some shoe leather work for me. What's your name and how much do charge for shoe leather work?"

"You can call me Faze. I charged the dude that owns this Stingray twenty-five bucks per hour for making this trip all the way out here from my usual place of business. For more serious work, I charge one hundred smackeroos per hour, with a bonus if I don't have to kill anyone. Know how I got that name, Faze?"

Vince never was one for guessing games and had little patience. So Faze answered his own question.

"It's because the Faze Does Favors. Watch you need from me, and what's your real name?"

"I need you to call some people and ask them to call me back. Some of the people will be cops. I might need you to go somewhere and get something for me. You OK with talking to Five-Oh on the phone and messing with them? And you OK with going and picking up things for me? My real name's none of your business, but it's OK if you call me Vince. That's the name I'm using for this job I'm doing."

"Vince, my man. We got us a deal. Who you want me to call or what do I get for you?"

"I'll call you tomorrow, or maybe the next day. You live in downtown Phoenix?"

"I do. Right now, just temporary you unnerstan, I live in a motel on Van Buren street; the Stage Motel. I change my cell numbers a lot, but the one I'm using this week is 602-488-2761. Who you want me to call first? What do I tell 'em when they answer?"

"Here's $100. For four hours' work. You just tell the people what I want and hang up. And I may also want you to buy some hardware for me. I'll front you the cash, you buy the stuff, and deliver it to me in Phoenix. You down on that?"

"Sure," Faze said.

Faze stumbled out of the park, walking like an old drunk. Vince loped out like he was on the track team.

CHAPTER 46

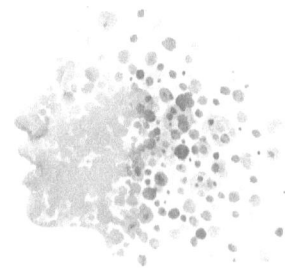

    Sally Lin was at her desk in the new highly secure Phoenix field office at 7th Street and Deer Valley Road when the switchboard operator told her an unnamed caller was holding. He'd asked for her by name and said he'd only hold for ninety seconds. She turned on her voice recorder and took the call.

"You be the FBI chick looking for Miss Vivian?"

"I'm sorry," she answered, "who are you?"

"You her or not?"

"I'm an FBI agent and am recording this call. We have your number in our database, but we don't answer questions about pending cases. Who is it you are asking about?"

"You playing with me. I ain't got time for this. If you ain't got no interest in talking to Miss Vivian, OK. Be fine with me. I'm just calling like she tole to do. I'm hanging up if you ain't interested. That's what she tole me to do."

"If I was interested, can you put me in contact with her?"

"No, ain't me involved. I tole you that. You interested, I can tell you where she will be at four o'clock this afternoon."

"All right, you have my attention. Yes, I would like to talk to Miss Vivian."

"Be cool. She gonna walk to the Starbucks on the northeast corner of 7th Street and Bell at four o'clock. She in a hurry. Don't you be late, you miss her. She be wearing some rags, sunglasses like from Hollywood. You late, she gonna disappear, again."

He hung up. She had nineteen minutes to drive three miles south. Racing to Cambridge's office, she quickly told him about the call and told him to follow her, but not to park at the Starbucks.

"Just watch me, I'll sit by the front window. You're my backup if this is not a friendly talk."

She got her car out of the underground garage, drove the three miles, catching two of the three lights, and got there at five minutes to four. She'd been in this Starbucks dozens of times and at least two of the baristas knew her by name. Neither was there today. She didn't order anything but just grabbed one of the two tables near the door with a good view of the parking lot. A minute later, she saw Cambridge pull up, forty feet away. He parked and trained his field glasses on her from behind the steering wheel.

Five minutes later, the women's restroom door opened. A girl wearing jeans with ragged holes and red Converse shoes came out. She wore oversize sunglasses in the shape of stars.

"Are you Vivian?" Agent Lin asked.

"Yes, are you with the FBI?"

"Here is my badge, and my card in case you ever need to call me. I'm very glad you reached out to us because . . ."

"I didn't reach out. I just want my backpack. Someone told me you have it. Do you?"

Agent Lin motioned to her table, "Why don't you sit down? We can talk about whatever you want."

Vivian took a step toward the table, then seemed to freeze, lifting one shoulder up, then the other, and rocking from side to side.

"Talk? I just want my backpack. May I please have it back?"

"Vivian, I'm on your side. I want to find out who killed your father and I know that's what you want. But your backpack is in Washington, DC, not here in Phoenix. Let's just sit down and talk about that and how I can help you get it back."

Seventh Street and Bell Road in Phoenix is not what you'd call a high rent district. The Starbucks was not very large because there weren't many people willing to pay $3 for a coffee and fuzzy milk. Agent Lin asked Vivian what she'd like.

"Water," Viv said.

"Not a coffee drinker," Viv responded, just trying to make conversation.

"No," Viv said.

Agent Lin decided that if small talk would not open her up, maybe hard facts would.

"Vivian, when you left your backpack in the hospital in DC, it was secured by a female police officer named Sgt. Wilsea. Do you remember talking to her?"

"A little. I just wanted out of there."

"Do you remember also talking to an FBI agent there at the hospital?"

"I did not talk to him. He can't make me and neither can you. It's his fault I left my backpack at the hospital. He was pressuring me, just an hour after my dad was murdered. He wasn't nice. You have to give it back, or else."

"Vivian, we are on your side, really we are. You're a victim and you have rights. We can protect you . . ."

"Protect me? You didn't protect my dad. You won't give me my backpack. And I want my dad's rusksack, too. You also have that. Since my dad's dead, it belongs to me. Why won't you give them back?"

"Vivian, please just let me try to explain things to you. Everything that was inside your backpack and your dad's rucksack was copied back in DC. Unfortunately, the originals and the bags themselves have been either misplaced, or stolen from FBI headquarters. I'm not supposed to tell you that, but I think we owe you that much. I have a digital copy of it here. You know what a digital copy is, right?"

"You lost our stuff, but you have copies? Now you're insulting me? You're what, thirty or forty? I might know more about digital copies than you do. I want the originals, but I guess I'd settle, for the time being, on a digital copy. Give it to me on a flash drive, OK?"

"Yes, I'll ask for permission to do that—make you a copy of everything in both bags, yours and your dad's. But first I really need to interview you about the case so we can find out who did this terrible thing to you."

"See?" Vivian said as she pushed her chair back. "You won't listen to us. I knew you wouldn't, but I still tried. I want my orange and black backpack, my dad's beat-up old canvas rucksack, and I want it bad. You're not investigating what happened before my dad was murdered. I need the stuff in those bags so I can find out on my own . . ."

"Vivian, I hate to interrupt you but . . ."

"Then don't interrupt. Just listen to me. I will make you a deal. I have this new red and yellow backpack, with the angry Indian face on the back. He's like me, angry with everyone in charge. I bought this in DC after I left the hospital. Now listen to me. I put some things I learned since DC in this bag. You take it. Read my stuff. I'll call you again in two days. I'll come to your office and you can interview me all stupid day. But you gotta give me those digital copies of our stuff, dad's and mine. And I want this Redskins bag back too. Can you at least do that for me? If you can, I'll give you an interview."

With that, Vivian took off her Washington Redskins backpack and pushed it across the table. She crossed the room and went out the opposite side from where Agent Cambridge was training his binoculars. Sally stood up and waived at him, signaling him to come down. She met him in the parking lot.

"Well that was interesting," she said. "I just made a deal to reveal file information in exchange for getting information for the file. Now I'm in the business of horse-trading with a protected victim. The boss is not going to like this. At least I got a new backpack; now if we could just find the two we lost in DC we might make some progress in this case."

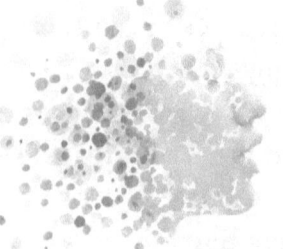

CHAPTER 47

Vivian walked across the parking lot to 7th Street and waited for the crosswalk light to walk east on Bell Road. She walked the five blocks to the garish sign welcoming everyone to Phoenix North-Mobile Home Park. Jumbo II was in the back row. No other trailers for five rows. She unlocked the door, went inside, and threw the key into the basket on the little kitchen table. Cambridge thought about following her, but decided against it. He'd rather have a Starbucks donut than follow that skinny girl.

Twenty minutes later, Vince came out, walked through the empty rows, and past the dozen or so trailers still in the park in July. There were no signs of life in them, but he could hear the AC on the two closest. When he got to Phoenix North's office he found the short guy at the desk.

"Hey, Shorty, the water tastes like shit."

"Name's Hector, like I told you two days ago, man. Don't call me Shorty."

"Hey Hector, chill. I'm just giving you some jaw, ya know. The water's got a stink to it."

"Personally, I think it tastes like piss," Hector said. "That's why we got Kirkland water right here for sale. Twenty-four bottles to the case, ten bucks per case."

"Ten bucks? I can go to Costco myself and get it for maybe $5.99 a case."

"Yeah, but you gotta get there in that old wreck of an RV. Where'd you get that bus, man? Looks like something in a history book."

Vince bought two cases of Kirkland bottled water, four bags of cubed ice, and asked Hector if he could borrow the wheeled cart to get them back to Jumbo II. Hector said he could, but he had to bring the cart back. Vince pulled the cart with the water and ice back to his space, got everything inside, and then pushed the cart a few feet into the row just south of him. He didn't come out for two days.

CHAPTER 48

Agents Lin and Sterndusky agreed to meet in the main conference room back at the office in fifteen minutes. That gave Sally time to stop at the restroom at the office, and Sterndusky time to buy an old-fashioned glazed donut and a tall coffee to go. Sally called the boss on her cell and asked him to meet her and Sterndusky in the main conference room as soon as he could shake fee.

"So, Sally, you finally got to meet the elusive young lady named Vivian. Is that her name?" the boss asked.

"Yes, sir, it surely is. Vivian is very focused, to put it mildly, on getting her old backpack retuned. She wants it bad enough to sort of loan this new Redskins backpack to me, so I can look at what she says is new material we will want to see. But she wants this one back too. She's willing to come here to pick it up and give me a statement in the next few days."

"What's in the bag?"

"Don't know boss. I called you from the Starbucks ten minutes ago. Haven't had time to even unzip this. Are you a Redskins fan, boss?"

"Is that relevant, Agent Lin?"

"Uh oh, Agent Lin," Sterndusky chimed in, "you don't wanna know the boss's favorite team—it's even worse than the Redskins."

Stan glared at both of them. Sally unzipped the bag and without fanfare dumped the contents on the conference room table. As they watched, Sally opened the five three-ring binders one at a time.

"Binder Number One is labeled Hurlitt International. Binder Number Two says Fritz Goshkervic. Binder Number Three doesn't have a typed label, but the ball point cursive writing on the cover page says 'Houston International Savings and Loan, Inc.' Binder Number Four has a typed stick-on label, marked 'Plankton Resources, Inc., Houston Texas.' 'Houston' is underlined with a red Sharpie. Binder Number Five is Autocrancis Currency, Inc. So, boss, we have five three-ring binders. Four businesses and one individual. Each binder has three-hole punched paper with tags separating some of the pages. I will get these copied ASAP and summarize each binder for the team. But, boss, two of these names are definitely connected to the underlying case, not the murder necessarily, but certainly to Mr. Manchester, before he was killed in DC."

The boss said he recognized Hurlitt International and Fritz Goshkervic, but not the other three names.

"Boss," Lin said, "Houston International Savings and Loan is a small loan company in Baytown, Texas, a suburb of Houston. Plankton Resources is a Texas corporation, also in Houston. You know about Fritz Goshkervic. The most interesting name in Vivian's new backpack is Autocrancis Currency. It's the parent company of Hurlitt International Services."

"What is its business and why is your Miss Vivian interested in it?"

"Don't know why she would have a file on it, but I haven't read the actual file yet. Autocrancis first came to our attention from the case agent at FinCEN. It is a global conglomerate and probably owns at least 200 other companies in the financial and insurance space. It is one of the largest currency companies in the world. It's home office is in Newark. FinCEN is watching it because it looks to them like a major player in financial crimes involving money laundering in the Caribbean, and Latin America, particularly in Panama."

"Did Mr. Goshkervic have a role in it? I know he worked for Hurlitt, but did he also work for Autocrancis?

"I'll get to that in a sec, boss. First, as I remember from our briefing with the agents from FinCEN and the CIA, Manchester, as he was known in DC—and Nau as WITSEC called him—testified at Goshkervic's first trial. At that point everyone just thought he was the financial manager for Hurlitt. He didn't do anything for its clients, or its related companies. But I think the file we got from DC said Goshkervic, Manchester's boss at Hurlitt, made several trips down to Houston where he did something with Plankton Resources. I think, although my memory on this is sketchy, that there were entertainment expenses for Goshkervic in Houston."

"Well, there was more to it than that," Stan said. "Listen up, everyone, we need to reread all those 302s and get back into the money laundering side of this murder investigation. Jesus H. Christ, we are in a fix here! The FBI Director himself told me two years ago that Manchester's back story and his relationship with Goshkervic were just a domestic financial crimes case coming up for retrial in federal court in Baltimore. But he said it smelled more like a South American money laundering case to him. Remember our briefing with the CIA operatives and FinCIN agents? Those boys were mounted up and way out in front of us. All we were concerned with was a missing protected witness down in Cranston. Now? What are the outer perimeters of this case now?"

Cambridge chimed in, "Boss, do we know whether Manchester ever knew that his company, Hurlitt, was actually a wholly owned unit of a Panama bank?"

Agent Lin, knowing full well she might be speaking out of turn, answered that question for their boss.

"Hold up, gentlemen. We need to look at these five three-ring binders. Yes, we need to know what Manchester knew because that knowledge may have been what got him killed. But the bigger issue is why he was killed. Why is his daughter digging into all of this, and what has she actually discovered? These binders may tell us that. I'm going to take Ms. Vivian's Redskins bag back to my office, and the binders to the copy room. Everyone, including you, boss, if you have time, should read these today. And then, with your permission, boss, could we meet back here first thing tomorrow morning and compare readings?"

Stan said he couldn't meet tomorrow morning but could meet with the group around four tomorrow afternoon.

Back in her office, with Vivian's Redskins backpack on the corner of her desk, Sally leaned her elbows on the desk, and leafed slowly through Vivian's three-ring binders. As she always did, she dictated her notes, rather than handwriting them, while she read background material. Punching the red record button, she accomplished two very different tasks; she recorded her observations on a digital card, and she formed judgments about what she was reading.

"Date, Wednesday, July 23, 2016, FBI File Number PHX dash 2014 dash 18519—Manchester slash Nau. Review of subject Vivian Manchester's Binder Number One labeled Hurlitt International. Binder has multiple segmented sections, separated by tags on cover sheets. First section appears to be corporate filings from the State of Delaware confirming Hurlitt's corporate status, officers, shareholders, and bylaws. Two annual reports for 2007 and 2014 are included. All have margin notes in red ink, with some sections underlined. Some paragraphs have little stars or checkmarks. No signatures. Second section includes job descriptions and employment data on Goshkervic and Manchester. Third section has a handwritten org chart connecting Hurlitt with Plankton Resources, and both with Autocrancis. A new name, not previously known to this agent, is North-By-North East Commodities, Inc.—Seattle, Washington—February, 2016. A handwritten line is drawn from this corporate name to a margin note that says, 'Dad's job?' Note to SAIC Marcellus, dash, we might need the Seattle Field office to point us on this new name and possible job for Vivian's father."

Sally set her dictator down, and read the rest of Binder Number One, but nothing else caught her attention. Opening the second binder, she picked up her dictator, announced the file number, and started describing the binder's contents.

"The file on Fritz Goshkervic appears to be newspaper clippings from the *Baltimore Sun*, three interoffice memos from him to Stephan Manchester, and trip reports for both Manchester and Goshkervic for two trips they took to Houston and one trip Goshkervic took from Houston to Panama City, Panama in 2013. The clippings only confirm what we already know about the underlying federal charges against Goshkervic, and there's a short article about his mysterious death in the 2014 plane crash in the Gulf of Mexico. The trip costs appear to be modest. The only connection seems to be that both men traveled on business from Baltimore to Houston. The word, Houston, is underlined in red, twice."

Just as she finished the second binder, Cambridge opened her door, "Got a sec, Sally?"

In his usual lumbering way, Cambridge took ten minutes to tell Sally two important facts that he knew, but were not actually in Vivian's third binder—the one labeled Houston International Savings and Loan.

"Sally, I know about that little piss-ant savings and loan down there in Houston, except it ain't exactly in Houston. It's in Baytown, a suburb on Galveston Bay. It's a front, and the so-called lady that runs it is a slick lawyer. She's got a law firm in the same little strip mall. She's mobbed up down there. I had a case there four years ago when I was in the Dallas Field office. We were tipped that the lawyer-lady who pretended to own the savings and loan operation was probably a hit contractor—she had a crew—a murder crew. Her name was Julia something, coulda been Santerra, maybe. Seems like she had a hyphen in her name. You know you can't trust women with hyphens in their last name, right? Anyhow, she's a piece of work. We never nailed her with anything and the whole investigation turned out to be a bust. Know why? Well it's mighty interesting. The only eyeball witness in the case was found feeding the fishes in Galveston Bay. Compliments of Julia baby. Well, that's what we thought, but it never mushroomed, and the Texas Attorney General, who asked us to co-work the case with them, just closed his file and never took shit before a grand jury. Bullshit, we thought, but it was Texas bullshit, so we closed our file too."

Cambridge finally left, promising to bring up the Houston connections at tomorrow's meeting. Sally continued dictating as she thumbed through Binder Number Four.

"Binder Four, with the handwritten label Autocrancis Currency, appears to be the largest of the five binders provided by Subject Vivian Manchester. Actual page count is 127. All pages are copies of originals. All are heavily annotated with margin notes, underlinings, and various cryptic notes from an unknown reader. All notes are in red pen. All appear to have been added to the documents by the same person. While the page count is high, much of the content is simple reporting on financial status, federal and state filings required by law, and newspaper articles either extolling the company, which is privately held, or suggesting that it plays a role in either money laundering or large-scale financial misdealing in the US and much of Latin America. This file will have to be reviewed by financial and corporate investigators. But from this examiner's perspective, the file seems to be sending us a message from Vivian. She thinks Autocrancis is somehow involved in her father's murder but cannot piece it together on her own."

Sally had spent three hours looking at only three of Vivian's five binders. She had far more questions than answers. So she did what FBI agents all over America do when faced with more file review and fewer answers. She called and ordered an extra-large pepperoni and sausage pizza for herself, Cambridge, and Sterndusky.

"Pizza coming to the conference room in twenty," she texted them. The pizza would come from Papa John's, only two blocks away. It would be left at the desk downstairs. So she got up, took the stairs down two flights, and gave the front desk guard three fives and three one-dollar bills for the pizza delivery kid.

When she got back up to the third floor, feeling a little refreshed by the stair climbing, she placed the five binders back into Vivian's Redskins backpack and trudged the forty-feet from her office to the internal—no windows—locked conference room. Cambridge was not there, but Sterndusky was.

"Where's Cambridge?" Sally asked.

"Downstairs, via the elevator, to wait for the pizza. He's a man who always keeps his priorities straight. Eat first, it makes investigating go down better, he says."

She put the backpack in the middle of the conference table and got herself a Dr. Pepper from the vending machine out in the corridor. Then, picking the middle seat, she asked Sterndusky how his review was going.

"Not bad, I started with the fattest one, number five. I have no freakin' idea what Autocrancis means. Is it just a made up name for a currency company? And what is a 'currency company' anyhow?"

"My friend," Sally said, "you've just figured out for yourself what Autocrancis means. It means the same thing Xerox, Kleenex, or Microsoft means. It's what you guessed—a made-up name for a company that will always stand out because the company has trademarked it. They own the name and they protect it with high-paid lawyers. It's in scores of domain names they also own. A currency company is a business. Its customers exchange one currency for another currency on a currency exchange. There are stand-alone currency exchanges. There are also currency services offered by banks. Either way, they make their money by adjusting the exchange rate, or taking commissions. In Europe they call them *bureau de change*. In Panama they call them gold mines; just kidding. But they are gold mines if you're mining drugs and need a way to sluice out gravel."

Cambridge showed up with the pizza. He and Sterndusky each chipped in five bucks. Together they ate 80 percent of the slices, leaving Sally with a bad financial exchange.

"So," she asked, "Cambridge, how far along are you on the Vivian binders? Sterndusky tells me he's done one out of five."

"I've read them all, not carefully you know, because I'm not lead on this, or writing the file report. But I see her plan clear enough."

"Plan? You think she has a plan that explains these binders?"

"I sure do. I think she's playing us. None of this stuff is really new, you know. It's all public domain stuff. All research most anyone could do. I don't see any big connections here. What I don't know is what her game is. What does she want?"

"She wants her backpack and her father's rucksack back. That's clear to me. I think she realizes she can only get those back by giving us something."

"But you told her the stuff in both bags was stolen in DC, right? We got copies, sure. But somebody stole that stuff in DC. My money's on her brother. I think he's one smart dude, that he slipped into HQ, passing as a cart-boy. But maybe they aren't speaking, and she doesn't know he's already got what she's asking us to give her. That's a game with some pieces missing, you know what I mean?"

"Yes, I told her the original documents that were in her bag and her dad's bag in DC were missing. And I told her I would give all her stuff back, except the bags themselves, in exchange for an interview."

"Seems a good trade to me. We give her Redskins bag back, which we don't want anyhow. We get an interview, which we cannot force her to give because she's not a suspect. Even if she was, she's entitled to her Miranda rights. Whatever we learn from her will be news to us, right?"

"Maybe, maybe not. She might say in an interview just what it says in her backpack. Both backpacks. If that's what happens, then you'll know she played me."

They ate the pizza talking about office politics and a new gun holster that Sterndusky was trying out.

"Works great at the range," he said. "That's the only place I want to use it anyway. I want to be among the vast majority of FBI agents—who've never even pulled their gun in the field, much less fired a weapon off the range."

Next day, they gathered once more in the same conference room. Sally used the Redskins backpack again to haul the materials, but she also had her recorded notes typed up and ready for discussion. Cambridge and Sterndusky brought their binders, but no notes. The boss, with his official SAIC voice, called the meeting.

"Okay, guys, and Ms. Lin, I hope your collective review of the materials provided by Vivian Manchester was more revealing to you than it was to me. Did any of you see anything new, or that might be helpful?"

Cambridge said, "Nah, boss."

Sterndusky echoed, by shaking his side from side to side.

Sally said, "Well yes, boss, I did learn something from the first read, maybe not so much from what I read as from the picture that kept popping up as I read all four binders."

"Enlighten us," Stan said.

"The picture comes from reading her files in the larger context of what she and her dad were looking for in DC. That part was in the digital copy we kept before someone walked out of HQ with two backpacks. That kept popping up as I read the not-so-new stuff in Vivian's new backpack.

Here's a summary. Goshkervic's retrial in Baltimore and Manchester's follow-up testimony were both tabled when Goshkervic plead out and avoided jail time. We knew that before, but Vivian knows it now. It's clear in the digital copies and in the print copies here in the Redskins bag. So, she can now see that her dad was operating out of a false sense of security when he and she surfaced in Boise, after disappearing from Cranston. They were gone a good long while. But it was a false sense of security because she and her dad had no idea what would happen only a month later when he was murdered in DC. Manchester probably knew about Goshkervic's death since the *Baltimore Sun* reported on it. But the DOJ still has an open filing on the case. Has it been dismissed? If not, why not? FinCEN told us in 2014 that the Panamanian bank was owned by Autocrancis. Likely neither her dad, nor Vivian knew that before they researched it in DC. That single bank dry cleans more than a billion dollars a year. But it's not their money. They are the middle segment—a drug cartel manufactures and sells cocaine, heroin, opioids, and other narcotics. For cash. They use cash to pay for operations, but they need credit and investment resources for their profit. That was almost surely news they discovered in DC. They found that Autocrancis, a worldwide currency company, has a side business. It holds, cleans, and invests drug money. But maybe either Goshkervic or Manchester suspected that. Maybe they stumbled onto that in their trips to Houston or during Goshkervic's trip to Panama. Is that why both of them were hit? Do both murders send the same message, and if so who is getting this message? Boss, we can piece together here in Phoenix what might be too elusive for the primary team in DC."

The boss, always impatient with long narratives, interrupted Agent Lin. Maybe 'getting that message' is not what's important now. What is Vivian doing and why is she willing to help us? Does she want all of this exposed, or does she have a more personal need? The only way we can find that out is to interview her here in our building. And to do that we have to give her the digital copies of what she has a legal right to, and the Redskins bag and her stuff, which is also hers, no question. So we give up nothing and get an interview. That's her deal. Let's accept."

Stan looked around the table for buy-in. Agents Lin, Cambridge, and Sterndusky all bobbed their heads in his direction.

"Agent Lin, you set it up. Give her stuff back, but make it happen here, inside the building. She talks first, and then walks out with the old files in digital format, and her new bag, and new stuff in print. But Cambridge, you're skeptical. You think she's playing us. So you sit in on the interview. Let Agent Lin take the lead, but you can challenge her a little. Don't forget, she's not a suspect and has federal rights as a victim as well as her basic constitutional rights. So, be eggshell with her, OK? I hate the cliché good cop/bad cop, but in this situation, if we are being played by a victim, we ought to know it, not just suspect it."

CHAPTER 49

Two days later, Vivian called the number Agent Lin had given her.

"Are you the lady FBI agent I talked to at the Starbucks on Monday?" Vivian asked when Lin answered her cell phone.

"Yes, Vivian, it's me. Thank you very much for calling back and for the information you gave me in your backpack."

"OK, do I get my stuff back now? It's still mine, you know."

"Yes, you do. But remember, you said I could interview you as part of the deal. You still agree to that, right?"

"I don't want to, but I said I would, so OK. When do I get . . . ?"

Sally interrupted, hoping that she could set the terms of the deal without an argument.

"Yes, Vivian, but let's do both together. When you come here, to the FBI Field Office for the interview, we can give you the Redskins backpack and a digital copy of what we found in the other two bags that went missing in DC. And we'd like to do it today, or tomorrow at the latest."

"OK, but only you. I didn't make a deal with the other guy, the one watching us at the Starbucks through his big old binoculars."

"Vivian, all FBI interviews are conducted by two-person teams. No exceptions. But if you have some reluctance to have Agent Cambridge involved, I'll arrange for someone else to sit in with me. But most of the questions will come from me, and it won't take too long. Can you come in today?"

There was a long pause. Sally was not sure she was still connected.

"Vivian, do I still have you?"

"Well, how long is this gonna take? I gotta go somewhere later today."

"Not long, an hour tops. Our address is . . ."

"I know where you are. OK, I'll be there in one hour. I don't wanna stay there long. I get dizzy, you know?"

"Dizzy, what do you mean? Vivian? Are you still on the line?"

Realizing the line was dead, Sally went to Cambridge's office to tell him about the call and the interview.

"In just fifty-seven minutes," she said.

Vivian walked from the Phoenix North Mobile Home Park to the FBI building. Took her twenty-two minutes. She paused at the turquoise-and-white building's big double doors, inhaled as much as she could, and stepped inside. She had the odd feeling she'd been here before but shook it off.

"I'm here to see Agent Lin," she told the security officer at the X-ray machine in the lobby.

"Yes, ma'am, do you have an appointment?"

"Yes."

"May I see your driver's license, please?"

"No, don't have one."

"Do you have any form of identification, a school card or a Social Security card?"

"No, I have a credit card. My dad's card, but I can use it."

The officer took it, passed her through the X-ray machine, and pointed to a bench.

"Just wait there," he said.

Vivian watched him sit down, pick up a phone, and talk, but she couldn't hear anything. He paused, the put the phone down, and put her credit card under the lid of an HP-printer on the desk. Then he picked the phone back up, mumbled something else she couldn't hear, and hung up. He walked back to her bench and handed the credit card back.

"Agent Lin will be right down."

It wasn't right down. Fifteen minutes later, Agent Lin came through one of the elevators on the far side of the lobby.

"I'm so sorry for the delay, Vivian. Please come with me. I have a room reserved for us upstairs."

"How long is this going to take?"

Agent Lin just smiled. They got out of the elevator on the third floor. She took Vivian lightly by the elbow and steered her into the conference room. It had no windows, a solid white door, and a table big enough to seat six people in swivel chairs around a circular table with a glass top. Vivian's red-and-gold Redskins backpack was in front of one of the chairs, along with a glass of water, an FBI notepad, and two business cards.

"Sit there, please. I just have to call Agent Cambridge. He's on this floor and will join us in a minute. I got some water for you, with ice, and there's a notepad there you can use, if you want, and . . ."

The white door opened. Lin, said, "Vivian, this is Agent Cambridge. He will sit in on your interview and may have some questions for you, or perhaps not," she said with a sideways glance at the heavyset agent in the dark-blue suit, carrying a legal pad.

"Now, Vivian, let me say, for the record, that you've agreed to come here voluntarily, and that you are not the subject of our ongoing investigation. You do not have to answer questions, but we very much appreciate your help and . . ."

"Is that a Miranda warning you're saying because . . ."

"No, no, it's not, Vivian. You are not a suspect and not a subject of any investigation. You are a victim of a federal crime and we will do everything in our power to protect you, as a witness and as a volunteer. We just hope you might be of some help in the investigation of your father's murder."

"I don't want to help the FBI. My father didn't trust you. I'm only here to get our stuff back, his stuff and mine too. So ask me whatever you want cuz I want to take my bag and go. Did you put the digital copies of my notes, and my dad's notes, in there?"

"We did, and . . ."

"Let me see. Is it a flash drive, or what?"

"Yes, it is. I have a notebook computer here with me. It's mine, but if you like, you can use the USB port and check to see that the files are on the external drive. It's quite a lot, because they are PDF files. You have Adobe reader on your computer, don't you?"

"Don't have a computer, but there's one at the library. I use it sometimes."

"Which library, Vivian? The big one downtown? I really like to go there too, and . . ."

"Don't matter which library I go to, does it? What questions do you have *for me* about my dad's murder?"

"OK, Vivian, let's just start with what happened in Cranston, Arizona, in the summer of 2014. Why did you and your father leave the federal protected witness protection program?"

"What's that have to do with his murder in 2016 in Washington? I thought the questions were about that?"

"It's just background, Vivian."

"Well, I don't want to talk about Cranston, or other places either. I know about evidence and relevance. I read up on it. You can't ask me things not relevant to your investigation, that's what I've been told."

"Who told you that, Vivian? Was it your brother, your father?"

"My father's dead, you know that. I don't have a brother. You should know that too."

"Who's Vince?" Agent Cambridge asked, sliding his swivel chair closer to the table. He was sitting on Vivian's left side, four chairs away from Lin on her right.

"Not your business."

"We think it is our business. We have your notes from the investigation and we have your father's book, the one that says *My Diary* on the leather cover. So we have some information about Vince. We'd like you to help us understand his role . . ."

"I was warned about this," Vivian said. "And I'm not here to talk about anyone except me and Dad. No one else. Please. Just ask me questions about who killed my dad, and give me our stuff back. Don't you understand?"

"Vivian," Agent Lin interceded, "we will respect your privacy and not ask you anything that you are uncomfortable about. Let me ask you some other questions. Did you or your father discover anything while you were in Washington that scared either one of you? Anything that remotely suggested he was in danger? Can we talk about that?"

"Dad said we went there to find out what happened to his friend, Mr. Goshkervic. He knew his friend might have been guilty of trading stock, or something, but that's all. But Dad also found out his friend was killed, and he thought they might be after him now, and that's why we were . . ."

"They? Who's they?" Agent Cambridge barked.

Vivian didn't look at Cambridge, or answer his question. She had been facing Agent Lin on her left side. She swiveled her chair even further to turn her body away from Cambridge. She reached up and put her left fist on top of her head. With her right hand, she moved her jaw and her face to her left as far as she could turn. She no longer had Cambridge in her line of sight. And he could not see her lips move, from his angle of view.

"Ain't talking to him anymore, Agent Lin. He's trying to put words in my mouth, like a forced confession or something. I read up on that too. I am going to get up and leave, and I'm taking my backpack with me. I never agreed to come here and get treated like a convict."

The interview lasted another fifteen minutes. Cambridge asked no more questions. Lin limited her questions to details about Washington, DC, and what had happened there. She learned nothing new, and terminated the interview as nicely as she could.

"I'm very sorry, Vivian, that we had to intrude like this. We're just trying to solve your father's murder. Please take my card with you. And call me anytime you think you might have something to say to us. And I promise to update you on our progress, but since you don't have a phone, that will be hard to do. Is there some place I can send mail to you? An email address maybe, or . . ."

"No. I don't need anything from the FBI. I just need my stuff. You can't bring my father back. But you can leave me alone. OK?"

Without waiting for an answer, Vivian reached across the table for her backpack. She grabbed one strap and slid the backpack toward her. She put the textbook she'd brought with her and the new USB flash drive into the zippered pack and squared her shoulders.

"I'm going now. Let me alone forever."

Lin said, "OK, Vivian. I only hope you'll call me if you need anything or want to talk more about your dad. We really need an address from you. The law requires us to give you notice of major events in the case because you are a victim. We talked about that, remember."

Vivian didn't answer. The security guard outside the door escorted her to the elevator and down to the ground floor, then walked with her through the exit line to the front door. She walked swiftly out, headed to the sidewalk, and then south on 7th Street.

Back upstairs in the third floor conference room the next morning, Cambridge gave the boss his summary of the meeting.

"Boss, she only took one sip from the water glass, and didn't make any notes. She left the office, walked to the elevator, and disappeared—that is, she walked south on 7th Street. We got shit. You should have pushed her, goddammit," he glared at Agent Lin.

"We should have arranged for a tail when she left the building. We got nothing; I checked the floor camera feed and the ground floor feed, and the exit feed. Our facial recognition software did not match her to anyone. The full forefinger and partial thumb print on the credit card was not matched in any state, federal, or Interpol database. Neither did the full thumb print on the water glass. We got nothing. But at least we gave her nothing."

Stan rubbed the back of his neck. "OK, we got nothing. But I'm wondering about what we gave her? Did we give her anything?"

"Did we what?" Cambridge asked.

"Did we give her anything? Anything to help her do whatever it is she's doing?"

"No boss, we didn't even give her a hard time. I started in on her, but Lin waved me off."

"So, she walked in here after giving us her bag and the crap in it. She left with her bag and our digital copy of what was left behind in Washington. Why did she give us the bag in the first place? And why didn't we get anything new from her? Something's amiss here. You two better find out."

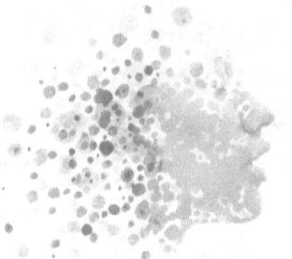

CHAPTER 50

Vince woke up just as the five p.m. news was starting. He didn't know how long he'd been asleep, but he was happy to see the Redskins backpack on the Jumbo II's kitchen table. Holy shit, he screamed, she did it!

He unzipped the flap, reached down into the bag, and removed the thumb drive with all the research and notes contents of his dad's rucksack and Vivian's old backpack. Screw that, I already got this in Dad's old analog version. Vivian had also stuck a copy of a barely used college textbook on some stupid course called *Nutritional Balance for Developing Countries in Equatorial Africa.* What's that about? he asked himself. What's this? Bait Viv had used to get the bag inside the F B I building?

Using a box cutter, he carefully slit the nearly invisible nylon fishing line all around the false bottom he'd created three days ago, before she hauled it to the freakin' F B I. In two minutes, he retrieved the Zoomer G9 carefully, checked the online display, and saw that the handheld digital recorder's voice-activated hard drive had over three hours of recording.

"Kiss my worthless ass, F fuckin' bee eye! Viv did it to you boys! She suckered you like a carny working a tent in Hucksterville," Vince boomed to the empty RV.

The Zoomer G9 was, as advertised by his new friend Faze, the best digital voice recorder in the audio business. Faze had given him the skinny on this fine looking piece of digital magic. "It's four-track recorder's removable, high-fidelity microphones, and four XLR inputs make it the monster for versatile snooping up the FBI's ass. Like the promo said, this baby's long as a dollar bill, weighs less than a brick, and is unbreakable, even when traveling and recording 'on location,' whatever 'n fuck that meant."

Faze, who turned out to be a good buyer and a better fixer, had modified it so the voice activation was silent, and the gain on the microphone was steady as long as the backpack was not moved around too much during recording. It was easy to use with track levels and EQ settings. And it came with two microphones: an XY microphone and a mid-side microphone. Sweet! It had monster storage. With SDXCs it could hold up to 2TB of data.

Like most millennials, Vince could not write, or under-stand cursive writing. Taking notes by printing longhand was for old farts. He typed, at 105 words per minute, whatever he needed. Four years of daily keyboarding had given him the skill to listen, and take notes without impeding either effort. Using an Ethernet cable, he moved the audio files from the Zoomer to his home-built computer. Then he used

Excel to make notes on a spreadsheet about what he heard on the Zoomer audio recorder feed, now resident on his computer. Then he moved all of the files to the Tor cloud bin, accessible only by him. When that was done, he wiped his C-drive clean, wiped the Zoomer hard drive clean, and began listening to the files in the cloud. And he typed his Excel notes while he listened.

> Probe 1—Redskins-recorded voices—FBI office?— Phx—Aug 1—female voice talking—2 male voices—talkin bout meet at SB with Viv—she says—will interview—read stuff in Redskins bag first—talkin bout Binder Nmbr #1 is Hurlitt International—binder #2 is Fritz Goshkervic— binder#3 bout Houston International Savings and Loan, Inc.—what's that??—binder #4 is Plankton Resources, Inc.—Houston Texas—binder #5 is Autocrancis Currency, Inc.—all 5 binders I did, left for Viv to deliver to FBI. Bait for the big grouper to bite—female voice talkin—"Autocrancis first came to our attention from the case agent at FinCEN—global conglomerate—owns 200 financial and insurance companies—FinCEN on it—looks like a major player—money laundering in the Caribbean, and Panama."—Unk voice says Goshkervic, Manchester's boss at Hurlitt—trips Houston—did something with Plankton Resources—entertainment expenses for Goshkervic in Houston.

Vince hit the esc button and sat staring at his monitor for two minutes, taking little short breaths. Then he hit play and started another note.

> Probe 2—Redskins-recorded voices—FBI cf room—multiple voices—1 female + 2 males—boss FBI and 2 agents—talking about Dad's murder—DC—new voice—maybe FBI boss man—pissed off—says "Listen up"—re-read all those 302s—now the Manchester murder investigation is tied the money laundering—Jesus H. Christ, we are in a fix here.

Vince hit pause on the audio feed and got up from his chair. He got a bottle of water from the little fridge and a Snickers bar from the drawer by the sink. Fuckin' what? Dad into money laundering? The FBI's in a fix? Fuck that, he thought. Dad's dead. It's me in the fix, not the fuckin F bee eye! He paced up and down Jumbo's fourteen-foot pathway from the driver's cab to the bed in back. Like livin' 'n a fuckin hallway, he thought. Cold water and candy always calmed him. He sat back down, put his headphones on, and clicked restart on the audio feed.

> Probe 2—continued—boss FBI talkin—remember CIA operatives and FinCIN agents—way out in front of us—FBI?—we thought case was a missing protected witness down in Cranston—that's Dad they are talking about—What now—FBI boss says?

> Probe 3—continued—female voice louder—one
> Viv met with?—sounds pissed—hold up, gentle-
> men—we need to know what Manchester knew—
> that's what got him killed—bigger issue—why was
> he killed—why his daughter digging—what's she
> know—am taking Redskins bag back to my office.

Vince always analyzed data and wrote code sitting down. Thinking was different—he thought best when pacing about, especially outside. Jumbo II didn't work for that so he went outside, in the dark, and paced up and down the empty rows at the North Phoenix Mobile Home Park.

So, the FBI ain't as smart as we thought. They are slopping in the wrong trough while FinCEN and the See Eye A storm troopers are eating their lunch. Dad was done in by the motherfuckers at that currency shithouse called Autocrancis and their captive bank down in Panama. But what's the cut? How n' fuck are those Houston companies laced into this deal? Who are they? But, hold the goddamn phone, man, none of those dudes, or that lady either, is asking the right question—it ain't *why* or *where*. Damn their sorry asses. The question I wanna know is *who!* Who killed Dad? Gimme the name and I'll take care of his ass—ain't going to be no pissy trial in pissy Baltimore. I'll off him just like he offed Dad.

After the fourth turn round the block of rows, Vince went back inside his trailer and logged back onto Tor. He fast-forwarded the audio one click so he could still distinguish the voice, but at a faster speed—one his age could fathom but fuzzed up old people's ears. It was the lady FBI,

Lin something. In a few sentences, he realized she was dictating to a recorder somewhere.

"Date, Wednesday, July 23, 2016, FBI File Number PHX dash 2014 dash 18519—Manchester slash Nau. Review of subject Vivian Manchester's Binder Number One labeled Hurlitt International . . . Third section . . . handwritten org chart connecting Hurlitt with Plankton Resources, and both with Autocrancis . . . new name . . . to this agent . . . North-by-North East Commodities, Inc.—Seattle Washington—February 2016 . . . Dad's job."

"What's this?" Vince thought out loud. Viv told that agent about Dad looking for a job up in Seattle? Why'd she do that? Was he? Never told me. Shit. But wait, maybe this is good. Maybe North-by-North East is part of the whole money-laundering scam those dudes were playing. Maybe Dad didn't know 'bout that shit. Maybe he did. Shit. He turned the audio back on.

> Probe 4—Goshkervic—newspaper clippings—Baltimore Sun—Stephan Manchester writes three interoffice memos—to Goshkervic—two trips they took to Houston—one more Goshkervic took from Houston to Panama City—2013—Goshkervic dies—mysterious death—2014—plane crash—Gulf of Mexico—both men connected—Baltimore to Houston—to Gulf of Mexico—word Houston underlined in red—twice.

"They." Vince kept bouncing the word off the computer monitor as he held his mouse steady over it on his screen.

This ain't good. Was Dad part of whatever 'n fuck his ratty ass boss Goshkervic was doing? Back to the audio, he told his homemade computer.

> Probe 5—new voice—door slamming—man—says Sally got a sec—tells her stuff—Houston Savings and Loan is a front—ain't in Houston—it's in Baytown—on Galveston Bay—run by lady named Julia something—probably Santerra—her law firm in same strip mall—she's mobbed up—she's a hit contractor—murder crew—old case from Dallas—dropped by Texas AG when only eyeball witness found feeding the fishes—Galveston Bay—compliments of Julia baby—Texas bullshit.

Vince took his hands off the keyboard, used the mouse to still the audio feed, and sat there like he'd been turned to stone. Then, shaking his upper body back and forth, he ripped the headphones off and threw them as far as he could down the hall. Closing his eyes, he slammed his fists down on top of his thighs, over and over. And he bit his tongue so bad he started spitting blood.

Julia probably Santerra! You bitch! You stinkin', smellin', whorin' bitch! You're the one! I can feel it. You went in that room Viv told me about at that fucked-up old folk's home. You killed him—I know you did—I know it!

Vince jumped up and spun around to the driver's compartment. As he tried to push away from the little table, his foot caught the power cord from the bulky computer to the outlet under the table. He dragged the computer off the table. It crashed to the floor, where he started kicking it. The monitor went off, and his cell phone began buzzing. He grabbed it and threw it down the hallway toward the rear of Jumbo II.

Two hours later, Vince found himself lying against the back fence of Phoenix North Mobile Home Park, staring out into the dark, wondering where he was.

"Hey man, you OK?" the stranger asked. "I heard you moaning all the way from my space, six rows up there," he said, pointing toward the front office. "You need me to call an ambulance, or what?"

"What?" Vince said.

"An ambulance. You fell, I think. Your knees are bloody, but maybe you're OK. Not my business, but man, you been moaning for a long time. I know you live in that old RV over there," the man said, pointing to Jumbo II.

Vince sat up and tried to wipe the blood off his right knee. "I'm OK. OK. Just let me be. I was just walking out here in the dark. Couldn't sleep. Fell down. Just tired, that's all. You go on. Just let me be."

Vince waited and watched the man walk toward the front of the lot and step up into his thirty-two-footer—the one with the dual AC units on the roof. Then he went back to Jumbo II and was surprised to see his computer down on the floor. The Zoomer was still on the table, but the cord connecting to the computer had been pulled out. He put everything back up on the table and was relieved to find that the knockdown hadn't damaged his computer. He booted up, fixed the restart, powered everything back up and, after changing his IP and DSCM tracks, logged on to one of his favorite websites on Tor. It took two and a half hours, but now he had glossy photos from Google Earth of the strip mall in Baytown, four references to Julia Santerra-Evans, including her bar license and official lawyer headshot from the Texas State Bar Association, and her Texas Corporation Commission file on the savings and loan she fronted. He also found the LLC documentation for her law firm, Withers & Associates, the Pac & Ship store she owned, and the tax records on her Galveston bay home.

"OK, Julia Santerra-Evans," Vince said to the dashboard of Jumbo II, as he started the engine and steered Jumbo II toward Bell Road, "I got you lined out, bitch. I'm coming for you. I'm coming."

CHAPTER 51

It took Vince nine days to drive the 1,200 miles from Phoenix to Houston. He averaged only 130 miles per day because he spent three hours driving, five hours sleeping, and the rest on the Internet accessing Darknet sites to build his front-line assault on Julia Santerra-Evans, Plankton Resources, Inc., Hurlitt International, and the Panamanian bank known as *Banco de Transfercias de Divisas*. He only used his personal computer in Jumbo II to find information that, if tracked, would lead nowhere. He stopped in Tucson for a day, El Paso for two days, and San Antonino for three days. In each city, he found Internet rental sites known only to hackers and the CIA. Some were beginners, some expert, and a handful, like him, at the top of their game. They rented dumb terminals with high-speed broadband at seventy-five bucks an hour. It was worth the price because the proprietors asked no questions but guaranteed no keystroke tracking. They operated out of what looked like buildings for lease in empty spaces in strip malls. There were no signs on the doors; if you didn't know exactly where they were, you couldn't look them up in the yellow pages or Yelp. Once you got inside, nobody looked anyone else in the eye. It was cash only. All computer booths were shielded from view. Usually, it had to be dark outside before you could even bang on the front door. Knocking was ignored.

Vince knew the basics and could guess how Hurlitt laundered its money through Plankton Resources by using *Banco de Transfercias*. The trick was that Plankton owned and controlled hundreds of smaller companies like Hurlitt, whose legitimate bank accounts in the US were sources of illegitimate transfers to foreign banks in places like Panama. When things went wrong and suppliers or customers went astray, Plankton had Julia to make everyone behave. And together, they had killed his father; he knew it. He would hit Plankton where it would hurt the most—in their bank accounts. But he couldn't think about her without screaming, so he resolved to not think about her at all. He'd just focus on her bosses at Plankton. For now.

By the time he got to San Antonio, he knew the names, addresses, and principal officers of all Plankton subsidiaries in the US, and which national banks they used in the US and Latin America. Julia Santerra-Evans's law firm, Wither & Associates, looked like an independent law firm, in good standing in Baytown. But the savings and loan she also owned looked like a private bank, not a public one. She also owned the building that housed all three of her businesses—law firm—savings and loan—packing and shipping. Saving what, he wondered? Loaning to whom, packing what, shipping where? All were questions the Internet couldn't answer. This would take shoe leather and patience. So, before driving the last leg south to Houston, he went shopping in San Antonio.

At Macy's San Antonio Rivercenter on east Bowie Street he walked through the men's department, paying attention to what young men were buying. Most bought athletic stuff, skin-tight jeans, hang-loose shirts, and running shoes with bright laces. But a few bought suits, dress shirts, shoes, and ties. So that's what he bought. One dark-blue suit, one brown sport coat with tan slacks, two pairs of lace-up shoes, two button-down dress shirts, both white, and a lightweight raincoat.

At the Harvil Camera Studio, twenty blocks away, he bought a new Nikon D-500. The camera nerd rattled off the specs so fast Vince knew it was the real shit. Guys who talked slow, like the suit nerd at Macy's, bored him. But this guy, wearing little Russian spy glasses, drooled over the D-500.

"It's got like your huge 20.9MP DX format CMOS sensor and an optical low pass filter; the processor is an Expeed 5; the multicam is a 20k autofocus sensor that trashes out at 153/99 AF points. And you're a computer guy, right? I can tell. So this freakin' ISO range runs from 100–51,200 expandable to Lo 1 and Hi 5. Dude, that a 50 to 1,640,000 equivalent! You wanna share your shots, right? This tiny box shares images instantly with built-in SnapBridge. You know 'bout that, right? It's Wi-Fi built in, Bluetooth out and, get this, it shoots cinematic 4K UHD video and hides your stuff inside dual card slots. XQD and SD media. Dude, you're gonna fantasize over this one. It's only 2,800 bucks, a steal, right?"

Vince added the D3400 Double Zoom lens kit, an AF-P DX Nikkor 18-55mm f/3.5-5.6G VR lens, AF-P DX Nikkor 70-300mm f/4.5-6.3G ED telephoto zoom lens, DSLR Travel Case, and a Nikon School Online class on how to hook up, manipulate, and navigate the package at another 500 bucks. He added a $200 tripod, bringing the total to $3500. He paid cash and couldn't wait to get away from the camera nerd who nearly exhausted him.

Vince drove crosstown to the Cabela sports store and bought a SIG Sauer Oscar3 Spotting Scope for the bargain price of $499. He liked it because it was designed to be used without a tripod. The salesman showed him its "simple one-handed" operation so you could open a stick of chewing gum while using this little beauty. It was lightweight and had a 10x to 20x magnification range. Just right, he thought.

The drive to Houston took just over three hours at fifty-five miles per hour on I-10, the same freeway he'd taken out of Phoenix a week ago. As always, Vince worried about traffic tickets, not for the money, but because there would be a record. He was using his Justin Bradley Luther Texas driver's license, with his picture on it. When he got to the west of Houston, he made a pit stop for gas, Fritos, and a thirty-two-ounce full strength Coke Zero. He used Google maps to pick a small town somewhere between downtown Houston and downtown Baytown. It turned out to be Lynchburg, Texas, a working man's town with cheap motels and one of the worst RV parks he'd ever seen.

Just right, he thought. He parked Jumbo II at the RV park, loaded up his computer and what he called his "necessaries," and walked three blocks to the first motel he came to. Rooms were $49 per night and advertised as "clean." He paid cash for two nights, said he had no ID, but needed a full size, working shower, with extra hot water.

The next morning, he ate breakfast at a local café and asked the cashier to call a cab for him. When it came he told the driver to get off I-10 and take him for a ride around Houston. It cost him $130 but eventually he spotted a used car lot twenty-five miles away that had ten barely clean cars in the front lot. All had big signs with sales signs ranging from $2,999 to $5,999. He bought a white five-year-old Chevy Cavalier Base for $4,600 cash. He used his Justin Luther license and got a dealer's plate good for fifteen days and a signed title from Butch Sunderson. The gas tank was half full, so he filled up at a Circle K and drove to the Plankton Resources office in South Houston, just off I-45. He could have rented a car for a lot less money, but it would have made a record, unlike the sale from the used car dealer. When he was through in Houston, he'd just leave it somewhere a thief might find it, with the keys inside and a half-tank of gas.

Plankton took up the top two floors of a three-story brick building. The ground floor was half-full with retail stores and a sizeable parking garage for Plankton employees. Once he located the building, he drove back to his motel in Lynchburg and changed into his blue suit. At 3:00, he arrived back at the Plankton building. Hoping he looked like a college student trying to look well-dressed, he went up the stairway and asked the lady at the desk where he went to apply for a job.

"What kind of a job?" she asked.

"Part-time. I'm taking a semester off and living with my aunt in Lynchburg. She needs me because she's got the cancer and no one else to take care of her. My mom's her sister but she can't come because she lives in Nebraska and . . ."

Waiving her hand at him to slow up, she said without a smile. "We don't hire part-time help here, except maybe in the garage, or in the mail room."

"The mail room? Really, that would be wonderful, I was in charge of my college mail room last year, and I know everything there is to know about mail rooms, like how to arrange incoming mail on a spreadsheet that sends alarms to . . ."

"Yawl don't need to explain so much to me. Go on back down to the main floor. You'll see a door marked Plankton Resources Deliveries & Parking. Just tell your story to them, and . . ."

She was surprised when he turned his back on her in midsentence and walked straight out the door. Within the next hour, Vince got hired by Plankton Resources as a part-time employee. They told him he could not work more than twenty hours a week, and they'd need his Social Security card, his driver's license, and his permanent residence address in Texas. He showed him Justin Luther's address, said he didn't have his SSN card because his mother burned it, but he knew the number. He made up one on the spot, and he gave them the address of the RV Park as though it was his.

He would be paid $8.75 an hour to sort mail and park cars in the garage. They said he'd get a Plankton Resources red and yellow vest to wear when he was on the job. Perfect cover. He was fairly sure he'd be out of Texas before he earned that first paycheck.

CHAPTER 52

It was 110 degrees outside in the glaring Phoenix sun when Sally got to the office. She'd spent the morning at the Phoenix Public Library. Sally opened the door to the FBI's third-floor conference room at exactly 1:30 p.m. that Monday afternoon, as per the schedule set by her boss. They'd been meeting every Monday afternoon on the Manchester murder for updates from the team. She was surprised to see her boss already there—he usually waited five minutes before he made his entrance. He was sitting with someone she didn't know.

"Sally, come on in and meet Ahmed, he's with the Boise Police Department."

The small, bearded man got up, offered a soft handshake, and said, "Agent Lin, it's a pleasure to meet you. Maybe I can be of some help. The SAIC tells me you're the lead agent on this case."

"Nice to meet you, Mr. Ahmed. I guess I'm out in front here in the Phoenix office, but the case is being run out of DC HQ."

"Ahmed is my first name, Ahmed al-Dosari is the full plate, but nobody in Boise uses my full name. In fact, I'm the only sworn officer to get to use my first name on DRs and interoffice stuff. I was the number-two investigator on the Jason Bloomington hit at Quinn's Pond in Boise."

"And you're tasked here to Phoenix, on that case, Ahmed?"

"No, not at all. I'm actually on vacation—relatives live in Tempe. But my boss thought I ought to give your office a call, since we have a new lead to follow. He called it in to FBI in DC and they said to let you know too. Since I'm here anyway, I thought maybe I could give you my take on it."

Agents Cambridge and Sterndusky came in, bringing a paper sack from Dunkin Donuts. Stan made the introductions and then asked Ahmed to fill them in on the new lead from Boise.

"Well, this is pretty much luck, I'd say, but we think we've figured out who the garrote killer, Chaco Hernandez, worked for. It was a woman named Julia Santerra-Evans. Lawyer. Practices in Houston out of a one-lawyer shop, but she seems to have only one client—a big company called Plankton Resources, Inc."

"Ahmed," Sally interrupted, "can I ask how you connected her to Chaco?"

"Sure, we ID'd Chaco Hernandez from his morgue fingerprints and stuff he had in his pockets, plus several hits on Interpol's database. He was a killer for the Sinaloa

Cartel. Very nasty guy. But we didn't know about Ms. Santerra-Evans until I spent some time at the Boise airport looking at video coverage from the gate and compared that with coverage at the taxi line in front of the airport. I had morgue lab photos of Chaco and his Delta ticket to Boise from Houston via San Francisco. I pegged him exiting the plane into the terminal. Then I spent some time looking at the cab line and found him again, this time with an unidentified woman. They were talking and got in the cab together. Then I went back to the gate coverage and looked at all deplaning passengers. There she was again. I got the manifest from Delta and finally figured both the woman and Chaco boarded in Houston. Eventually I eliminated all other passengers and zeroed in on her. She has almost no hits on crime databases, but she shows up on hits connected to Plankton Resources. They show up in a few places as players in the money laundering world. Finally, I got some more info about her. She claims to be the owner of a savings and loan in a little town called Baytown. But the Texas AG's office thinks it's a front for Plankton. And they were suspicious about the lady because she showed up as a person of interest in two open homicides—gang related—by gang, I mean the Sinaloa Cartel out of Culiacán, Mexico. That's pretty much it."

Cambridge asked, "OK, Mr. Ahmed, I gotta say that's some slick police work. Connecting the boarding gate film to the street in front of the airport. Slick. But I didn't hear how you connect the lady with the man. They both came from Houston, but couldn't that be a coincidence?"

"Maybe, but not likely. The lead investigator in our office, Bill Amsterdam, dug deeper and found that both tickets were paid for in cash at a small travel agent's shop in Baytown, Texas. One telephone call there and they gave up Ms. Julia Santerra-Evans. They said she buys lots of airplane tickets for Latin America types. She has their names, DOBs, license info, and even their frequent flyer numbers, which track back to her law firm. She comes in by herself, never brings in the ones flying out of Houston. And this particular trip was the only one the lady travel agent could remember where she went on the trip *with* the guy she fronted on the tickets. We got the idea there's no love lost between Ms. Santerra-Evans and her travel agent. She was cold, the travel agent said."

"Cold? What'd she mean by that?"

"Dunno, just cold like a cold fish, or maybe stuck up. Can't say. But I can call Billy, he might be able to add something, since he's the one who talked to the agent in Baytown. Where's Baytown, anyway?"

Cambridge answered, "It's south of south Houston, on Galveston Bay. That's a huge port down there. Did you connect Hernandez to Plankton Resources?"

"No, not directly, but the lady lawyer is on Interpol as a person of interest in several contract hits in the drug and money laundering trade. No arrests, but a lot of smoke. And she's definitely connected to Plankton both as a lawyer and through her front in the savings and loan business."

Sterndusky chimed in. "Boss, this fits some early leads. Hurlitt is owned by Plankton. Hurlitt employed both

Goshkervic and Manchester. And now we got Hernandez and Julia Santerra-Evans on the same scope. But how do we tie them directly into the Washington, DC, hit on Manchester?"

Stan raised one palm up and pointed at Sally Lin with the other hand. She took the cue.

"They are connected by what Stephan Manchester and his daughter Vivian were doing in DC. They were looking into the Goshkervic killing because they thought it might help them understand why Chaco Hernandez killed Mr. Bloomington in Boise. If they could follow that track, maybe they could tell somebody, maybe even the FBI. They did find out something, although we don't know what it was. But it was enough to get Mr. Manchester killed. What I'm wondering is whether Julia Santerra-Evans was in DC when Manchester got hit."

Ahmed had an idea. "Hey, my sergeant, Billy Amsterdam, could call the travel agent in Baytown. They helped us before, maybe they will again."

Ahmed excused himself, went out into the lobby, and called Boise. Five minutes later, his cell rang in the conference room. It was Billy. He had talked to Baytown Travel.

"They confirmed that Julia Santerra-Evans bought a round-trip, first-class ticket to DC, the day before the Manchester hit. So, we got her in the same town when Bloomington got hit, and in DC when Manchester got it."

"Sally," Stan said, "you need to go to Houston in the morning. I'll task you to that office for as long as you need. The answers might be there waiting for you. Hell, maybe your friend Vivian will be there. You can have a little reunion."

CHAPTER 53

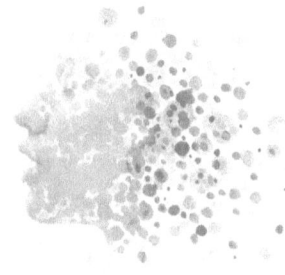

Agent Lin flew coach class to Houston and used the three-hour flight time to read about the famous case of Shirley Ardell Mason, the real woman who was the subject of a book called *Sybil*. The book generated several movies by the same name, most recently in 2007. It prompted her to make a telephone call from her hotel room at the Magnolia Houston on Texas Avenue, not far from the convention center. She'd stayed there before and liked the pool up on the roof. It was five in Houston when she got there and sticky hot. So, she took a quick swim in the pool and then called Dr. Socorro in DC.

"This is Eliana, Sally, how nice to see your name on my caller ID. How can I help you?"

"Well, if you've got a few, I could sure use some insight. Of course, I am calling about the young girl we talked about at your hospital. Remember? She was apparently diagnosed when she was nine or ten with DID. Now she's nineteen.

I actually met her twice recently in Phoenix. By the way, I've been reading *Sybil.*"

"Yes, Sally, we all know the book and the movies based on it. While it was good medicine at the time, most psychiatrists today think it triggered an epidemic of the diagnosis. Many young children were misdiagnosed because of the notoriety of one patient. Some of the attending psychiatrists in my residency thought Sybil was a brilliant hysteric, others disagreed and thought she was correctly diagnosed, despite the lucrative publishing rights that sprang up from her early treatment. But that's old news. How did she strike you? As a mental patient? Or just a confused young woman?"

"Well, neither really. She was quite focused. But I did have the feeling she was somehow using me. It was really odd. Mostly, young people are uncomfortable with police authority, but she seemed relaxed when a colleague and I interviewed her in the FBI building in Phoenix."

"Can you give me an example?"

"No, it was not any one thing. She didn't help us at all. And she didn't seem curious enough about her father's murder. She just focused on getting back some research notes she and her father had made in DC."

"Did you think she was making things up?"

"A little, I guess. But it wasn't things, it was people."

"People, you mean she was making up people, someone in her life, or strangers?"

"I couldn't say—it was not a judgement, or even an opinion on my part, just a feeling. What I wanted to ask you about was, assuming the diagnosis of DID was correct ten years ago, would it still be accurate today?"

"No way to say without seeing her and learning whether she'd been treated at any time. Was she?"

"We don't know that, or much of anything about her. But it's possible she had a brother. Others have seen, or heard, about a brother."

"Well, the brother could be an alter. Or perhaps you were interviewing an alter and did not know it. Therapists often have trouble, especially with new patients, identifying personality states. Sometimes the problem is that the host personality may not be the true identity of the patient. One of the most difficult problems in treating a DID patient occurs when you are treating the host but an alter appears and seems belligerent. The therapist might not know that she's talking to an alter rather than the host. Or if she does, she might not understand that the alter would naturally feel the doctor is trying to eliminate the alter, thereby restoring the host personality to normalcy."

"So, how would you suggest I deal with it if I come across Vivian—that's her name, Vivian—here in Houston? I'm here because we think she might be acting as an investigator into her father's murder. A sort of policewoman without a badge, so to speak."

"Oh, I could not begin to offer advice. But I can say you should be very careful if you come in contact with her to try to clarify whether it's the same personality state you talked to in Phoenix or a different one in Houston. Alters are often identifiable by how quickly they come to anger if they think someone is trying to eliminate them."

"Does that mean an alter actually knows they are just a different personality state and not . . . well, not a real person?"

"No, I'm not saying that. An alter always believes he or she is real. And they sometimes feel, but do not actually know, that they are helping another person. Or hating another person. Or any one of a thousand different scenarios. Here's another thing to remember: the primary identity is a trauma victim. Most trauma victims feel empathy for others. But an alter rarely feels empathy because the alter has no memory of the primary identity's trauma. The primary identity might be mild mannered, timid, and even loving, while the alter could be hostile, boastful, and hateful. From a therapeutic perspective, it is the primary identity you're trying to help, not the alter. Because it's rare for a primary identity, sometimes called the host, to actually know that an alter is coming in and out of her life, effective therapy is a huge challenge. That would be even more challenging if the primary is a girl and the alter is a boy. We talked once about who you might arrest for a crime committed by an alter, remember?"

"I do," Sally said, glancing at a text message which just crossed her screen.

"So, now you might have a different problem, you might be investigating the alter, rather than the host."

They talked for another minute, then Sally begged off to call her boss. The text had been abrupt: "SL call me."

"It's me, boss. I just got off the phone with that child psychiatrist, Dr. Socorro, and . . ."

"Tell me later, Sally, I just talked to my boss, Director Kahn. I brought him up to speed, told him I'd tasked you to the Houston field office. He thinks you need a full-time partner there because a single agent cannot watch her own back. He's on the phone now talking to my counterpart in Houston. So I want you to go to that field office right away. They've got some intel that can't be shared over a cell tower. It's at 1 Justice Park Dive. Are you close by?"

"Sure, boss, I'll be there in fifteen minutes."

CHAPTER 54

When Sally Lin showed her badge to the security guard manning the X-ray machine in the lobby of the Houston FBI field office, she got a pleasant surprise.

"Right, Agent Lin, we were told to expect you. Here's a temporary ID card so you don't have to get scanned as long as you're here. They are expecting you in conference room 209 on the second floor. Quickest way up is through the stairs, right over there." He pointed to a double-wide set of stairs leading up to what looked like a mezzanine overlooking the lobby.

As directed, Sally went to room 209 and eased open the door. Three women and a balding man were huddled at the end of the conference table. The man shook her hand vigorously, "Agent Lin, I'm the SAIC here—Slater Blakey, they call me Slate. We'll brief you on the status here in Houston, but first we need to check in with DC."

The other agents identified themselves. They also shook her hand, but less forcefully. They were not testing her, just saying hello. After the terse introductions, Slate said, "Let's get Phoenix and DC on the speakerphone and up on the video screen so we can all get briefed at once."

Her boss appeared on the split screen from Phoenix. Then, DC made its digital appearance in the upper right corner of the screen. She could see a grey-headed agent in a dark coat and tie, sitting at a desk piled high with folders and three-ring binders. She'd heard about him, but had never met him. Assistant Deputy Director Davis D'Angelo. His face was deeply lined and his eyes were dark behind thick, black plastic-rimmed glasses. He looked to be in his mid-sixties. He was known in every field office as the senior officer leading the FBI's task force on money laundering in the Americas—North, South, and the Caribbean. After a thirty-second introduction and a rollcall of the agents from Phoenix, Houston and DC, Agent D'Angelo took charge.

"I know that you all know about the good work done by the Boise office in unearthing a viable suspect in the garroting of Jason Bloomington. Her name is Julia Santerra-Evans. Day before yesterday, we linked Santerra-Evans to Washington, DC, on the day before the Manchester hit. It's a thin link—we think she was here in DC on the day Stephan Manchester was murdered. By thin, I mean no bigger than a single thread, but it's a silk thread. Here's what we did—we used the Boise playbook. By running the photo of Santerra-Evans that Boise secured in their airport, we discovered the same face, walking through the exit from the gates to the baggage area at Dulles airport. A different camera picked her up at a baggage carrousel; the one offloading bags from the Houston flight. She picked up two nondescript roller bags and got a baggage handler to help her take the bags to the airport train station. They picked her up again on video disembarking the airport terminal train and entering the Amtrak terminal. That's the end of the video tracking. So we can place her here in DC the day before the Manchester murder."

Sally waived her hand at the monitor, "Mr. D'Angelo, I'm Sally Lin, from the Phoenix office. I'm on temporary duty here in Houston on the Manchester case. Can you tell me whether Santerra-Evans is currently under surveillance here in Houston? Her law office is close by—in a suburb called Baytown, and . . ."

Slate interrupted, "Mr. D'Angelo, good morning. I can tell you that Santerra-Evans is not under surveillance by our office. We have files and background details about Plankton Resources, Inc., and it's possible Santerra-Evans shows up in those files, but no, we're not tracking her."

"Well, I think your office ought to ramp up concerning Ms. Santerra-Evans," D'Angelo said.

"Find her and sit tight on her location while we decide how best to approach her. If she is in any way complicit in the Manchester murder, we need to know everything there is to know about her before your office brings her in for questioning. My guess is that will be a Miranda event. She'll be advised of her rights, refuse to waive, and out your door she goes. Comments anyone?"

Sally made the instant decision not to comment, but her stomach was howling at her. She sat out the rest of the meeting. Between the three field offices, they set up a new team of three agents; two from Houston and herself. But, Sally thought, is Vivian here? If she is, did she come here because she knows about Santerra-Evans? Why has she disappeared, again?

An hour later, one of the two Houston agents confirmed by telephone that Santerra-Evans's office was closed, at four o'clock in the afternoon. But a car parked in the lot was registered to her. The Pac 'n Mail office was closed, as was the Houston International Savings and Loan office. The agent, a rookie named Montoya, was told to park close by and watch for any activity, especially anyone approaching the parked car. They set up a surveillance team composed of two agents in a black standard-issue Ford Explorer with heavily tinted windows to relieve Montoya two hours later.

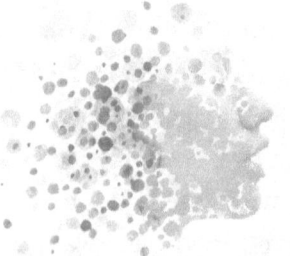

CHAPTER 55

Vince was parked a half-block down the street from the Berkley Apartments building on North Third Avenue in Baytown as the black Ford Explorer drove into the parking lot across street. A man in a dark suit got out, walked up in front of the building, and looked in the windows of the mail store, the savings and loan office, and Julia baby's law firm. He saw the man pause and take down the license plate of the only car in the lot, a bright-yellow Jeep Wrangler Rubicon Recon. Then he got back into the Ford and drove a half block away. There he made a U-turn into a driveway and parked facing the three offices. From his position, Vince could not see how many people were in the car, but he took several still shots and spent a few minutes with the spotting scope on it. Three hours later, another black SUV pulled up behind the first one. No one got out of either car, but the first one pulled out and headed west toward central Houston.

Motherfucker! You guys are the freakin F Bee Eye! You're watching for Julia baby and I'm watching you.

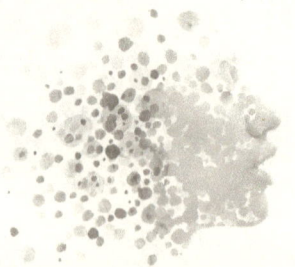

CHAPTER 56

The FBI stakeout of Julia Santerra-Evans' office ran from seven a.m. until seven p.m. for three days. They used two-man teams, literally. Sally Lin was not assigned to either team. At the end of the second day, Houston SAIC called it off.

"Yes," Sally answered, when Slater Blakey asked whether she thought it best to cut off the close surveillance.

"If Julia Santerra-Evans is either the killer, or the organizer, she'll be constantly aware of her situation. Like a good cop, she'll notice everything around her that seems off. Black SUVs with tinted windows will spook her."

Sally kept her cell phone close by and the pager on her belt that Agent Blakey had given her for as long as she was TDY (temporary duty) in Houston. She spent part of the second day masquerading as a job applicant at Plankton Resources. She drove a rental car to the Plankton Resources garage. It was not a self-parking operation. Rather, they simply gave you a ticket and took your car to the garage from the front entrance.

Without either knowing it was happening, Sally actually saw Vince, when he returned her car to her at the garage. As he stuck his hand out for her parking receipt, she felt something she could only later describe as a small creep in her spine. A day later, she would guess who the young man really was. Her description matched perfectly the look of the parking attendant.

CHAPTER 57

Vince spent a half day riding around Baytown in his 2011 Chevy. Most of the cars he saw were a lot like his: cheap, white, and dirty. His blended in with traffic on every street. He made two trips to Julia Santerra-Evans's building on Third Avenue, once in the car and once on foot from a parking lot five blocks away.

Now that he'd gotten a front view, he walked back up the street and around the block. When he came back down the opposite street, he could see the small parking lot on the west side of the building. There were spaces for six cars. Each was marked reserved and warned violators would be towed away. He walked across the street to the Berkley Apartments; he'd parked on the street opposite from it the previous day and thought then that it might be a good place to stake out Julia baby. It was a two-story frame building that looked like it was a good fifty years old. They had a small sign on the front porch—Studio Apartment for Rent—Furnished—$90 per week.

The young dark-skinned woman sitting on the porch eyed him suspiciously until he spoke the magic words.

"I'm looking for a small apartment on account of I just got a job here. It's a three-week job, but they told me it could take an extra week to finish up the drywall. I'm a drywall hanger and I walk on stilts. Are you willing to negotiate a little on the rent? I got eighty dollars in cash on me, right now. What do you think?"

The woman got up with difficulty. She had a knee brace with a silver hinge thing on both sides.

"I think my grandfather would go for that. You want to see it first?"

"Does it face the street or the back?"

"Faces the street. Fact is, it's right on top of this office. Same view as looking outside from here. Only you go up the stairs from the back. We only have eight apartments, one that me and my grandfather live in, and seven for rent. Number 5, the studio, is the only one available. But you got to put up a $50 security and cleaning deposit. Which ain't refundable. One month's rent is $480 plus the security deposit of fifty dollars. That makes it $530 for four weeks. You got $530?"

"Not on me. But I could go get it back at the motel I'm in now. They charge forty-nine bucks a day and don't clean all that much. Let me look at it, and I'll give you twenty to hold it for a day. I'll come back tomorrow morning with the rest. OK?"

"Yeah, OK."

Vince went up the back stairs to look at Number 5. One room about the size of a cheap motel room, but with a bigger bathroom. It had a cast-iron bathtub, a hot water heater, and a clean sink; it smelled of Lysol. The room had two windows facing the street, directly across from Julia's three businesses in the ugly concrete block building. Vince estimated the distance at no more than fifty feet. Perfect, he thought. He went downstairs and told the lady in the knee brace he'd be back tomorrow. Then he drove up Third Avenue for a few blocks until he hit Highway 330, which took him back to Lynchburg and the trailer park where he'd left Jumbo II. He spent the night there researching all savings and loan institution rules and regulations at the Texas banking department's website. They listed Houston International Savings and Loan as inactive but in good standing. There was no listing for Julia's Pac 'n Mail store, except under the online Yellow Pages, which listed the correct street address but did not list a phone number or an email address. There were no Facebook pages, Yelp reviews, or BBB references. Her law firm was listed at the Texas State Bar site, but she didn't belong to any bar sections, committees, or have a disciplinary record. She was not rated by any of the half-dozen rating sites covering lawyers in Houston. Maybe she's practicing ghost law, he thought.

Next day, he moved into Unit 5 at The Berkley Apartments. Their parking lot was in back, not visible from the street. He lugged two bags up the back stairs. One held clothes, the other his new camera, tripod, the spotting scope, and snacks. He set up the tripod, locked down the camera, and took a half dozen still shots and one short video of Julia's three businesses across the street. Perfect. He could see who parked in the lot, who went in the front doors, and who went in the side door at the back of the little parking lot. He set the camera to video, used the widest angle lens he had, and turned on auto record. Then he went down the back stairs, got his car, and made the circle around the block to park in Julia's parking lot. Giving his camera across the street a discreet nod, he walked to the front concrete pad.

First, he went into Julia's Pac 'n Mail store and asked if he could make a phone call because his battery died and he had to call his grandmother. They said no. He went back out to the car and drove off. He changed his shirt and put on a floppy hat and sun glasses at a gas station two blocks away. Then he drove back to the same parking lot. This time he went into the savings and loan office.

The name, Houston International Savings and Loan, etched in gold on the front door, was impressive. Vince opened the door, stepped inside, and surprised two people. It was a twenty-by-twenty-foot room with four metal desks, a row of tan-colored filing cabinets lined up against the back, and four fluorescent light fixtures on the ceiling. There were no windows, no teller's cage, no reception area, and nothing that resembled a place to save money or make a loan.

The large woman sitting behind a desk piled high with stacks of what looked like stapled batches of letter-sized documents, said, "Sorry, we're not open."

Looking at his watch, Vince said, "It's quarter to eleven and the door was open."

The man at the desk behind hers stood up.

"Well, yes sir, that's my bad. Shoulda locked it behind me. We are not a walk-in place; we only make appointments for new customers. You don't have one, do you?"

Vince noticed that his desk had almost nothing on it, except a blotter pad, a telephone, and what looked like a daily newspaper. The man was bulky and dressed like a tourist, with a Hawaiian shirt, untucked, and jeans.

"Sorry, I just came in because it's quarter to eleven in the morning and I'm looking to open a savings account. No appointment. Don't want one. Just a savings account."

"Well, we are sorry, young man," the woman said, not looking the least bit sorry. "We don't have savings accounts."

"The gold letter on your door says savings and loans. How come you don't have savings accounts?"

The man motioned the woman to sit down and walked up to face Vince.

"She just said we're sorry. I'll say it too. We're sorry, OK? Door shoulda been locked. We arrange savings as collateral for loans, but they are not the kind of savings account you are probably looking for. Our customers are corporate, not individual. There's a Bank of America, two blocks south on Third Avenue. Just turn left out of the parking lot."

The man stepped around Vince, opened the door, and waived his hand out to the parking lot. Vince turned around, stepped out onto the concrete pad, and then turned to face the Hawaiian shirt man.

"OK, man, sorry to have bothered you. Tell Julia I said hello and that I'm sorry I missed her."

"What? Julia? Do you know her?"

"I know her, man. I know her. She owns the place. She probably owns you too."

He got in his car and started the engine. He could see the man pull a phone out of his back pocket, tap the screen, and hold it up to his ear. Vince moved slowly out of the small lot and turned right toward Third Avenue. In his rearview mirror, he could see the man had followed him to the street and was now writing something on his wrist. Good for you, man, now go check my license plate out and see what it gets you. Motherfucker.

Vince made the full loop around the block to get back to the Berkley Apartments and parked the Chevy behind the building. Taking the stairs two steps at a time, he bounded up and hurried into Unit 5 to check his video. Turning the dials to view video on the two-by-three-inch viewing screen, he watched himself park his car and walk up onto the concrete pad. He saw himself give a little nod up toward the window where the tripod and camera still faced. He watched himself go into the Pac 'n Mail store, then through the fake savings and loan door, and finally his slow walk past the front door of Withers and Associates. Then he smiled at himself, on camera, as he got into his car and made that loop out of sight of the camera. He deleted the eleven minutes of video that showed the two other cars in the lot across the street and waited to see the results of the Hawaiian shirt man's phone call.

It took twenty-seven minutes, but it worked. A yellow Jeep Rubicon pulled up into the parking lot with a screech of brakes, and a short woman in jeans and a white T-shirt jumped out. She ran to the side door of the building, took out a ring of keys from the canvas briefcase hanging from her shoulder, and opened the side door. He got all of it on camera. Fifteen minutes later, the fluorescent lights went out in the savings and loan and the Hawaiian shirt man and his lady came out the front door, got into their cars in the parking lot, and turned north on Third Avenue.

"OK, Julia baby, you ready for me?" Vince said to himself, as he straightened his tie and buttoned the jacket on his blue suit coat. He made sure his video was on and recording before he went out the back door, down the steps, and around to the front. As he crossed the street, he turned his head and gave his camera another nod. When he got to the other side he knocked loudly on the front door of Withers & Associates. No one answered. He banged again on the wood door. Nothing. He just kept hitting the door with his knotted fist.

Finally, the door cracked open a few inches and a high pitched voice said, "Hey buddy, we ain't open. Get away, or I'll call the cops."

"Call the cops, Julia. Go ahead. But first, you ought to hear what I know about you. About Chaco Hernandez. About Boise."

The door opened about a foot. Vince jammed his shoulder into it, knocking the little woman in the white T-shirt to the floor. He pushed his way in, kicked her in the stomach, and pulled the big .44 Mag revolver from the waist band of his suit pants.

"God damn you to hell, Julia fuckin' Santerra-Evans!" he screamed.

Then he realized she'd been holding a black pistol in her other hand, but had dropped it when the door slammed back into her. He kicked her again in the hip as she held both hands over her stomach. Scooping her gun up in his free hand, he aimed it, and his gun at her.

"You ready to die, bitch, for killing my father? To die for the dumbshit you killed in Boise? For all the money you stole from whoever 'n fuck those assholes in Panama really are? From your bosses across the bay at Plankton? You ready, Julia? Open your mouth. I'll shoot you in the mouth so you can taste your own blood in the split second you got left on this earth!"

She shut her eyes and clamped her jaw shut.

He slammed the door shut and crossed the room to the reception desk. Julia, on her back on the floor, could see his chest heaving up and down as he leaned backward against the desk. Then, to her surprise, his locked jaw seemed to relax, and he started shaking his head at her.

"No, Julia, I don't think I'll shoot you in the mouth yet. I think I'll wait until you help me get even with Plankton. Then I'll shoot you in the eyeball, two times. Once with my gun and once with yours. And I'll leave you outside in that stupid Jeep of yours to wait for the fuckin' F Bee Eye. They'll come get your body when I'm done with you. You ready for them?"

Julia pushed herself to a sitting position on the floor. "Them? Who's them? Who the fuck are you? Do you know what's gonna happen to you when my people get here?"

"Ah, Julia. You're flat on your skinny little ass on the floor. Your belly hurts, right? Your hip is killing you, right?

You thought I was gonna kill you a minute ago, but now you're asking questions and threatening me? I'm the guy with the big gun. A .44 Mag. If I shot you in the knee cap from here, it'd blow your leg in half. That's who I am, bitch. I'm the man with the big gun. That's all you need to know 'bout me for now. So here's what we're gonna do. I can see this shitty little room is for your secretary, or whatever. Let's go in the back to your real office. Roll over. Get on your hands and knees, like the bitch you are. You're gonna crawl back to your office, bitch, crawl, goddamn you!"

She crawled. When she got to the office door, behind the reception desk, she pushed open the door with one hand and crawled in. Once inside, on a dark red shag carpet, she vomited before she reached her desk. He stepped around her, reached behind his back, and slid his red Washington Redskins backpack onto the desktop. Then he kicked her again. In the head. She fell over and closed her eyes, moaning, with spittle coming from her mouth. Loosening the zipper on the top of his backpack, he took out the Zoomer G9 recorder that Vivian had used to tape the FBI in their own conference room in Phoenix. He turned it on, set on the desk. Then he dug out a two-foot length of one-eighth-inch diameter seven-by-nineteen galvanized cable. He looped one end around her left wrist and locked it down with a steel wire clip.

"Get up," he ordered.

"Why should I, you shit! You're gonna kill me anyway, right? Go ahead, I ain't afraid to die."

"Get up,' he repeated. "I might give you parole, maybe even ninety days. You tell me what I want to know, I might parole you."

Grabbing the end of her desk, she pulled herself upright. She was still weak from the blows and steadied herself with her left hand. Vince stepped behind her and pushed her big black executive chair into her backside. She fell into her chair and he quickly looped the other end of the galvanized cable around the adjustable stem below the seat. Then he pulled the cable taut and locked down the lower loop.

"OK, Julia, now you're a prisoner in your own chair. You can use your right hand, but not your left. Scoot your chair so your knees are under the desk and your right arm is on top the desk. First things first, open your safe. Right now."

She just sat there. Her belly still hurt, as did the side of her head, but she was focused on survival now and decided to test him. Again.

"Why? Are you a thief, too? Is that what this is about? My money?"

"It's about your life. And your money. And your asshole bosses over at Plankton Resources. And their money too. You want parole? First step in that direction is your safe. If you refuse, then I'll kill you in your chair and open your safe the hard way."

She stared at him, but she could smell death all around him. He had started to bead sweat on his forehead and on his upper lip. His eyes seemed inflamed and he blinked constantly. So, she took the easy way.

"My safe is inside my desk, here on the right side. I can't reach it with the stupid cable thing you've got around me."

He took three steps to her, and pushed her and her chair back five feet. Opening the large door on the right side of her desk, he saw the twenty-four-inch stainless steel safe. It had both a digital combination, and a key lock.

"Where's the key? What's the combination?"

"The key is in my wallet, which is in my rear pocket. I'm sitting on it. The combination is 94 dash 07688. Help your fucking self."

"Good girl, you're cooperating."

He moved to the chair, slapped her across the mouth, and said, "Use your right hand to get the wallet. Toss it on the desk."

He fished through the wallet, found a small slot behind the driver's license holder, and stuck the small bronze key in the safe. That caused a small light to come on over the digital keyboard. He entered the combination and the door swung open. He turned back to Julia's chair and wheeled her around to the opposite side of the desk. Then he reached into his backpack, took out a second cable, and used it to chain her swivel chair to the right table leg on her side of the desk.

The safe had a foot-high metal tray in the middle. He took it out and dumped the contents on the desk. It was cash, in dollars and Euros.

"How much?" he asked pointing to the currency on her desk.

"Maybe six or seven hundred thousand. It's getaway money. You're welcome to it, as soon as I get my parole," she said.

"So, you're saying I can get away with six or seven hundred thousand getaway dollars? If I do and let you live, how will you get away?"

"It's just money. I can always get more."

"Yes, I know you can. Let's see what else you got in here."

He saw two steel drawers, each about two inches high. The first drawer had a stack of bearer bonds. The second had two notebooks, one with ledger paper, and the other with plastic sheet covers, holding what looked like a half-dozen typed letters with inked signatures.

"How much in bearer bonds?"

Smiling for the first time, she answered, "Exactly two million dollars, American. Do you know about bearer bonds? I mean, how to use them?"

Ignoring her question, he continued, "And what are these letters, with inked signatures. They all say 'To Whom It May Concern.'"

"They are letters of introduction, signed by six bankers in six different foreign countries. As you can see they introduce the person who has the letter, not by name, but rather by the fact they have the letter."

"For what?" Vince asked.

"For protection. These letters are almost better than money. They can keep you alive and safe in a new country. Sometimes, in my business, safe harbor is much more valuable than a safe full of cash."

"OK," Vince said, after sitting in silence on the hardback chair on the executive side of the desk. "I'm considering parole. You keep these letters. I'll take the cash and bearer bonds when I go. What's the notebook with the ledger entries?"

"Things you'd never understand, asshole. But if you did, what's in this notebook would kill you. It's my life insurance policy, and your death warrant."

Vince sat on the end of the desk and started flipping through the ledgers. A quick glance is all it took.

"These are American companies and South American banks. The account numbers and monthly deposits are arrayed in double-entry accounting schedules. This is Plankton Resources' laundry list, reduced to numbers, right?"

"What would a dick like you know about double-entry accounting schedules?"

"My dad was an accountant, remember? And I know as much 'bout the names in this notebook as you do. I been studying them for several weeks."

"Studying them? What 'n fuck you mean by that?"

"Meaning, I know how the currency exchange business is used by Plankton to launder drug money. That's what I know. I'll keep it a secret when I go."

"When you go, where?" Julia asked.

"Actually, that's the wrong word, bitch. I won't go. I'll disappear. But there's one more condition to your parole. You have to execute some electronic transfers for me. Two of them. For two million USD, each, payable to an account I'll write down for you, in a bank you'll recognize, down in Panama City."

"No, I won't do that. If I execute a transfer of their money to you, they'll kill me. If I don't transfer the money, you'll kill me. Either way I die. So, just shoot me now, take the cash, and see how fast you can disappear, you little prick."

"Prick? I call you a bitch and you call me a prick? So, we're speaking the same language now, you and me. But the electronic transfers are not to me. And they won't ever be executed because each transfer is from one of Plankton Resources' subsidiaries to another of its subsidiaries. And they are delayed transfers, effective three days from now. Here's the deal. I know you got other getaway cash and a getaway plan. Killers with law degrees always have a plan A and a plan B, right? When Houston sees these transfers, they'll know they have three days to hunt you down. They'll know you might have more numbers than these two, so they will work hard to find you. But they won't find you, Julia. I know that for sure."

"For sure? You don't know shit for sure. I'm telling you those notebooks are your death warrant. Even touching them will execute that death warrant."

"Julia, you haven't taken a good look at me, even now. I'm wearing surgeon's latex gloves. No finger prints on whatever I touch today. My face is nowhere. Not in any database in the world. And you're the only person in Houston to actually see me, or talk to me. If I parole you, you'll jump in that banana yellow car of yours and execute your getaway plan. By dawn tomorrow, if you're still alive, you'll be a million miles away from here, right? And you won't be you, anymore, right?"

"You are stupid. Why should I run? My friends at Plankton trust me. My friends in Culiacán and Panama City trust me. It's you who will be on the run. You can kill me, but you'll never hide from my friends."

"Julia, here's why you're going to run. Because you're smarter than them. Right? You've never fully trusted them, right? You've always known they might turn on you. And you have a foolproof plan, don't you? I myself am an expert on disappearing. But you're even better, I know that. Which is why I don't need to kill you to keep you quiet about stealing the cash, and the bearer bonds in your safe. You can't tell the fuckin' F bee eye, can you? They'd arrest you. You won't tell your bosses, either—they'd kill you. And you won't hunt me down, because that won't help you. The only thing that will help you is to disappear. Me too. But not together. Hopefully on different continents."

Vince wheeled Julia back around to the executive side of her desk, powered up her computer, and stood behind her as she logged on, opened a secure browser, logged on again, and executed the first electronic transfer of a million dollars. It took one minute, thirty-seven seconds. The second transfer took three minutes, flat. Vince used his iPhone to video all of it—the screen shots, the voice he used to tell her which accounts, and which banks to use. And everything he had said to her, once she agreed to cooperate, was recorded on the Zoomer G9 digital recorder.

"Ok, asshole, now you should get the fuck out of here. I'll give you my money and a one-hour head start. Then I call and warn my friends that you stole my money, a little of theirs, and my notebook. They'll hunt you down. They always do."

"Julia, Julia, what about your parole? I promised, remember?"

"Yeah, and I earned it. I did the transfers. You should get the hell out of here right now."

"Sorry, Julia baby. I lied."

Vince hit her on the back of her head with the butt of his .44 Magnum. She slumped forward onto the desk top. He pushed the chair as far into the keyhole as he could. He took the extra-large role of red Gorilla duct tape from the red backpack and taped her entire right arm to the table top, with the strips running all the way across the forty-eight-inch desktop. Then he taped the executive chair to the desk with tape tightly wound around all four sides of the desk. He also ran the tape around her upper body several times and twice around her legs and the swivel chair. She, her chair, and her desk became unyielding objects, in bright red stripes.

He waited for her to come out of the stupor of her head bang; it took five minutes.

"You bastard, you rotten bastard! I did everything you asked. Now you tie me up? With red duct tape? Jesus, you are sick."

"No, Julia, we're not sick. We know you killed our dad and we got one more thing to do before you get parole. Confessed killers get parole after they serve their time. But killers who don't confess, die. So, now we're down to your choice. Confess or die. You confess right now, speak clearly into this audio recorder, and I'll cut you free; well, mostly free. You can work yourself out of the duct tape in an hour or so. By then we'll be gone. Or refuse to confess, and I'll hit you with the front of my .44 Mag. Two bullets in your forehead. Painless but permanent. Oh, I almost forgot. I promised I'd shoot you at least once with your own gun. I'll shoot you in the left knee cap—they say that's one of the most painful places you can take a bullet."

Julia rolled her head to one side, then another. She gritted her teeth, and tried to spit on the desk top. And she visibly leaned forward into the cushion of 3-inch wide red duct tape stripes across her chest. Her shoulders sloped, head down, she started talking to her own desk.

"OK, I'll tell you. But I didn't kill your dad, or the dope in Boise. I was the planner and paymaster for both. That's why I was there, but I didn't kill anyone. I'm a lawyer and I know about felony murder. So, my statement here, into your fuckin' zoom recorder, will get me life in prison. I know that. But that's not so bad for you. There's a lot more I could tell you, about other cases, about Plankton, about all of it. And somehow, I think that's what you really want. You want me alive, to be a snitch, to be an FBI informant. That's what you really want, asshole, ain't it? I'm going to take that bet. That's why I'm confessing what I did in Boise, and in Washington, DC. I can bring down the whole thing; you know I can. So, you got my money, my electronic transfers, and my ability to shut down Plankton. That's why you taped me up instead of shooting me. Go on, asshole. Get out of here. I only ask one thing. Tell the FBI I'm here before Plankton's inside people figure this out."

Vince turned the recorder off, placed his iPhone on the desk, and took his backpack off. He took out four digital video cards he'd used to film the FBI stakeout. He left the Washington Redskins backpack on the table, facing

Julia. She couldn't reach it, but he knew who would. In five minutes, he was back at the Beverly. Still wearing the latex gloves he'd worn every second he was in the Beverley Apartments, he boxed up his stuff, loaded it into the Chevy, and drove to the trailer park in Lynchburg. There, he transferred everything from the car to Jumbo II and drove north toward Beaumont, on I-10.

Ten minutes later, he pulled off I-10 onto a freeway off ramp with a big truck stop. He bought a Cricket phone without giving an ID. He used it to call the FBI field office in Phoenix.

"Phoenix office of the FBI, how can I help you?"

"Give Agent Lin a message. Tell her to go to Attorney Julia Santerra-Evans' office in Houston, Texas. Right now; I know she's there, but I don't know her number. Julia baby is waiting, and anxious to confess that she killed Jason Bloomington and Stephan Manchester. Oh, and I left a tape recorder there on Julia's desk, along with a backpack she'll recognize. It still has the recording of her meeting in Phoenix with my sister."

He had been watching the second hand on his watch while he left the message. It took exactly nineteen seconds. Using the lug wrench in the trunk, he destroyed the Cricket phone and dropped it into a dumpster. An hour later, he pulled into another truck stop near Lake Charles. He gassed up, bought a bag of junk food at the Circle K, and looked at his map. Then he drove another three hours to New Orleans. He found a cheap trailer park, paid for a three-day stay, and never left Jumbo II.

Three days later, just a little after five a.m., Vivian stepped down onto the concrete pad from Jumbo II, dressed in jeans and a hoodie. She had a new bright-yellow suitcase. The taxi cab she'd ordered from her new Cricket phone was waiting. The driver tipped his cowboy hat in her direction as he opened the trunk of his cab.

"I'm taking you to the airport, right Miss?" he asked, smothering a yawn with his elbow.

"Yes, please," Vivian said as she settled herself in the back seat.

"You must have an early flight, Miss. Which terminal you want?"

"American Airlines, please. And please don't play the radio; I hope to take a little nap before my flight to New York. It leaves at 8:05 a.m. We'll be there in plenty of time won't we?"

"Yes, Miss. Will you be paying by credit card?" the driver asked with a nervous tone.

"No. Cash."

When Vivian got to the airport she gave the driver a hundred-dollar bill against the $40.50 meter reading.

"Thank you for not playing the radio. I hope my sixty-dollar tip is not the best one you'll get today. My husband is wealthy and waiting for me in New York. He is a big tipper."

Once safely inside the terminal, she went to the American Airlines desk and bought a first-class ticket for San Diego.

CHAPTER 58

Sally Lin and Agent Montoya were having coffee in the FBI employee lounge when their phones buzzed. Within five minutes they were on their way to Baytown. The Houston County Sheriff's office had been alerted and already had two units standing by when they pulled up in front of the concrete building on Third Avenue. All five officers were geared up, with Kevlar vests, stun guns, and one deputy with an AR-15. The sheriff's deputies had done a quick check on doors, windows, and exits. They said the place was "quiet—no signs of distress or criminal conduct."

The deputies led the way—knocking first—then forcing open the door to the law office. Once inside the reception area, Agent Montoya led the others into Julia's office. Other than the obvious fact that she was duct-taped to her desk, she also looked like someone had beat the crap out of her. Furious and obviously scared, she insisted that they arrest her immediately and give her safe passage to FBI headquarters.

"That bastard robbed me, kidnapped me in my own office, and threatened to kill me. And I made a true confession about two murders to him . . ."

"Him?" Sally asked. "A man did this? Did you know him?"

"Know him! He's a maniac. He hit me, kicked me, and damn near killed me. But you'll have to wait for me to give you a full statement. I'm a lawyer. I waive my Fifth Amendment rights. He said the FBI would want the recorder and those digital photo cards. And I think he wants you to take that crappy Washington Redskins bag. Don't know what he meant, but he said the fuckin' FBI would want to examine that bag very carefully."

Sally arrested Julia, and declared the whole building a federal crime scene. Agent Montoya called for a full forensic workup. Over the next three days, Julia Santerra-Evans gave a detailed statement of the murders of Mr. Bloomington and Mr. Manchester, along with a very complicated story about the eleven years she had helped Plankton Resources launder money for the Sinaloa Cartel. She was put into WITSEC's custody as a cooperating witness and a confidential informant. After a day-long debriefing in the Houston Field office, she was put in the hands of the US Marshal's office in Houston for transfer and further debriefing in Washington, DC.

CHAPTER 59

When the FedEx delivery truck driver brought the large box into the Cranston Public Library, Perry Ricketts, the head librarian, was not at the front desk. His assistant Cynthia was. Her twin, Cecilia, was working with Mr. Ricketts in the basement, trying to solve a cataloging problem.

"Morning, Miss Cynthia," the uniformed driver said, "this one requires a signature by Mr. Ricketts himself, no exceptions. That's the special instructions on it. Pretty rare, but we got a rule on it."

"Well, Daniel, he's not here, as you can plainly see. I always sign his name to things, so you just give me the clipboard."

"Miss Cynthia, you trying to get me fired? I got instructions, you know. I can wait a few minutes or I can bring it back tomorrow morning. If he's out of town or something, we'll hold it for redelivery when he gets back."

"No, just wait till I call him; he's downstairs with Cecelia. They have fun down there while I have to stay here and handle instructions. Is there no trust in the world anymore?"

Two minutes later, Perry Ricketts and Cynthia's twin came to the front desk. He signed the clip-boarded form, and then used his pocket knife to slice the packing tape around the heavy box. One by one, he lifted out six hardbound copies of the same book and a cream-colored envelope marked, *Personal for Cranston Library Staff and Mr. Nettles.*

The dustcover on the hardbound books startled Mr. Perry, amused Cynthia, and nearly took Cecelia's breath away. The title, *Let's Disappear,* by *Vivian and Vince* was in deep-blue embossed font, embedded in a cover of soft wafting clouds that varied from grey to white over the entire front and back cover. The back cover's blurb read.

THIS IS THE STORY OF A YOUNG GIRL AND HER BROTHER'S ADVENTURE INTO THE LAND OF DISAPPEARANCE. THE STORY OPENS IN A SMALL TOWN PUBLIC LIBRARY. SHE REVEALS HER DEEP NEED TO LEARN ABOUT HER OWN IDENTITY, AND HOW TO CHANGE IT. IT'S A STORY OF AWAKENING AND RESOLVING. A STORY OF TRAGIC LOSS AND LEARNING THINGS ABOUT YOURSELF, YOUR FAMILY, AND YOUR WORLD THAT SHOCK AND SOOTHE IN UNEQUAL PROPORTIONS. SOME OF THIS STORY IS TRUE. THE WRITER'S NAMES ARE

PSEUDONYMS DESIGNED TO PROTECT THEIR
DISAPPEARANCE. AT LEAST ONE OF THEM
IS REAL.

Mr. Ricketts asked the only staffer on duty that day to cover the front desk. Then he and his twin assistants took the books and the letter into his office immediately behind the front desk. Mr. Ricketts read the letter aloud to Cynthia and Cecelia.

Dear Mr. Ricketts, Mr. Nettles, Cynthia, and Cecelia,

Today is March 9, 2017. Exactly three years ago today, I walked into your library in Cranston and asked for Mr. Ricketts' help in finding a book. I can remember almost every moment of that day. I was not quite eighteen then, but I told Mr. Ricketts I was. I don't think he believed me, but he still gave me a library card under the name Vivian Shortfield. That wasn't my real name, then, or now. I told him I wanted to borrow a book that would help my character disappear.

Of course, I didn't tell him it was me that wanted to disappear; he might have believed me and called the booby hatch to come get me. I told him it was a book about Vivian and why she wants to disappear from things. Vivian, my character, wanted me to figure out how to disappear. I told Mr. Ricketts a little fib about my character writing a book inside my book. He didn't understand. Or maybe he did. Either way, what I meant was that it was a book about writing a book.

Well, I did it. I disappeared and I wrote a book inside a book about disappearing. I want you to have these six copies, fresh off the printing line. Sorry I didn't inscribe them, but that's because it's hard to explain who did the writing, and who lived the story. You know what I mean, I hope. There is a book for each of you and two for your lending library. I hope somebody in Cranston reads this book, even though it's kinda sad, and the chapters Vince wrote have awful language. I'm also enclosing three checks. Two are for Cynthia and Cecelia—these are dividend checks because they invested in a company called Disappearance, LLC. That company is out of business now. The other check is to The Cranston Public Library. You can use it for books or whatever you need. I don't think I could have written this book without the one you lent to me three years ago.

I know the FBI probably bothered you, but they meant well. I didn't send them a book because, well, let's say I still don't trust them. If one of them wants to borrow your books, make them take out a library card. I still have mine.

Most sincerely yours,

V

Mr. Ricketts, who always kept his composure, had to gather himself when he looked at the cashier's check, drawn on a bank in Perth, Australia, and made out to the Cranston Public Library for $250,000. The dividend checks to Cynthia and Cecelia for $25,000 each took away their collective breath away. When Mr. Nettles came to the library to get his book the next morning, he took it to a library table and spent the whole day reading it.

EPILOGUE

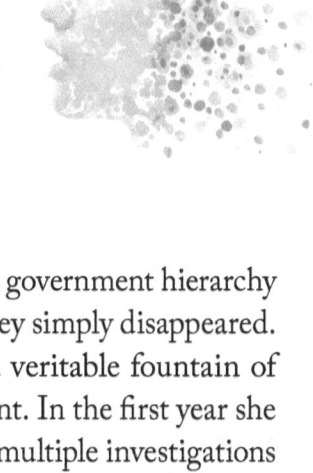

No one in the federal government hierarchy was able to track Vivian, or Vince. They simply disappeared. Julia Santerra-Evans proved to be a veritable fountain of information for the federal government. In the first year she spent in WITSEC, she cooperated in multiple investigations which resulted in charges, convictions and forfeiture of almost $500 million in laundered money in a dozen different countries. But in the process, Julia created another getaway plan built on the same principles she explained to Vince just before he duct-taped her to her own desk in Baytown. When she disappeared from WITSEC, the FBI and the US Marshal's office searched for six months without success. The last known country that spotted Julia was England; they posted it on Interpol, but by the time the FBI got it she was gone. But she left tracks.

MI6, England's vaulted spy agency, learned that Julia discovered Vivian's alias in London. She had apparently created an entirely new persona—Vinessa DiAmonte—and a new UK corporate structure—Emergence Inc. The MI6 agent told his CIA counterpart that Julia knew where Vivian was. He also said her focus was not on Vivian, but on her little brother, Vince.

Two months after Julia left England, on the hunt for Vince, a luxury cruise line's newest and most elegant ship, the *Ovation*, docked in Sydney, Australia. The bright spring sun shone brightly off the Sydney Opera House as the ship maneuvered through Sydney Harbor. This was the last big port before the *Ovation* would sail across the Pacific to Los Angeles, her disembarkation port on the 2018 World Tour. Most of the passengers were headed to the Mercedes-Benz Airstream tour busses for the day's on-shore excursions. Only one passenger bypassed the busses. She was met by a chauffeured car, chartered to take her to Sydney's Kingston Smith International Airport. She carried only a slightly oversize handbag while pulling a small carry-on bag for her flight to Singapore. She picked up her UK passport before decamping the *Ovation*. But when she arrived at the airport, there was no record of her boarding the flight to Singapore, or anywhere else. The Singapore flight manifest identified only twelve women traveling alone, none of whom boarded with a UK passport, or identified as Vinessa DiAmonte.

The Singapore flight also carried seventy-three men, under thirty-five years of age, but none had UK passports. Once the plane landed in Singapore, half the men got on connecting flights to other countries. The other half disappeared into the high tech—big data center that was the "new" Singapore. It was at the forefront in Asia, quickly positioning itself as the region's big data hub. Some said its data analytics industry contributed at least one billion US dollars to the Singapore economy annually. Perhaps more telling, an Internet metrics company, Ookla, claimed Internet speeds in Singapore as among the fastest in the world. It was a welcoming hub for young, ambitious techies, given the city-state's significant infrastructure investment as part of its *Smart Nation* initiative.

Ms. DiAmonte had been the only guest in the Grand Wintergarden Suite for the last eighty-seven days. That was the *Ovation*'s second most expensive suite, and this would be the only time that a single guest would occupy it. It's six-figure cost for the World Tour always meant that at least two, and sometimes four, very rich people would occupy the two-bedroom, 1,300 square-foot suite.

The suite had been booked three months earlier by a London-based travel agent representing a newly formed American nonprofit corporation called Emergence, Inc. The name of the company's CEO had not been initially disclosed until shortly before she boarded at Dartmouth the day the ship departed on its maiden World Cruise. Two days before departure, the ship's tour director was informed that the company's CEO would be occupying the suite. No one told Seabourn that she'd disembark in Sydney. Her departure was only learned when Ms. DiAmonte did not rejoin the ship as it sailed out of Sydney Harbor bound for New Zealand, before the long cruise to Los Angeles. The fee for the balance of the cruise to Los Angeles was forfeited.

Ms. DiAmonte had aroused great interest the moment she stepped on board in England. Part of her hair had become loose when she stepped off the gangway onto the teak deck. Half covered her cheek, the other half blew briskly in the offshore wind. It was a dark brown with red tints and a rich warmth, but lacking the popular gloss of younger women's hair oils. She wore low heels, was deliciously slim, and had a worldly sense about her. It was rumored she was twenty-eight but she could have passed for twenty. The maître d'hôtel would later describe her as lithe as a hazel wand, and elusive as a shadow cast across a darkened glass. She mingled with only a few passengers. Those few agreed, in later interviews, that Ms. DiAmonte was a lovely conversationalist, but one they learned little about.

A very different-looking young woman, named Julia Joyce, an American, boarded the *Ovation* at Sydney just for the trans-Pacific crossing. She had booked a Veranda suite on the same deck as Ms. DiAmonte. Ms. Joyce was short, compact, and glared at everyone in her path. Once settled in her Veranda suite, she gave the deck-butler a note to be delivered to the occupant of the Grand Wintergarden suite the morning *after* they disembarked. This note and the new guest's temper tantrum would be the talk of the voyage from Sydney to New Zealand, where Ms. Joyce furiously stomped off the ship. Ms. Joyce apparently thought she knew Ms. DiAmonte. The note was never delivered because, by the time the butler tried to deliver it, Ms. DiAmonte had flown to Singapore and was met at the airport by a chauffeured limousine. The note, when opened by the *Ovation*'s director of security, said:

> You do not know me, but your brother Vince called me Julia Baby. I mean you no personal harm, but I intend to find and kill him. He has destroyed my life. I am a hunted woman by the law, and by my former employers in Mexico and Panama. If you do not help me find him, I will kill you.

The *Ovation's* Chief of Security, Solo Artremis, sent the original hand-written note to the London-based travel agent for Emergence Inc. explaining that he thought the note should be given to Ms. DiAmonte, since she had disembarked before the butler could deliver it personally. Mr. Artremis suggested that the original note might be of value as evidence since it confirmed the threat of mortal harm to a British citizen.

Ms. Julia Joyce got off the *Ovation* in New Zealand, where she was met on the dock by New Zealand police. She was arrested for threatening a British citizen, Ms. DiAmonte. As far as MI6 could ascertain, Ms. Vinessa DiAmonte had disappeared, again.

www.ingramcontent.com/pod-product-compliance
Lightning Source LLC
Chambersburg PA
CBHW030343120726
47901CB00007B/1896